HEART, WINGS, AND FIRE

BOOK ONE OF THE 27 KINGDOMS

Trisha J. Wooldridge

Imprint
Coinjock, NC

Copyright © 2022 by Trisha J. Wooldridge.

All rights reserved. No part of this publication may be reproduced, distributed or transmitted in any form or by any means, including photocopying, recording, or other electronic or mechanical methods, without the prior written permission of the publisher, except in the case of brief quotations embodied in critical reviews and certain other noncommercial uses permitted by copyright law. For permission requests, write to the publisher, addressed "Attention: Permissions Coordinator," at the address below.

Chris Kennedy/New Mythology Press
1097 Waterlily Rd.
Coinjock, NC 27923
https://chriskennedypublishing.com/

Publisher's Note: This is a work of fiction. Names, characters, places, and incidents are a product of the author's imagination. Locales and public names are sometimes used for atmospheric purposes. Any resemblance to actual people, living or dead, or to businesses, companies, events, institutions, or locales is completely coincidental.

Cover Art and Design by J. Caleb Designs

Ordering Information:
Quantity sales. Special discounts are available on quantity purchases by corporations, associations, and others. For details, contact the "Special Sales Department" at the address above.

HEART, WINGS, AND FIRE/TRISHA J. WOOLDRIDGE -- 1st ed.
ISBN: 978-1648555275

Get the free Four Horsemen prelude story *Shattered Crucible* and discover other titles by Seventh Seal Press at:

chriskennedypublishing.com/

* * *

Get the free Eldros Legacy anthology *Here There Be Giants* at:

dl.bookfunnel.com/qabsr57lq3

* * *

Discover other titles by New Mythology Press at:

chriskennedypublishing.com/new-mythology-press/

* * * * *

Dedication

To the dragons and dwarves of Clans Driscoll and McCarthy,
who were always kind to kender
and protected their *lit chuar* and bard-sister.

To my beloved, souljoined mate,
who puts up with all my storysinging—
even when it's off key—
and carries me on flaming wings
when I need.

* * * * *

Acknowledgements

Acknowledgements are hard!

I am a very lucky and blessed author to have an awesome team of my publishing family, writing and editing family, related family, and chosen-family who support my dreams—and put up with a lot of crap.

And a lot of wordiness.

And forgetfulness: Apologies ahead of time for those I don't name. I have an ADHD brain, and this has been years in the making.

For helping me free Hawush, Byria, Koki, Mokin, and this lot of characters upon the world, a dragon's share of thanks goes to my editor, Rob Howell, of New Mythology, and my publisher, Chris Kennedy of Chris Kennedy Publishing, along with Tiffany Reynolds and Zach Ritz, my editor and proofreader. I'm honored and thrilled you saw my heart in this story, these characters, and this world and allowed me to share them with others. Thanks for welcoming me to the CKP family!

Because making my character's experiences as authentic and respectful to victims of abuse as possible matters to me, I offer special thanks to my friends and colleagues who are professionals or experienced in this and helped: LA, Mellisa, Deborah, Suzanne.

My Southbridge and Northbridge writing groups also provided me with excellent feedback through all the early drafts. (Yes, I really do have writing groups in towns of those names!) As well as my long-term and late-night writing friends and colleagues: Kim, Paul,

Sery, Shielding, Christy, Kristi (also my volcano informant), Suzanne, Laura, Matt; Cat, Cat, Cat (yes, three of you!); Val, Morven; Mike Jack, Len, Jessica, Megan and the Late Night Monday Zoom Crew; Venessa and the TWT crew... I know there are more of you, too. I love you even if I don't name you!

Thank you to my friends in Broad Universe and the New England Horror Writers, who have been excellent resources for almost twenty years. Especially My Other Scott (r)., who puts up with my convention shenanigans and organizational misadventures.

Many thanks to the fantastic Dante Saunders, who designed my covers and also had to listen to all my worldbuilding during our barn adventures. (He gets his full name so others might try and offer him money for great art!)

This book also wouldn't exist without the Tribe behind Superstars Writing Seminars, where I met Rob and Chris, the cool CKP team, and pitched this! On top of all the other great learning and networking and Tarot reading that happens regularly during the conference.

I'm also very grateful to my editing team at The Writer's Ally and my clients for all I've learned from them—and the flexibility to work on my own writing.

Not all writers have a great family who supports them, especially if they are geeky, but I do. Thank you, Mom and Travis, for all your support and understanding my weirdness.

Most of all, uncountable thanks to my husband, Scott, who is my soulmate and brings me food, water, and makes me go to bed when deadlines make me forget to do all that.

I love you all, and I thank you all!

* * * * *

Maps

World Map

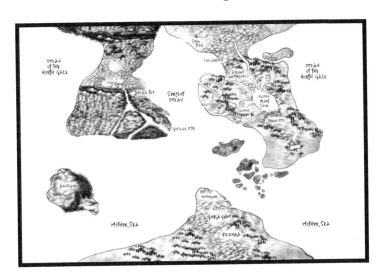

* * *

Regional Map

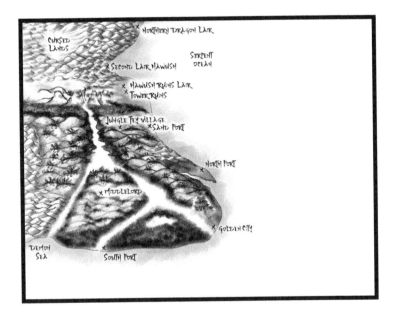

* * * * *

Book I

The Princess and the Dragon

* * * * *

Chapter One
Dressing for Scars

A woman should be happy on her wedding day. Byria's mother, the queen of Huotaro, had told her this many times. *She's probably still trying to convince herself*, Byria had thought on several occasions.

I should be happy. She'd thought that more than once today, *the* day, as her maids were binding her into the silken gown. Other occasions, and also throughout this day, the young woman had wondered if there was simply something wrong with her. Perhaps she truly *should* be happy, *should* take her place as princess to her husband.

Her father approved. Her mother was happy over the whole affair, thoroughly enjoying every aspect of planning this great event. Huotaro was one of the richest kingdoms in the Twenty-Seven Kingdoms Treaty. None dared challenge them in war, and all wished to trade with them—in their markets, with their merchants—despite the travel over the ocean. Byria should want for nothing.

She should be celebrating every moment of her special day.

Instead, the moments disappeared into the blur where many memories went, the ones she couldn't differentiate between dreams, stories, nightmares, or actual events. More and more frequently, she'd found herself blending these things together to soften the edges. There was a reason she'd developed this habit, but that reason was lost between those blurry edges.

Her maids exchanged smiles and giggles as they carefully arranged the fabric, covering her arms and back. The fabric around her neck nearly choked her, but she knew a woman must be modest—especially upon the day she was promised to her man.

And there were all those scars to cover.

Scars and… Byria let herself fall back between fuzzy edges, trying not to wince as one of the women tightened her beltcloth a little too hard.

The maids, of course, knew to avert their eyes as they dressed her. For modesty, again. Only a husband should cast his eyes upon so much of his wife's skin.

She should enjoy the moment. It was her own fault she didn't recognize the small joys of life. Forcing a laugh and smile, she selected ribbons for her maids to braid into her simple brown-black hair. It wasn't a raven black like her mother's, nor the hued, deep browns and blacks of the other women's. It was dull and heavy, no matter what her maids did. So she selected the most expensive ribbons, laced with threads of gold and bronze, to help make it prettier.

"The sun shines brightly with nary a cloud, my princess. A fortunate sign for the parade." A younger maid smiled as she braided the gold and white ribbon in a loop by Byria's temple.

Parade? She didn't recall rehearsing for a parade!

"My princess, are you all right?" asked Syng, Byria's personal attendant. She remembered Syng's name because Syng was always there, always knew the right thing to say when Byria forgot. She was a few years older than Byria, with beautiful, black, straight hair kept in a slightly more intricate style than the other maids. "Loosen the tie on the wrap, Mohi!"

"I... I'm forgetting the practice for the parade." Heat flushed her cheeks. That was bad. Sweat would cake the makeup used to pale her skin like fine dishes and sculptures. She wouldn't be perfect for the wedding. She had to be perfect!

And she was forgetting the parade! Her hand shot out, clenching the long cuff of Syng's sleeve like an eagle grasping a mouse. "Remind me what I must do for the parade, my Syng."

"You must simply sit beside your husband in the coach behind the dragon statue," Syng crooned, using her free hand to stroke Byria's hair. "There's nothing you need to practice for today. Breathe. Remember to breathe. I'll have Mohi keep your dress a little looser. It can't be too loose, you know—"

"It would be improper." Byria shut out the world, thinking only on her breath as it came in through her nose, brushing her upper lip like the kiss of a tiny wind. "But... but Syng..."

She found herself unable to let go of the woman's cuff. Though Byria's eyes were closed, the rustle of Syng's silks indicated her beloved maid was shooing the other girls out; she wouldn't let her princess be embarrassed with another episode. Byria loved Syng dearly for her kindnesses.

The delicate patter of feet and swishes of dresses left the room. Byria found it a little easier to breathe.

"What is it, my love, my princess?" asked Syng.

"If I shall be sitting beside my husband, then is the parade happening after my wedding?"

Her answer was silence. Breathing became hard again. What was she forgetting? What was she getting wrong?

"Syng?" Her voice squeaked like the sound of baby chicks.

"My princess…" Syng lifted Byria's chin and ran her thumb over each of Byria's eyebrows.

Byria blinked, and then looked at her maid, hating the pity in her eyes, hating the delicate edge that always seemed to cut—but needing that cut, needing that focus, sharpness. It cut away at the comforting blurry edges. Sometimes it helped.

This time it didn't. She shook her head, begging for the explanation this time.

"My princess, today is the Parade of the Family Dragon."

There was a nudge in Syng's voice. The tone pushed against some memory stone—she pictured her mind as a broken mosaic, each stone hiding a memory, each memory a piece of her life story—but nothing loosened free.

"It's the celebration of the day your husband freed you from the dragon, before he was your husband, of course."

I was captured by a dragon? Dragons are truly real? But… "Before he was my husband? I… my wedding?"

"My princess…" The edge in Syng's eyes now sharpened her tongue. "Your wedding was five years ago, the day before the second Parade of the Family Dragon."

* * * * *

Chapter Two
Parade of the Dragon

Syng's earlier tones had cut away some of the fuzzy edges. Byria remembered she was married, though hardly the five years since.

She remembered nothing of any dragon.

Syng had explained, "Your husband's sword brought its power to your family seat, making him the ideal husband."

"Rescuing me wasn't enough to make him an ideal husband?"

There had been that sharpness in Syng's eyes again.

Byria remembered making note to never ask such a question again. Syng always could tutor her with just a look. Sometimes she would even remember the lessons.

Like at this moment. With her husband catching her eye, she gave him that shy, woman's smile he loved. The one she painted to tell him he was a good husband, and she was a good wife.

He returned the smile, touched his hand to the many-faceted gem of her family upon his chest, and turned to the crowd gathered along the main street of the Golden City, waving to greet their applause, noisemakers, and firecrackers.

Byria mimicked the pose—minus touching the necklace; a woman didn't wear jewelry of power—and his smile. But her mind slipped back to the preparations and the memory.

Syng's face had softened, and she'd caressed Byria's hair, careful of the face paint, repositioning an enamel barrette, delicately sculpted into a moon moth and appropriate for a woman. Byria touched it in her hair now. Her maid had said, "It's the dragon's fault you have this memory issue, my beloved princess. And the scars. We cannot imagine what horrors the monster visited upon you in your captivity."

Syng's words had nudged a different memory stone, one that caused a lurching, ill feeling that sat in her stomach still, even as she waved for the parade.

Fuzzy memories dulled pain. That made sense. Byria kept the world blurred and soft to avoid painful, sharp, cutting edges and points. Ripples like the gentle edges of a lake or stream could keep a blazing fire contained.

Sometimes, when she accepted the loosening of a thought, it made a memory real. This thought—the thought of the dragon and why she had problematic memories—though she knew it was true, didn't ease the sickness she felt. There must be another memory, buried deeper still. She wanted to explore it, find it, since the world was being clear—she remembered she always wanted answers and memories when things were clear.

But there were so many people!

Byria could feel them all, each clap as if it were a pat against her body. It wasn't a hard slap, not a strike, but even just a "pat" from so many thousands could wear away tender human skin.

The sulfur scent of the firecrackers also gave her clarity. Her husband—*His name is Tain*, she reminded herself—wrinkled his nose and hardened his eyes at those who set them off.

Seeing that glint, sharp like the facets of the stone he wore, made Byria's stomach lurch again; she knew to hide it. She set her face into the smiling mask, positioned her hand as if she were working a puppet, and tried to find a balance between blurry-in-between and clear-and-important.

She looked upon the dragon statue. The ornate float carrying her and her husband was drawn by eight war horses. Directly in front of them, twelve men carried the six-sided platform holding the gold dragon. At each corner was an ironwood post, twelve feet high and carved with magical runes. Between the posts, magepriest magic darted like lightning, shimmering against the golden scales, and making the whole display resemble a glass cage from the menagerie.

Such precautions were necessary to keep the crowd away. None should ever touch the statue, lest they tarnish the family power.

Memory: The dragon statue was a likeness based upon the corpse her husband had brought to the Golden City, the capital, when he'd returned her to her family. She'd been a child, too young to marry, but was promised to the man.

Byria didn't remember any of this herself, but she knew the stories, and the pictures in her mind from the stories were clear. The corpse of the dragon had been given to the magepriests, and they'd performed all the rituals necessary to instill the power of the beast in the city and its ruling family.

Byria remembered none of the rituals, either, but most women weren't allowed into the presence of the magepriests outside of the sacramental rites—such as birth-calling, naming, and fealty-swearing to one's husband.

The dragon was coiled, like a snake. She remembered being told it was twice the length of a tall man, but the coiling made her think it was bigger. Pictures of dragons on tapestries and paper blinds had curled horns, like those of deer, sprouting from their heads. This dragon didn't, though its bat-like ears matched the paintings. Its snout was not so long nor so thin as a crocodile's, but bore similarity. Perhaps the muzzle of a fine horse—like those that drove the carriage—mixed with the crocodile would make a better comparison.

He, not *it,* came another thought, perhaps a memory, but she couldn't find what it attached to. She couldn't recall anyone referring to the dragon as anything other than "it." A genderless, sexless monster made of magic and evil.

His face didn't look evil to Byria. Perhaps the sculptors had taken pity and given him a neutral face?

The thought of sculptors gave her the same *no* sensation as calling the dragon an *it.*

One of the firecrackers from the crowd sizzled against the magepriest lightning. Her husband stood to admonish the person, calling the guards for an arrest and to confiscate all fireworks, adding that anyone hiding them would also be arrested.

When he stood and shouted, a thought that felt True reminded her she shouldn't flinch or cower. It would be unbecoming of a princess.

You would be hurt. That thought felt True, too, but she didn't recognize it as hers.

Something pulled her attention to the dragon.

Sparks still sputtered where the firecracker was caught in the lightning. A few danced along the side of the statue. The gold darkened to a copper tinged with green. It moved. *He* moved. Closer to the tiny sparks of fire, but not too close…

She gasped.

"It's all right, my love," her husband Tain said. He placed an arm around her shoulders. "They will be dealt with."

"The dragon—" she hissed.

"Don't look at the dragon, my princess. Look at me." His thumb and fingers grabbed her chin and pulled her face toward his. Her neck tightened; she knew not to pull away, but instinct tugged otherwise.

He squeezed harder, and pinpricks of pain blossomed along her jaw. His eyes were sharper and colder than the royal fish knives.

"Look. At. Me."

She closed her eyes—a foolish, rebellious act that resulted in more pain. His other hand snaked around her, and fingers dug into the spot just below where her silken beltcloth tied. Where she remembered it hurting when her maids had tied it.

Pain made things clearer; that was the edge fuzzy memories dulled. Byria knew what she'd seen.

"The dragon!"

It was hard to speak with the way her husband clenched her face. She supposed to the onlookers, he might appear to be caressing her, calming her from the recent excitement of the wild firecracker. Everyone knew the princess was delicate.

"No, my love." His voice was soft this time, and his grip grew gentler, as if he were cradling a child. "You do this whenever you see the statue. I know the memories are hard for you, but what you see isn't real. It's just the fear of what it did to you."

The dragon would never hurt me!

A wave of guilt made her swoon. She took advantage of her husband's soothing attempts and looked once more at the dragon. Gold, all gold.

Her mind wasn't right. She could have imagined it.

No!

"My princess..." Her husband's fingers dug into the bruise again. "Can you make it through the parade? It would be embarrassing to you and your family if you had to be brought in. Again."

"I... I will be fine. My love." He liked it when she called him "my love." She gave him her sweetest smile; he always liked that, too. "You know how I get. You take such good care of me."

She leaned her head on his shoulder, avoiding his gemstone. Something—a lost memory or a feeling—told her even brushing against it would cause more problems, more pain.

Tain relaxed, loosening his grip, and kissed her on the temple. "I do. I only want what is best for you, my love."

She smiled again, eyes lowered, then turned back to the people and waved. Out of the corner of her eye, she saw her husband resume waving, though his eyes kept flashing to her.

A sadness welled in her mind that she didn't understand. She glanced at the dragon once more, and the tiny, broken stones that hid memories moved just a little, trembling, shaking as if from a great wind. For half a moment, she thought she saw the sides move with breath. This time she didn't react.

Instead, she used her thumbnail to make a tiny cut in her first knuckle. It was a pain *she* chose, an edge she kept sharp so she could remember.

* * * * *

Chapter Three
A Choice

Byria lay awake in her bed. Her husband was out with the other men, warriors and soldiers, drinking to his victory again. He would flirt with serving women who could wear loose, unbound clothing in bright colors. Then he would come to her room and demand his marital rights.

He would always come to her room. He never invited her into his.

If she were very good, and reminded him how much she appreciated his sacrifice and pain to save her, he wouldn't hurt her past the marital rights.

Perhaps.

Women were permitted no weapons. They couldn't even touch them to hand them to their men. The eunuchs even prepared food in such a manner that no lady need ever touch a knife.

But she had access to her embroidery—proper women should create beautiful things—and embroidery needles were sharp. She'd tucked one into the corner of her mattress, concealed. When she'd dug her nail into her knuckle at the parade, it had helped her remember. It made the blurry edges fit together, and she'd avoided angering her husband.

He'd praised her well, saying this was the first parade she'd finally made it through without embarrassing him and her family. That was good. There was no need to be punished.

It occurred to her that if she could remember things that kept her from being punished, there would be less need for blurry edges and memory problems.

Except memories still hurt. She didn't like what she remembered. And now that she'd remembered a particular thing, it frightened her.

"Why have you given me no children? What's wrong with you?"

Syng had reminded her that she'd been married for five years. There were no children. Surely a good wife would have provided a child—preferably a son—by now, no? Her husband thought so. When he came tonight, he would expect her to grow pregnant.

Byria didn't want to become pregnant. The thought made her ill, though she didn't know if it made her more ill than the thought of being punished again.

When her husband came to her that night, slobbering and drunk and demanding she give him a baby, Byria didn't let her mind grow fuzzy. She told herself it was her choice to experience the pain.

And there *was* pain. He was rough; he slapped her with a man's leather belt to soften her muscles—he said the problem was that she was too tight, that she clenched so hard, his seed couldn't get in her.

She clenched because the belt hurt, but she let it hurt this time. When he was done with the belt, he twisted her breasts and bit at them. Bit at her neck. He pushed her onto her back and shoved her legs apart, and she let him. That made it easier. She still felt his painful shove into her, and the tearing. And with each thrust, the rubbing of her welted back and buttocks against the dry sheets. The maids, of course—even Syng—would say nothing of the bloody sheets, nor comment on how stiffly the princess moved. Life would simply continue.

But it won't *be the same,* Byria decided.

When her husband was done exercising his marital rights, he rolled over and fell asleep. Byria made herself breathe slowly through her nose. Breath was a gentle kiss on her upper lip. As she just breathed, she reached for her hidden embroidery needle. As she just breathed, she made tiny stabs in her thigh with the embroidery needle—a pain *she* created and controlled.

* * * * *

Chapter Four
A Secret Gift

As Byria walked through the moonlit gardens, the smile on her face felt foreign, as if she were training her mouth to speak a language from across the sea. Yet she didn't want the smile to leave.

It had been a most wonderful day, and she would remember all of it.

Tain had been inside, with the other men, sewing Between Moon gifts for their women. Many times throughout the day, Byria had imagined him poking a thousand holes in his hands, and his blood ruining his work over and over. That wasn't her favorite memory, though.

Today she'd fought.

It hadn't been a *real* fight, of course; the Between Moon women's fights were a game, nothing more. Except Byria had *wanted* something real—and had received a gift.

Her mother normally discouraged her from partaking in the fight games with the other ladies of the court, and previously, she'd obeyed. As far as Byria could remember, she'd listened to her mother, the queen of Huotaro. She didn't know why, but the thought of disobeying her mother had always filled her with the same fear as disobeying Tain—though she had no memory of her mother hurting her as Tain did.

But my memories still like to hide, Byria thought to herself, pausing before a still fountain bed. She dipped her hand in the shallow water to run her fingers through the stones, to make ripples, the way she pictured her mind working. Like the small silver wishing coins, her memories often hid beneath mental stones she couldn't easily move. Or things became blurry, as if the surface had been broken, and she couldn't focus.

Ripples twisted the faces of the two moons upon the water. During the Between Moon festival, all the fountains were stopped so the pools would reflect the silver Seal Moon and copper Stormbringer Moon.

Around the many palace gardens, night-blooming flowers seemed to glow, dripping a perfume almost as heavy as midsummer, and leaving a fragrant path for the Demon-Wife Hero herself to walk among them. Stories and songs said she did so on this night, granting wishes or causing chaos, depending on her mood.

When the women had gathered to play-fight, Byria had kept her mind clear with her stolen embroidery needle. She'd come up with an argument. Perhaps she hadn't borne her husband a child because she sat out these games and displeased the God.

The queen of Huotaro had intoned that playing among courtesans was beneath a princess's rank, Byria had pled that she wished to join the fights *only* because she would do anything, *anything*, to please her beloved husband.

"And I am bleeding, Queen Mother…" she had added, eyes lowered as she bowed in supplication. "It's an auspicious time for me to do all I can, that I might best perform my duties as wife."

Finally, her mother had relented.

In making herself remember more, Byria had discovered a talent for acting—or rather, remembered the talent more readily. It was a good defense when Tain was angry.

She *was* bleeding; that much was true. The blood wasn't *that* blood, however, but blood caused by Tain, who believed if he *made* her bleed before the celibate time of the Between Moon festival, it would have the same effect. Byria doubted any auspiciousness to an injury's blood rather than a woman's regular blood. Her mother hadn't needed to know the distinction for Byria to make her argument.

Byria slipped a hand inside her belt pocket and pulled out a shard of green glass. The "weapons" the women had been given to fight with were dull wood shaped like men's swords, but decorated with gilt, colored glass jewels, and dyed leather. The moons' light glinted upon the glass's ragged edge, widening Byria's smile. The glass was only half as long as her smallest finger, and only as wide as one of her hair comb's teeth.

It was the most beautiful thing she'd seen in a long time. And it was hers.

During the play fights, no one had wanted to—or *dared* to—strike the princess. Certainly not with the queen watching over the "battles." That had infuriated Byria. She'd come to fight!

After the fourth woman had bowed out of Byria's challenge, Byria had lunged at the fifth woman before she could do the same. It was poor game etiquette, as it would be for fighting men, but Byria had wanted to *hit* something.

For her part, her opponent had held her own. While not attacking Byria, she had defended herself. Cruel whispers buzzed among the court ladies. Byria would send the low-ranking woman who had fought her a gift and good fortune prayer before the festival was over.

Surprised at her own strength, Byria had broken the woman's sword not but a minute into the match (She would send a *generous* gift). The broken weapon had permitted the woman to bow out honorably.

Knowing no other woman would play with her that day, Byria had paid her respects to all the "warriors" of the games, the mistress of the games (the wife of the ceremony master who oversaw combat challenges between men), her esteemed and blessed queen mother, and the direction of the sunrise to honor the God.

With the fighting, and then turning and bowing, Byria's robes had become tangled. When she'd taken a step to leave, she had fallen in a most undignified and unprincesslike manner.

A sharp pain had cut into her arm. She hadn't cried out. It took far more than that to make the princess voice pain. The soft titters of the court ladies had been cut short by her mother's glare. As she'd stood, she'd palmed the cutting object. After carefully adjusting her robes to hide any potential injury and her illicit find, she'd bowed again, leaving with more collected grace.

A different wave of feminine laughter and whispers brought Byria back to the present. She thrust her prize into her belt pocket and ducked behind the fleshy vines and lattice of a moonflower plant.

Listening, she heard no approach. After a moment of breathing to calm herself, to convince herself it was not a good time to test the sharpness of her glass—others might see!—she left the shelter of the plant.

Keeping to the shadows of lattice and vine, Byria followed the sound of the other women. The tones of their voices sounded more like servants than courtesans. As she got closer, she heard the soft lapping of water.

They must be in one of the baths. During equinox night, when both moons were full and night was exactly as long as day, women servants could use the royal baths. Most took advantage of the luxurious bath house within the palace's walls, but a few knew of these hidden hot baths amid the gardens and chose to use them.

Byria's smile returned as she made out what they were saying.

They were talking about Between, the hero of the night. The magepriests, of course, insisted the Demon-Wife stories were nothing but folk tales and had prohibited their public singing during the festival, but they couldn't stop the people from retelling the stories to each other.

As she crept closer, Byria thought she recognized a few of her handmaidens' voices. Peering through the jasmine hedge at the bath, she recognized their faces. Among them were a few young girls—too young to be servants. Byria wondered which of her personal servants had children. It bothered her that she couldn't remember any of them speaking of children.

Syng began to sing.

Byria recognized the song, too. The First Cycle of Between. One of the formal songs, the forbidden ones.

Byria fingered her glass shard, pressing it between her fingers hard enough to hurt, but not cut, as she listened carefully to the storysong. She'd heard it many times before, she knew. This time, this time she wanted to *remember* it—just as she wanted to remember which of her servants had children, families, and lives beyond caring for her.

* * * * *

Chapter Five
Between

A tailor and his wife were expecting twins to be born when the Stormbringer Moon eclipsed the Seal Moon, hiding its light for much of the night.

The magepriests say—and the sorcerers before the magepriests, and the wisemen before them—that children born before the eclipse will start life strong and end weak. Children born as the Stormbringer Moon covers the Seal Moon will be plagued by evil and bring evil into the world. But if a child is born as the Seal Moon is revealed after the eclipse, that child will be a beacon of light.

The woman's belly grew through nine cycles of the two moons, swelling even when they waned. Finally, the night of the eclipse was there, and the woman started her birth pains. She fought with the coming children, not wanting them born when the moons were getting dark.

The older of the twins was strong-willed. Despite her mother's attempts and wishes, she came just as the eclipse hit the halfway point—neither in more darkness nor in more light. The younger twin daughter came easier, though slower, and the Seal Moon was more than three quarters revealed at her birth.

The girls grew, and as they did, they showed their personalities. The younger twin did, indeed, bring joy wherever she went. Her skin was pale, and her black hair reflected any and all light. Upon her entrance into a room, people would smile just in her presence—and her manners and grace were impeccable.

The older twin, however, was not so fair, nor so sweet. But she had many friends, for what she may have lacked in manners, she had in laughter, stories, and schemes. She never meant to hurt people, though sometimes in her thoughtless fun, she would.

One day, the older sister had been sent to wash the laundry in the river, a task she hated and found boring. A water demon swimming by heard her sighs of lament and approached her.

"Oh, what is a lovely lady such as yourself doing sitting by the water, attending to something so mundane as laundry?"

The demon, like most when interacting with humans, wore a handsome face and spoke with perfect manners. While the older sister could tell what he was, the flattery still touched her. After all, it was usually her sister whom everyone called lovely, and who would not be a little jealous of that?

"Thank you for your kind words, sir, but I am not a lady, as you say, but a humble daughter of a tailor."

"With a face so beautiful, you cannot be. Are you sure he is your father? That you were not a stolen child?"

"I am very sure I'm not a stolen child. My parents can recount my birth. It was during the Seal Moon's eclipse."

"So you *are* a special lady, for it's auspicious to be born during an eclipse."

"It's auspicious if the Stormbringer Moon is passing from the Seal Moon's face. I was born in the middle, so that is not so auspicious."

"Ah, but it is! To have equal measure dark and light is auspicious, indeed."

"Perhaps for some, but not most I know," she said demurely, for while she could tell she spoke to a demon, she knew better than to insult him. A demon, of course, *would* find being born with darkness auspicious.

"Perhaps, then, you don't belong amongst those who don't appreciate your special birth. Come with me, and I'll show you what it's like to be not only appreciated, but adored. Would you come with me?"

"I thank you for your kind invitation, but my parents do adore me, in their way. I have never wanted for food or clothes or affection."

"Oh, dear girl, you should know better than to lie to one like me." The demon's eyes grew dark. "I can see you have wanted for affection, and I can give you such beyond any means your parents could ever give. Would you but walk with me, that I might show you my affection?"

"Once more, I thank you. You are too kind, sir. But they have given much to raise me. It would be disrespectful for me to just leave them." She was careful not to lie this time. While it was true she was well-loved by her parents, she did want the affection they more often showered upon her lovelier, sweeter, better-mannered sister.

"You insult me to suggest your parents—a tailor and his wife—could care for you the way I would, maiden."

"I did not mean to suggest that, sir, but would you have me disrespect my parents for your offers of affection? They have already given a first payment to a matchmaker."

"Would you have them sell you to a man who couldn't adore you as I would? Would you let them disrespect you so?"

The older twin lowered her eyes and inclined her head, as she knew a modest woman should do—and her twin sister always did, but she herself so often forgot. But in the presence of a demon, she knew she needed to play the game while scheming of a safe escape—a thrilling feeling, she had to admit. One could not be too demure or too yielding or too sweet, lest such a creature trick a person and steal them away to the demon realm.

"Dear sir," she said again, for she also knew to call a demon what he was would anger it and bring its wrath upon her family, "you are far too handsome and clever to adore one such as me. Besides my simple face and simple manners, would you want a partner who would blemish your grace in defying her parents? But if you find beauty in one so lowly as myself, and if you were to ask my parents for their blessing, and they to give it freely, I would be ever so honored to be that which you adore."

The demon growled at her, his expression twisting and revealing his true face for a moment. He knew no loving parent would freely give blessing to their child's union with a demon.

When he regained his visage, he looked even more handsome than before. "I see you respect your parents, and the God sees that as good. I will distract you from your chores no longer, but if you would be so kind and mannered as to allow me to kiss your hand before I go?"

The older twin clasped a robe to her chest, her eyes still lowered in respect, and said, "Dearest lord, as my parents' livelihood is clothes, and they promise the lords whom they serve that their valued clothes are touched only by the hands of their virgin daughters, I must respect that, as well. I thank you once more for your kind and gracious attention, and I bid you the safest travels on your way."

With his third invitation declined, the demon transformed again and gnashed his teeth. The older twin had been mannered and clever, doing nothing to give reason for retribution, so he could do nothing against her but dive back into the water and leave.

The older twin finished washing as quickly as she could, not daring to breathe even a sigh of relief until she was near home and far from any chance of the demon seeing anything that might appear as disrespect.

While she would never admit as much—for she could be somewhat proud—the older twin had been shaken by the meeting and kept the event to herself. Though she was glad to know she'd been clever enough to escape, she was gladder when her sister offered to wash the next day.

When the shadows had grown to afternoon lengths, and her sister had not yet returned, worry grew in the family—but in none more than her twin. She wasted no time running to the river when her parents sent her to check on her sister.

Her fears were confirmed when she found only a basket and clothes upon the bank.

Falling to her knees, she gasped out a cry and stared into the waves of the river, searching for the face of the demon. Her sister was kind and well-mannered, but she could also take those traits too far. Not wanting to be rude, if she were caught unaware, she might have accepted one of the demon's invitations—leaving her open as his prey.

She gathered the clothes, washing them with her tears, and slowly made her way home. She knew she was clever, and she knew she was stronger; why had she let her twin go down to the water today? The older twin lamented that she could have prevented her sister's abduction. Demons work in threes. She should have known he'd come back and tempt her twice more.

When she returned with the clothes, she did not tell the whole story. Her parents, seeing her tears, did not press. They alerted the town, and search parties were sent, but the older twin knew such things were in vain. Only *she* could release her sister now.

Eating herbs that stole sleep, she waited for her parents to retire, and she snuck back down to the river. With the proper offerings in hand, she invited the demon to speak.

Sending a tray of honey-sweetened rice and cream on a small boat to the handsome-faced demon, the older twin asked, "Dear sir, I offer this to you for knowledge of my twin sister. My parents are distressed, for as I'm sure you understood, she is their favored child. What would it take for you to release her?"

"What do you speak of, dear girl?" The demon reached for the food, but a shock stopped him. He glared.

"The offerings are given in exchange. They are yours when you answer my question in full and with honesty."

His face twisting once more with a growl, the demon stared at the older twin with a gaze so hot, it burned. She did not flinch and waited patiently, head bowed and eyes lowered in respect.

"Your sister accepted my invitation to kiss her hand, and her touch allowed me to take her to my home. She refuses food or drink from my unending cups and plates of gold, and is not nearly the smart company I want by my side, so if you were to join me, instead, I would free her."

"Is there no other way for me to convince you to release her? Will you take no other offering?"

"The cut-out hearts of both your parents, perhaps? Nothing less than that or you by my side."

The older twin replied, "Then I will join you by your side, but I need to prepare. Will you allow me to do so? I will return tomorrow night."

"Then I will see you tomorrow night." The demon took the offerings and disappeared back into the water.

The next night, the older twin once again stayed up until her parents were asleep. She knew part of what trapped people in the demon realm was eating or drinking that which was made there, and stories told of poorer people who fell victim to promises of cups and plates and bowls that never emptied. Taking the robes meant for her wedding, the older twin hid food and drink in its folds, and went down to the river.

The demon was waiting, her twin on his arm, and he smiled as the older twin approached. "I am here, good sir, and I will join you once I see my sister walking the path to my parents' house."

The demon stared at her for a long time. "I wish to see you as I would on our wedding night. Disrobe and cast your clothes into the water, and I will let you see your sister walking the road home before I take you below."

The older twin said, "This is my wedding robe. To simply discard it into the water would disrespect the work my parents put into making it for me. If you would have me throw it away, may I change and leave it for them to resell the fabric?"

"Can you leave and return before the sunrise?"

"I will return tomorrow in my oldest robe, that I may cast that into your water and come naked to you as I would upon our wedding night."

"You would leave your sister to me for another whole day for the sake of *clothing?*" The demon hugged her terrified-looking sister closer to him.

"One must always hold one's parents above siblings and friends, and so I do. As you know, my sister is favored by my parents. She has eaten and drank enough that another day without food or water will be little for her to bear." She hoped her sister understood her and would not eat or drink—for if she did, the older twin knew, she would be lost to the demon realm forever.

"Tomorrow night, then. And if you are not ready then, your sister will be mine forever."

"I understand."

Once the demon disappeared into the water again, the older twin left, only she did not head for home. She headed to the butcher's and cut away the skin of a pig that was left to cure. Leaving the silken sash of her robe as payment, she snuck home, stealing her father's best needle and thread. When her parents awoke, she told them she was sick, so they would leave her. When they did, she took the pig skin, needle, and thread, and with the practiced hand of a tailor's daughter, she sewed the pigskin pockets to her own flesh. Then she pressed a healing paste and used her mother's makeup to hide her work. Once her parents went to bed, she hid food and water in her new pockets, and returned to the river for the last time, wearing her oldest robe.

"Lord, I am here as your wife, and I cast my robe into your water. Set my sister free as you promised."

She stood there, naked and pale, praying that her handiwork was good enough that it was undetectable to his demon eyes.

"You are a woman of your word, child of the half-eclipse, equal parts darkness and light. I will keep mine."

Her twin's feet touched the ground, and she ran to her sister, but the older stepped away from her embrace. "Go home and tell our parents what has happened, that I loved them and respected them properly. Be happy in your life, and know I will always love you. But go. Now."

The younger twin's face cracked with sobs, but she did as she was told, and the older twin watched her leave down the road. When she could no longer see her twin, she walked to the water and stepped upon the path the demon made. The older twin took her place by his side and let him bring her to the watery demon realm below.

Everything in the demon's realm had a sumptuous façade and glamour, though the older twin could see better—as one might see the muddy bottom of a pond below its shining surface.

When he offered her food and drink in a cup and bowl he said would be hers, she asked if she might have her first meal alone, that she may have one last memory of her family before becoming his wife. Pleased as he was that she was with him, he granted her request.

When he was gone, the elder twin emptied the food and refilled the bowl and goblet with food and drink from her realm and ate that. As she took each bite and each sip, she saw that her food was what refilled the vessels, and she felt a tie, an anchor to her own realm.

When she let the demon take her to bed, she hoped her scheme would not be undone. He was a surprisingly gentle lover, for a demon, and she felt her tether still. She tested the link and found she could return to the mortal realm at will.

So, when her husband traveled to play his games, she would return home and watch over her sister and family. Sometimes she would help others, exchanging advice for more food from the mortal realm to put into her bowl and cup—strengthening her ties to the mortal realm.

Her scheming won her favor even from the demon she had tricked. And so the clever twin, born in perfect split of darkness and light, grew to live between the mortal and demon realms.

And now, if one is clever enough and brave enough... if one brings the proper offerings, and shows the proper respect... the older twin might still answer cries for help—particularly for those regarding demon troubles.

* * * * *

Chapter Six
An Offering

After the story was sung, the women made their way out of the water. Byria pulled away, eyes on the flowers to allow them their modesty. No one said anything, but she heard the sounds of moving stones and clinking porcelain.

Byria had no siblings. The storysong made her wish otherwise, made her wish she were the older twin sister. While the younger twin brought light and grace wherever she went, the older twin made her friends laugh, created mischievous schemes, and fixed problems she found. She remembered this was not the first time she had felt kinship with the Demon-Wife, Between.

With wet, shuffling steps, the women left the hot pool. Byria counted to one hundred before leaving her hiding spot.

Nothing seemed out of place around the pool. Puddles and drips of steaming water marked the women's path back to their quarters. No one else was around.

Byria knelt by the flat stones that more hot water usually ran over, directed by hidden pipes from the bath house to waterfall into the pool. Without the water running over them, she noticed a space where two rocks didn't quite fit against each other. In the opening between the stones were plates and bowls from a children's tea set filled with tiny servings of cut fruit, honey, and sticky rice.

Byria smiled so widely, she felt the night air against her teeth. An idea hit her. She pulled out her embroidery needle, the one she kept hidden in her robe when she needed to feel pain, to take a little control, to keep her mind sharp.

Holding the needle out as an offering, Byria let the moons kiss it, and then she tucked it between the tiny plates and bowls. Today had been a gift, and she wanted to give thanks. After hearing the story again, making sure she remembered it, she felt the needle was a most appropriate gift.

She had no duty to return to her bed. Sex was forbidden during the festival's three days; it was believed the wait made for stronger children. Instead, she found another shadowed path to follow the water trail of the women. Syng had only performed the first cycle of the forbidden songs. Hidden in the servant's area, she might be bold enough to sing another.

* * * * *

Chapter Seven
Conversing with a Dragon

It was the Parade of the Family Dragon again. Byria was aware of it as her servants dressed her. There were still fuzzy edges to most of her memories, especially the old ones—and even those from the past year.

It was hard to tell if there were fewer new scars this year than last. She wished she had some point of comparison, to see if her experiment in pain had made her suffer less punishment.

As she let her maids dress her, she concluded it had made her suffer less in other things.

Knowing and remembering gave her power. A secret power. The tiny cuts she made regularly with her piece of glass signified nothing to anyone but her; they looked no different than the cuts Tain made. A secret was power.

And she had *two* secrets.

Her belly had begun to swell, and it was *her* punches that had made the miscarriage happen. No one knew better. Of course, Tain had punished her, but he'd have punished her for having a miscarriage, regardless.

She'd made a decision that affected the kingdom. Her husband would have no heir. At least, not from her body. No child of *hers* would suffer his cruelty.

It was their sixth year of marriage. If she didn't produce an heir tonight, he had the right to take a handmaiden as a concubine.

Byria pitied the concubine, but it would mean he paid less attention to her.

In her layers of dresses and material, she found it easier to climb their royal float behind the dragon. She also found it easier to shape her mask into a smile and wave her hand. She'd tucked the colored glass shard into her sleeve; she welcomed its rub against her wrist with every movement.

And she found it easier to look at the dragon.

No.

She *wanted* to look at the dragon. It would give her power over whatever it had done to her that she couldn't remember.

When she'd made herself look at the statue for a full minute, she thought, *"Greetings, Dragon."*

"Greetings, Princess."

She gasped. She hadn't expected that.

"My love?" Tain grabbed her wrist, the gem on his chest flashing facets of angry sun. His grip made the glass dig in, and she smiled at him, lowering her eyes demurely.

"I-I apologize, my love, but I felt…" She touched her stomach and thought of the most powerful thing she could say to keep Tain from hurting her, from disturbing her moment and this unexpected discovery. "Tonight, I believe, our prayers shall be answered. I've never felt like I do in this moment."

Her husband's eyes widened, and he changed his grip, putting one arm around her middle. "What is it you felt?"

"I… I can't explain, but…" She looked up at him through her lashes, lips slightly parted. "I look forward to your visit tonight."

He bent down and kissed her, a rare kiss that didn't hurt. The crowd cheered at their embrace.

She smiled when he was done, flexing her wrist so the glass point stuck her—*let there be pain*—and she let him raise her arm, hand clasped in his, to show their union to their people, making them cheer even more loudly.

He kissed her cheek once more, and then returned his attention to the crowd, smiling, waving with one hand as the other brushed the royal gemstone. Fortunately, that meant he released her hand. He didn't see the tiny, disgusted flick she hid in the billows of her sleeves, even as she scratched herself again.

Re-affixing the smiling mask and letting her hand wave itself, she turned her attention once more to the dragon. Had she imagined that thought, that greeting?

"*No.*"

She kept her surprise, her fear, well behind her mask this time. Then she imagined a mask over her mind, hiding her thoughts, too. This was neither the place nor the time.

But in the corners of her eyes, whenever she looked away from the dragon, she saw it. What she saw, she wasn't sure. Sometimes it was the movement of a flank in breath. Other times a swirl of copper, green, and stone. The twitch of an ear or tail. And once—just once—it, no *he*, tilted *his* head just enough to look at her.

She kept all these things behind the mask of her face and mind and continued waving and smiling at the crowd. She was the proud princess of the warrior husband who'd slain the dragon and taken his power for himself.

For the second year in a row, she made it through the parade without an "embarrassing" incident.

* * * * *

Chapter Eight
Another Secret; A Passage

Byria didn't lie in her bed waiting for her husband that night. She sat and waited. She waited for everyone to lose themselves in drink and celebration, and then she snuck to the bedroom door.

She left her room to explore halls she didn't know by heart. She had barely an idea of where she was going, just that she was going toward something True, something different than the story she'd been told was hers.

She took her shard of glass with her. It wasn't a weapon, but it made her feel safer. Inching the door open, she listened carefully. Nothing but the usual sounds of the palace. She crept into the hallway.

Picturing the dragon in her mind, she started walking in a direction. Her silk slippers and robes made no noise against the stone floors. Her eyes, her feet through the silk, her nose, her ears—even her tongue, like a snake or lizard—attended to her surroundings. She would remember this path.

The hall she followed didn't go to the main stairway, but Byria hadn't expected it to. She was also unsurprised when the hall ended with a tapestry covering a wall. Of course the way would be hidden.

The tapestry was one of her favorites, one of the few of the Demon-Wife Between that hung in the palace. That fact seemed fitting in Byria's mind. This particular piece showed the woman hero calming an angry water dragon that had brought chaos and ruin to all the lands. At least, that was how the tapestry depicted it. A trickle of thought moved a memory stone, and Byria heard the bars of a different song, one where Between had rescued the dragon from a demon lover who'd trapped it.

Byria wasn't here to admire the tapestry or remember music. She willed her senses to find some clue, some hint. There would be a secret passage. Stories or tales frequently had secret passages and hidden stairways.

There was a brick that smelled different, *felt* different. She touched it, and a vibration shot through her fingers. She pulled back, then pressed her fingers once again to the stone.

It *was* like a vibration, but one she could manipulate. Again, she didn't know how she knew this, but she did.

The princess moved her fingers, curling them into a pattern that *felt* right. A giant breath sighed from the wall, fluttering the tapestry and Byria's hair. Edging her fingers behind the tapestry, she drew it aside. A solid slab of granite opened inward, revealing a slice of darkness. She pushed the door wider.

Looking deeper, she found only more darkness. Warm darkness that breathed. She'd brought no candle or lamp; such a thing would be seen, and she didn't wish to be seen.

If she explored this darkness, would she fall, hurt herself? What would be her punishment for wandering, for not being ready and waiting for her husband to exercise his marital rights?

Byria dug the edge of glass against the inside of her forefinger. She chose to accept the consequences, whatever they were. The princess lifted her chin, a rebellious gesture to the very darkness itself, and slid her foot forward until she found the edge of a stair. She stepped.

When she closed the door behind her, there was no light. There was nothing for her eyes to adjust to. One more dig of glass. She would move forward, follow the staircase.

An energy, not unlike the one she'd sensed from the secret passage's trigger, pulled like a spider-string attached to her breastbone. A warm spider string. The feel of cool, rough stone against her fingers pleased her. She smiled a real smile, not a mask, though she wasn't sure why. She compared the air current to a breath because it had an underlying warmth.

Keeping a hand on the curving wall, she moved—*slip foot forward, find edge, step; slip foot forward, find edge, step*—down a spiral staircase.

Spiral like the seashells in paintings. She had a memory of holding a shell, an actual shell. Purple-blue and perfect.

When had she been to a beach? Had someone brought it to her? No, she'd been on a beach at one time. A scent she recognized as the ocean—only so much cleaner, *purer* than the scent at the docks they passed during the parade—traveled on the darkness's breath. Ocean, sand, stone smelling hot in late afternoon, the burn of hazy and sharp sand and rocks and shells on bare feet.

There had been many different bird calls. The waves pounded and hissed—things she could feel as well as hear. And one sound, one sound stood out: a *hawoosh* of wind past her ears.

It was a real memory, sharp and edged like her glass, like jagged rocks and sand and broken shells. It was real. Just as she'd known the dragon was real, and a *he*, and that she had *not* imagined what she'd heard and seen at the parade. The ocean memory was beautiful, soothing, yet it hurt. Byria found herself sniffling and felt the itch of unexpected tears.

She squeezed her glass again, hard, possibly drawing blood, but she didn't want this memory—or the memory she was making of walking blind down a spiral staircase—to fall between fuzzy edges. They'd be added to her trove of secrets.

Slip foot forward... slip, slip. No edge. Byria hesitated, then slid the other foot to meet its partner. She stood solidly on two feet, slid her hand against the wall, and found a corner. Another press of sharp glass reminded her she could be brave, that she was choosing these consequences, and she shuffled silk slippers around a corner.

She saw a thread-thin light edging around what looked like an arched doorway down a hall.

The spider-silk tugged at her chest again, and the darkness seemed to breathe faster, excitedly. Through the silk of her slippers came a similar vibration to that trigger stone. It called her forward.

Would there be traps? Would they hurt? It was a secret passage, after all; only certain people were supposed to be here.

You belong here. It "sounded" like the dragon in her mind again. But... it also sounded like something she knew she should know. It made her memory stones hum and move—like what she felt beneath her feet. What was calling her to the doorway?

She chose to move forward.

One more drag of glass to remind her she was making this choice, having this thought.

I belong *here.*

She entered the room.

* * * * *

Chapter Nine
Freeing the Forbidden

Even in this hidden room, mage-lightning surrounded the dragon statue. Byria couldn't quite tell if it was the lightning that cast the glow, if the dragon himself glowed, or if it was a combination of both.

The darkness had stopped breathing. It was holding its breath, as was she. It hurt her lungs, so she slowly blew out air until her body forced her to breathe in again.

Her stomach churned, both sick and excited. Fear and... joy? The joy of a child, a child laughing on the beach, avoiding the waves, climbing rocks, and feeling safe. Safe.

She knew what "safe" meant; she'd felt it once.

A lurch from her gut to her nose, as if she were falling, made her stumble. She reached out, grabbing the marble countertop along the wall to keep her balance while a wave of dizziness passed. She leaned on the glass in her sleeve. She would *not* faint!

Byria focused her attention on breathing, just breathing. And staring at her hand on the marble counter.

Its beveled edge had a pattern similar to the ornate carvings in the temple she could now remember from her wedding day. Another sharp memory came: she'd worn a blue silken dress with an embroidered train that had spread behind her in a circle almost as large as her bed coverlet.

It wasn't a happy memory. It wasn't like the ocean, though the dress shared the ocean's color on a sunny day.

But the memory was clear, no fuzzy ripples.

Byria gripped the corner of the counter harder, using it to press the glass into her palm. She felt the sticky sensation of blood. Her blood now marred this pristine place where she knew she shouldn't be.

Where they *say you shouldn't be.*

The princess looked at the dragon. Shimmering mage-lightning, the dim light, her own wooziness made it look like he was moving—coiling around himself so he'd fit into such a small space. His tongue, forked and black, flicked and flicked. He could taste her blood in the air, and that agitated him.

"What did you do to me?" she asked. "Why can't I remember?"

"Forgive me, my princess."

The words pierced like a knife to her chest. She looked away, looked at the dark smear of her blood on the counter that now stained her robe's sleeve. Tain would notice *that*. And if he noticed, he might find out her secret.

Panic fluttered like snakes in her belly. No. She must keep her secrets. They were all the power she had.

"No. No!"

She chose not to look at the dragon, though she felt truth in his words. A heat flowed through her body, a different kind of power. For a moment, out of the corner of her eye, she thought she saw mage-lightning on her skin, beneath her robes.

With a gasp, Byria stepped from the counter, running her hands over herself. Blood smeared whorls like the dyed designs in the most expensive silk robes.

Tain would *definitely* notice that.

She looked at the door. If she left now, she could change, bind her hand, say she was already embroidering a baby's name-choosing sash and had simply pierced herself. Certainly that would allay any punishment, preparing for a baby and awaiting her husband's arrival to her bedchamber. She should leave.

"Please!"

Another knife stab came from the emotion in that voice. It wasn't a voice that begged. It had *never* begged, but it would, just this once. The sensation of this Truth nearly doubled Byria over.

She chose not to look at the dragon. He wanted her to look at him, and it was an act of rebellion, not doing so. Choices she could make were powerful, important. Instead, she looked upon the counter past the blood smeared on the corner.

Her attention split between two things.

Within a silk-lined box near the back of the counter was a collection of ornate knives, set out like tools, but beautifully worked. Layers of metal arched and waved like ocean waves painted on the paper walls. Written characters between magical creatures—phoenixes, spear-horses and water horses, manticores, things she didn't recognize, and of course, great dragons—decorated the hilts.

She wished to touch such forbidden objects. Open blades decorated with the symbols of power and writing she recognized and almost understood, despite knowing full well women were not permitted to read such characters.

What stopped her was a second thing, more macabre, more unsettling than such a wide collection of blades.

An eye floated in a jar of clear liquid. A full eyeball with veins lining its white roundness and flowing into a thick purple cord that dangled like a tail. The eye was *looking* at her.

That it was looking at her was another thing she felt was True.

It had been watching her since her arrival; that was True, as well. Yet no guards were on their way to her in this forbidden place. No danger came from being watched, not by this eye. Byria studied it as it studied her.

The color of its iris was unlike any other she'd seen, a golden amber like honey. It appeared to have an upside-down triangle carved into it, inside the black pupil. The triangle reflected—no, it *glowed* a warm red, like embers from a fire.

She didn't know why, but watching the eye watch her boosted her confidence, made her feel stronger, jostled more memory stones. Good ones. It felt *safe*, the way she had often wanted her mother's eyes to look when she shared her fears about Tain—the way her mother's eyes *never* looked.

Solid, sharp, real memories. The look in this triangle-etched eye told her she could face the dragon. She *should* face the dragon.

Byria first took a knife. A small one—that was hard enough, but it fit in her hand. Standing straighter, she loosed her robe just a little, and gently ran the tip down her inner thigh, where she would often cut with the glass, alongside new and old scars—some with memories attached, others without. Tain, like her handmaids, couldn't tell the difference between his cuts and hers.

It didn't hurt, but she *felt* it. The line of blood, her blood that she'd chosen to draw, made her smile once more. As she lifted the blade to look at it again, she watched a bead of blood run from the pointed tip down the blade. It reflected the mage-lightning like the edge of a fire, or the line of lava seeping through a crack in volcanic stone.

I've seen lava. Her thought. Another True memory. *I've been in a volcano.*

She remembered the smell of sulfur, the feel of heat burning inside her nose, the prickle of sweat on her skin, and the almost-painful warmth beneath her feet. That was also a *good* memory.

Byria looked at the dragon. He'd stopped moving so much, but for the flick of his tongue, and she only saw that when she focused on the mage-lightning. If she looked directly at the dragon, she saw nothing but the golden statue.

When she stepped, she felt the line of blood down her leg. She saw the stain on her silk slipper and the drops on the floor. The princess chose not to panic because she had no plan for how she'd hide her slippers or the stained robe. She took another step toward the dragon. And another.

To keep stepping, to keep breathing, she had to explore the room and the dragon in pieces.

Step. The dragon's eyes sparkled like a blanket of embers or a pool of lava.

Step. There was a low table like a bed with straps that filled Byria with dread and jostled memory stones she didn't want jostled.

Step. The dragon *did* breathe. *And* he changed color.

Step. There was a door on the wall that did, in fact, have exactly the same carvings that decorated the temple. Byria had the sense it led to the sacrosanct area behind the altar where only magepriests could go.

Byria stood at the dragon statue, so close she could touch the nearest corner column surrounding the dragon if she dared. Mage-lightning flickered between the columns, which were carved, though not in relief like the counter edges or the archway of the door that would lead to the most secret part of the temple.

The princess had a feeling if she stared long enough at the carvings, she'd be able to read the characters.

Byria looked at the dragon. He had five claws on each of his feet shaped like human hands. She could taste the dragon's breath, hot like a volcano, salty as sand, and metallic as blood. It escaped through the waves of mage-lightning. Letting her eyes lose focus in the blur of the magic, she saw the dragon watching her.

She lifted her hand and reached to touch. The lightning walls pricked shocks of pain against her palm.

Byria had become quite good at bearing pain. She kept her hand there and asked, "What did you do, Dragon? Why did you ask me to forgive you?"

"I failed you. It is my fault you suffer so."

Gripping the knife with two fingers, she loosened her robes more, revealing the scars. "Did you do this to me? With your claws and teeth?"

"Yes. And no, save for once."

"I don't understand."

"That is my fault as well. I failed you, and I failed my oath, save for the scar that saved you once."

His "voice" was in her mind. And it *hurt* him to speak. Byria felt *that*, too.

"You can't tell me plainly." She knew she hadn't spoken a question once the words were out. The hand she still held to the mage-lightning was beginning to burn. It was the hand she'd stabbed; she was aware it no longer freely bled.

The dragon lowered his head, affirming her statement.

Byria had another choice she could make, a powerful one, and one that was entirely hers. "I forgive you, Dragon." No pain, no blood, not hard-edged, but still clear and True.

Heat—a good heat—bubbled up from her stomach and filled her chest. Tears prickled her eyes once more. The vibration beneath her feet grew, moving into her, shaking her bones and blood.

"I forgive you, Dragon." Like a temple chant, the words had power, and more when she repeated them. Tears flowed down her cheeks freely, but not due to pain. There were memories, True things, but they were emotions. There were no pictures, no tactility, no taste nor smell to go with them, but they were real. "I forgive you."

No pain, but it still *hurt*, and she didn't know why. Byria was losing control—too many emotional memories, and no ground for them. She'd made a choice, but it was too big... too big yet. The princess needed to control these things. She needed...

Byria pushed her hand to the mage-lightning cage. Shocks froze her. Terrified her. Another real memory. A bad one, an awful one.

"No! No! No! No!" Her thoughts or the dragon's? Or both?

The dragon lunged. She knew it hurt him. The force of movement, of air, wind, a *hawoosh* like from great wings—she saw no wings upon the dragon—pushed her away from the wall. She stumbled backward, falling, dropping her forbidden knife.

A dragon's scream was a thing that shouldn't be forgotten.

How had she forgotten it?

To cause so much pain to such a powerful being renders a cry that could split earth, air, flame, water, and more.

The whole room shook. The knives clanged metal notes. The jar with the triangle-etched, motherly eye tinkled. The stone groaned. The low bed to the side that Byria could see without looking sparked with more metal clanks and a soft buzz.

And the dragon's scream hung in the air like ash from a volcano.

He coiled more tightly. No, no wings, but she'd *felt* wings. He appeared smaller now, and not metallic. Shifting colors like stones and lava. Byria could see him clearly.

The mage-lightning wavered and crackled outward from her tiny handprint, a smear of still-sticky blood.

The dragon's tongue flicked in her direction just before his head snapped to the doorway and the stairway.

"*Run. Hide!*"

Voices echoed. They were coming down the stairs.

She would be punished so horribly, and the dragon feared so as well.

Body shaking, Byria stood. There was the door to the sacrosanct area of the temple. Would the God actually strike down a woman for going there? Would such a fate be any worse than what Tain and the priests would visit upon her for what she'd already done?

She took two wobbly, jogging steps to the sacrosanct door and stopped. "No," she said.

The dragon snapped his attention to her. She felt his command, his emotions urging her to leave—he couldn't even put together words. His fear for her hurt worse than the cage's magic.

There was still a choice she could make, before the God struck her dead, or her husband did worse. There was one more powerful thing she could do.

She dove for the small knife. Clutching it tightly, she ran it across her palm, drawing fresh blood upon its blade.

The pillars containing the mage-lightning were carved. They wouldn't be metal. The lightning was magic, not needing the conduction of metal. More information Byria didn't know how she knew, but useful information. She plunged the small, bloodied blade into the ebon-wood pillar, splintering it, prying at it, wanting more than anything in that moment for it to break.

And it broke.

The lightning scattered across the room. Byria dove to the floor, fear of the loosed power all but making her heart stop. Two mage-priests, a soldier, and her husband had come through the door. They, too, dove to the floor to avoid the explosion of the dragon's cage.

For to cage such a creature required the most powerful of magic, and to break that cage…

The room shook harder and longer than when the dragon had screamed.

Byria heard the crashing of metal and glass. The eyeball was on the floor with the knives, other containers, and broken glass. For a moment, Byria hoped it wouldn't be cut by the blades or broken glass.

The roar of the dragon snatched the princess's full attention. He flew. He *did* have wings—but wings of pure flame. Fire billowed and flapped from his sides, making a *hawoosh* sound she recognized. The dragon flew and circled toward a ceiling that was higher than Byria had imagined.

So big and so small. Eyes on the dragon, she was paralyzed in awe. Seeing such a creature stabbed Byria with a different fear.

It was, after all, a dragon.

A dragon she'd freed. A dragon now reveling in his memories of power. Despite his fiery wings, he moved more like a snake in the air, diving over the now-cowering men. He paused, hovering above Byria.

"Come with me, my princess." His words were spoken in a voice of fire upon coals.

In her mind, she cried, *Yes!* but she said, "No. Leave me. So I command!"

The dragon hesitated, and a wave of sadness descended in his heat. In that half moment, she *knew* he would never force her—had never forced her—to do anything against her will.

Reptilian quick, he darted to the ceiling. A blinding flash of flame and magic weakened the stones and shingles. They fell, some landing hard upon her prone body. The dragon's shadow flitted briefly over the face of the blood-copper-red Stormbringer Moon, and then he was gone.

Byria could smell the piss and shit of the men who now surrounded her. They grabbed her arms and lifted her from the ground painfully. Her husband clasped her face, hard, in his hand.

"What have you done?" He was furious.

She should have been trembling, perhaps have even soiled herself. No memory, not even vague ones, showed him in such a rage.

Yet Tain didn't frighten her. She'd seen a True Dragon, freed him, felt the awe of his presence and the heat of his flame.

She'd forgiven him for sins she didn't even remember, and meant it.

A smile snaked across her lips. Her mouth cracked open, and laughter poured out. When was the last time she'd laughed? It didn't matter. She welcomed the laugh; it was hard around the edges and hurt her throat.

She welcomed the pain from Tain's strike just before she welcomed the darkness that followed.

* * * * *

Chapter Ten
Consequences of Power; Consequences of Choice

"Will it work again?" Tain's voice, displeased. Byria had heard it far more times than she'd ever wanted to in the past... week? Few days? Month?

Time was slipping between fuzzy edges to dull the pain. She had to let the edges get fuzzy again; she remembered why she'd given in to forgetting so often. Even remembering that fact hurt.

Besides, there were too many pains to differentiate now, and none of her own doing. Or, in a sense, all of her own doing, but none within her power or control.

Her arms ached from her chest to her wrists from bearing her weight as she hung, not quite on her knees, but unable to stand. Her skin wept blood and pus from the untreated lashings that screamed pain. She doubted more than a flash of the bruises from his fist showed through the torn flesh.

Not that she could see herself. Both eyes were swelled shut from blows and the acidic fumes held below her face.

And then there'd been the brands. Multiple brands, for she was a traitor to her husband, to the throne, to her people, to the God. Each of her sins had been burned into her flesh between the lashings.

Worse, Tain had still taken his rights as husband upon her body that night, and uncountable times after. Punishing her had always excited him in that way.

He had taken her in ways that wouldn't produce children, she was certain. The way a man would take a whore, not a princess. She remembered that forbidden knowledge. Syng had shared a picture book of such things with her the night before her wedding. Pain had loosed that memory stone, and it flowed clearly.

"I'm not sure, my prince." That voice belonged to the high magepriest. He'd supposedly been chosen by the True God to be the greatest keeper of magic, and to train the other priests.

People placed his age at over a hundred, possibly a hundred and fifty. All his hair was silver and white, and he wore a long beard, but he walked with the bearing of a man only in his fifties or sixties. Byria pictured him speaking to her husband just off to the side, not even thinking or caring that she heard. "She may forget everything again, and we'll have no information on where the dragon has gone to ground."

The dragon. He was real. He'd once protected her, but failed.

Byria would *not* let that memory slip back into the blurry-edged whirlpools that dulled the pain. In that moment of hesitation, before he'd left as she'd commanded—he'd done as she'd commanded!—he'd hovered for not even time enough to draw a full breath.

He had been *magnificent*.

It was the greater sin to allow a being like him to be held and tortured, captive to mere mortals. Horrible mortals, at that.

She'd made that choice. That choice was her power, and she *would not* forget.

"What other choice have we?" The anger in Tain's eyes was tangible. Even their voices struck upon skin so raw. "Our best scouts returned to the cave and found nothing. Absolutely *nothing*."

Some time must have passed since the dragon's escape, Byria guessed. His cave was certainly not near, and it would take time for scouts to go and return.

The high magepriest sighed. "There's still the black fire witch in the dungeons."

Black fire witch? Another memory stone loosened, but not quite enough. She sensed a change in Tain's posture; the heat of his fury lessened. "She's still alive? I thought she died."

"She hasn't."

"What would you do with her?" Tain asked. Byria felt his eyes on her again. "She was no help in finding the princess or the dragon before, and she shouldn't have survived your questioning."

"But she did. We did nothing with her once you returned with the princess and the dragon." The high magepriest's voice smoothed into a poisonous tone that made Byria's stomach twist. She barely kept from gagging; that would hurt even more, and give away that she was listening and conscious. "She worked so hard to hide the child princess, fought all our questioning of her. How would she feel to see one she apparently cared so much for suffering like this?"

Someone cared for her. Someone with honey-amber eyes—only one eye?—set in a dark face.

Byria saw that memory in a flash before she had to fight another wave of illness. She would be used to torture someone who'd once cared for her to find the dragon for whom she'd chosen to suffer this punishment. This *questioning*.

She remembered the questions now. They'd slipped between the pain-dulling edges of her mind. *Where did the dragon go? Why did you release him? Where is he hiding? What direction did he fly? Would he return to the same cave?*

Byria had refused to answer, even if she'd known. Her forgetting was a gift. She had no recollection of where the dragon had once lived or how he hid. She remembered he could change his skin like a chameleon, but she didn't even share that information.

Would this black fire witch break upon seeing her? Would her choice to free him be lost? Would the pain be for nothing?

No. No, that must not happen.

Tain moved in front of her. She could smell his sweat and feel the heat of his body. She gave no reaction. His hand grasped her face and lifted her head so she might look at him. Well, as much as she could with swollen eyes.

His voice was soft as he spoke this time. "Why?" He brushed his thumb over her cheek. "You were so happy at the parade."

Byria expected her silence to be punished. Instead, Tain walked away, returning with healing salve. He began to rub it over her body, his touch gentle and the salve soothing.

Memories like this bubbled up, too. A soft touch, a pleasant kiss, an arm cuddling her after he'd taken his marriage rights. She'd enjoyed those moments, treasured them, even—when she could remember.

"Did he steal your tongue? You've hardly made any noise at all." His voice was still sweet. He carefully unstuck her hair, piling it on her head and fixing it with sticks so it wouldn't get clotted into the injuries he now cleaned and treated.

Injuries *he'd* caused.

The dragon stole nothing from me. The dragon gave me a gift. Byria had felt it inside her, a well of her own fire deep in her belly. Perhaps not literally, but it was there. Burning. Smoldering. When she let it, its heat kept the edges of her memory sharp.

"What did he do to you?" His lips were by her ear, brushing it. The edges of her ears were a part of her that wasn't injured, and his breath and touch caused a pleasant shiver.

She hated that worse than the pain. Would that he'd beat her again! Byria focused her attention on the pain caused by the weight on her arms and any movement of her skin.

"My prince, should I fetch the witch?" asked the high magepriest.

Byria hoped the tensing of her muscles would be read as a reaction to the salve.

"Can she *do* anything? Is it safe to bring her up here?"

Byria imagined Tain looking at the broken prison the dragon had escaped from and realized she thought similarly. What might a fire witch do if brought to this hidden room behind the temple?

"Of course it's safe, my prince." The high magepriest scoffed. "We've removed her power thoroughly."

"Mmmm..." was all Tain said.

"It was your wife who set the dragon free." The high magepriest spat as he spoke now. "You saw her blood on the post. It's still blood of the Most Holy Royal line, chosen by the True God to rule us. The dragon must have tricked her in some way."

Of course he must have tricked me. A delicate princess would never *think to do such a thing.*

Byria liked the edge that grew on her mental voice, like teeth. It was like donning a long lost robe. Perhaps, in the memories she still hadn't found, she spoke with a knife for a tongue sometimes. That would have certainly caused plenty of punishment. And she had many, many scars.

"If the dragon was able to trick my delicate wife, it wasn't completely contained. It would've had to get through your barriers."

"You placed the brands upon your wife." The high magepriest spoke in tones of snake venom. "You know she's a traitor. Perhaps she weakened the bonds herself and allowed such vile trickery. Women's minds are easily twisted to the darker side of magic. You know this too, my prince."

"I know what I was taught." Tain's voice was hard to read, and that unsettled Byria. She listened extra closely to the words he chose. "But I also know my wife. She's betrayed us—that much is true—and I punished her for her actions as the law directs."

The rest of his statement went unspoken, but Byria knew it. *The law directs death to traitors.*

"Unless they atone and submit." Tain ran his fingers down her arm. "If she leads us to the dragon, that would be atonement and submission. If it could be shown she wasn't in control of herself…"

"The dragon was suppressed, its power fueling our kingdom for seven years. It wasn't until she interfered that there was a problem. With most reverent respect, my prince, do you doubt the might of the magepriests?"

"What man would?" Tain's question answered that he did, in fact, doubt the magepriests' power.

Or that he may not actually wish to kill me, a softer voice in her head said. *No,* responded that sharper voice that was also her own. *Of course he wouldn't want that. He could no longer hurt me if I were dead, and he would miss that greatly.*

"Shall I bring the fire witch up here so we can question her, too?" the high magepriest asked. "Though, of course, if it's the fire witch who leads us to the dragon, I'm not sure that would be the same as the princess atoning and submitting herself."

Tain stood up. She knew the posture he'd be using, the one that reminded everyone he was, in fact, the warrior who'd rescued the princess and slayed—no, captured—the dragon. "Where is the witch being kept now?"

"The southern dungeon. It would be some long minutes to bring her here—"

"Don't bring her here. There are other cells down there. Place my wife in a cell the witch can see. Use your magelight orbs so they can see each other. Place two guards at the door down there, and a black mirror outside the cells, just in case."

"My esteemed prince?"

"The southern dungeon isn't directly below the palace. If my wife somehow manages to also incite a witch—who should have died years ago—to try to escape, a fire would be contained there, and the mirror will let you retrieve my wife, should she need extrication."

The tone of Tain's voice said he'd chosen his words to jab at the high magepriest. "That's my order. You may ask my father-in-law for his blessing, as well, in case this goes beyond his decree that I am to handle all things regarding my wife and the dragon."

"I don't question your orders, my esteemed and holy prince," the high magepriest said with matching voice.

"Good. I'll inform my guards, they're at your disposal."

Byria listened to Tain's steps as he walked away, and the *swish* of him donning his royal robes—he'd left them far from where any blood or other fluid would mar them.

Two guards entered shortly, unbound her wrists from the poles she hung between, rebound them behind her back, wrapped her in a rough cloth, and carried her to the southern dungeon.

Byria hurt too much to even consider fighting.

But moreso, she wanted to meet this witch and weigh her loyalty to the dragon.

* * * * *

Chapter Eleven
The Fire Witch in the Dungeon

"In here," Tain directed.
Of course he's here, making sure all happens as he planned, she thought.

"And you two, place the mirror there."

Byria hardly moved when the guards dropped her in the cell. Perhaps it was due to her lack of response that they cut her hands free. She still lay motionless, listening to the cell door *clank* shut, the boot scuffs, the heavy shuffle and grind of whatever the "black mirror" was being placed exactly as her husband directed.

They'd left the sheet around her. She pulled it closer. Some comfort. She did her best to pry her eyes open. The swelling seemed to be going down in this cool dampness.

Shadows moved solidly from steady sources of light. She remembered a last-minute order from her husband to bring *only* magelamps, nothing with fire. He was taking no chances.

Though the lights were dimmer than torches or lanterns, her eyes soon adjusted. A loud *clang* of metal striking metal, and then *cla-cla-clanging* down the row of bars finally caused her to flinch. Neither Tain nor the guards were looking at her, though.

"Witch, are you really still alive in there?" Tain asked.

A glowing orb over her husband's hand illuminated the cell across from her. Not by much, but enough to see movement through her lashes and irritated mucus. There was a person, and the person indeed had dark skin, as in the brief flashes of memory that were returning to Byria.

Foreigners, many the slaves of the merchants and farmers, were dark like that. Byria saw them occasionally on the parade route. In the palace, the servants weren't so dark, and some were especially pale. One of her mother's handmaids even had hair the color of maple leaves.

The other prisoner stopped moving, but Byria could feel herself being stared at. She pulled the sheet around her more.

"Sit up and take off that sheet, my wife, or I shall remove it," came the cold, angry voice of Tain.

She raised herself as best she could and let the sheet fall to the floor. If the purpose of this exercise was to make the woman speak of the dragon because she cared for her, Byria would give them no excuse to torture the woman more. Tain would see to it Byria's compliance with his orders was most painful.

Lowering her head, she let herself tremble, but through her swollen eyes, she peered hard at the witch where she figured her eyes—no, eye—would be. She must see that the princess was *not* broken, nor would be. If she did know anything of the dragon, she *must not* be persuaded to reveal it.

"Come closer, or do I need to drag the princess to where you can see her?"

"I can see her well enough, you fucking monster."

The witch spoke in a low voice with a thick accent, and Byria was quite sure the descriptor for "monster" was in a foreign tongue, though she understood it. A memory slipped through like a bubble. The woman had taught her many coarse foreign words that Byria knew the meaning of—but she had no recollection of their equivalent forms in her language. Proper ladies would never use such language, and men would never use it around proper ladies.

"Even with one eye?"

"Even with one eye."

Tain's posture stiffened, and he puffed his chest out more. His hand shifted just a little closer to his royal gem, which caught the light, shattering tiny twinkles inside. His other hand rested on the hilt of his knife.

This woman unnerved him, and Byria had to fight the urge to smile. She lowered her head further and pretended to tremble more, as if she, too, were terrified.

A thought came to her. That the witch saw her "well enough" was a message to Byria, as well. She understood this game.

This witch could be trusted.

"I will leave you two to catch up, then." Still in a defensive posture, Tain headed toward the door.

Another thought came to Byria. She threw herself against the bars, reaching out to her husband. "Please, my love!" Her voice scraped against her throat, making her sound more pathetic, broken, helpless. "Don't leave me here! Why am I here? What have I done?" A sob broke into more pitiful coughs.

Tain hesitated, staring at her. His dark brown eyes flashed a second of warmth before turning cold again. "Do you not remember what you've done? How you freed the dragon and betrayed us all?"

"D-dragon?" Byria could remember herself in the moments of not remembering, and she wore that role like a mask now.

Tain came to the bars and slapped her hand down, squatting in front of her. She shook her head as if confused. He stared hard into her eyes, and she was relieved that they were still quite swollen, making it harder for him to see through her mask.

He said nothing more before standing again. Then he turned to the witch. "If you have any care left for her, you may wish to spark her memory of where the dragon might live, else she face the five different deaths of a traitor. I'm sure the magepriests will find any way they can think of to allow her to experience as many deaths as possible."

Byria watched him leave, and the two soldiers stood on either side of the exit that Tain locked behind him.

She turned her attention to the witch, who settled down at the back of her cell. She said nothing to Byria, but the princess could feel her gaze. Now was not the time to speak. Taking her sheet, a tiny shred of dignity, Byria wrapped it around her shoulders and lay on her side, where the least amount of her body touched the floor. She didn't need to cause more pain than necessary to keep her memory sharp and clear.

* * * * *

Chapter Twelve
Breath and Fire

"Byria?"

Byria blinked her eyes open upon hearing her name. It occurred to her that she couldn't remember the last time she'd heard her name. Not once from her parents' or husband's tongue, and certainly no servant would dare speak her name.

But she recognized it as her name. Upon hearing in the fire witch's accent, she realized it fit better there than in the native tongue of Huotaro.

She didn't know how to respond, though. There was something altogether frightening about hearing her name. Frightening in the way seeing the dragon fly had been frightening: a welcome sensation.

"Byria?" Concern touched the woman's deep voice now. "Do you even remember—?"

"That *that's* my name? Yes." Her voice scraped thinly from her throat, sounding smaller than Byria wanted. She still lay on the ground, sheet covering most of her body. She was cold, and she hurt, but all that was overshadowed by the fire witch speaking to her, by the emotions the woman's voice stirred. "But I only remember you calling me that."

"No one else?"

Byria thought. "No one in the palace."

The woman spat. "Well, of course not. *They* wouldn't know it."

"What do you mean?"

"I gave you that name to hide you, and you asked me if you could keep it. So I said you could. I told *them* nothing of you. Not any name."

Byria blinked her eyes. While not as swollen as earlier, the remaining puffiness still trapped tears and blurred her vision. "I don't remember that."

Hearing movement in the other cell, Byria tried to clear her vision. Mage orbs floated near the ceiling and cast dim light. The woman knelt near the bars now, staring at her.

Biting her lip, she glanced to the door; both guards were asleep. She gasped. Surely palace guards would know better than to fall asleep at the same time! Byria looked back at the woman.

The witch smiled a sharp grin that flashed teeth. "They won't bother us for a while."

"You still have witch magic?" Byria swallowed hard, unsure what to think of that. On one hand, if the woman had power, why was she still trapped here? On the other, a woman using magic both intrigued Byria and gave her an unexpected sense of comfort.

"Some. I've been saving it for a while. They nearly forgot I was here."

"I didn't know you were here. Not until the high magepriest said so."

"Did they tell you I was dead?"

"They told me nothing. I didn't—I still don't mostly—remember…" Byria looked to the floor in shame. How could she forget the woman who'd given her the only name she knew?

The woman was silent for several moments. When she spoke, her voice was soft and gentle. "What have they done to you, Byria?"

The gentleness of the fire witch was like the sharpest scalpel lancing a boil. Byria hiccoughed once, gasped, and choked a moment before giving into sobs that poured from her body like diseased pus and infection.

As when she'd faced the dragon, there were no pictures, no sensations. Only emotions. They all fought to be released in that moment. Byria could do nothing but lie down and let them loose.

The fire witch said nothing. She didn't have to. Her silence wrapped around Byria like an embrace.

When she finally cried out all the warring emotions, Byria rubbed her eyes on the sheet's few cleaner spots and stared at the woman, not quite ready to move. After a moment of gasping, she said, "I... don't remember. I can't even remember your name."

A soft chuckle came as gentle as the prior silence. "Don't worry yourself about that. I never gave you a name. You just called me Patch." She tapped her closed, hollowed lid. "I used to wear cloth over it. You were little, and that's what you called me."

"Patch." The name felt familiar on Byria's tongue. It brought back memories. Good memories. "You had a few different cloths of different colors. One of them was the color of the sunset."

She chuckled again. "I remember you liked that one. I left it with him when I left you."

Byria tried to retrieve that memory, but couldn't. She shook her head.

"Doesn't matter now. What matters is, we get you out of here. You set *him* free. Now it's time for you to go."

Byria widened her eyes. She understood the woman's words. They were in her tongue, but they confused her as if they were a foreign language.

"Sit up for me. Let me see how badly you're hurt."

Swallowing, Byria moved, or tried to. Every inch of her skin hurt. Even the sheet stuck to her injuries. She whimpered, fresh tears flowing down her cheeks.

"I'd hoped it wasn't as bad as it looked, or that you'd healed more while you slept," Patch said, her voice sounding much sadder now. "I'm not a healer. That was never something I was good at."

She sighed. "You can't leave in that condition. We'll have to come up with a good plan to give you time to heal."

Byria still didn't know what to say. Patch looked as if she expected an answer. What answer could *she* give? She could hardly move. It had taken all her strength just to *keep* from talking, to look at her husband. She thought of the prior night, trying to convince him she knew nothing—that it was useless to torture another person to get her to talk. Even that had drained her, and she wasn't sure it had accomplished anything.

What would she do outside of the palace?

I wasn't always in the palace. The thought came to her. *Not even for most of my life.*

"I don't have any plan," Byria whispered, swallowing and finding only blurry edges and sharp light when she reached for any specific memories outside of the palace.

"Don't you worry, child," Patch said softly. "We'll think of one. Now, just heal. As I said, it's not my talent, but I've seen you heal yourself before. Focus on that."

Byria drew her brows together. Even that hurt, pulling on the raw skin around her face. "I healed myself?"

"It wasn't a power of yours specifically. I never saw your magic the way I saw it in others, but you definitely healed faster than any person I know."

"I have magic?"

"*He* seemed to think so, and I know you could heal yourself. When you were young, you did it as you slept. When you were older, you were beginning to do it on purpose."

"I don't remember." Byria wanted to cry again, but only dryness scraped her eyes. She was out of tears.

Patch paused, and Byria could see the white of her one eye as she studied the floor. Then she looked back at her. "Close your eyes, Byria. Just listen to my voice. Can you do that?"

"Mmm-hmm." Byria did as directed.

"Listen to my voice and feel yourself breathing. Feel your breath moving from your nose or from your lips."

Byria smiled. This was familiar. Was it Patch who'd taught her to do this initially?

"Feel your heartbeat. Around your heart, picture a golden fire, burning and powerful. See it grow bigger with each beat. Feel it grow hotter… hotter… hotter. Do you feel it, Byria?"

"Mmm-hmm." The light around her heart was warm against the cold of the dungeon. She wanted it hotter still, and it grew with that desire.

"Keep growing it, stoking it. It should almost burn your chest."

"Mmm." *Even hotter. Like the dragon's fire. Let it burn right through me.*

"Now, pay attention to your breathing again, just knowing that fire is there."

Making another affirmative noise, Byria found herself smiling despite the cracks around her lips.

"Now, with each breath, listen to your body. Feel your body." Byria whimpered. This was not so pleasant.

"Find where you hurt the most. Find it, acknowledge it, and *own* it, Byria. Take that pain as your own."

She did. She knew this, too. Hearing Patch say it validated her experiment of the past year. All her choices had been correct, had been right. Had been *hers*.

"Once that pain is yours, send your fire there. Send your fire to where it hurts the most. You have a lot of fire in your heart, Byria. You can send it to all the worst pain."

Yes, Byria thought. *I can do this.* Patch repeated her instructions. Byria sent it to the skin on her back, her swollen eyes, the torn ache between her legs, deeper, and behind that.

Eyes closed, she watched that copper-bright fire burn at the scars, at the ruined skin, at the shame that clung to the injuries. She burned it all away with fire as bright and powerful as the dragon had been, and with heat like that which he breathed.

The flame around her heart dimmed, unable to grow, when Patch finally said, "Rest, Byria. That fire is always there. Remember. Keep it burning. Don't forget to tend it, and it will always be there when you need it, but let it rest now. And you rest. Bring your energy back to your breath. Feel that and own that, and let yourself rest as you need."

Byria nodded, sensing Patch could see that. Fresh exhaustion lapped at her, but it was comforting, like the ocean waves from that memory. That *good* memory. The *True* memory.

* * * * *

Chapter Thirteen
The Map Plan

"I know where the dragon hides, but I will say nothing until the princess is fully pardoned and reinstated to her proper place."

No! Byria's eyes flew open upon hearing those words.

Tain stood between the two cells, looking down at Patch.

"Ah—" she managed. Tain turned to look at her, and Patch shook her head, her one eye sharp. Swallowing, Byria looked up at Tain with tears in her eyes. "My husband, have... have you come for me?"

He knelt in front of Byria's bars and reached one hand in, gently brushing her hair from her face. "Will you tell me where the dragon has gone, my princess?"

"D-dragon?" She shuddered and flinched as she had always done whenever the dragon had been mentioned.

"Look at me." He dug his fingers under her jaw and pulled her closer. The facets of the royal gem seemed to reflect red sparks in the dim magelight. She couldn't focus on that in his painful grip. "Do you mock me? Are you playing games with me?"

"I—"

"My cooperation hinges on the princess being hurt no further." Patch's voice was calm and even, yet it carried clearly through the dungeon halls.

Tain dropped her. Byria let herself fall, though she might have had the strength to catch herself. She even released a cry, though she felt much less pain than she'd expected.

Her husband's attention was back on Patch. The fire witch stood naked and unflinching in her cell. The glowing orbs showed scars up and down her dark skin, too. She paced in her cell like the tigers in the menagerie, every bit as commanding.

Tain stood taller, chest puffed. He wouldn't be intimidated. Or at least, he wouldn't show it. Though he stood alone, she noticed six guards by the door.

"I could even draw you a map if you brought me a writing utensil and paper." A wicked smile showed her teeth. Though they were yellowed, rotting, they still seemed bright between her dark lips.

Women, of course, weren't permitted to write. The thought of one drawing a map, among the women Byria knew, was laughable.

She had no doubt Patch could draw a map.

But she mustn't! The dragon must remain safe!

Tears filled her eyes, and she tried to subtly shake her head, to keep Patch from doing this. Her safety wasn't worth the life of the dragon!

But the slightest piercing glance from Patch froze her.

Byria's heart pounded. She thought of Patch's words. Had it been this morning? Last night? She could still feel the fire around her heart. It was stronger now. There was no hay nor anything else in the cells. She didn't remember doing so, but it appeared she'd crawled to a corner to clear her waste, leaving a stinking, liquidy puddle; it had probably hurt, though at the moment she didn't feel the pain so much. Could human waste burn?

She had the sheet. Would this heart fire affect anything besides her body?

The sheet. Her tiny bit of comfort.

Byria pinched the corner of it between her thumb and forefinger.

"Don't!"

She couldn't stifle the cry of surprise at hearing Patch's voice in her head. When Tain turned to look at her, she gave him wide eyes. "May I come back home with you, my love? Please?"

He tightened his lips and narrowed his eyes at her. His look was disgusted, but not entirely. There was still that one glimmer, that potential kindness she'd noticed when he'd carefully treated her injuries, and on those rare occasions when he would gently kiss her.

She hated that glimmer. It was as tempting as a demon's face!

But she couldn't show it. Byria reached her hand out to him. In her mind, she thought loudly to Patch, *"You mustn't betray the dragon!"*

"Trust me."

Byria had little memory of those words ever being trustworthy, but she had so few memories of Patch.

"Do you want my help or not?" the fire witch asked.

Tain turned to Patch. "Once the dragon is recaptured, my wife will be pardoned."

"And you will never lay a harming hand on her again." Patch narrowed her eye at him.

"She's headstrong. Were I not to discipline her, she would get herself killed!"

Patch glared at him.

"You may not think I do, but I love my wife. I want nothing but the best for her, just as you do. The dragon keeps all of us safe. It's in all our best interests that we recover it. I can get the magepriests to drop the charges against her. I'll tell them you stoked her memory, and she'll be forgiven and returned to her rightful place by my side, as future queen of Huotaro."

Patch only glared.

Tain took another step closer to her bars, standing taller and leaning close, though he kept one hand guardedly on his gem as if he expected her to steal it.

Byria noticed Patch was taller than him. Her height and smirk undermined any intimidation Tain might have been attempting. Or perhaps that was only Byria's perception.

When he spoke, his voice was as quiet and even as Patch's. "I offer you this bargain only once, witch. I'll bring a map and one of my soldiers down, and you'll show them where to go. If they find the dragon and recover it, my wife is free and forgiven. If not, she'll be put to death in the worst way the magepriests can find for a traitor. If you decide not to help now, we'll use more severe methods to interrogate her, and if that fails, then she'll be put to death. Am I clear?"

"Abundantly," Patch said. "Send your man with his map, and I'll give you specific instructions. The princess will *not* be subjected to your cruelty further."

"I'm glad we're in agreement."

With that, Tain turned on his heel and marched out of the dungeon, boots clicking. Four of the six soldiers followed him out. Two remained at the door.

After some time, one of the magepriests came down with a map. Byria leaned against her bars and whimpered, doing her best to appear confused, lost, and frightened.

The magepriest cast her a sympathetic look or two, but did nothing. He carefully drew upon the map, writing the directions as well as plotting out the course with a dashed line.

Byria had no memory of any map, but as she saw the course laid out, she knew it was a lie.

* * * * *

Chapter Fourteen
Healing: A Rebellion

Between the minimal deliveries of food, the changing of guards, and Tain's visits, Byria estimated her time imprisoned to be around two weeks, give or take.

Tain reminded Patch that she'd better not have led him wrong. He asked Byria what she remembered of the dragon. When she answered that she remembered nothing and didn't understand why she was down there, he'd stare at her for several minutes as if deciding how he felt about her answer. Then he'd leave wordlessly.

She would've barely healed but for Patch's mostly-regular ministrations, leading her to use her heart's fire upon herself.

Sometimes Patch would say they were being watched and tilt her chin ever so slightly in the direction of the large mirror of black glass that stood not far from the guards. During those times, Patch would speak in Byria's mind, as she had during Tain's map negotiation visit. When it was safe for them to speak freely, according to the fire witch, she explained that such communication was also difficult for her now, though it hadn't been at one time.

"What time was that?"

"A time well before you were born. When I had two eyes."

"I saw… in the room where the dragon was… an eye in a jar. It had a triangle on it. Is that your other eye?"

"How are you feeling today, Byria? How well can you move?"

Byria frowned at Patch's change of topic but didn't press. She stood, dropping the sheet around her, and bent to touch her toes. She stretched from side to side, then walked quickly from one side of the cell to the other.

"Can you run?"

Pursing her lips, Byria moved to the corner where she hadn't been leaving her waste and ran the diagonal of the cell back and forth twice over before she stumbled, feeling winded.

"Better. Better than most any other person should be after what he did to you, but we must continue to work on your healing and your stamina. And we must not let them know how well you are healed."

"Do you really expect me to leave the palace?"

"I do. And to find the dragon and never to return to these abuses again."

Byria sucked in a breath. "You expect me to run away forever?"

"Yes."

"Will you come with me?"

"I may, but only if joining you doesn't compromise your escape."

Byria didn't like the sound of that. Before she could voice that opinion, Patch had her run two more diagonal laps, and once more across just for good measure. Her chest burned from the exertion, and she gagged on the cell's stench, but as she leaned on the bars, Byria saw Patch smiling proudly. She matched the expression.

If she were to escape, she would find every way to ensure the fire witch joined her.

* * * * *

Chapter Fifteen
Blood-cut Plans; Secret Fire

Four more visits from Tain passed, with the only change being how many times Byria could run back and forth across the diagonal in her cell. That, and her nails. Once manicured, with beautifully painted tips, they'd grown long enough for Byria to file to points on the rough stone. Most of them, anyway. It was no easy task, and she'd broken almost half. But her thumbnails were long and especially pointed.

Like dragon talons. The thought made her smile and fed the fire she'd been tending in her heart.

Patch had seen her filing and had made no remark. Byria sensed her approval. In the long, dark, quiet time between them, Byria had learned to read more of what was said in silence and in the shadows of one's face. She counted such knowledge, like the knowledge of her heart's fire and her sharp nails, as more powerful secrets.

It was only for short periods that Patch could put the guards to sleep, and when she could tell no one watched them through the mirror. She didn't explain how she knew, and she spoke very little but to coach Byria on her healing and her running.

Byria wanted to know more; she wanted to know the many things she'd forgotten. She wanted to know who this fire witch was besides the one person she could ever remember feeling as if she could trust. A feeling that grew even more as her heart's fire strengthened.

But there was so little time. As the days had passed, she sensed Patch's anxiety. The fire witch pushed her harder and harder.

When they were free, they would speak freely. Byria would take the woman's hand and feel a touch that she had no fear would hurt her.

The guards had begun to nod off again. Patch achieved this by putting her hand down on the stone in the corner of her cell closest to the soldiers. As Byria's eyes had adjusted to the constant darkness, she now picked up a shimmer in the air, like heat waves at noon rising from tiled paths in the sun gardens, that drifted up from the floor in a line from Patch's hand to the two men.

A slow count to ten was the wait time from when the guards fell asleep before the women were free to talk or move. Byria stood, ready to run. She felt she could accomplish forty laps between the two corners before their short time was up. Patch held up one finger, collecting herself. She seemed to be growing more tired with each time she put the guards to sleep.

"When was your last woman's blood?" the fire witch asked.

Not expecting the question, Byria chuckled mirthlessly. "Just before he brought me to you. He punished me doubly for being unclean and not becoming pregnant. I preferred the punishment to the pregnancy. Why do you ask?"

"It's harder for a woman to travel because of our blood, and you were too young for me to teach you what plants can be used to catch your blood while moving, what to eat to keep your strength, or what roots might aid you if you have pain. Animals are attracted to the scent of blood, so you will need to be extra vigilant."

"But you'll travel with me, and you can show me when we leave. We'll be leaving soon. I can see it in your face."

Patch said nothing.

"I won't leave without you. I will *not* leave you to their cruel hands again—"

"You will leave whenever you can leave, however you can leave, Byria."

"No."

"You *must*, or all I've done thus far is a waste."

"It's not a waste—"

"Please."

Byria shook her head. The softness of the word moved her heart and pulled from her eyes tears she hadn't cried since her first day in this cell. Taking a deep breath and letting it out, she said, "I've only just found you, and I don't even remember… anything, and you're asking me to leave you to the torture I *do* remember?"

"I'm far better equipped for torture than you, and I still remember more than a few tricks. Just because I can't come with you doesn't mean I'll be stuck here, or that I'll fall victim to their inquisition again. At the very least, I can promise you I shall have a quick death before your fear happens."

Byria swallowed. Patch's words were only slightly reassuring.

"I promise you have no need to worry, my child," continued Patch. "Will you promise me you won't hesitate when you have the chance to run? Please?"

Byria stared at the fire witch for several moments, then said, "I promise I won't hesitate when I have the chance to run. *But* I also promise that, once I'm healed and wiser, I'll find a way to ensure you're no longer suffering on my behalf."

Patch tilted her head, regarding Byria. "I'll get no other promise from you, will I?"

"No."

"Then attend to my instructions. And remember them."

Byria couldn't suppress a whimper. *Remember?*

"You *will* remember these instructions. You must."

Byria bit down hard on her lip; the sharp pain drew the taste of blood. Yes, she would remember. Cleaning her thumbnail as best she could to prevent infection, she folded her arms, raking the pointed end against her skin.

"When they come in angry, you'll cower near the door, clinging to your sheet, as you already do. When they open the door, you'll rush them, and rush to the black mirror. On the mirror, you'll draw this symbol with your blood."

Byria knew she could make herself bleed easily. Patch traced a symbol in the dirt. When she was done, it glowed briefly. Byria carved that into the inside of her elbow so she wouldn't forget. Patch nodded when she saw what Byria was doing.

"Then you'll go through the mirror—"

"What?"

"You'll go through the mirror. Trust me. It should bring you to the high magepriest's room, or the room where they kept the dragon—I don't know which. From there, run. Find some servant's quarters or a place to steal clothing. Steal any weapon you can, and any food, water, and money. Then leave. Quickly. Leave the palace. Head northwest from the city. Stay off the roads. Stay hidden."

Byria made a cut in her arm with each instruction, repeating it in her mind. She'd travel by night. She had pictures in her head of foods, places for clean water, and she'd keep moving no matter what.

"Until when?" Byria asked.

"You'll know when."

Byria started to shake. She'd trusted Patch, but she wasn't so sure she trusted this last instruction.

"*How* will I know when?"

"You will. I have faith in that. You can do this, Byria. If you can't remember, ask the fire in your heart where you need to go, and go there. No matter how frightening it may seem."

Trembling as if chilled but without the cold, Byria couldn't find any further words. That was for the better, as a soft snort from the guards signaled their waking.

Patch settled back into her cell with a small nod. Their conversation was over.

Byria focused on the fire in her heart once more, drawing on it to help stop her shivering. As it grew hot all the way out to her fingertips, a thought, a memory came to her. When she'd feared Patch would betray the dragon, she'd thought of creating a distraction, and the fire witch had stopped her. They hadn't spoken of that moment, but would the woman have stopped her if nothing would've happened?

She wanted only a spark, or the heat of only a spark. Too much, and it wouldn't be a secret. Her time with Patch, as short as it might be, had only branded in her mind the importance and power of secrets.

It took longer than she expected, and she had to fight to keep pinching into the burning pain. Finally, she felt a wave of exhaustion similar to the look on Patch's face after she'd put the guards to sleep. Byria had accomplished her goal.

A scorch mark the size and shape of her fingertips marked the corner of her sheet.

* * * * *

Chapter Sixteen
Forging Shit into Shine

When the next chance came, Patch paused Byria, indicating they needed to speak.

"But I need to move!" she said, not expecting her own protest.

Patch smiled. "You do, and you will. But take this first."

A glimmer of motion and a clatter brought a small stone, like an unpolished gem, rolling to Byria's cell bars. She picked it up. It was warm and light, but small facets reflected the mage orbs—No. Not just the mage orbs.

Byria looked closer. In one of the larger facets, she could see the glow of an inverse triangle, like the one she'd seen on the eye in the dragon's room.

"What is this?"

"A token. Keep it safe. Once you get to the jungle, you'll find help." Patch sounded tired, very tired.

"You still speak as if you're certain you won't be able to escape with me." Byria blinked in surprise that her own tone was stronger and more chiding than she'd expected.

Patch chuckled. "I'm fairly sure, Byria, that for many days now I've been strongly suggesting I won't be able to leave with you."

Byria frowned. "You will at least try?"

"I'll ensure you escape. You'll get no more from me than I can get you to promise to never return here looking for me."

Pacing in her cell, she scowled. "You are most stubborn."

"As are you. It's a trait that serves both of us well. I promise you that, too." She still sounded out of breath.

"Are you hurt?" Byria asked, furrowing her brow in concern.

"No, but I am tired. I'm out of practice in using so much magic."

"I'm sorry—"

"Don't you dare apologize. I should have stayed in better practice..." Her voice trailed off.

"Why didn't you? Especially if you were forgotten down here."

"I grew lazy. I'm human. And..."

"And what?"

Patch sighed, and Byria heard a catch in her throat as she said, "I lost hope. I lied to myself, saying perhaps you escaped, or perhaps you were at least being treated well. But I knew *he* was in pain, and there was nothing I, alone, could do. I gave in, Byria. And I almost gave up, except I'm stubborn, so I couldn't. Not all the way."

She shook her head, biting her lip. After a moment, she looked at Byria with the wicked smile the princess had come to love, the one that made Tain wince whenever Patch wore it. "So I'm still here to help you now, and that's why you *will* escape this time, like you promised me."

Byria nodded and began pacing again, regarding the small gemstone. "Where did you get this?"

"I made it. I've been working on it since you arrived."

"You *made* it? From...?" Byria didn't finish the question. There was nothing down here but dirt and their own excrement. Even the walls were solid, no small stones from wear or weakness. Perhaps it was best left unsaid what Patch may have "made" anything from.

Patch didn't answer, confirming Byria's suspicions. Still, it currently looked and felt like a small, just-hewn gemstone. That would be how she'd think of it. And certainly such use of power to create a thing like this from... well, from *anything* would exhaust an unpracticed witch. That was why Patch seemed so tired.

"Now, before we run out of time," Patch said. "Repeat my instructions to you."

Still pacing from the anxious energy that seemed to only build inside her, Byria repeated them back to Patch's approval. Then she returned to her still-in-pain cower beneath her sheet and beside the bars so whoever was watching them would be none the wiser.

And as Byria lay there, she continued practicing her scorch marks along the sheet's edge.

* * * * *

Chapter Seventeen
Underestimated

Tain came down to the dungeon, furious, with eight soldiers behind him. Patch and Byria only had time to share a look.

It's time.

Byria dug her thumbnail into her palm to make it bleed. She held Patch's token in a tight fist.

Tain had the keys out.

Keys!

He unlocked the door.

Byria rushed him. She grabbed the keys, and then she performed the step of the plan she'd created herself.

She willed all her heart's fire into the sheet.

It caught with a *hawoosh* like small dragon wings.

She threw it at the guards. She threw the keys into Patch's cell. She ran to the mirror.

Blood already dripped from her hand. She smeared the symbol on the black glass. She paused to look behind her.

"Run!" Patch was out of her cell.

The flames of the sheet danced like a serpent, binding the soldiers and Tain. "Come!" she called but began to jump into the mirror as she'd promised. She'd only hesitated a moment—to make sure it was safe—

Two hands grabbed her and pulled her *through* the mirror. Once more, the world went black.

* * * * *

Chapter Eighteen
Lightning Crown and Burning Robes

"You promised me the witch was secure."

"You left a flammable object in the dungeon with a fire witch."

Fools, Byria thought as she fought the blinding pain in her head. *You left a flammable object with* me. She tried to move and found her hands bound. Her token was gone.

No!

"Have you at least secured her now?" Tain asked.

The high magepriest responded, "We collapsed the entire tunnel. She should be *dead*."

Dead? No! The feeling on her back and arms was familiar. *Why am I feeling this?* Very familiar. *Patch!* Terrifyingly familiar. *If Patch is dead, they can't torture her.*

Byria's heart beat like it would jump from her chest. Her instincts told her it wasn't fear for Patch. It was something else. Something horrible. Breath fought in her lungs.

What am I remembering?

She blinked. She was in the dragon room. His prison appeared to be repaired, awaiting him. The high magepriest was putting balm on Tain, who was angry that his soldiers were still down there.

Well, there *was* something he cared about.

I need to get out of here! Her feet were also bound. There was wood behind her. That scared her, too. Why? Where was she? Something about the angle of the view. Her mind didn't *want* to remember.

I must escape.

"The collapse was complete. We rigged it as a security measure for the witch," the old man said. "None could survive."

There were burns all over Tain's chest and back. Were it not so hard to breathe, and if she wasn't fighting blinding fear, she felt she'd be wearing Patch's wicked smile. He even still wore the royal gemstone around his neck, unable to give up his claim of power, though she was certain its heavy chain and sharp facets were agonizing against his seeping, blistered skin.

There was another sensation. It yanked Byria's mind back to her own body. Like tiny insects crawling over her skin. It itched. Somewhat. More than itching. Buzzing? Most awfully familiar.

No! No! No! No, what? What was in her mind? Was it even her thoughts? It *felt* like her thoughts, but why did they feel distant? Were the memories so deeply buried?

"Enough!" Tain's face was also half-burned. He should've let the magepriest treat him, or perhaps seen the healers, but he was too furious. Byria knew that look; nothing would stop this now.

"That fire is always there, remember." Patch? Was she still there? Alive? Or was it just a memory?

A burning in her chest told her only the message mattered now.

She still had fire.

Tain stormed over to her.

Byria closed her eyes and breathed. Only breathed.

He slapped her across the face.

She breathed. She felt the breath, but she didn't send the fire to the pain.

Another slap. "You whore. You'll tell us where the dragon went, or we'll drag it from your mind."

Drag it from your mind. She remembered. Panic stole her memory to breathe. That was what they'd done to her before. They had made holes in her memories so they could fill it with stories.

The magepriest was fastening something to her head. A metal thing that made the itching, the buzzing grow. It captured stormlightning and sent it into her mind.

She fought, she writhed, she squirmed, only to be struck more by Tain.

"Tell me, you little bitch."

Tend the fire!

Breathe. Breathe. She could control her breath. That was all. She didn't have to speak. She didn't have to fight. She just had to breathe.

"Tell me."

She ignored the ugly words, the punch to her stomach, the punch lower, and another slap, and she breathed. She wouldn't even look. Behind her eyelids, she watched the fire in her heart.

A thing she knew: Women needed to stay away from fire in their best silks because some of the bright dyes could catch fire.

"Shall I, my prince?"

"This is your last chance, my love." Tain caressed her stinging, swelling face. "Just tell us, and we won't have to do this."

Another thing she knew: The high magepriest had the honor of wearing the best silks in the brightest colors.

"My esteemed prince?" The high magepriest sounded excited.

A memory: The switch that did this, that worked the device that tortured her mind and memories, was on the wall behind her left arm. She wriggled her left wrist to see what movement she had. So very little. Could she reach him before he pulled the switch?

"Your last chance," Tain growled.

The magepriest needed to come closer.

Tain grabbed her face. He was naked but for a fresh cloth for modesty. It wasn't silk, and not dyed, and she couldn't reach it. He dug his fingers into her cheeks, prying her jaw open. She relaxed her mouth, then bit his fingers.

"You filthy whore!" He slapped her again, shaking out his hand.

She opened her eyes and spit the blood in her mouth at the high magepriest.

The high magepriest grabbed her face, leaning over her on the angled wooden "bed" to which she was strapped. The edge of his robes brushed her fingertips.

That was all she needed.

They went up faster than the filthy sheet in the cell. He screamed, flailing. Byria gripped the cloth, though it burned her hand.

The straps that held her were leather, and leather burned. So did wood. She hoped they'd burn faster than her flesh. It was little comfort, in the burning pain, that the high magepriest burned, too.

But it was some comfort.

As she gripped the flailing, burning robes, she kept yanking her wrist. Could her very flesh scream in agony, it would, but Byria refused to give into the panic. She felt a give. The small metal buckle broke, melted. She released the mage just as Tain pulled him from her grip. She unbuckled the other wrist, yanked the lightning crown from around her head, and freed her feet before Tain had helped the high magepriest disrobe completely.

Already hurt, she grabbed the still burning over-robe from the floor and threw it at them.

She ran to the table where she remembered the knives had been. They were still there, as was her token from Patch, and the triangle-etched eye in a fresh jar of liquid. She grabbed the token, the jar, and the biggest knife in the box—the one with the dragon handle.

With a scream, she brandished it at Tain and the high magepriest. Her attack surprised them, and she drew blood from both. She ran up the secret stairs she still remembered, and through the tapestry.

The palace on the other side of the tapestry was quiet.

Pain had temporarily subsided in the rush of her escape. She fled to the servants' chambers before it could return and slow her escape.

She had her instructions. She had a plan.

And she had a dragon's fire in her heart.

* * * * *

Chapter Nineteen
Meditations on Pain and Memory

Byria stared up at the stars. She lay hidden in long grass, upon ground far outside the palace, and beyond the city boundaries.

Everything was a different burn. Her skin suffered fire burns and the stinging stick of cheap cloth against them. Her lungs burned from breathing harder and faster than she could ever remember doing. Muscles blazed pain from pushing so hard. Hot sores bled from the soles of her feet; she'd kicked off the shoes that were too big for running some time ago. Perhaps she'd regret it later, but the cool night eased her feet.

She'd run until she could only feel the tiniest ember of her heart's fire left. Then she'd stopped, found herself in grass nearly as tall as her shoulders, and decided it was safe to hide and rest.

Byria was free.

She took a deep breath in and nursed the tiny fire in her heart. It would take some time to bring it back so she could heal.

The sparkling whorls of stars in the black silk sky were more beautiful than anything she could remember seeing. Except for the dragon and his wings. Nothing could be more beautiful than that.

A tiny thought told her she shouldn't sleep yet. She should see to her wounds and eat something. Drink something.

With a sigh, she slowly edged her right arm, the unburnt one, and reached for the bag she'd tossed to the ground with her hat when she'd let herself collapse. A shoulder bag, stolen from the kitchens, and laden with the food made for those who worked in the rice paddies for the palace.

It had occurred to her that the rice workers left before sunrise and returned at sunset, and likely got few breaks, so their food would be suited for her to travel with few breaks. And it was meant to be carried in the steamed bamboo stalks.

She'd stolen a manservant's clothes, sneaking into and out of his room as he slept. Men were the ones who left the palace for errands. It would make sense for a man to leave the castle with a shoulder bag in the early hours of morning. She'd also found a messenger's hat and had added that to her disguise. Using the sharp dragon's knife, she'd cut her hair, hiding the loose bits in her bag. Were anyone to be found near such evidence, they would be punished for "helping" the traitor princess.

She'd bided her time, hiding in a closet, waiting for the chaos of the earliest morning hours. It hadn't been long, either. The healing balm she'd stolen from the servant's room had helped the burns some, enough that she could handle the pain enough to escape.

Strangely, she'd heard nothing of any search for her, nothing about a part of the castle collapsing, nor even a word about her husband. Once the morning's work started, she'd heard whispers, but she'd kept her head down and pretended she was part of the normal process. It hadn't been very hard. Everyone moved with purpose during the morning rush.

As she smeared fresh healing balm on her burnt arm and neck, Byria let the memories of the city at street level play in her head. It had seemed like a blur as she'd left, but she was surprised by what details she remembered.

The streets—the streets had been *filthy*. She was glad she'd kept the oversize shoes on during that portion of her travel. And the streets stank. Even the heavy incense from the temples she'd passed couldn't hide the smell of filth and death.

She'd seen beggars, a dead man and a dead woman with her dead baby, when she'd left the rich market area and headed into where she'd figured the various non-palace workers lived. There'd been many stray cats and dogs, most skinny, and some dead or nearly dead. Rats, very much alive, had feasted on the bodies. Had she eaten anything but the scant portion of food sometime the prior day, Byria would have puked.

Guards and palace soldiers had been at every city exit, all carrying dragon sticks. Byria had shivered upon seeing them. Four times a year, the palace guard put on a show of force that included the use of the deadly arms that shot a stream of fire—like that of dragons, thus the name—up to ten feet in front of them. The guards had slowed the exit, checking the people as they headed out to the fields or roads. She'd panicked a moment, having come so close and still possibly failing. Then she'd made herself breathe, and she'd made herself watch.

After all, many workers regularly went out to fields. Many merchants headed north, and checking each carriage and traveler took time.

The well-dressed men who oversaw the paddies and fields had grown impatient first, for this was cutting into the workday. They'd argued with the guards, wanting to know what the search was for. The guards and soldiers hadn't answered, simply pointing their dragon sticks at the argumentative ones. The rest had waited with quiet resignation in their eyes.

Dampening one of the clean cloths she'd also taken with water, Byria cleaned the filth off her. She thought of the people. These were the people she was meant to rule over? Had been meant to rule over? Well, had been meant to parade over—what rule would she have had, anyway? And if Patch was indeed dead, there was no reason for Byria to return. No, they weren't her people any longer.

But as she looked at the sky, their eyes seemed to look back at her. Not quite dead—for she'd seen dead eyes—but not quite alive, either.

She sighed and broke open a bamboo stalk to eat the portion of rice and dried fish.

In the packed queue of people leaving, she'd edged her way to one of the side roads. It had taken little effort to find another beggar and ask him to trade clothes with her. Of course he'd agreed. Even servants of the palace had some quality to their clothing.

Changing, however, had been problematic. The man had stripped naked in the street, and had expected Byria to do the same. It had taken brandishing her dragon knife to convince him to allow her to take the clothes and change behind a thick drain. The old man had been shocked, arms up as if expecting her to stab him, when she'd returned to give him her clothes—along with a ration of food.

She'd felt sorry for having to point a knife at someone who was frightened of her, someone even skinnier than she'd become, someone who'd hardly had the strength to stand and strip. Giving him food had been a poor choice in regard to her survival, but she didn't regret it. Before returning to the queue, she'd cut small bristles from her hair, dumped the rest, and smeared her cheeks, chin, and neck with filth, stubbling it with the short hairs.

Not only had that made her stink, it had made her look like the poor men in the queue. The hat further shaded her face and blended in with the many other hats men wore to keep the sun from their faces.

Over two weeks in the dungeon had certainly made her look starved. The palace guards had wrinkled their nose at her and shoved her out with the rest of the masses.

Once the men had begun to disperse themselves in the fields, she'd followed a little ways, and then she'd run. The well-dressed men had yelled. Some had given chase, but she hadn't stopped. She'd run until she was far from any rice paddies, avoiding the small communities constructed of wood, cloth, and nails, and avoiding the roads and people.

She'd run until all she could see was tall grass in every direction, and until the last light of the setting sun had disappeared, making it hard to know if she was going north anymore.

Byria found a memory while she was chewing a last bite of rice—sailors and travelers knew north by the stars. Such things were not, of course, things learned by ladies of the court. Had Patch taught her to do so?

The stars gave no answer. She picked out a few bright ones and remembered that, at one time, she'd known their importance, but she couldn't shake those memory stones free.

A damning curse upon Tain and the high magepriest! If the True God were so real—for she'd begun to doubt even that now—and not but a demon worshiped by the magepriests, may he send every plague upon them!

She knew what had destroyed her memory now. In the depths of her bones, beneath the cool air upon her burning skin and muscles and organs, she felt the memory of *that* particular pain. She wanted to fight it, bury it again.

But Byria was done with that.

To survive, she had to let all the memories, whatever she had left, come out and be sharp and *hurt*.

That she *must* do this resonated as another True and Important Thing.

So she did.

Byria began to shake. That buzz that had crawled upon her skin, the sensation of so many crawling, stinging insects, burrowed deep, deep into her bones until it hurt. Her jaw clenched painfully. The inside of her ears popped in tiny, aching explosions. She couldn't breathe.

Memories had been stabbed with that pain, pulled, inspected, thrown away; bright lights pierced eyes straining to pop from her skull. Tain and the magepriests had thrown a storm into her head, tearing apart the sails of thoughts, splintering the masts of knowledge and True Things, and rending the ship of her mind asunder.

It had hurt from the inside of her bones outward.

Byria took another breath. And another. She could breathe. She wasn't writhing, though her mind felt as if her body was. The only pain was from the burns and the day's running.

Except in her head.

The light of the stars ached now, so she closed her eyes, feeling a wetness that stuck to her lashes and ran down her temples and into her ears. With a sniffle, she wiped the tears away.

That was enough of that memory for tonight. There would be more nights of freedom and running north. She'd take each memory in its time.

* * * * *

Chapter Twenty
Tribulation of Travel

The sharpness of the tall grass didn't surprise Byria, so she figured she must have known, a memory not totally uncovered. She did remember she needed to keep her wounds clean to prevent infection. That lesson had been repeated enough.

She'd begun wrapping her feet in cloths to protect them, but the grass tore at the cloths, too. After enough walking, fresh cuts on her feet turned the cloths perpetually red.

Despite her openness to memories, even the ones that hurt, so many still wouldn't come. The painful ones kept repeating, and that was no good, as crying pulled water from her body, and she had so little left.

Two waterskins—all she'd been able to steal—only held so much, and emptied quickly when one was trying to clean so many injuries. The heat drew even more moisture from her skin.

How did Patch think I'd survive this?

Byria pulled out the jarred eye and stared at it as she walked. Both moons were showing crescents now, so she could find north from their rise and fall. Though she was tired and hurting, she was restless. If she didn't find a spring or something, she'd die from lack of water.

Was this Patch's eye that she looked at? However she turned the jar, it looked at her. She found that comforting. Perhaps the woman wasn't dead and had escaped. Perhaps she might meet Byria somewhere along the way. She would know a better escape route than Byria had taken.

With that hope, she kissed the glass jar—surprising herself, for she couldn't remember the last time she'd kissed anything—and re-wrapped it in the cloths she'd used to protect it.

Once it was secured, she moved her hand around the inside of the bag, now roomier for empty waterskins and fewer portions of food. She ate very little. Why hadn't she thought to bring twice as much water and half the food?

Because she'd remembered nothing of survival outside of the palace. Even now, with all the remembering she tried, she knew very little more besides the fact that she needed water, and needed it soon.

Finally, her fingers found what she sought. She pulled the small thing from the bag. A little grin teased her lips as she figured her token ought to be called something. *Shit gem* had been her first thought, because she imagined it would make Patch laugh, especially considering the vulgarities she'd openly called Tain.

"Shit gem," she whispered. Her throat scraped with the use of her voice. How long had it been since she'd spoken aloud? Since negotiating to trade clothes with the beggar. How many days was that? She mouthed the words again and giggled. A woman of the court, much less a princess, would never let such a vulgar word pass her tongue. She whispered it one more time, "Shit gem."

As ready as she was to rebel against anything related to being a princess, perhaps that wasn't the best name for the woman's last gift to her. But Byria *wanted* to remember where it came from, that someone had used magic to create a magical token from shit. Good or bad, Byria wanted control over *all* her memories, even the ones from the palace.

And there had been small memories she'd cherished. Syng's care for her, the woman's jokes, and her patience in teaching her things—often many times over, because of Byria's faulty memories. Syng had been a source of good memories, of being cared for. Syng would remind her how to be a graceful lady, and how grace could have power—power to make people treat you a certain way, do things for you. The Demon-Wife Between had had *grace* when negotiating with the demon she would marry.

One who was graceful didn't say "shit" in reference to such waste. She said *pyut*. It was a delicate little word that could dance off a lady's tongue.

Approving her name choice for Patch's gift, Byria held her pyut-gem up to the night sky. Though both moons were but crescent slivers, they gave off quite a bit of light. Particularly the smaller Seal Moon, so named for when it was its biggest and brightest in the winter, and many hunters would sail north to hunt the animals before they headed to the colder water with their pups. Plus, one was most likely to see the sea animals during the full Seal Moons, for the fish they ate seemed to swim closer to the surface during those times.

Byria smiled. The little pyut-gem seemed to help the nicer memories come out more. Not that the thought of hunting seals and their pups was "nice," but it was hardly as painful as other memories.

The tiny triangle in the pyut-gem's center glowed more in the moonlight. Another memory: Certain rituals of the magepriests were based on the phases of the moons. Byria concluded the moons must affect magic.

That realization made her stop walking and press down enough grass to rest. If her heart fire *was* magic, as Patch had suggested, perhaps now that she could see the moons, she should use them to help with her healing.

She could move faster if she were in less pain.

Her heart's fire sprang to flame within a breath of Byria focusing on it. Imagining Patch's soft, deep voice instructing her, she repeated the exercises the fire witch had taught her, making her heart's fire so hot it might burn through her chest, then pushing it out to all the things that pained her.

The moons were heading toward their setting horizon by the time Byria was done with the exercise. She smacked her dry lips, feeling thirstier, but in much less pain. She decided to sleep for the remaining hours of the night. Patch had told her she healed even more when she slept.

Tucking Patch's gift away safely, she rolled to her side, and followed the woman's advice like she was, indeed, still there with her.

* * * * *

Chapter Twenty-One
Raindrops and Laughter

The sun didn't wake Byria in the morning. Something better startled her from sleep. A fat drop of rain upon her nose.

She sputtered, coughed, choked… and then laughed as another fell upon her head, and another upon her arm.

More than she could count began to soak her clothing. She turned her messenger cap upside down. It was cloth, but it could hold some rain!

Reaching into her bag, she pulled out every cloth. Some were still clean, as she always made sure the jar with the eye was wrapped and protected, so she loosely folded them so they'd absorb as much rain as possible. With the bloodstained and filthy ones, she rubbed and wrung and washed them in the downpour. She stripped to her skin—what modesty had she left or did she need in nothing but tall grass?—and held out her hands.

Then another thought hit her. She began to dig. The earth was soaking up the rain, but puddles were forming. She dug several holes and lay the flat, sharp grass—more pliable, now it was wet—within them.

Water filled the holes.

Byria laughed.

She laughed like she hadn't in so long. She laughed like she had in the moment the dragon had flown away. She laughed like she was a child and tipped her head back to let the rain fill her mouth, swallowing and swallowing and swallowing.

The rain cleaned off layers of filth and blood, it fell so hard. She rubbed with the stained cloths to wash as much of her skin as possible.

She'd drunk her fill and cleaned much of her skin before it tapered off. Quickly, she wrung out all the clean cloths into a waterskin, and then soaked up the water in her holes before it slipped through the grass blades and into the thirsty dirt. She managed to pour most of what had collected in her hat without spilling. She only managed to fill one of her two waterskins, but that was better than nothing.

When the rain stopped, she wrung out her clothes and the rags for her feet, put them back on, and repacked her bag. The clouds were dissipating, and she could see the slightest glow of the sun through them. With that, she continued northward.

*****

Chapter Twenty-Two
Darkness in the Daytime

All of a sudden, there was jungle. A wall of trees and vines.

Byria had expected a gradual change between landscapes, perhaps a tree or two as a warning, but no. There was tall grass, then there were vine-dripping trees, as if a line was drawn between them, separating their vastly different kingdoms.

The jungle was still north, so in she went.

She hadn't walked very far—at least it didn't *feel* very far—before her heart started pounding. It was dark under the trees' canopy.

Without the sun or moons to guide her, how would she know which way to go? Even looking behind her, she was unsure of the direction she'd come from.

Where is north?

A few of the words Patch may or may not have meant to teach her some long time ago filtered into her head. She paused, appreciating the newly loosed memories...

But where is north?

She took a breath, and then another. Holding out her arm, Byria looked at the ladder of small cuts up the inside and thought back to their discussion. How would Byria know when to stop? It also worked, she realized, for knowing where to go.

"How will I know...?"

"You will. I have faith in that. You can do this, Byria. If you can't remember, ask the fire in your heart where you need to go, and go there. No matter how frightening it may seem."

And the token, the little pyut-gem. Patch had *specifically* said it was for the jungle! She'd known Byria would make it to the jungle, and she was here. She was where she needed to be.

Making sure she was still breathing, Byria reached into the bag to find her little token. Clasping it in her hand, she closed her eyes and sought her heart's fire. It appeared in her mind almost immediately.

As the flame grew with her breaths, another sensation came to Byria's mind that made her open her eyes with a snap and press a hand to her heart.

Someone was watching her. Definitely some*one*. That felt like a True Thing, like the dragon being a *he* was a True Thing. Byria looked around, circling in her place. She saw nothing.

Not ready to close her eyes again, Byria kept her hand on her heart. Would her heart's fire work like this?

As she kept turning, she felt a pull in a direction. She paused, turned a little. *Tug.* Same direction, stronger. Like the sensation of spider-silk that had drawn her toward the dragon.

That way, she thought.

* * * * *

Chapter Twenty-Three
Eyes in the Jungle

The sense of being watched didn't abate. The jungle grew darker and darker. Byria was tired, but she couldn't stop and rest. She wasn't frightened. It was nothing like when she'd felt Tain's eyes on her.

It was still unsettling.

So she walked in the dark. Coal dark. Black glass dark. Darker than on the grass, for the moonlight hardly penetrated the leaves.

It wasn't until sometime later that she realized, while she could hardly see, she hadn't stumbled or tripped. There was no road beneath her feet, and the trees and plants grew in unpatterned patches of lush foliage and root-ribbed earth. She frequently moved fallen branches, ferns, and other things from her path, but she never fell, and she never stepped on anything that bit or stung—and she was certain such things would live in a jungle.

Pausing, she held out the hand that clutched her token. It didn't glow enough to give off light, but enough for her to be able to see it if she were to drop it. She closed her fist around it, unwilling to take that chance.

As she took a deep breath, squinting as if that might somehow help her see better, she heard another familiar sound.

Water.

The refilled waterskin was empty again. The day had been hot, and the trees seemed to trap the heat even more. Very little wind seemed to pass through, unlike in the grass. While moisture stuck to her, slowing her movement enough that she'd considered discarding the uncomfortable, chafing clothes, it did nothing to slake her growing thirst.

Pressing her hand to her heart again, she breathed. It was a good choice to go in the direction she heard the water.

She found a clearing—perhaps the size of her bed back in the palace—amid the thick vegetation on the shore, where everything competed for the ribbons of sunlight. The area was comprised of small stones, big stones, and one massive, flat stone that pushed aside most plants, giving Byria clear access to a fast-moving stream.

As she approached the water, the sensation of being watched seemed to recede. She breathed deeper; she hadn't realized how tense her chest had become.

Wincing, she walked over the sharper, smaller stones. The now-larger crescents of the two moons slipped through the slits of sky that cut between the parasol-like treetops. Their light glimmered on the water and on the thin footprints of blood Byria left on the larger rock at the water's edge.

She frowned. Patch had said animals could smell blood, so bleeding was bad. By her calculations, she wasn't due for her woman's blood for at least another week and a half, not until the moons were at least half-full or just more than half-full, but any blood was problematic.

The cloths upon her feet pulled away in shreds. She threw them directly into the water. Removing her hat, she scooped up water, poured it over her feet and the rock, and splashed it as far behind her as possible to wash away her footprints. Walking back over the stones would likely cut them further, but she felt like she was doing something useful.

She drank several handfuls of water and refilled her waterskins, almost collapsing to sit as she did so.

She made herself eat one more bamboo stick of rice, which ended up becoming two. She hadn't eaten once since she'd entered the jungle, between the heat and the feel of being watched.

While that watching sensation had lessened, it hadn't *completely* gone away.

* * * * *

Chapter Twenty-Four
Hunters... Friends?

Dim light, a horrible feeling, a low growl, and the stink of animal musk woke Byria. The low light gave her the opportunity to aim the large stone she threw even as she jumped to her feet.

It was a cat, large and spotted. The stone struck its side, and it snarled, arching its back.

Byria shouted and threw another stone. And then another. She crouched just long enough to pull the knife from her bag, then grabbed a fourth stone. Howling and jumping, she bared her teeth, keening in fury.

As a fifth stone struck the cat right in its face, it arched with a hiss and ran away.

Tears ran down Byria's face as she gasped in ragged breaths, not quite ready to move yet—

Her token!

She didn't recall throwing something so small. Dropping to her knees, still clutching the knife, she patted the ground with her free hand. She couldn't have lost it!

It was right at her feet. She snatched it up and cradled it to her chest with the knife, letting a few sobs escape her.

Jungle cats. A lesson from Patch. The memory came clearly. The woman, seeming ever so much taller than Byria, saying that one must convince the cat they're not easy prey, that it was too much of a risk to try to kill them. That they were bigger and meaner, and unafraid—so the *cat* should be afraid.

She'd scared it away. For now.

As she calmed down, she felt more burning in her feet. She sat, feeling very tired all of a sudden. Very tired, and very sore. Keeping the knife near, she crossed her legs to look at her feet in the growing light.

She frowned. Still bleeding. What she walked on hardly looked like a woman's feet anymore.

Biting her lip, she edged back to the water and decided to dip her foot in. Byria wasn't aware of having observed the slight movement until after she'd yanked her feet from the water and grabbed her knife. Without knowing she was doing it, she skewered the toothy fish that had jumped at her. She didn't remember breathing until after she'd smashed its head with a rock.

Byria thought there should be a memory as she stared at the fish, which still flopped its tail, despite its crushed head. She didn't remember killing anything before, but she felt she must have. A lady of the court didn't have such reflexes.

Patch had said they'd lived out here for some time.

Why couldn't she *remember*? She rained curses upon Tain and the high magepriest once more, fresh, hot tears trailing down her cheeks. Wiping them away with a vengeance, she regarded the fish.

Most palace meals included fish. During very special occasions, the fish were sometimes killed right at the table and served over seasoned rice and with vegetables cut and folded to look like flowers and animals.

This monstrosity looked nothing like the fish cut at the tables, but could she eat it? There were only three bamboo sticks of rice left, and no memories had come loose of what other things she could be eating.

Squeezing her token stone and asking, Byria received no answer from her heart's fire.

With a grimace, Byria cut into the fish's belly. The cutting didn't feel right; the knife wasn't meant for culinary use. Cutting out a chunk of the stomach, she frowned as a purple-black liquid dripped out. It was thicker than the reddish blood that had splattered from the fish's head.

Her stomach rumbled. She poked the ragged piece of flesh with the tip of the knife and lifted it to her face. A sniff gave no bitter or sour odor. She opened her mouth.

"Na! Nanana! Na!"

Byria jumped to her feet again, casting the fish aside and brandishing her knife at...

There were memories attached to this... person. Little person. It—she?—was the height of a child of eight or ten. Her hair was cropped short like a man's, but green, and looked like the fluff from milkweed. Her skin was pale, but also tinged green.

"Who are you?" she asked. The memories were stuck. Were they about this particular person, or persons like this one?

The small woman stared at Byria as if she, too, were trying to remember. However, she carried a spear and wore the skin of one of the jungle cats over her torso. Byria shook the knife at her again. The purple liquid from the fish splashed near her.

"Na! Na!" The woman put the spear down and held out both hands, showing back and front. Next, she pointed at Byria's knife and then to the ground.

Byria shook her head, not ready to disarm herself. "Who are you?" she repeated, eyes glued to the woman's hands—weapons in and of themselves. They seemed too large and were tipped with greenish claws.

The woman said something Byria didn't understand. Some words sounded familiar, but not enough to make out what she was saying.

After a pause, the small woman pointed even more at the knife. "Na! Nana!" She made a sharp gesture at the knife, and then down to the ground, as if she were throwing it.

Byria saw the purple liquid dripping down past the blade. She put the knife down. The woman nodded, showed the front and back of her hands again, then made a fist in her left hand and brushed it open with her right hand.

Byria shook her head once more, and the woman repeated the gesture, pointing at Byria this time.

Byria looked down at herself, noticing she was still clutching her token stone. Biting her lip, she slowly opened her hand. The stone seemed to glow more, its tint greener than she remembered.

"Ah. Aa-ah?" The woman nodded, then held up both hands, switched them back and front, and took a step toward Byria. When Byria winced, she stopped and repeated the hand gesture. She stepped forward once more, though a much smaller step, then repeated, "Aa-ah?"

Taking a deep breath, Byria pressed the stone to her heart again. She didn't *feel* anything wrong, anything warning her. She gave the woman a nod.

Continuing the slow movement and the repetition of showing her hands, she moved toward Byria's knife and drew a thing from her belt. Byria almost fell, staggering away.

"Aah. Na-ah."

After another breath, Byria saw the woman was giving her the handle of a stone knife. She made an offering gesture, and Byria snatched it, not quite ready to touch those animal-like hands.

She cringed a little more; the woman was between her and the dragon knife. The woman showed the back and front of her hands once more, took a deep breath, and turned her back to Byria. She tugged at one of the cloths and folded it, wrapping it around the dragon handle. Then she plunged both the cloth and the knife into the water, shaking it, cleaning it.

The woman stayed away from the fish.

After the small woman cleaned the knife, she used it to poke and push the fish back into the water, avoiding the purple liquid that seeped from the belly very carefully. Once more, she thoroughly washed the knife.

She let the cloth float away in the river and pulled a clean one from a pouch on her belt to dry the blade before handing it, handle first, back to Byria.

With better manners, Byria took her knife back (still managing to avoid *touching* the green claws and extra-jointed fingers) and placed the handle of the small woman's knife in her outstretched hand. The woman nodded and gestured at the rest of the cloths, the bag, and the hat still scattered on the stone.

Beginning to understand, Byria gathered the items back into her bag, stowing her hat as well, for it was hot and she wanted nothing blocking her view. With one more nod, the woman retrieved her spear and looked at Byria. She made another gesture that was similar to what Byria recognized as "follow me."

The woman said, "Koa?"

Shrugging and unable to think of a reason not to, Byria returned the nod and followed the small woman.

* * * * *

Chapter Twenty-Five
Another Gift of Healing

Byria moved at a much slower rate than her guide was used to. The small woman slipped through the pathless greenery, disappearing, only to reappear, arms folded, as she waited for Byria to catch up. The impatient sigh was no different among Byria's people.

"I'm sorry," she said, hoping her tone communicated what she figured her words didn't. Her feet hurt. There were more stones, more roots, and more sticks, and each now seemed to seek out her feet. Why was this different than the prior night? Had she just been so tired and afraid, she hadn't noticed? The injuries she'd seen at the stream would support such a thing.

Hungrier and more tired than she'd been since leaving the palace, her every step was agony.

One root, just a little higher than Byria had calculated to step over it, brought her to the ground in a fall that splayed her on her stomach, and echoed pain from her nose and head, all the way down the rest of her body. Her messenger bag spilled its contents across the floor of the jungle.

"O-o-ooh!" What started as a cry wrapped into an exhausted moan as Byria rolled to her side and curled her elbows and knees, shaking her head. She squeezed the pyut-gem, comforted to still feel it in her grip.

The little green woman chattered around her, looking anxious.

"I'm sorry," Byria murmured again. "Just a moment, please?"

The woman sighed again, laid down her spear, and then walked around Byria with a more critical eye. When she got to Byria's feet, she hissed out a breath and a noise that definitely sounded bad.

She went to Byria's bag and took several of the cloths. As she yanked one, the jar with the eye came rolling out. The woman let out a squawk upon seeing it.

Byria found just enough energy to stretch and grab the jar, cradling it to her chest with the pyut-gem.

A stream of clicks and "Kah" noises came from the woman's mouth. Byria stared at her face, sensing the woman was distressed—afraid, even. She pointed one of her claw-like fingernails at the jar, eyes wide.

Byria shook her head and hugged the macabre thing tighter, but she didn't know, even in her own language, how to communicate that this was important and not dangerous.

Well, not dangerous to Byria and anyone helping her. That was the sense she had, another Truth that was free in her mind. And the small woman *was* helping.

With a frown, the woman shook her head and returned to gathering the cloths. She also took the waterskin and went back to Byria's feet. She dampened one cloth and carefully began to clean her soles. Byria hissed in pain and did her best not to wince or pull away too much. With each gentle (though very painful) pat, the cloth became redder and filthier.

Holding up a small waterskin of her own, the woman gestured pouring it on a clean cloth, then touched her arm with the cloth, making a face of twisted pain. As Byria cringed in response, the woman gestured a gentle patting motion, her face relaxing with each touch. Then she held up her arm, as if presenting it, and showed her own unmarred skin.

Biting her lip and closing her eyes, Byria nodded shortly in understanding. The woman would put something on her feet that would hurt a lot before it would heal.

The woman brushed her ankle again, so Byria opened her eyes and looked. The woman was gesturing once more. She took in an exaggerated deep breath, opening her arms around her belly as if she were catching all the air, then blew out, lifting her hands as if pushing the air from her.

Nodding once more, Byria took a deep breath of her own and turned her attention to just breathing. With her eyes closed, on her inhale, she noticed the rich, wet, green smell of the warm earth she lay on.

On the exhale, she realized she'd been hearing a small but beautiful cacophony of birdsong all day. They'd been there this whole time, but she hadn't *noticed* them. She recognized some songs from the birds kept in the palace gardens, but many crows and deep calls were not so clear in her memory—though they weren't entirely foreign, either.

The searing pain in her foot made her cry out, quieting the nearer birds. Byria kicked reflexively, and though her eyes squeezed shut, she could feel the woman jerk to avoid being hit.

"Sorry! Sorry!" she said between gritted teeth. It was like liquid, salted fire was worming into her skin.

The woman squawked out impatient and almost-scolding noises, but that was all. Byria repeated her apologies once more. With another sigh, the woman braced her knee on one of Byria's ankles, then firmly grabbed the other one and continued with her agonizing cleaning process.

Bringing her attention back to breathing and nurturing her heart's fire, Byria managed the pain and didn't kick out again.

The woman's deliberate touch on her ankle again pulled Byria's attention back. Byria blinked her eyes open, feeling warmer and a little more energized from her heart's fire. Her feet still hurt, and tears stuck in her eyes.

The woman pointed at Byria's feet, which were now wrapped in fresh cloths with leather pouches tied over them. Next, she pointed to many things strewn on the ground, and then to Byria's shoulder bag.

Nodding with a smile, Byria said, "Thank you," hoping at least the tone of her voice and the look on her face would communicate how she felt.

"Mmm." The woman nodded back, also giving a small smile—revealing what looked like a mouth of fangs!

If she saw Byria flinch, she didn't react as she filled the messenger's bag. Curiosity redirected Byria's attention to the things the woman was packing.

There were stones tied together with long strips of leather, a skein of shiny string thicker than embroidery thread, some folded banana leaves tied with that shiny string, and several small clay pots topped with wax seals. The woman also carried some small brushes and a few yellowish-green cloths of her own, though of a coarser material than what Byria had. She also had a roll of leather that looked like it held tools.

Noticing Byria watching, the woman opened a banana leaf and offered what looked like a small biscuit of nuts and fruit. Byria's mouth watered, though she hesitated. The woman broke it in half, took a bite of her share, chewed, swallowed, and held the other half out to Byria again.

Byria took it with a hasty "Thank you." Though it was hard to bite, at first, it dissolved in her mouth with a surprisingly tasty mix of savory, sweet, and a little spicy.

And familiar! She'd eaten this before! She finished the offering in a single bite. "Thank you," Byria repeated, blinking rapidly as tears threatened again. She had no way to explain why eating something delicious would make her cry. Instead, she focused on the still-open banana leaf, trying to see how many were still inside, and wondering if she was looking too covetously or rudely.

With a smile, showing her wickedly pointed teeth again—Byria managed not to flinch—the woman offered Byria one more before rolling the leaf back up and retying it.

Byria savored this one, eyes closed as she chewed slowly. While she wanted the act of eating to bring back more memories, she didn't want them *right now*. Not in front of this person, who might or might not be a stranger.

Byria opened her eyes to see the woman studying her almost wistfully. She offered Byria another smile, and from a pouch still on her belt, she pulled out a bamboo stick. Delighted at the familiarity as much as the offer of more food, Byria couldn't contain a wide grin, further thanking her and bowing her head for added emphasis.

When Byria cracked the bamboo open, however, she was surprised. Instead of rice and dried fish, it contained what looked more like mashed sweet yams and nuts.

But like the biscuits, the unexpected insides pulled at more memories. The smell drew out other images of the jungle, faces like the woman's—perhaps even this woman's face—but they all came so fast. Byria wasn't ready for them all, not yet, not now. She took a breath and consciously acknowledged the memories, storing them for later.

The woman made a questioning noise, tilting her head and looking at her with concerned eyes.

Byria had an idea to avoid trying to explain how the food was affecting her. She pointed to her bag and gestured to reach something out of it. When the woman held it closer, Byria pulled out one of her bamboo portions and handed it out to the woman, nodding. Byria was already eating hers when the woman bit hers open with her sharp teeth, and the emotions tied to the smell and flavor overwhelmed her.

Before the threat of tears returned, she made an "mmmm!" sound, rubbing her stomach and nodding. She hoped she was communicating her compliments.

The woman regarded the inside of what Byria offered her with the same curiosity, but ate with little hesitation. She made a surprised face while chewing, then mimicked Byria's response as she finished it. Speaking slowly, the woman issued a string of *coo* and *loo* and *aah* noises, and made a gesture over her heart before pointing at Byria.

Byria nodded in understanding. "Thank you," she said in her own language, but imitated the woman's gesture.

With a concluding smile and nod, clearly ready to get moving again, the woman finished packing the satchel. She tied a knot in the strap before twisting it over her own shoulders in a way that Byria couldn't quite follow. The bag was still enormous against the woman's small body.

"I can carry that," Byria began, reaching for the bag.

The woman stepped away and shook her head. Picking up her spear from the ground, she made the "follow me" gesture once more and said, "Koa. Koa."

Gingerly, Byria got to her feet and took a few wincing steps. It was far from pleasant, but she could do it. After breathing a few more times, she headed toward the woman.

With a grunt, the small woman readjusted the shoulder bag and continued walking. Whether it was the weight of the shoulder bag or knowing how difficult it was for Byria to walk, her speed stayed close to something Byria could keep up with.

* * * * *

Chapter Twenty-Six
Hunter and Healer

The two traveled together for another three and a half days. Byria learned her guide's name was Koki. Koki had a hard time saying Byria's name; it came out more like Beelheah, with a trill to the *l* sound, but they began to forge understanding.

She started to recognize—and repeat with reasonable accuracy, per her guide's excited approval—more of Koki's words and phrases. Easy things: yes, no, please, thank you, follow, stop, quiet, danger, safe, hurt, feel better, eat, drink, are you all right, do you need to rest, and the various names of foods, as well as some birds, plants, and animals they saw.

The woman also had a very expressive face, Byria noticed. It was lined, as if she were perhaps middle-aged, but her eyes and features were bright and energetic, like she wasn't much older than Byria.

Koki remembered Byria from when she was a child, little more than a baby, according to Koki's gestures. And she remembered Patch, who'd watched Byria like a mother. *That* detail, "like a mother," she emphasized—Koki had cradled an invisible baby in her arms, looking at it with absolute joy and love.

The more they spoke—or rather, communicated mostly through gestures and limited speaking—the more memory stones came loose in Byria's mind. The face of Koki and another person like her, a man, perhaps, who smiled with love and comfort, albeit with fangs for teeth.

Warm, savory broth over shredded meat, and that sweet potato-like stuff inside Koki's bamboo, with little eggs cracked over the top. Lots of beads, strings and strings and strings of necklaces, moving, clacking, in bright colors.

The smells of so many herbs.

Unfortunately, Koki kept their conversation to a minimum as they traveled, only for necessary communication while they moved, and only a little more when they stopped to rest. Byria got the distinct sense that the woman didn't rest nearly as much in her normal travels.

A good part of their limited communication while resting was due to caring for Byria's extensive injuries, and only the ones Byria let the woman see. For her part, Koki never pressed Byria to show more than she was comfortable with, and she took a lot of time making sure Byria understood what she was doing. For each step of unwrapping, cleaning, rubbing salve, and rewrapping, the woman patiently waited for Byria to nod her understanding and approval for the woman to continue.

The first few times Byria realized what Koki was doing, asking her permission even to help, she'd been struck with fresh tears. Koki acknowledged the tears, but respected Byria's request to carry on as if she weren't crying. That meant more to Byria than she could have communicated, even if they spoke the same language.

The triangle-marked eye in the jar unsettled Koki deeply. Byria tried to make the connection between Patch and the eye, but that seemed to bother her guide even more. Byria kept it wrapped and tucked in a separate pocket so the small woman didn't have to touch or see it, since she still insisted on carrying the messenger bag.

She kept retying it in different ways, and clearly had opinions about its design. Byria thought she recognized a few more of the words Koki growled every morning and evening when she put it on and took it off.

On their second day of traveling, Koki made camp early, and insisted Byria stay there, promising she was safe several times, but making it clear she needed to not move while she was gone.

Byria agreed, using the time to go through what memories were coming loose and tend to her heart's fire. As it got darker, her anxiety slowly overtook every other emotion and thought.

Then she heard a whistle that wasn't birdsong—but definitely sounded like a song. The whistling turned into a hum, then words recognizable as Koki's language.

Byria's joy at seeing the woman, at hearing her lovely song, was cut short when she saw the woman carried two dead animals without skin, a rabbit and… a giant rat?

The small woman raised an eyebrow at Byria's horrified face and gestured to her stomach. "Hungry?"

Byria *had been* hungry.

The woman rubbed and stuffed the rabbit with several herbs, stuck a stick through it, and kept turning it over the fire. She cut the giant rat-looking thing into many strips, rubbed it with herbs and salt, and threaded it on several sticks that she balanced on stones around the edge of the fire. She crisscrossed the skewers, building almost a wall around the edge of the fire.

It took some time for Byria to stop gaping at how the cooking rabbit, though delicious smelling, still *looked* like a dead, skinned rabbit. Head and all.

As she watched, she remembered. She'd seen this before. The smell, the heat, sitting on the ground were all familiar. All things Byria had experienced. When or how, she didn't remember. Was it with this woman? With Patch?

But she'd eaten freshly killed animals, cooked over a fire, before. That was a True Thing.

Though she appreciated the pieces of freed memory, Byria was thankful Koki did no more hunting while they traveled. She'd been able to eat the rabbit, and was able to eat the other meat Koki had let cook overnight while they traveled, but was glad not to have to watch again—especially later, when Koki had cleaned the blood off her spear.

In lieu of hunting, Koki spent the rest of their travel time collecting plants, bark, fruit, roots, mushrooms, and other things. She tried to explain to Byria what each thing was for during their resting times, when she would sort her things and wrap them in leaves or put them in the small jars. More understanding came attached to memories still not fully unearthed in Byria's mind. *Good* memories—she knew that as True.

Like watching the meat cook, Byria had once sat and watched these actions before—sitting on the ground, looking at the plants, the *sound* of the words, if not their actual meaning. She'd sat and watched, and felt *safe*. More than that she didn't know, and that lack of knowing ached in her heart.

The heartache came on top of the mental exhaustion of trying to understand the woman's language. She sometimes did and sometimes didn't, with no clear reason why. There were more emotions that felt as if they *ought* to be tied to memories—but Byria couldn't reach those memories, either.

She tried to ask the woman more about what *she* remembered about Byria and Patch, but the woman clearly had a job to do, or she thought it was more important Byria know about what she was doing. The frustration of that, as well as the more difficult communication, fought with the *lack* of fear and anxiety.

It hadn't occurred to Byria how frightening it could be to *not* be afraid. More often than not, out of nowhere, her heart would start pounding, her chest would constrict, and she'd look everywhere, searching for what was about to hurt her.

When that would happen, Koki would put down what she was doing and stare at Byria. She'd reached out to take her hand the first night, but when Byria had jumped back, she'd stopped and laid her hands in her lap, palms up so Byria could see. And she'd spoken slowly and softly, almost singing or chanting.

By the third night, Byria recognized the woman's words—whether she'd learned them or remembered them, she couldn't tell. She *heard* them in her ears and heart.

"You're safe. No danger. I'm here. You're safe."

The cadence of her words reminded Byria to breathe, reminded her of her heart's fire. Then her heart's fire would blaze up upon hearing the woman speak. Byria came closer to believing her each night.

On their fourth day of traveling together, only an hour or so after they'd started walking, Koki held up a hand. "Stop. Quiet," she whispered.

Her sharp posture, her darting head—cocking from one side to another like a bird of prey, the firmer grip as she drew her spear from its holder on her back—

Panic hit Byria again. *Something dangerous!* Her chest tightened. She breathed in gasps.

"Sssshhhhhh..." Koki relaxed her posture some, looking at Byria out of the corner of her eye. She lifted one hand slowly, up and down her torso, miming breathing.

Byria understood what she wanted, but even as she was trying to help Byria relax, her moss-green eyes, which sometimes reflected copper rings, continued to scan the area.

Switching her calming gestures to herding ones, she waved Byria toward a tall, straight tree trunk as wide as a horse and had her press her back to it. "Stay. Don't move."

Byria nodded.

The woman started to go, then paused. "Beelheah. Breathe. Breathe."

A slightly annoyed scowl crossed Byria's face, surprising herself because she didn't know why she felt that way. But it gave her impetus to take a few exaggerated deep breaths.

"Good. Stay." She unhitched the messenger bag and put it at Byria's feet.

Byria's lips scrunched once more. Did the woman really think she was going anywhere?

The unexpected emotions kept the fear and panic at bay as Koki jumped onto draping, woody vines and scampered up and out of sight. She was gone for several moments, but when she came back, she had an irritated frown. Picking up the satchel, she only tied it so it wasn't too long, and draped it over her shoulders. "Safe. Come."

They'd walked maybe an hour or two more, with Koki maintaining a much faster pace, when she stopped again. While she was still tense, she didn't draw her spear.

A masculine-sounding voice called out the woman's name, followed by words that Byria guessed were asking if it was her.

Koki relaxed, jutting out a hip and releasing a beleaguered sigh. She turned slightly toward Byria and rolled her eyes with a playful smirk.

"Gyotan..." The rest of her response sounded similar to what the other man had said.

Seeming to appear out of nowhere, a man about the same height as Koki, possibly a little shorter, and definitely stouter, approached and greeted the woman with a big hug before stepping back and looking Byria up and down with wide eyes. He wore a basket over his shoulders, a loincloth, a belt covered with embroidered beads, and so many necklaces of beads attached to wood over his shoulders and arms and intricately woven together, he could have been wearing a shirt.

His expression and words sounded like a question, to which Koki nodded and said, "Yes, and hurt."

"Oh!" The man said something else, and then moved to hug Byria.

With a gasp, Byria stepped back, landing hard on her still-pained feet, and nearly falling.

Koki stepped between them, and said more, reiterating "hurt," as well as "danger" and "safe."

The man nodded slowly and said something else, making Koki groan and roll her eyes again. He took her hands and said something else that sounded both pleading and apologetic. Byria recognized "no danger here."

Koki nodded emphatically and patiently, pulling the man into a hug and kissing both his cheeks.

Byria tried not to stare, wondering if the man was her husband or a close relation. His face didn't resemble the one from her memories associated with this woman, but her memories were still blurry. The details of their faces were as if looking through smoke or water, or like a painting that had gotten wet.

The two spoke further, and finally, the man gave her another hug and set of kisses—he had to be her husband? Who else kissed so often!—and headed further into the jungle, disappearing as if by magic.

Before Byria could ask anything, Koki said something to her punctuated with several sighs, an eye roll that made her tilt her entire head, and the command to follow.

Byria frowned. If the woman said that much, she ought to know. "I understand 'come,'" she said, letting her own frustration come through her voice.

Koki paused, apologized, and frowned in thought.

After a moment, she held her hands out and made the outline of the man they'd just met. "Gyotan." She touched herself. "Koki." Pointed to Byria. "Beelheah." Then she made another outline in the air. "Eluta." And another. "Komati."

And then a few others, running off names, and then just rapidly circled herself and made an encompassing gesture. "See *you*." She came at Byria, arms open, as if to embrace her, as the man—Gyotan—had.

Instinctually, Byria stepped back again, wincing in pain, and nearly tripping as she stepped on one of the ties for the leather pouches that had come undone.

Koki sped to her side, holding her arms as if to catch her. In the half-moment of falling, Byria thought the small woman seemed ridiculous, but as she flailed, she grasped the woman's hand and shoulder, finding her especially solid and strong. As soon as she had her balance, she pulled away, trying not to look ungrateful. She tried to thank the woman in her language, but followed it up in her own.

"You're welcome. Always. Understand?"

Byria nodded, hugging herself.

"No danger. No hurting. I will..." Koki dodged around Byria, showing she would try to get between her and others. "But..." She repeated her gesture showing many people. "But no danger. No hurt. Understand?"

She nodded again, though she looked only at her sleeves, as she still held herself. They were stained and drenched in days of sweat, but at least that made them less likely to slip up her arms, which she'd kept hidden from Koki's attempts at treating her injuries. The woman had just given her salve and cleaning brushes and cloths, turning away to give Byria privacy.

"Beelheah." The woman moved closer, waving her hands to get her attention. "No danger. No hurting. Understand?"

Again, Byria nodded.

"Understand, please?"

Blinking a few times, she swallowed, and then said, "I understand. No danger. No hurting from people." She weakly imitated Koki's signing of many people.

"No danger. No hurting. Safe. With me."

"I'm safe with you," Byria repeated, trying to smile to show she at least believed Koki *intended* to keep her safe.

Koki nodded reassuringly, started walking, and paused. "Come? Yes?"

"Yes. I come." It took her a moment of deliberate thought, but she picked up one foot, put it down, and then picked up the other. She had to consciously think, like when she'd snuck down the stairs to the dragon, but she continued taking consecutive steps after the small woman who seemed certain Byria would be safe with her.

Unlike the change of grasslands into jungle, the change from jungle to jungle village was subtle. That appeared to be the intention.

The first thing Byria noticed was that the path grew brighter. She looked up to see more breaks in the tree canopy, smiling at the swaths of visible blue sky. With fewer trees, the air seemed to move even more, helping with the humidity.

And then, as Koki and the man had seemed to appear and disappear with magic, Byria noticed the first structure when it was only a few paces away. Bamboo and ferns created a border, behind which three palms stretched toward an opening in the jungle canopy. Between the palms was a little house of grass, more bamboo, and leaves. The house had a few levels, all woven together and to the trunks, supported by platforms of bamboo built upon more woody vines.

She could hear singing, speaking, and the sound of a child's laughter behind the borders. Koki led her around a bend, but an excited cry came from behind the vegetation.

As promised, Koki stayed between her and the people who approached, sharing a conversation similar to the one she'd had with Gyotan.

The houses weren't terribly close together, nothing like the homes and businesses in the Golden City, and Koki seemed to be trying to take a less populated route, but there were still plenty of people. Upon seeing Byria, their voices grew louder and more excited. Which, of course, drew more people.

And many of them looked upon her with some level of recognition—albeit surprised, many of them gesturing about her height. A few, particularly older people, regarded her with more wariness, but no one seemed hostile. There was no "danger," as Koki had promised.

That didn't mean Byria was remotely comfortable.

Besides the many who had to be intercepted in displays of affection toward her, nearly everyone greeted Koki with some form of touch, if not outright hugs and kisses. And just about everyone she saw was cuddling or snuggling with someone else. There were very few children, but every one she saw was snuggled in the arms of a parent or leaning against someone.

At the palace, still the most vivid memories Byria had, her maids would touch her for preparation and dressing, but not with any particular affection. Even Syng, to whom Byria had felt the closest, had not been "affectionate" outside of occasionally holding or squeezing her hand when "her princess" was especially hurt or frightened.

She had no memories of any touch from her parents—though, sifting through the conversation with Patch, she wondered if they even *were* her true parents. And any "affection" from Tain was suspect and could turn to pain.

Besides all the affectionate display and attempts, the people wore hardly any clothing. A few were in animal or leather tunics like the women, but even they had mostly bare arms and legs. For the rest of the people, their primary wardrobe appeared to be loincloths or skirts of soft leather or that coarse yellow-green cloth.

And beads. So many beads. Men *and* women wore multiple necklaces—or whole collars and shoulder plates, like Gyotan, hung with strands and strands of multicolored beads—rather than any shirt or robe.

Yes, the jungle was hot and humid, but how immodest!

As they walked, and Koki kept repeating her conversations, Byria focused on her and tried to understand more of what she said. Besides the various forms of "hurt" Koki used to describe why she was hurrying with Byria, she understood they were visiting a particular healer—one a lot of them really liked, particularly those with children.

And that perhaps this healer was related, close, or married to Koki. Married or a lover? At least from some of the looks and responses. Named "Mokin" and something else she didn't understand. Other words, "lhulhokya" and "ulhyoken," sounded familiar, and Koki kept repeating them. They seemed to reference "child" and "adult" in regard to her, and that *felt* correct.

Eventually the houses grew further and further apart. There was a break with no other homes—though many people continued to follow them—before they got to a somewhat larger clearing, where another grass-bamboo-and-leaf home filled a gap between two curling trees. Bordered by what looked like ginger plants, if Byria was recalling correctly from the palace gardens. There were several rows of gardens, as well as even more plants growing in pots near the house, attached to the exposed tree trunks, and within the border of ginger.

Competing scents of cooking broth, spicy flowers, and musky rose filled the air.

Because of the cleared garden area, Byria got a better idea of the home's construction. Window-holes were lined with braids of grass or green branches and hung with strands of beads. The trees themselves had a dark brown bark that almost shone, and they flourished in the clearing, with many branches of waxy, dark green leaves, and small, fleshy flowers. More bead strings decorated the front door. These clattered musically as the door swung open and shut. A man came out to great them as Koki pulled her inside the ginger border—giving a look to their crowd of followers that kept them on the outside path.

This man's face more closely resembled the blur in her memories.

Byria didn't get to study it too long before Koki grabbed him in an embrace with a kiss that clarified he was definitely a husband or lover.

She looked away, blushing at such a flagrant show of affection. A glance at the crowd, some of whom were edging between the ginger plant border, showed not one of them found such public affection noteworthy. Granted, they were all mostly still staring at her.

When Koki and her lover were finally done with their shameless ardor, they spoke, but too quickly and softly for Byria to pick up anything besides that she was hurt. Then, arms around each other, they approached.

He was dressed similarly to Gyotan, minus the basket, but with plenty of beads over his chest to warrant the wood over his shoulders to which they all attached. And while his chest was almost entirely covered, there was still an awful lot of him that showed. That was even more outstanding after such a show of affection—and with how close he and the woman embraced as they walked.

Both looked around Byria at the people, and she heard them shuffle away some.

"Beelheah," Koki said, gesturing to her. Then she pressed her hand to the man's chest. "Mokin." She hugged him again to show she clearly loved and trusted him, and he returned the hug, staring intently at Byria. Then Koki asked another word Byria recognized and hated. "Remember?"

Biting her lip and feeling tears sting—all too aware of the gawking people—she gave a shrug and tilted her head sideways, back and forth, to indicate she wasn't sure.

"All right," the man, Mokin, said. He stepped away from Koki and bowed deeply. "Safe. Here," he repeated Koki's promise. Then he fixed the onlookers with a firm look and addressed them. Byria understood his "thank you" and her name, and what definitely sounded like a dismissal.

Koki stepped around Byria and repeated something similar while he gestured for Byria to follow him. He held the door open for her to enter, pointing to her head and miming for her to duck.

She did so, making another attempt at "thank you" in their language.

While Byria had always been considered petite and delicate among her people—signs of beauty, where Byria knew she lacked in other ways—she still had a difficult time fitting into the house. The tallest among the people, Mokin in that group, were no larger than almost-adolescent children she'd seen in the Golden City. Inside, her hair brushed the ceiling. The man frowned and gestured for her to sit, which she did.

They continued to communicate through signs and gestures. The man spoke even less than Koki had, but something about the way he moved, his calm confidence... the very air around him soothed Byria. He brought in a bowl and pitcher of water, and then he brought her a bowl of broth served over shredded meat and that sweet potato. There was no egg, but she recognized the look of it. The smell. She swallowed hard, and the tears she'd been fighting all through her jungle walk released in force.

"Sorry. Please. Sorry..." She didn't want the man to stare at her. "Remember—I remember."

* * * * *

Chapter Twenty-Seven
Safe For Now?

Byria didn't know where the man went, but he'd left her as if he understood. Only when she started eating did he return.

Then he simply sat in front of her outstretched legs and waited for her to look at him. He'd brought in a flat basket of bowls, cloths, brushes, and small pots, similar to what Koki had carried in the jungle. One of the bowls steamed, and the cloths and brushes looked softer.

"Thank you," she said in his people's tongue again.

"You're welcome. Always," he said, just like Koki. He gestured to her feet. "Please?"

"Thank you." She nodded again. "Please, yes?"

As he removed the leather pouch "shoes," which now had holes in them, and the cloths wrapping her feet, Byria noticed he kept his nails short and smooth. His movements were even quicker than Koki's, but gentler. More practiced. A line deepened between his brows, and he breathed out through pursed lips.

"Still bad?" she asked.

He looked up and tilted his head as she had earlier, but offered a half smile and touched his heart. "Better..." He moved his hand in the air to say "in time," or so Byria understood.

She gave another nod. "Thank you."

Then, also as Koki had done, he explained each thing he would do, gave an idea of how much it might hurt, and then waited for her to give him permission to continue.

I am safe here.

Her heart's fire warmed more with that thought, so Byria took it as an affirmation.

Mokin cleaned from her feet to her knees as she allowed, but didn't wrap them as Koki had. When she tried to ask, he signed that she was staying here, not walking. Then he pointed to different parts of her body, but she shook her head emphatically, hugging herself.

She pointed to his tray of things, then to herself. "Please? Koki...?" She nodded and pointed between his items and herself again.

Giving her a small bow of assent, he stood. Touching his chest again, he lifted his chin toward one of two doorways in the corner—one dark, the other somewhat brighter, both strung with beads, shells, and hollow bamboo—and called, "Mokin!" before stepping away.

Byria smiled, made a sweep over her body, and put a hand to her mouth toward the beaded curtain, and repeated calling his name.

He chuckled and bowed again before leaving her. The beads clicked pleasantly in his wake. In the shafts of sunlight that came through the doorway he exited, the swaying strings of color were mesmerizing. Byria watched for a moment before she began her own ministrations.

While she did her best to clean and put the healing salve on the rest of her body, she heard the low voices of her hosts speaking. They weren't near, but close enough they'd hear if she called. While she attended to her hurts and the glyph on her arm, she kept glancing furtively toward the beaded curtain, but it remained still. Their voices stayed at a distance.

The balm he'd given her, which cooled her skin, smelled of grass, lavender, and camphor. After spreading it over the burns she could reach, she grimaced upon feeling the bottom of the small pot. Would the small man be upset that she'd used all his healing salve? She chewed her lip until she tasted blood, then pressed her lip until she felt a scab, before finding the courage to squeak out "Mokin?" in the direction of the beads.

More musical clacking suggested Mokin had passed through another beaded doorway before the one into the room where she sat, and that Koki followed behind.

"Sorry!" she said as soon as she saw him. She held up the empty clay pot in a shaking hand.

His eyes widened, but not in anger. "More?"

Byria looked down and away, giving a little shrug that made her wince. Parts of her burned shoulder were sticking to her shirt, and it was becoming uncomfortable to lean on the woven wall.

"More," he stated and slipped back through the beaded curtain.

Koki remained, leaning on the corner between the two doorways, and looking nervous herself. Half illuminated and half in shadow, she made Byria think of the Demon-Wife Between. It fit. The woman was obviously an effective hunter, yet she'd cared for Byria, protected her, and worked with—was clearly in love with—a healer. She offered a smile to the woman and looked to the floor beside her in invitation.

A hopeful smile broke across the woman's face. As she sat, Byria noticed darker circles around her eyes, and tearstains. She reached a hand toward Byria, stopping herself just as Byria uncontrollably flinched, eyes on those large, taloned fingers.

"Sorry," they both murmured to each other.

Byria squeezed her eyes closed and shook her head. "Not you..." Had she not invited the woman near? Spent days without her purposefully hurting her—no, *healing* and *protecting* her. Why couldn't she stop the fear that made her jump even from affection?

I'm safe. Here.

Safe. That feeling, in and of itself, was foreign; Byria didn't know how to trust it. She wasn't even sure she knew *how* to trust, though she'd trusted Patch.

But this small woman who sat in front of her? She'd had barely a glimpse of memories about her, but her heart's fire said she could trust her. Shouldn't that be enough for her body and mind to stop reacting in fear?

"Mokin said you remember food?" Koki asked softly.

Byria chuckled. "Food. Yes." Food, but not the people who'd made it or shared it with her. Tain and the high magepriest had stolen these people from her mind! She dropped her face into her hands to hide the fresh tears. "Sorry."

"Beelheah?" Mokin's voice.

Byria separated her fingers to look at him.

He held up another clay pot, this one bigger than the first, and then put it on the ground beside her. No, not *ground*, grass mats. The house had a grass mat floor. It was more comfortable than the ground, softer.

"I remember *food.*" She sniffled and wiped her face on the sleeve of her less painful arm. "Food. No... no..." She repeated Koki's gestures for people and many things. "I'm sorry."

"No," Mokin spoke again. He kneeled beside Koki and waited for Byria to look at him. "Beelheah no sorry. No you. This—" He tapped his head. "Hurts. Heal." He motioned as he had earlier to mean "in time."

She looked away, about to cover her face again.

"Beelheah. Please." He handed her a damp, clean cloth.

She took it from him.

While she still looked, Mokin angled his head to keep her gaze. "Understand? Healing..." He pressed his lips together in thought. "Healing not... this." He pointed to his body. "Healing is this." He gestured up and down himself. "And this." He pointed to his head. "*And* this." He pressed a hand to his chest.

"All..." He repeated the encompassing circle with his arms. Again, he glided his hand like a fin to indicate taking time. "*Aaaaand...*" He folded his hands together and then drew them out. "Understand? Please? No sorry."

Nodding again, Byria pressed the damp cloth to her face, wiping her tears into it and sniffling.

"Beelheah?" Koki's voice now. Byria peeked over the cloth. "Mokin correct. Yes. No sorry. Safe here. To heal. Stay." She repeated Mokin's mimes for taking time. "Understand? Yes?"

"Yes, I understand." Byria whimpered. "Thank you."

"You're welcome. Always," she said, as Mokin nodded emphatic agreement.

After a moment, Mokin mentioned sleeping and resting. Koki nodded, stood, and disappeared through the beaded curtain over the darker room.

"Beelheah." Mokin waited for her to look at him. He held up the pot of salve he'd brought in. "This. You. All. No sorry. Yes?"

"Thank you. Again. Always."

He smiled at her, gentle enough she hardly noticed the sharp tips of his teeth. "Always. You're welcome."

Byria tried not to jump when Koki came back through the beaded curtain with a pile of animal skins. She and Mokin piled them evenly on the other side of the room, nearer where the wall was tree trunk. Koki then held up a finger and said, "Oh, wait!"

She glanced at Byria and kept from moving too quickly. Disappearing through the brighter beaded doorway, she quickly returned with Byria's messenger bag over her shoulder, while also carrying another flat basket with more water and broth.

Mokin shot her a wide smile. "Good, yes," he said, along with words that were a strong enough compliment to make the hunter woman with claws blush and giggle. He kissed her again, softly, on the lips. Not the passionate greeting of earlier, but sweet. Loving. Nothing more, nothing less.

The act both warmed Byria's heart and made it ache again.

The small woman nodded and turned her attention back to Byria with a smile on her lips. Putting a hand on her hip, she pointed to each thing. "Drink. Eat. Sleep. Rest." She bowed and backed away. "You're safe here." Then she said something else Byria couldn't remember her teaching her, but she understood. "Home."

Byria bit her lip hard. Unable to stop the prick of even more tears, she looked away.

"Rest," Mokin echoed after a pause that was almost uncomfortable. Then he repeated, "Home."

Managing a nod, Byria covered her face again, listening to the rhythmic, almost chiming *swish* and *click* of beads as the two left the room. Alone, she let herself cry as she arranged the skins to lie upon.

The full length of the room was barely more than that of her bed, but she could fully recline.

She'd spent over a year choosing to feel pain, create pain. Now, she chose to feel *safe*, to let the pain heal.

As she drifted toward a comfortable, unafraid sleep, Byria's heart's fire grew warmer, spreading out to her body, healing her unbidden. This was where she needed to be right now. But something else moved within her.

For now.

This was not an end to her journey.

The realization came suddenly, but not jarringly. Byria opened her eyes wide and sucked in a breath. A True thought rang clear in her mind:

My journey ends with the dragon.

* * * * *

Book II
Village of Lost Memories

* * * * *

Chapter One
Making Promises and Healing Trust

"Ko-od mohnink."

Byria blinked, trying to place where she was, and the soft, male voice trying to speak her language with the tongue of a bird. The small village... running from the palace... Patch and her instructions... the dungeon...

The dragon! Byria barely kept herself from gasping. The soreness in her joints and over her skin caused her to wince upon sitting up.

"Good morning," she said back, rubbing her eyes, trying to adjust to not only the dimness of the jungle, but being inside the small hut, and then repeated the greeting as Koki had taught her.

Mokin—pride and relief filled Byria upon remembering his name—beamed like she was a student who'd tested well after a lesson. He stood by the brighter beaded curtain, which swung with its pretty-toned clacking, and held out another steaming bowl of broth. Byria licked her lips, making a delighted sound when she saw the little egg cracked on top.

"I remember!" she said, pointing. Then she added, "Thank you. Always."

He bowed, beaming. "You're welcome. Always." He said something else, also pointing to the egg, and then asked, "Remember, too?"

Looking down at the soup, Byria shook her head shamefully. "Sorry," she murmured between sips.

"No sorry. Remember, 'no sorry.' Understand?"

"I understand." Byria nodded and slurped up the egg, which made her smile again. Shifting to stretch her legs and flex her feet, which were noticeably less sore, she grimaced at the results of the quantity of water Mokin and Koki had made her drink the day before. She put down her bowl and made an uncomfortable noise, crossing and squeezing her legs.

Mokin nodded and gestured for her to follow him outside. There was an area behind the hut of strategically placed leafy branches around a hole. After thanking him again, Byria took care of her needs and returned to the house.

With her soup sat another pitcher of water. She hadn't realized how thirsty she still was until half the pitcher was already gone before she'd touched the soup.

Mokin had been nowhere around when she'd returned, but Byria soon finished her soup and her water. As if he knew, Mokin returned with another bowl and pitcher, taking the empty ones.

"Thank you," Byria said again.

Mokin bowed, and after repeating his perpetual, "You're welcome," he added, "no 'thank you.'" She didn't understand the rest of his words, but he repeated the gesture for *all things*. "Here. Safe. Home."

Blushing, Byria bit her lip to keep from doing exactly the opposite of what he'd said. She sipped at her fresh bowl of soup.

Mokin pointed to the flat basket of cleaning and healing supplies. "Please?" He reached, but waited for her to nod before coming close enough to take it. "Eat. Drink. I will return." He pointed his chin at the soup and water with those commands, then gave a small bow before leaving.

When he was gone, Byria closed her eyes and slowly slurped her soup, taking time to breathe in its scent and savor it on her tongue. While that freed no new memories, each taste triggered her shoulders, back, and neck to remember how to relax, and her chest and lungs how to breathe easier. She wanted to remember more, but the comfort growing in her stomach and feeding her heart's fire allowed her to feel content for the moment.

She'd finished both her soup and the fresh pitcher of water, and was doing her best to fold and neatly pile the skins when Mokin returned, carrying an empty tray.

"Good! Thank you, Beelheah!" He smiled, shifting the tray to one arm, and pointed to her empty bowls and pitcher. "Please?"

"You're welcome, thank you, please, always?" She tried to answer his words and gestures, scooting out of his way while still on her knees. The fast movement reminded her how much she still hurt, especially as her shirt ripped away from her burnt arm and shoulder, where it had stuck while she slept. She couldn't contain a yelp and hiss of pain.

"Beelheah?" Mokin put the tray down and squatted in front of her, but not so close that she felt the need to pull away.

"All right. I all right—" Byria said while trying to unclench her jaw.

"Na." He changed his pronunciation more to how she said it. "No. Not all right. I know."

Byria cringed at the more serious tone of his voice, squinting at him as her skin continued to stick, pull, and burn.

Mokin sat back on his heels and backed half a step away, relaxing his posture. "You're safe. You're hurt, not all right, but you're safe. No more hurt to you in this home. *Never* hurt to you in this home."

He said another word in his language that she didn't understand, but he pressed both his hands to his chest, and then held them out to her, cupped in offering. "Understand?"

Looking between his hands and him, she shrugged and shook her head.

He repeated, "*Never* hurt you more in this home. *Never.*" Once again, as he said the word she didn't know, he pressed his hands to his chest—his heart, Byria realized—patted them there several times, and then offered them cupped. After a moment, he made a tossing motion and pointed to her chest. He tapped his own chest, then pointed to her—her heart—and repeated the word.

She nodded, saying "Promise" in her language, and then repeating it in his.

Mokin smiled, touched his chest, and offered again. When she only nodded, he pointed to her, and then reached out, as if grabbing something from the air between them, and pressed it to his chest. Then he made both the offering gesture and then the receiving gesture. Tilting his head, he looked at her with wide eyes. "Understand?"

Byria studied him a few moments, for which he waited patiently. His face had more lines than Koki's, almost as lined as an elder, but like Koki, his expression and movement made her think he couldn't be much more than ten or fifteen years older than she. Perhaps it was his larger eyes—a darker green than Koki's, though they sometimes reflected more silvery circles than copper—that made him look younger. Or his physique.

Finally, she nodded, mimicked his offering gesture, and repeated the word he'd used that seemed to mean "promise."

"Yes!" he agreed emphatically, catching her offering and pulling it to his heart with a smile. "*Never* hurt you more in this home," he repeated, speaking slowly. "Never. Promise." He offered her his heart, and this time she caught his promise, pressing it to hers.

"I understand. Thank you."

"*Always.*" Mokin paused and then stood slowly, reaching toward the tray and waiting for her approval before picking it up. As he headed toward the beaded curtain, he said, "Now, come. Please." He waited, watching her with concern as she stood, nodding in encouragement as she took a few steps.

Byria followed him through the curtain and couldn't repress swatting it a little extra so she could hear all the tones of the beads, shells, and bamboo clicking. In front of her Mokin chuckled and waited by another curtain, running the backs of his nails across it to produce even more sounds.

Between them was another small room with a folding wall of more beaded strings, several grass mats piled, and what looked like children's playthings—blocks, large puzzle boxes of cut-out shapes, and little wheels on strings. Byria hadn't seen or heard any children around the house, but didn't know how to ask about the toys.

Mokin led her outside through the other beaded curtain. A door of woven branches and grass, like the one on the front of the house, was propped open from the beads. They entered a patio where more woven branches and bamboo made two walls that stuck out from the house like an enclosed corner. Covered in the same roof as the house, overlapped leaves and thatch, each wall held many shelves full of jars, bowls, baskets, folded or rolled banana leaves, tools, mortars and pestles, and more things Byria either didn't recognize, or felt she ought to recognize, but couldn't.

The rest of the patio area was open, the ground set with a floor of flat stones. In the center of the patio was an intricate fire pit with a number of wooden bars over it, each hanging with a pot or two, and a grate that looked like woven clay high enough over the fire that more burnables could be added.

On the grate, to the side, was a large pot that smelled of the delicious broth. Its scent mingled with many others from more simmering pots. Sweet floral notes and savory spices mixed with acrid bitterness and soft grassiness.

Beyond the patio were paths between raised gardens and the small structure Mokin had sent her to earlier to relieve herself. Jungle foliage bordered more closely at the back of the house, several very tall trees rising high and spreading full umbrellas of leaves that covered most of the sky. Byria could see a few clearly traveled paths into the jungle.

Mokin put the basket tray down by the fire and directed Byria to a far corner on the open side of the patio, where there was a pile of woven mats similar to, but thicker than, what covered the little hut's floor. He put two end-to-end, creating a resting place where Byria could fit, and motioned for her to sit on them.

She did so, and he brought over another flat basket resembling the one from last night, but with even more things on it. It held a steaming bowl of water, a cool bowl of water, brushes, more cloths, some fresh leaves, and three different covered pots—all three larger than the ones she'd gone through yesterday. Mokin pointed between her body and his supplies, a questioning look on his face. Byria sighed, acknowledging how much better she felt than the night before, but not looking forward to the pain that would have to come first, and nodded.

He knelt at her feet first, reaching to ask if he could pick one up. When she allowed, he shifted so he was on one knee, and rested her ankle on his thigh. She couldn't keep from cringing again at the thought of her bare skin against his, even though it was for healing.

When he saw her face, he put her foot back down, stood slowly—his every movement seemed deliberate and preceded by a pause so as not to startle her—and grabbed what looked like two small stairs from near the shelved walls. He put that down by her feet, asking with a look and his hands if that was better.

"Yes! Please! Thank you!" She looked away in embarrassment, hoping she hadn't offended him.

"All right," he said, then reached for her ankle, waiting again for her permission to touch her.

She nodded as more tears stung her eyes. Even her handmaidens at the palace, who were supposed to defer to her in all things, had never been so patient. "Thank you. I—" She gestured between them, sniffling, wanting so hard to tell him why she was crying so he wouldn't worry. "Say 'thank you, no, home,' but... please, *thank you*." Though she was making no promise, she repeated his heart-offering motions because it seemed to fit.

He motioned to catch it, pressed his hand to his heart, and kept it there while he held her gaze for a weighty moment. "I understand."

More tears came with his response, with what it might mean. She sniffled and took the cloth he gave her. She hoped, truly hoped, he *didn't* understand, not really. No one should truly understand such things. It would mean they had suffered, and Byria didn't want to think of anyone—much less this very kind person—suffering as she had. But though she covered her face as she wiped her eyes, she could still feel the heaviness of his gaze on her.

When she finally moved the cloth enough to look at him, he offered another gentle smile and pointed to her foot. "Please?"

"Yes, please."

He rested her foot on the small step block and studied it. A surprised smile grew on his face, and he declared, "Healing! Good!"

Byria couldn't repress her own grin at his excitement and the little sense of pride that she might be healing even faster than he'd expected. "Good!"

He carefully cleaned her foot. Though he was definitely slower and gentler than Koki, the liquid he patted against it still burned, and it took all her focus not to pull away or kick in pain. After a moment, she realized her foot was securely gripped in his hand, though she hardly noticed the pressure.

To distract herself and prevent any panic at being held, she pointed to the parts of her foot. "Words?" She leaned and touched her toe, saying her word for it.

Mokin understood and repeated what he called it. They continued the vocabulary lessons through him naming the liquid he used to clean, the minty-grassy-smelling balm he rubbed over her sole and between her toes, and the leaves he wrapped around her foot that numbed the pain.

Besides the interest in their language lessons, Byria found herself intrigued by his movement. While he didn't have the claws of Koki, his hands still seemed too big with extra joints.

He rapidly and smoothly shifted between kneeling and squatting on either side of her leg to get the best angle to inspect the various injuries, and to clean and apply balm or leaves. The pressure from his touch was never too much, sometimes hardly even perceptible, outside the relief from the salve and leaves.

When he reached her knee, she insisted he stop. He didn't argue, and let her switch feet herself. When he finished with her other foot and calf, he stood and approached her face and neck. Byria allowed him to take care of those injuries, too, but pulled away when he requested to move her collar much more.

Stepping back, Mokin sighed and furrowed his brow as he walked around her, studying the way her shirt had begun to stick to her burns again.

She shook her head, hugging herself and grimacing from the pain of the action.

Mokin squatted beside her. When she looked at him, he said pleadingly, "Bad. Hurt bad, bad, bad. Very bad." Then he twisted to each side, showing his limited reach on himself, and pointed again to her back. "Very bad. Please?"

Byria looked down, understanding what he meant. She couldn't reach far beyond her shoulders or up too much past her waist, and she could feel the oozing and burning worse where she couldn't reach.

A whimper was all she could manage for an answer, though.

After a thoughtful noise, he said, "Wait," and returned to the little hut. He came out with a cloth tunic, similar to Koki's, but larger. Putting it on over his beads, he lifted the back over his head, keeping his arms in their holes his chest offered. "Good?"

Byria considered while he removed the tunic, folded it, and placed it on top of the mat pile. He clearly preferred just his beads, loincloth, and beaded wide belt of large pockets and pouches. He squatted, waiting patiently for direction from her.

My choice. Still my choice. I can choose to hurt or not hurt. I can choose which pain is mine, and which I don't want. I trust he will stop if I ask him to, and he won't do anything I don't want.

Her heart fire agreed with her thoughts.

Byria made a decision. She pointed to her left arm, first her forearm, then the top part and shoulder. That one hadn't been burned, but still had cuts from her travels and Tain's lashings beyond her back. If she was comfortable with how he treated that arm, she'd let him look at the right. Then, if she was still comfortable, she had a different idea for her back and shoulders.

Mokin nodded and moved to her left arm, letting her roll up the sleeve to her shoulder. He continued naming her finger and hand parts, and what he was doing and using. When he got to the back of her arm, where she knew the lash wounds still were, he only hesitated a moment before wrapping them with leaves, not veering from his explaining and their vocabulary practice.

He slowed as he reached her shoulder, but she let him continue until her sleeve didn't move any more. When he stepped back, indicating he was finished, she offered a small smile and another nod as she carefully rolled down her sleeve.

Byria fiddled with her right cuff, cautiously peering at him. Mokin gave a nod and shifted his attention to cleaning his brushes and cloths, letting her know he could wait. Taking a few slow breaths, seeing him nod in approval out of the corner of her eye, she slowly rolled up her right sleeve. "Mokin?"

This time he couldn't keep from flinching. His face tightened, and his jaw clenched as his eyes lit on the glyph she'd carved into her arm. She pulled it to her chest defensively.

"Sorry! Sorry!" he said quickly. Putting down his cloth and brush, he leaned back, holding his hands up and flipping them back and forth, as Koki had done so many times on their trip.

It was meant to be reassuring, showing there were no weapons, but she was all too aware weapons weren't necessary for hands to be dangerous.

"Sorry. Please?" He held out his empty hands.

She bit her lip, shifted, and held out her right hand. "Me? Heal? Please?"

After a moment, Mokin frowned, scrutinizing the rest of her arm. "Wait..." He went over to the shelves and brought over two much larger pots. Pointing to the angry, seeping blisters, he said a few words Byria didn't understand.

When she shook her head, Mokin pursed his lips and scrunched his brow more, thinking a moment. He pointed to the cuts on her arm and said, "Bad," and then the burns on her upper arm, and intoned deeply and more forcefully, "*Baaaaaad*," and then moved his hand to show the much worse injury was over everything.

Byria pressed her lips together, noticing Mokin kept looking at the glyph on her arm, clenching his jaw, and then deliberately looking at the other injuries. His breathing sounded like hers when she was trying to focus on her breaths and stoke her heart's fire. He clearly recognized it, and it frightened him.

It *frightened* him. That was a True Thing.

She wanted to ask him more, ask him what it was, but they didn't have the words for that yet.

I can trust him. He won't hurt me. Those thoughts still felt True, too.

"Mokin?" she asked.

"Yes?"

"What? Explain... healing things?"

He nodded. Pointing to a fresh bowl of water he brought over, he mimed patting her arm with that. Then he indicated one of the larger pots, opened it, dipped in a stick, and handed it to her, miming she could put it in her mouth.

She smelled, then tasted it. "Honey?"

He restated it in her language and again in his, nodding, and then mimed spreading it over her arm. When she made a confused face, he nodded harder and repeated, "Healing."

Byria shrugged, motioning for him to continue.

Mokin opened the other two jars. One had what looked like giant, flat mushrooms; the other had some type of moss. He motioned layering those on top.

After making another face, she considered. Nothing sounded like it would take the marks away. The burn itself had already faded and twisted them, so perhaps treating the burn would preserve them. Finally, she reached her arm out to Mokin. "Yes. Heal, please?"

"Yes," he agreed, and did exactly as he'd explained, though every time he came near the glyph on her arm, he tensed or clenched his jaw. Only when he'd covered it with the mushrooms did he begin to relax.

And so did Byria, who hadn't realized how tense she'd become until she felt her muscles loosening as Mokin did. She noticed the returned prickling anxiety up and down her spine as it faded again.

When he was done, he rolled her sleeve over all the layers he'd placed and offered a weak smile.

Byria returned the expression.

Mokin pointed to her back. "Heal?"

Her smile fell. Tain had put brands across her back; she'd felt them all last night, when she'd put the healing balm everywhere she could reach. It hadn't been comfortable, and it would be a little more difficult with all the things layered over her arm, but she felt certain she still could. What she wasn't sure about was how Mokin would react upon seeing the symbols of the brands. She thought a few more moments.

"Mokin? Um…" She raised a finger and spun it, hoping it meant the same here as it did in the palace.

He nodded, picking up the dirty and used cloths and taking them to the other side of the patio, keeping his back to her.

Byria tugged a few times at the neck of the tunic she wore. Checking her reach, she worked around to the back. Using her own sharp thumbnail, she sawed somewhere in the middle of the back until she heard a rip. Then she tore until the shirt was split to just above where she could reach, which she verified by smoothing more of the balm over each of the brands. Satisfied, she called Mokin back over and opened up the tear for him.

He raised his brows, but brought the tray of supplies behind her, and continued his work, still explaining and exchanging words in their languages.

While he was layering the moss and mushrooms over her shoulder, it occurred to her that quite some time had passed, and she still hadn't seen Koki. She asked Mokin.

He chuckled and moved to where Byria could see. "Ka-kaw-tooa." He moved his hand, making stabbing motions as if he held a spear. "More. Need more food."

"Ooh—"

"No you sorry!" He pointed with a smirk. "You here. Safe, Koki…" He said another word and smiled widely, eyes sparkling as one finger circled his face. "More than anything, you safe is good."

Byria blushed.

Mokin returned to layering things over her burns. When he was done, he stepped to the side and pointed to the rest of her and the tray. "You?"

"Yes."

"Good. I…" He gestured toward the fire, then pointed back to her, and mimicked how she'd put her hand to her mouth to call. "All right?"

"All right. Thank you."

"You're welcome." His smile returned, and his eyes were sparkling again. "Always." He bowed again before leaving her. True to his word, Mokin kept his back to her the whole time.

He seemed to have a lot to do. He checked all the pots on the fire, moved around other things, took many things off the shelf and sat down, back still to her, and spread out herbs, bowls, and tools and attended to those, humming softly.

Byria covered nearly the whole rest of her body in the healing salve, as she still had so many remaining injuries. She wondered how bad she'd still be, how horrified Mokin would be, had Patch not taught her how to use her heart's fire.

Once she was done using another significant portion of what he'd left, she adjusted herself to sit comfortably and practice with it more.

When she'd used it down to almost embers, she opened her eyes, feeling both more energetic and exhausted. "Mokin?"

The man stood, bringing another tray of food and water. In addition to the soup—with another little egg cracked over it!—he'd added a bowl of figs and nuts, and one of purple sweet turnip, different nuts, and honey. Two portions of each. He gestured to the pile of mats and gave her a questioning look.

Waving to the patio stones beside her, Byria said, "Yes, please."

She had so many questions for him, and he kept looking at her as if he had them, too, but they ended up only exchanging words for food and how to say one really enjoyed food.

Mokin blushed a little, admitting that he enjoyed cooking. Good cooking used herbs, so feeding people good food was part of healing.

Byria liked that philosophy. While soups and teas were part of the medicinal practices in the palace and the Golden City, magepriest healers placed more emphasis on their magic and strong-flavored herbal tinctures in alcohol, or special ingredients added to food and eaten with specific instructions.

Though she didn't learn much more about her history with these people, and no more memory stones loosened in her mind, Byria enjoyed sharing the meal with Mokin. When they were finished eating, he packed up all their bowls, stood, and pointed firmly to the mats she sat on, wagging his finger over their entire length. "Now rest."

Byria frowned, that same odd irritation as when Koki had ordered her to hide rising. Had she not only just eaten lunch? "I'm fine."

"Na," Mokin said firmly, pointing his finger at each and every injury he'd tended, then making a wide gesture over her whole body.

Standing tall (for his size), with one hand on his hip, he jabbed his finger at the mat again. "Rest."

His eyes held no room for compromise.

Byria couldn't help but smile. She imagined him keeping a herd of small children in line and found herself thinking of the toys in the other room. Unable to keep from first giving an exaggerated sigh and eye roll, as Koki had done to that other man in the jungle, she reclined and closed her eyes as directed.

"Good," he said in an amused voice. "Rest good, Beelheah. And heal."

* * * * *

Chapter Two
Curiosity and Consent

On her third day with Mokin—Koki hadn't yet returned from hunting—Byria convinced him to let her help weed the front gardens. She'd successfully weeded everything behind the patio the day before, and felt the need to do something in return for all he and Koki had done for her, and how much of his healing salves and balms she'd needed to use.

He looked concerned at her request, but before she could try to rephrase with more gestures, he drew her to one of the windows.

Pointing outside, he motioned for her to wait. It didn't take long for her to notice the cause for his concern.

Several of the villagers kept walking up and down the path outside the house. She even recognized some of the faces and necklaces of those who'd been the most insistent in their attempts to embrace and speak to her despite Koki's intervention.

Mokin gestured for her to back away from the window; some of the passersby had begun to pause and glance toward the house more directly—some more obvious than others.

It hadn't occurred to Byria until that moment that Mokin had been trying to give her privacy and time to recover. She swallowed, warmth spreading from her heart's fire at his concern. He gestured her further away from the window and then made a sweeping wave before pointing at her.

She nodded. If she were to go out front, *everyone* would want to come by and see her, speak to her—embrace, her even. And no Koki to keep them away.

Byria wanted to ask if they really all remembered her, or if she was just an odd, large person who drew their curiosity. The ones who'd tried to embrace her *must* know her or remember her. Would they talk to her? Would speaking to them loosen more memory stones? Could she handle that onslaught?

"Beelheah." Mokin reached his arms out as if to embrace her, and stopped, eyebrows raised. She hadn't flinched, but she'd stiffened. He nodded, letting her know he understood.

She knew he did, likely more than she wanted him—or anyone—to.

Byria sighed and stood up as straight as she could in the small house, pointing to the door outside. "I want to know. Memory?" She shrugged and tapped her head. "I don't have. Still. Maybe…" She waved her hand toward the window again. "…remember?"

He scratched his smooth chin—no hint of stubble, contributing to how young he looked despite the lines in his face—and chewed his lip. She sensed from the look on his face he was trying to figure out how to say what he wanted in their still-limited communication.

After another sigh, he pointed to the wooden disk that hung from his belt. There was a glyph burned into it, one Byria didn't recognize. "Oma-ku-mama." He pointed at her injuries, to the animal skins, the various plants, all the beads over his chest. He then gestured to the back patio and the room leading to the back patio—the one with all the toys Byria hadn't figured out how to ask about.

Byria nodded, understanding. "Healer. You heal people."

He nodded. "Yes. I'm a healer." He pointed at the door and to the curtain that led to the small room again.

"People must visit you. For healing." Byria pointed to his glyphed disk. "But you're healing me. Just me. Days, now."

He nodded again, pointed to the front door, and walked back and forth between it and the curtain.

"Healing another person, can't watch me," she tried. "Everyone—" She added gestures to clarify her attempts at speaking more of his language. "—might talk to me. Hug me…"

While he smiled and nodded once more, worry still filled his eyes.

Byria pressed her lips together. Trying to match her voice to the jungle people's tongue, she said, "I say, 'Excuse me, waste house, no follow me?'"

Mokin covered a chuckle and gave an approving nod. "Would work."

Escape plan ready, Byria moved to weed Mokin's front gardens while he saw to his patients.

* * * * *

Chapter Three
Mothers and Children

Mokin stayed outside with Byria for a few minutes, showing her what weeds to pull, and giving the passersby a good, firm look. A few cast their eyes to the ground and decided they had important work elsewhere.

After Byria assured him she was ready, he picked up a pot containing a spicy-smelling jasmine bush and moved it to the front of his gardens. He explained to Byria that meant he was available to see people. The second the pot touched the ground, a very pregnant woman (Byria had seen her pacing most frequently), wearing so many beads they clattered as loud as voices, made a waddling jog between the rows of herbs, dragging a small child behind her.

She barely greeted Mokin before she launched herself at Byria and fully kissed both her cheeks. It took a lot of effort, but Byria managed to not cringe, and even smile—though it was forced. The woman didn't seem to notice as she clutched Byria's fingers and started chirping and hooting in their language so quickly, Byria didn't even understand a word.

Even if Mokin had tried to translate, he couldn't get a word in edgewise.

The child hid behind the woman, peeking out at Byria with eyes that looked even bigger in the small head. Byria couldn't tell if it was a boy or girl, because it wore what almost everyone seemed to wear—a loincloth of some animal skin and several necklaces of wooden and stone beads that covered the chest, including quite a few necklaces, more than some of the other adults who'd passed.

Byria gave the child a shy smile and waggled a wave with the fingers not being squeezed by the woman. The child returned the smile and the gesture. Byria pointed to the child's necklaces and whispered the word she remembered for "pretty." The child gave a giggle and thanked her.

The woman finally chirped a few words Byria understood—the need to go to the waste house. With a quick turn to the child, she said something, pointed to Byria, and dashed into the house by herself.

Mokin's eyes widened, and he smacked his hand to his face. Muttering "Sorry" in five different phrases she mostly understood, he asked, "All right?" and gestured up and down.

"All right," she said, surprised to find it true. The hug had shaken her at first, but now that the woman was gone, she realized she'd actually liked the moment of unbridled and honest affection. She made the heart offering gesture. "Promise."

Mokin caught it with a sigh of relief that nearly doubled him over. "Thank you. Sorry! I must see her. Baby in only a few months and important friend. Thank you for patience! And sorry!" He reached a hand out for the child. "Come…" She couldn't quite make out what he called the child.

The child's eyes widened, and it looked nervously at the door, at Mokin, and at Byria before taking a tiny step closer to Byria. The small brow furrowed in concern.

Byria took a guess at what the woman had said based on the child's actions, and inquired as best she could. "Woman say me watch this one?" She pointed between her and the child.

Mokin gave a small nod and muttered more apologies.

Byria thought a moment, looking at the very small child and wondering how old—he? she?—was. She hadn't spent much if any time with children, but this little one looked so worried and out of place, she felt a kindred connection. And she certainly didn't want to cause trouble. "Can stay with me."

Mokin looked at her with surprise. "You're sure, Beelheah?"

"Yes." She smiled down at the child and knelt between the rows of plants—which still left her taller than the little one—and she touched her chest. "Byria." She pointed at the child and asked, "You?"

"Owi." The child sounded even more like a little bird than anyone else she'd heard and perked up significantly at her attention.

"Owi help with weeds?" She looked at Mokin to make sure he trusted her to make sure the child didn't damage his plants.

"Thank you, Beelheah-kau. Owi-ki." He bowed at both of them. Through the house, Byria heard the bead curtains clacking again. Mokin looked at Owi. "Be good for Beelheah, yes?"

"Yes!" The child enthusiastically threw him the promise gesture, which he caught with a laugh before hugging Owi and kissing the child's head.

"Good. Thank you!" He bowed once more before disappearing into the house.

Byria pointed to the first row. "Pull weeds?"

"Pull weeds," Owi agreed, plopping to a knee and waiting for instruction.

Byria did her best to explain with the words and gestures Mokin had taught her yesterday. Fortunately, the child was a quick study, and the two swiftly made their way down the first row of plants.

By the time they started the second row, a different villager approached. It was another woman wearing many necklaces. She had no child with her, and she spoke softly and slowly. Her hair was a paler green than Koki or Mokin's. Strands of white and silver numbered almost as many as the green.

Byria's gaze went to her hands and feet. They were sharp, like Koki's, and though her hair had the look of age, her face and stride didn't. Her movement was graceful and strong, and her face—though lined like Mokin's—didn't look old.

Byria couldn't help but glance at the woman's breasts behind her necklace. They weren't swollen like those of Owi's pregnant mother, but small, like Byria's own.

Not that she had much experience for comparison.

Byria's most vivid memory of nude bodies, outside her marriage requirements with Tain, was the night before her wedding, when Syng had shooed out all the other handmaidens and shown Byria a forbidden book with pictures of men and women. Syng had sworn her to secrecy—both of them would be executed for such an act—but she'd wanted Byria to be informed on her wedding night. Despite her anxious and stern words, Syng had become quite giggly only a few pages into the book.

Heat came to Byria's cheeks with this memory. The woman paused in her speech and raised an eyebrow at Byria. Fearing her face might catch flame in embarrassment, she looked back at the weeds.

Owi, who'd paused to look between the women, said something about "know," "learning," and "words."

The older woman nodded. She pointed between Byria and herself. "Remember me?"

Byria lowered her eyes again and shook her head. Cooing slowly to see if she could better imitate their language, she said, "Memory nah. No memory for, most all things. Almost everything," miming appropriately for further clarification.

The woman's face fell, but she made no move to touch or embrace Byria.

She sensed this woman was kindred, like Koki and Mokin, so she lifted her left sleeve and dropped the collar to show her right shoulder. "Hurt," she said. Then she touched her head. "Hurt, too."

The woman's eyes widened, and while they were sad, they didn't hold pity. Byria appreciated that.

"Um..." She pointed to herself, "Byria," then to the child, "Owi," and to the woman, she asked, "you?"

The woman gave a little smirk, and the child giggled once more.

Byria held out her hands with a questioning shrug. She'd thought she'd said the word correctly.

"Kau-ah," the woman said.

That sounded close to what Byria had said. She also wasn't sure if the woman was trying to teach her the correct word for "you" or if that was her name.

The woman gave a gentle chuckle and touched her chest. "Ama." She pointed to the child. "Owi-ki." And then to Byria. "Kau-ah?"

Before Byria could answer, the woman said, "Bee-lhee-ah-kau," pointing at her, and then exaggerated her tone as she asked, "Kau-ah?"

Byria waggled her head to show she was unsure, but at least the woman was coming closer to making the "r" sound in her name.

She wondered if the "ki" at the end of Owi's name and the "kau" at the end of hers were some added honorific. People needed to show extra respect to the royal family and magepriests, so they added extra words at the ends of their names. And parents often used affectionate versions for their children. Perhaps the woman was Owi's grandmother? No, she remembered when Mokin addressed the child, it *had* sounded like Owi-ki.

With a tilt of her head, the woman then asked, "Lhu-lhoo-kee?"

Byria remembered hearing Koki use that word to people when they'd come into the village. Then she imagined the word or words with the "r" sounds where the woman slurred similarly when speaking her name. *That* word she remembered! It was in Patch's language.

"Yes! Nah." Byria tried to explain. Crouching to one knee, she waved her hand as if making a line from Owi's head. "Rurokye. Um…" Had she heard the word for "child" in this language? She must've, but didn't recall, so she made another gesture as if to encompass Owi, who was looking at her with amusement. Gesturing at Owi once more, she repeated, "Rurokye," then gestured to herself and the woman and said, "Urukyen," the word for an adult woman.

"Uh-lhoo-kee-en!" the woman said excitedly. She made a gesture up on her toes as if reaching for the sky, scooped up some of the dirt from the garden, and brushed it on her arm to make a smear of brown. "Uh-lhoo-kee-en. Iwah-kao kaueh." She pointed to Byria and made a cradling gesture.

"Oh! Patch." Byria smiled. The woman was asking after Patch, who was far taller than Byria, had much darker skin, and whom Koki had said had treated her as a mother would.

The woman looked at her questioningly, shaking her head to indicate she didn't understand.

Patch had seemed to want to keep their names a secret, calling them only Child and Woman, if Byria were understanding correctly. Tears pricked her eyes as she thought of the woman. Was it possible she might have escaped despite the high magepriest saying the whole dungeon had collapsed? She looked away, shaking her head and wiping her eyes.

The woman reached out her hand.

Biting her lip, Byria took it, feeling it would be rude not to.

Byria recognized the phrasing of an apology, though what the woman said sounded more elaborate and more somber.

"Thank you." She looked down at their hands. The woman's grip felt almost as strong as Koki's, and as gentle as Mokin's. And, surprisingly, her long nails didn't even touch Byria's skin. She didn't flinch from the strange hands or their touch.

The woman nodded, squeezing her hand. She gave Byria two small tugs downward and gestured for her to move so she could reach her. Pressing her lips together nervously, Byria took a knee again. The woman had acted kindly and not overly affectionate thus far. She didn't want to be rude, and if lots of necklaces meant a higher status, she especially didn't want to be rude to this Very Important woman.

The woman warbled a few more words Byria didn't understand, and then blew upon Byria's forehead through pursed lips, finishing by gently pressing her thumb right between Byria's eyebrows.

It made Byria think of a blessing; she bowed and gave her thanks. The woman nodded and turned to the child next to her. She said a little more to Owi, but then repeated the blessing.

The child smiled, bowed to the woman, and thanked her with the same words Byria had used, which relieved her. She hadn't given offense.

Once the woman left, Owi turned to Byria with a much bigger grin and puffing—his? her?—chest proudly.

As soon as the woman was well away, and the two were halfway done weeding the second row, three more women, one with a child who looked a little older than Owi, came up through Mokin's gardens.

The one with the child accidentally stepped on one of the neat rows.

"Na!" Byria said quickly, making a motion for the woman to move away.

Owi added a little more, and the woman stepped off the crushed plant, trying to make it stand and muttering apologies.

For the rest of the time Owi's mother was in Mokin's house, which felt like a very, very long time to Byria, Owi kept the villagers from getting too close and informed them Byria was helping Mokin clean the garden of weeds.

The number of people on the path between the rows that led to the door grew. Besides the clumsy woman, another also had a child in tow, hers younger than Owi. The mothers urged their children to help Byria with the weeding, or so she understood from the gestures. They waved and blew her kisses as if they knew her well.

Byria noticed the two mothers, like Owi's mother, wore the most beads in the most colors around their chests—enough so their breasts were almost completely covered. She saw no one else dressed as Koki had been, in a full spotted cat skin, but only about half of the women had long, clawed fingernails and toenails like Koki. The mothers had rounded nails similar to Mokin's. Perhaps they didn't want to accidentally scratch their children, or needed smooth fingers for work; she could understand Mokin not wanting to scratch his patients.

Few of the women actually spoke to Byria, though they all stared. The non-mothers looked at her rather uncomfortably, *hungrily* even. It made Byria's stomach writhe as if it were filled with worms.

The children who'd been sent to her, on the other hand, were quite happy, and very helpful. They collectively worked on the third and fourth of the twelve rows on that side of the entrance path—but weeding had become difficult with the attention.

The older child who'd been with the plant-crushing mother, Iaki, looked more boyish and wore fewer colorful necklaces, but Byria couldn't tell for certain. And the one younger than Owi, whose name was Iyiti, was just as mysterious in its gender.

Despite how awkward she felt, not knowing if they were boys or girls, it didn't hinder the pleasure of their company. She engaged them in a game similar to what she and Mokin did, naming her body parts, his actions, and his tools.

Byria would point to things, asking, "What?" and the children would tell her the things' names. They complimented or corrected her repetition, or if she was especially mistaken, they'd giggle as if she'd said a particularly naughty word. Sometimes she'd purposefully say something very wrong just for their reactions. They all insisted she must teach them her words for the things she asked about as well.

The simple joy of their company pricked her eyes with more tears, but the children were laughing so hard at some of her speaking attempts that they had tears of their own.

Unbidden, she thought of the child she'd made herself miscarry. There was a small twinge in her belly, and she paused to touch it. She expected to feel more tears, different tears, but she didn't. There was an emptiness, but it wasn't unpleasant. The child would likely not have survived their escape from the palace. Worse, if Byria had stayed, the child would have known the cruelty of Tain. She wouldn't wish that on any being.

A questioning sound from Owi drew her attention. She smiled and pointed to a brightly colored bird squawking and preening in a nearby branch to continue the game. Even if she'd had the words, she wasn't sure she was ready to share her more painful and hidden thoughts with anyone—definitely not children she hoped would never know the feel of a striking hand or belt, or worse.

As she and the children moved to weed the next garden row, her laughter turned to a yelp of surprise as three of the women all reached to touch her.

She stumbled back with a sharp, frightened "Na!"

The women looked hurt and angry. The children stopped laughing.

Owi was the first to stand in front of her and say, "Beelheah is hurt! Mokin said don't touch her because she's hurt!"

The women's anger melted into shame and mumbled apologies.

Embarrassed, she whispered her thanks to Owi.

The other two children looked at her in concern. The older child, Iaki, looked between the women and Byria, then leaned close and murmured the words Byria recognized as "mother" and "baby."

Byria blinked and shook her head; she didn't understand. Iaki pointed to his—she decided to think of him as a boy, not an "it"—

mother and reached out a hand as if to touch her, stopping before doing so, then nodded questioningly, asking if she understood.

Byria shook her head again.

Making a face, Iaki said "mother" in both languages and pointed between himself and his mother, then reached as if to touch Byria, nodding questioningly.

Biting her lip, Byria shrugged and shook her head more. She had no idea what the child was trying to explain.

Iaki pointed to one of the women who wore very few beads and pointed to Byria, touching her hand, and then pointed between his mother and him again. The non-mothers, or so Byria now figured, nodded eagerly, their eyes regaining their hungry look.

Byria couldn't keep from cringing as she finally pieced together an understanding. The women who had children seemed to know her well. The non-mothers' touches weren't embraces—they just wanted to *touch* her. They didn't care how or where.

But their children looked so young! Once she'd counted the years she must have been married to Tain, she figured she must be nineteen or twenty years old. If she'd been only a baby or toddler when she was last here, any child born shortly after her leaving should be perhaps a few years younger than she.

Owi was, perhaps, a few years away from adolescence. Iaki was likely about to be adolescent, and Iyiti, the youngest, was only just barely out of toddler years. For as young as they all seemed—and Owi's mother being pregnant—how could they assume she had anything to do with bearing children?

"Na. Na. Na." Mokin stood in his doorway, shaking his head with his arms folded. She looked at him with relief. He must have heard her yelp and seen the "conversation."

Owi's mother waddled out, glowing with happiness. She waved and blew more kisses at Byria, calling her child to her.

"Goodbye, Beelheah-kau! Thank you!" Owi said.

Byria nodded with a big smile. The child hesitated, and Byria held out her arms to allow an embrace. Owi had been a good friend. "Goodbye, Owi-ki. Thank you, too. Much help."

The pregnant woman squealed in joy as the child thanked Byria several times with a few more bows.

From the door, Mokin groaned and shook his head, rubbing his face. He addressed the group of women sternly. Byria understood enough to get the gist of what he said.

While the women slumped in dejection, she felt a different sadness that made an ache in her heart. He and Koki had spent the most time with "Uh-lhoo-kee-en" and "Bee-lhee-ah," and they had no children. There was no magic to touching her. He beckoned all of them to wait for their turns inside, then cast a look at Byria and the two children.

"Do you need rest?" he asked with a pointed look at the children and other villagers who were passing close to his gardens.

Byria looked at the two children, who were biting their lips uncomfortably, and shook her head with a smile. "We're all right. Thank you."

Mokin nodded, giving one more particularly harsh glare to the people outside his gardens. Walking down the entrance path, he picked up the jasmine pot and placed it at his door. The rest of the people began to disperse. Shaking his head again, he muttered something about Koki and returned to his waiting patients.

Not knowing what else to do, Byria apologized to the two children.

Iaki looked particularly sad.

Byria gestured to his face and asked, "What?"

Iaki rubbed his belly. Brushing Byria's hand with his fingertips, he murmured, "I want a baby someday."

"Oh." She apologized again and decided not to assume the gender of another child.

Iaki shrugged and returned her attention to the weeds for a moment. Then, giving herself a little shake, *she* pointed to the jasmine plant and asked, "What?"

* * * * *

Chapter Four
An Ill Magic

Iaki and her mother had already left when two men and one woman approached Mokin's home. They wore many beads and striped skins around their waists.

Byria noticed they wore wooden disks similar to Mokin's, though different from his. One man with silvery, pale hair had a different symbol than the other two. She brushed her shirt's sleeve against her hip, making sure it fully covered her cuts and glyph.

While one man and the woman didn't look unkind, she didn't like how they *felt*.

The man with the paler hair lingered behind and had eyes as hard as emeralds but without sparkle. Something about his face seemed both wrong and familiar. Worms burrowed in her stomach upon looking at him, and she noticed an odd, disorienting hum in her ears.

Iyiti, the child remaining, bowed and kept his or her eyes lowered.

Byria matched Iyiti's bow and posture, then nudged with her foot and made a soft questioning sound, hoping Iyiti would understand she had no idea what to do in this situation.

Iyiti looked at her sideways, eyes wide, and gave the tiniest headshake.

"Lhu-lhoo-kee-ki?" asked the man with kinder eyes. He stood in the front of the group, and his voice was soft, but firm.

Not knowing what else to do, Byria touched her chest and said her proper name. The sharp cut of Iyiti's toenails informed Byria such a response was clearly not proper. Not knowing what else to do, Byria lowered her head in another bow.

"Hooa-oma-sshahek. Koa-hoo omawu."

In front of the house's path, Koki bowed. It was a low bow, but quick, and her voice didn't sound particularly reverent. Small splashes of blood stained the spotted skin Koki wore, and she dragged the carcass of a deerpig upon a sled of bark.

Relief washed over Byria.

The men and woman addressed Koki. Their words swam together like a chorus of birdsong.

When their attention left her, dizziness made Byria waver. She barely kept from falling—or perhaps Koki had moved that fast and had caught her. Byria couldn't tell. She pursed her lips, trying to think as the roar of faraway fire rose in her ears.

Koki spoke a few more words to the important people and ushered Byria and Iyiti into the house, frowning at the women still in there. "Mokin," she called and uttered a few more words Byria felt she *ought* to understand, but her mind was no longer making connections. She leaned heavily on Koki, despite worry about how small she was, as the woman led her into the house's third room.

It was the smallest room and had no windows. She was already dizzy, and the darkness didn't help, as Byria tried to crouch. Koki helped her lay down on a nest of mats and skins. After a few deep breaths, Byria turned her attention to her heart's fire.

She didn't know what it was about those persons, but it had made her chest cold. She imagined herself blowing upon the embers of her heart to get it to flame again. Once she'd done that, the dizziness was gone, and she felt stronger.

As she tried to sit up, Mokin was already *na-na-na*-ing at her. He offered her a steaming cloth that smelled of lavender, mint, and chamomile. She took it, and he gestured for her to put it on her face and lie back down.

Not wanting to argue, she murmured, "Cloth over my face. Rest. Be good. I understand."

He chuckled and said he'd return. It was too dark to see if he'd made that promise gesture, and despite her tone, Byria welcomed lying down and doing nothing. She made a noise of consent, so he knew she understood.

It *had* been a long morning, and she *was* tired.

Byria hoped she never had to see those people again. As she dozed, she pressed her nail into her arm so she'd remember to ask Koki and Mokin about them… and about children being boys or girls… and about what that other important woman's blessing meant.

*****

Chapter Five
Difficult Words for Difficult Conversations

It was dark when Mokin roused Byria to eat on the patio. Her mouth was already watering from the smell of roasting meat. The dizziness and fatigue were gone, so she had no problem moving.

As Mokin checked skewered meat and stirred a few pots, he was more animated than usual, though he still spoke slowly, making sure Byria understood him. He was quick to answer the questions she managed to put together with her growing vocabulary.

Byria found out Koki had killed six deerpigs—what Mokin called the fat little deer with snub noses. They roamed in herds, and were best known by Byria's people for being particularly delicious, especially stupid, and easy to catch. However, their numbers had dwindled due to excessive hunting, and thus they'd become a rare dish served primarily in the courts.

That Koki had killed six spoke well of her hunting abilities, and suggested the animals had at least grown smart enough to move into deeper jungles and mountains, which her people generally avoided. Koki had distributed one to her parents and brought the rest to the village's shared kitchen, where the meat would be given out based on one's rank.

As Byria had guessed, the more necklaces one wore, the higher their rank. Since Mokin was a healer for the village—particularly for women and children—and as, per Mokin, Koki was the best hunter of the village (Koki later denied such nonsense, claiming it was her father who held that honor), they had enough rank to keep an entire deerpig.

"Nothing with having magic big-person who makes mothers?" she couldn't help but try to ask.

Mokin raised an eyebrow with a mix of bitterness and amusement.

Remembering his comment about he and Koki having no children, Byria wished she could take back such a thoughtless question.

Before she could apologize, he said, "Nah," and explained the full deerpig—or something of equal value, depending on what Koki killed—was their usual allotment.

Byria stared at the patio stones, ashamed for hurting his feelings and unable to think of another question to change the topic. Having children was clearly an Important Thing to the villagers. The little bit of darkness and pain Mokin hadn't hidden in his admission of being childless was plain as leaves on an evergreen.

Apparently, the concern on her face was also obvious. She could hear it in Mokin's voice as he said, "Beelheah."

"Yes?" She looked up at him.

Putting down his wooden spoon, he approached her and offered his hands, green eyes intense.

Biting her lip, she put down her bowl and placed her fingers in his palms.

He bit his lip and closed his eyes a moment as he gently squeezed her fingers. A warm wave passed over her, similar but different from what she'd felt from the visitors. Instead of dizziness and nausea, it brought a sense of tranquility and... understanding? She gasped when she found herself perfectly comprehending his words. "You have nothing to do with if or how anyone might have a child. Nothing. Not helping. Not hindering. That's not a worry or concern you need. You have your own healing to do."

After one more burst of warmth in her chest, she felt Mokin shiver. He released her hands and took a deep breath, closing his eyes. Wetness touched his lashes.

"Mokin?" Byria pressed one hand to her heart, feeling even more strength and fire to its beat. "You do... something?"

His second deep breath wavered. He murmured a word Byria knew she hadn't learned yet, but understood its meaning like the shadow of a loose memory. "Something..."

She didn't get a chance to ask more before the clattering beads drew their attention.

Mokin's expression went from tired and hurt to an overjoyed glow as Koki stepped out to join them. Byria's eyes widened as she took in Koki in only a loincloth and many necklaces. Like Mokin and the villagers who had large quantities of necklaces, hers were attached to wooden shoulder pads strapped around her neck and upper arms. One necklace draped around her neck; Byria had noticed she'd worn it even in her animal skin. The other strings of beads mostly covered her breasts, but as Byria *knew* Koki, she felt more uncomfortable seeing so much of her.

Mokin, as one might expect of a loving husband, didn't mind at all. He skipped over to pull her into a very intimate embrace and kiss.

Byria had to look away. Besides being uncomfortable to witness, such intense affection between two people—their kiss and their placement of hands upon each other—gave Byria sensations in her body she certainly didn't want to think about.

Their chuckles drew her attention. Each with an arm around the other, both Koki and Mokin covered their mouths. Koki apologized first, pulling away from Mokin. "Your mother also uncomfortable." Byria didn't understand the last bit of what she said, but she guessed it was words for affection or kissing. It gave her a sense of relief that Patch hadn't been comfortable with their open intimacy, either.

"Come. Eat. Food is ready," Mokin said. His eyes kept straying to Koki with wicked glints that, when Koki caught him, made her giggle even as she said something that sounded like a reprimand.

His words began to have that foreign feel again. The feeling of understanding, as if she spoke their language, had faded away. It saddened her to realize it. As thoroughly improper as they acted with each other, she couldn't help but giggle at their affections—which didn't need any words to be clearly understood.

Crackling deerpig fat and crispy meat over a spicier mix of another shredded root went exceptionally well with Mokin's broth and was a welcome distraction.

Watching their passionate affection made her heart hurt. Her marriage had been so far from their reality that one *needed* words in different languages to describe the two states. Even as they ate, Koki and Mokin sat so close one would sometimes jostle the other with an elbow.

Each time they paused to touch or kiss, Byria felt another pang of sadness and, even more unwanted and uncomfortable, that blossom of *other* sensations in her body.

Staring at her food, hoping for a distraction, she requested, "Please, I ask another question?"

"Ah, Yes! Yes," they both affirmed. Both sets of large green eyes fixed on her, flirting and teasing temporarily abandoned.

"The people, the last people who came, made me sick. Who? What?"

Both sighed, deflating. Mokin's expression darkened like a shadow fell over it. Koki spoke first, though it sounded like she chose her words carefully, even beyond ensuring Byria's comprehension. Byria still only understood two words, and those words worried her. "Magic. Healer-with-magic..."

Byria pursed her lips. "Healer? Like Mokin?" She pointed to his belt where his circle hung.

"Not like Mokin—" Koki began with a sneer on her lips.

Mokin put a hand on her arm. "Akka and Hooulin heal. Like me, but with magic. I heal with herbs." He gestured to the plants.

"Magic, too." Byria frowned. She was sure her fast healing, despite her own abilities, wasn't something normally accomplished with herbs. And when he'd held her hands earlier, when he'd helped her understand his words as if they spoke the same language, herbs alone couldn't accomplish that.

Mokin shook his head quite emphatically. "Not magic."

Koki made the big circular gesture that Byria understood as "all" or "everyone" and said, "People have abilities. Not the same as magic." She pointed at Byria. "You—" Byria didn't understand the word, but Koki's gesture clarified it as meaning larger people "—have a different magic. You don't understand."

Pressing her lips together, Byria considered her words. After a moment, she asked, "Akka. Hooulin," and held up a finger for each of their names. "Healer." She held up a third finger and asked,

"Who? What?" She felt certain the unnamed person was the lighter-haired man with the hard eyes.

A deeper wave of darkness—similar to when Mokin had seen the glyph on her arm—flitted over their faces. Mokin glared at his bowl, and his lips screwed into repressed hurt and anger.

Koki's eyes were on Mokin. She squeezed his arm and said, "Magic. Hides us from danger…" She made a gesture as she muttered a few other words Byria figured meant "other things," and that Koki thought very little of these "other things."

Mokin took a deep breath and looked like he was about to speak.

Koki squeezed his arm again, which stopped him, then looked pointedly at Byria and her empty bowl. "More food?"

"Yes, please." Byria found herself staring at Mokin after handing Koki her bowl. The look on his face was too familiar and gave her stomach nervous jitters—the kind she associated with Tain approaching. She didn't want to think that of Mokin at all, certainly not with how much he clearly loved Koki.

I understand. He'd understood her fear of being touched, of being hurt. She didn't want to think of him suffering, either.

As Koki refilled Byria's dish with more food, topping it with a spoon of broth, she said, "I saw my mother."

Byria looked up, relieved at the subject change, and curious about her new friends' own families. Especially good things about their families. "Happy. See you…" The rest of the words Byria didn't know, but Koki mimed out the blessing the older woman had given her.

"Your mother?" Byria asked in surprise. She tried to remember the woman's face to recognize any family resemblance.

Koki nodded proudly. "Spoke with you about Uh-lhoo-kee-en and your new name."

New name? It took Byria a moment to remember the conversation and what Koki's mother likely understood from it. "Adult name," she clarified.

"A-ah!" Both nodded. Koki added, "Big change."

"Um…" Byria didn't know what to say to that, so she decided to change the subject once more. "First woman with child Owi? Important?"

Mokin chuckled, shook his head, and rolled his eyes. "Child…" He counted upon his fingers to three, then half raised a fourth with a smile. "No one has so many children. And her family makes all the necklaces." He jiggled the beads around his neck, and then Koki's. "Most bead things." He touched his wide belt with beads embroidered on it.

"… Gyotan," Koki added, squeezing her hands together against her cheek as if cuddling, but then rolling her eyes and laughing. "Even more than us!" She touched the necklace around her neck, which looked to be made of many polished stones of darker blues and blacks, save for a few yellow-white ones and a single, larger, red one.

With a sweet smile, Mokin ran his finger over the single string around his neck, too. Its beads were a yellowed white, save for the same brilliant red stone and matching darker ones that looked like those mostly comprising Koki's necklace.

Once they finished eating, Byria helped clean the bowls and put them away. She tried to ask about boy and girl children, but couldn't phrase the question in a way they understood. She'd already learned the words for "man" and "woman," as well as "mother" and "father," but when she'd asked what one would call a child who would grow up to be one or the other, they gave her the same answer—the same word for "child." When Byria asked about using "he" and "she" for the adults, Koki and Mokin used "ti," an entirely different word, for the children.

Eventually she gave up and lay back on her mat as Mokin checked the other pots around the fire, straining some, adding things to others, transferring contents to various clay or wooden bowls and jars. She'd come to enjoy their quiet time together after dinner. Sometimes she'd ask about his work; other times, he'd work while she'd stare up at the jungle's canopy, looking at the stars and for the moons in the gaps between leaves.

Tonight, Koki and he chattered back and forth with each other too fast for Byria to understand. On top of that, there were more and more giggles and kissing sounds. Their affections overwhelmed her with a distressing swirl of feelings.

One part was the sensation in certain parts of her body that, despite being pleasant, made her the most uncomfortable. Another part was sadness; she'd never felt the way they clearly felt about each other.

As the bright Seal Moon, almost a quarter full, winked through the leaves, she recognized the other emotion—jealousy. And there were plenty of tales that spoke of the dangers of jealousy.

Koki and Mokin deserved to be happy and in love. They were good, kind people who'd welcomed her into their home for a second time in her life.

She just wished, sometime, she might have that kind of happiness, too.

* * * * *

Chapter Six
Where Dragons Are Free

The dragon hovered above her. His wings of flame were outstretched, covering the ceiling. His body writhed in the air, like a great serpent, despite the fire-made wings that suspended him.

That moment. Longer than Byria remembered.

The dragon's scales caught glints of the lightning dancing around the room. His eyes smoldered like coals. Smoke curled from his nostrils. Feelers twined and wove around his face like the beard and moustache of an old man—wayward, moving of their own accord.

And Tain cowered. Cowered! Cowered upon the floor like a spineless beast. Along with magepriests, men who made rules even the king must follow. And soldiers, men trained for battle. Cowered. All of them.

Terror wound 'round Byria—as it should upon seeing a dragon. Her heart grew hot, hotter. This had happened before she'd known to search for her heart's fire, yet she noticed it now. Paralyzed, she'd never felt more free. More powerful.

She had released a dragon.

Byria knew there was—had been—shaking and breaking glass and shouting. All she heard were the great wings. *Hawuuusshhh*. And then his voice.

"Come with me, my princess."

The sound of moving coals, of shifting fire and earth. She *knew* that voice. She recognized it. Many memory stones quaked, trying to come loose. The voice brought tears to her eyes.

Her heart's fire had cried *Yes! Yesyesyes!* Her voice and words, her paralyzing fear, betrayed her.

"No. Leave me. So I say!"

The dragon hesitated, but left as he'd been commanded. He'd followed the command of a princess who commanded nothing. He broke the roof and flew away with another *hawuuusssh*.

And then Byria heard the stones falling, glass breaking, and men screaming. Pain bloomed in many places, but mostly her heart. When she clutched her chest, she felt hot, burning liquid. She pulled her hand away and looked. From her chest fell flaming chunks of red flesh. Her heart, its fire, broken, spilled to the ground in a smoldering, bloody heap.

Why didn't I go with him?

Byria awoke with a start, clutching her chest, still feeling that pain. Checking her hand, her chest, she saw no blood or gore.

Her heart hurt as if it'd been struck with an arrow, or punched. She gasped for breath. Tears made her lashes tacky and stuck to her cheeks in the humid night.

There were still noises. Cries and grunts. She didn't recognize them at first and was frightened.

They came from behind the beads in the room where Koki and Mokin slept—Byria realized where she was now. In their home, not the palace. A winding giggle was punctuated with another cry, and Byria's whole body flushed.

She'd gone to bed early, letting them flirt and cuddle as Mokin had done his usual evening preparations of herbs. Byria had felt it best to give them privacy.

It was perfectly dark now. She knew where things were based on sound and the direction she chose to sleep in. Apparently, they'd waited to truly enjoy each other's company until she'd fallen asleep. They couldn't have planned for her to wake from the nightmare of a broken heart.

Why didn't I go with the dragon? Closing her eyes, Byria lay back down and fluffed her shirt over her chest to move the sticky air, wrinkling her nose. She smelled awful. She'd washed regularly as she and Mokin had tended to her injuries, but her clothing… She wondered about going outside, where it might be a little cooler, but she didn't want to let her hosts know she was awake or interrupt their very happy reunion.

She scowled. Despite being hot from the humid night, now there was another warmth inside her in places she didn't want to feel that kind of warmth. Byria brushed her fingers against one of those places out of curiosity. A shudder ran through her, and she snatched her hand away.

No. She wasn't ready to explore that.

* * * * *

Chapter Seven
Unwanted Visitors

After breakfast the next day, Mokin removed his many pots and dried bunches of herbs from the fire, then disassembled the crossbars for hanging those things.

Koki filled a large basket that strapped over both her shoulders with small jars, strings of beads, tied bunches of herbs, and small cloth packs in which Byria figured were more herbs. They said very little to each other, save for short bits that sounded like questions for verification.

"What are you doing?" Byria asked, trying her best to speak their language. "Can I help?"

"Ah!" Koki motioned her over, pointing to various things on higher shelves. Byria got each one as Koki explained that it was Trade Day, where people paid debts for services or goods, or purchased new things.

After that explanation, Koki handed Byria a piece of rope and motioned for her to wrap it around her hips. She did so, and Koki pierced the rope with a long splinter. Then she had Byria hold a rope up to her shoulder, marking it, too.

When she was done with that, she kissed Mokin (in a manner that required Byria to look away again), grabbed several large, flat, empty baskets, and left.

Mokin called Byria over to the rain barrels at the corners of the patio roof and pointed at the dark sky. Heavy, gray clouds churned in the space between the leaves. With a gesture to indicate that he expected rain soon, he had her help him reposition the empty pots and bring the half-full one to the grate over the fire.

Despite his small size, Mokin was much stronger than he appeared. He lifted the half-full barrel faster than Byria, nearly spilling it. He squawked what sounded like a rebuke, and she apologized several times.

On his count of three, Byria lifted—and was promptly scolded again.

"What?"

He indicated she was doing something that would hurt herself. After an unexpected lesson in how one must lift heavy things—this was not among the things she would've learned as a princess—Byria and Mokin placed the half-full pot of water on the fire grate. Not quite as gently as Mokin would have liked, she could tell from his face, but the woven clay platform held.

With a sigh, he pointed to the other clusters of pots around the hut. Thunder rumbled overhead, and fat drops plopped through the thick leaves. The two were still moving the empty pots of the next-to-last cluster when the sky opened. When they were done, rather than going in the front door, Mokin had them jog to the rear patio—careful of the plants—and stay under the roof and near the fire.

Byria started apologizing again, but Mokin waved it off and offered her a gentle, albeit weary, smile. With his fluffy hair pasted flat against his head, his lips and eyes looked even bigger, almost doll-like. He gestured upward, then to the rain pots and his gardens with a firm nod and an affirmative smile. A few drops penetrated the roof's overlapped leaves and woven branches, spotting the patio's flat stones, but far fewer than Byria expected. Outside the roof, fat streams of water rang musically into the pots—loud enough to be heard over the din of rainfall and thunder. Lightning cracked through the jungle's canopy, brighter than the height of day, with a *boom* that resonated through Byria's body.

Byria shook uncontrollably, squeezing her eyes closed. The little hut held against the roaring thunder and pounding rain that bounced from the ground outside into the patio's perimeter. She sensed Mokin near, and she opened her eyes to him standing beside her. He offered his hand.

Biting her lip, she shook her head and hugged her arms around herself. He took no offense at her rebuff, but gestured for her to move closer to the house, as the wind blew sheets of rain into the patio. Gusts whistled through the woven walls, clattering the shelves of pottery and herbs.

Motioning for her to wait at the door, Mokin returned to the fire and, using a long stick, moved the ashes around, added more fuel, and then stacked bricks up around the pit. Lips pursed, he inspected his work, nodded, and returned to Byria.

Asking her to wait just a little more, he slipped into the house and brought out a large piece of cloth, similar to what he'd wrapped her injuries and feet in. He handed it to her after a quick mime of toweling off. She nodded and did so, making sure to kick off the slippers lined with soft cloth Mokin had made or acquired to keep her from further injuring her feet, which had been a pleasant surprise for Byria on her second day there. No one else in the village, that Byria had noticed, wore anything on their feet.

Mokin grabbed a mortar and pestle, more dried bunches of herbs, and several jars, and then followed her inside, wiping his bare feet on a textured grass mat. Byria appreciated the fact that even a house of branches and leaves, with woven mats over dirt and stone floors, had such rules to stay clean.

They sat in the main room, and Mokin began separating leaves from stem, placing the leaves in one jar, and breaking the stems and putting them in the mortar. He offered a small bunch to Byria. "Help?"

She nodded, eager to help, and finding the simple task relaxing. So much so, she didn't notice the thunder fading, or the rainstorm lessening to patters, then to nothing. When she found herself squinting from a brighter light, Byria paused to look out the window and smile.

"Aaah! Good, no?" Mokin smiled back at her, then stood and stretched, heading to the window.

Byria followed suit, then paused as he held up a hand. It wasn't the gesture that stopped her, but the expression on his face. The gentle lines around his eyes and face grew hard, almost beastly, and his eyes darkened. His lip curled in a sneer that revealed the tips of his sharper teeth.

A shiver ran through Byria as he practically growled, "Stay. Here." He spoke slowly in both their tongues. He didn't want to be misunderstood.

Byria nodded, eyes glued to him as he headed out the front door. She shifted so she might look outside to see what had caused him to change so.

Up the path, head high, strode the older man of yesterday's trio. The magic user she suspected wasn't a healer. Mokin spoke first, but his voice was such a low growl, she couldn't understand him.

She knew his posture. She remembered wearing exactly the posture he wore as he faced the other man. Mokin stood as tall as he could, shoulders squared—braced as if prepared to take a hit. His body trembled and vibrated in equal parts fear and fury.

Byria's heart jumped into her throat. She looked toward the patio, ready to run. She then glanced to the front door, ready to throw her heart's fire at this person who'd made her new friend feel the pain and terror she knew well. As she clutched her clothing in indecision, she smelled smoke. With a gasp, she released the shirt hem, seeing scorch marks.

It was probably not a good idea to set fire to oneself while in a branch-and-leaf-made house.

When she looked back out the window, she saw the older man looking in. Not just in, but *at her*, even though she wasn't near the window. A sick chill hit her chest like a stream of rain falling on her heart's fire, and she hissed through her teeth, backing away and closing her eyes, trying to keep some glow to her flame.

No, she was no help to Mokin. That thought dampened the embers of her heart even more. All he and Koki had done—not just now, but in a time she'd been too young to remember—and she couldn't return a fraction of the favor.

Mokin's voice rose with a word she almost recognized, but his growl and tone kept it foreign to her. She felt the older man's attention leave her. He said something back, loud enough that he likely meant for Byria to hear—if she could understand the language—and then he left. There was a physical sensation to his leaving, like the lifting of pressure had been pushing the edge of being painful. Byria gulped a deep breath.

"Beelheah!" Mokin said, his face filled with concern for her. "You're all right."

Letting out the breath she didn't realize she was holding, she nodded and fixed her eyes on him.

He sighed, frowning gently, one eyebrow raised in question.

She waved her head from side to side to suggest, perhaps, she wasn't entirely all right, then shrugged. She *would be* all right. She had to keep believing that.

Mokin gave her a weak smile. They were still looking in each other's eyes. He seemed to be considering his next words carefully.

Had he recognized what they shared before when he'd tended to her wounds? What she'd suspected? Did he realize that Byria now recognized *his* hidden torture? Byria wasn't sure how she felt about how much Mokin knew of her abuse. How did he feel about what she now knew of him?

She found herself breaking the silence first. "Who?" That was all she managed.

His face fell, hardening in a pained scowl. After a deep breath, he said softly, "My father."

Byria lowered her head, feeling the hurt his words bore, and remembering the darkness in his face when she'd asked about the man last night. How he'd let Koki do almost all the explaining.

"Mokin…" Byria began, then took a deep breath when he looked up at her. He'd seen some of her scars, but far from the worst. Pressing her lips together, she lifted the back of the shirt entirely, thinking quickly to fold in the scorch marks—though she didn't know why.

As she rolled up the fabric, keeping only her breasts covered, she turned around so he could see. The hiss of breath through his teeth made her wince, but she finished turning before covering back up again. Biting her lip, she found herself without words in any language, and unable to meet his eyes.

"Beelheah," he said. The gentleness in his tone gave her the strength to look at him. He closed his eyes a moment, and a shimmer like a heat wave moved over his body. His skin twisted grotesquely as the illusion lifted. It was Byria's turn to gasp as he turned, eyes lowered to the ground.

Scars disfigured most of his back, arms, and legs. They stretched over his stomach and chest where he moved aside beads. There were even lines of scars up his neck and onto his left cheek. Worse, sending those sick stabs through her stomach that she'd come to associate with the magic users, most of them were jagged marks that looked like runes and glyphs—some Byria recognized—darkened to stand out as if with ink or dye.

Mokin studied one particular mark on his arm with a ferocious sneer. "Magic powder. Stops proper healing."

"Why?" Byria asked.

Mokin met her gaze with a bitter look and nodded in her direction. "Why?" he asked back.

Byria didn't know the word for "monster" in any language but her own. She tried, "Beast. Worse," in their two partially shared languages. "And I was wrong—"

"Na," Mokin stated. "You weren't wrong. I know." He took another deep breath, and the shimmer returned his flesh to its earlier pristine, uninjured appearance. He shivered some, closed his eyes, breathed, and looked at her again. "Who?"

Byria tried to remember what Koki and Mokin called themselves, the word Koki had used for the relationship between Owi's mother and Gyotan. Her gaze caught on his necklace, the one that matched Koki's with the brilliant red stone, the only one worn around his neck. She pointed at it. "That mean?"

The slight smile curling his lips as he touched it answered her question. In that same moment, his smile vanished as he looked with horror between her and the stones in his hand. Squeezing the beads, he whispered, "Koki and I..." His eyes met hers, and she saw the glimmer of tears.

After another breath, he said, "*Yoo-wah-hoo*. Koki and I. You...?" His gaze went to her arms, the easiest scars to see, and he shook his head.

Brushing her arm, lifting her sleeve to reveal the scars again, she nodded, repeating the word, "Yoo-wah-hoo," figuring she understood its meaning enough from his reaction.

He wrapped his own arms around himself with a shudder. Then his lips pressed into a hard line, and he looked at her again. "You left. You live." Mokin nodded vigorously.

"Yes. Difficult."

"But you left!" He lifted his chin proudly, and his eyes glistened with tears again. "Good! Very good!"

Byria gave him a weak smile and shrugged. Then it occurred to her. If his father had hurt him so...

"Your mother?" blurted from her mouth. She regretted it immediately.

Mokin froze, hard as a stone again. After a forced breath through his nose, he shook his head. "Na," he said, then stepped closer to her.

Byria couldn't help but flinch.

He apologized, hands up, flipping them back and forth. His posture was still rigid, and his eyes still dark, not quite looking at her. "Your injuries. I see no magic remains." He pointed to her arm with the glyph and her back. "The burn is better. I can heal more?"

He obviously didn't want to speak about his mother.

But Byria wasn't ready for anyone to touch her scars yet. "I-I not... no. No healing now." However, she was fine with changing the topic. "Your father. What want me?"

Mokin sighed deeply again, then made a face of consternation. Byria wondered what he was thinking about. His expression looked deeper than when he was trying to find the right words to use, but thoughtfulness melted away the pain and hardness in his face.

After another deep breath, he pinched the bridge of his nose and gestured for her to sit again, then held his hand up to indicate she wait. His own sniffles explained his lack of spoken words.

She nodded and sat.

He barely whispered thanks and headed through the back room. The patio door snapped, and if she listened hard, Byria could hear the sound of pottery being moved around. She considered going back to separating the herbs; instead, she unrolled the hem of her shirt to look at the scorch marks from her fingertips.

The material had worn thin with her travel; it had been worn long before she'd stolen the shirt. She ripped off the edge with little trouble and tucked it into her satchel, which had found a home in a corner where the woven walls met the irregular tree trunk to which they attached with shiny, rose-smelling dried sap.

Part of her wanted to tell Mokin of her abilities, but another wanted to keep it secret, her little bit of power. She rationalized that the magic these people used made her feel ill, so perhaps hers wouldn't agree with them. And while she'd test such a theory on Mokin's father, perhaps bring upon him the painful illness she'd felt in their two encounters, she wished to bring no discomfort to Mokin or Koki.

After she hid the evidence of her heart's fire, she started separating the herbs once more. The heat had returned, and the humidity stuck to her face. Even pausing to unstick and fan her clothes often, she was surprised at the progress she'd made when Mokin finally came back with two steaming bowls.

He paused and smiled at her work, thanking her again and saying she'd helped a lot. Then he asked her to move the herbs, mortar, and pestle aside.

When she did, he set down the bowls and sat near her. She studied his face, noting more green in the whites of his eyes, and darker shadows, evidence of having cried. Byria wondered, if he could hide such gruesome scars, how much more he might disguise. Was there a limit? Could he hide his emotions if he wished?

Mokin seemed unbothered by her scrutiny and waited, taking a moment to swirl the bowls beside them.

With a few breaths, she edged even closer and faced him. He placed a hand on his heart. "Beelheah." His tone had returned to its usual gentleness, only even more serious. "Trust me?"

Byria took her time considering the question. As always, Mokin showed no impatience.

What did he mean by trust? Was he going to do something that might hurt? No, she didn't believe that at all. But what would he want to do that required him to ask?

She looked at the steaming bowls. They smelled of grass, an earthy pungence, and a touch of something floral. Medicine of some sort?

Did she trust him?

"What want do?" she asked, hoping that wouldn't sound too much like a "no."

"Talk. Speak. Communicate." He said the words in both their languages.

She thought of the prior night, when he'd taken her hands and she'd understood him, and how tired he'd looked after that. Though they'd made good strides in their communication attempts, there was still so much they couldn't say. Byria nodded and pressed her hand to her heart. "I trust you."

He smiled and passed her one of the bowls, taking the other for himself.

She sipped the steaming liquid carefully. A honey sweetness softened the bitterness that curled her tongue. They said nothing while they drank.

Byria finished hers first. The bowls had held the same amount. When Mokin put his down, she asked, "Still work same bigger me?"

"Ask me that in your language."

* * * * *

Chapter Eight
Necessary Magic

Byria understood Mokin as if he spoke her language.

After blinking a moment in surprise, she answered as he'd requested. "I wondered if it would work for me, since you gave us the same amount, and I'm bigger."

"It appears it has." Mokin gave her a shy smile and a shrug.

Byria's sigh of relief broke into delighted laughter. There was so much she wanted to ask him! So many things she hadn't had words for!

As her mind spun, he started speaking. "You wanted to know why my father was so interested in you. That's complicated, and I didn't know how to answer you the way we were speaking. I don't *like* being unclear or not understanding someone completely."

Byria nodded.

He made a face. "He senses your magic, giant magic, and that intrigues him. He sensed it on you and your mother when you were here before. We wouldn't let him near you then—only Ulhokeyen was fairly intimidating on her own. With Koki beside her, and Koki's parents supporting our choice to keep you safe..." Mokin's mouth twisted into a wicked grin. "No one in the village challenged us."

Byria chuckled. She hadn't seen Koki's father yet, but Koki had said *he* was the best hunter of the village, and her mother was a priestess, or "Godspeaker." She could imagine what they'd looked like alongside Patch.

"But Ulhokeyen isn't with you now, and he *knows* Koki is out paying our debts and obtaining things we need. That's why he came now."

"Will he come back?"

"He might. And he might try to find you if you're out alone again. As I don't know what your magic is—and you needn't tell me—I don't know if your reactions yesterday and today are from his attempt to harm you through magic, or if your magic interacts poorly with ours, or—" he gave another bitter smile "—it just allows you to sense how awful he is."

"I don't need magic to know he's awful," Byria said, the bitterness in her voice matching Mokin's.

"I would guess not."

"So, I need to be careful around him and make sure I'm not out alone."

"That would be the safest." He pressed his lips together. "How do you feel now?"

"Well. Very good, actually." Tears pricked her eyes. "How long will this last? I have so much I want to ask you."

"A few shadow-widths." He made handprints in their shadows to show them growing shorter. "That's all. It might help some later, but it also might not, which will be frustrating."

Byria nodded. "It will."

"But you're not feeling ill at all now? Or faint?"

"No, why?"

Mokin's lips tightened. "That means you and your magic likely aren't adverse to our magic, either."

"Oh," Byria said. That left only the worst option for why she'd felt ill around Mokin's father.

Before she could ask more about his monstrous father, he apologized. "I'm sorry. I wasn't entirely truthful last night. I *can* do magic. I *choose* not to, and use herbs, roots, and other methods to help my visitors."

"Why would you choose not to do magic?" Byria furrowed her brow.

He gave a short, dry laugh. "Many reasons. I'd say because my father chooses to, but that's not the main reason..." His face had that "looking for the right words" expression again.

Byria smiled. Clearly, even magic had its limits.

"Our village and others like us have never been very big. We've never grown or populated as giants do. But some time back, before I was born, we noticed there were no women having babies. None. Before then, we'd used more magic to help with births. To help with everything. We grew dependent on it, was what my mother told me. Our numbers were bigger then, but with no children, people would take their last walk, and we grew fewer and fewer."

"That explains the not-mothers touching me in the garden."

He nodded. "The Godspeakers thought we'd upset the gods by an abuse of magic. That magic in our medicines was keeping us from having children, so we pulled magic from anything having to do with pregnancy and childbirth. Then we removed it from most other healing, and anything with food. And then someone became pregnant, finally. So, to do what I do—and what my mother did—to heal and to help bring more babies to our people, we avoid magic as much as we can."

"And this?" She gestured to the bowls.

"I used magic to enhance the herbs' properties, and herbs strengthen my abilities."

"And hiding your scars? That isn't magic?"

Mokin shook his head. "Glamour? All of us can do that. Some stronger than others, but so can lizards and fish and other animals. That's not *magic*."

Byria pressed her lips together. She'd seen the dragon's camouflage, and that of lizards in the menagerie. His "glamour" looked like magic to her, but she had more pressing concerns. "So, your father isn't pleased your people choose to avoid magic?"

Mokin tilted his head. "Of his many faults, that wasn't among them. He understood the need for our separation. My mother had her space to work, her own separate hut, and while she was there, he'd never defile that place. His problem was with *me* for preferring her path to his."

"He wanted you to *be* a magic user like him? Like…" Byria tried to think of a word in her language. As far as she knew, the only people allowed to use magic were the royal family and the magepriests. Echoes of stories that she could sometimes remember suggested others could and did use magic. "Sorcerers." The word came, but nothing with it. She knew it was her language, and the right word for what she meant, but it felt foreign. She scrunched her face.

"What?" Mokin asked.

"My memory…" She sighed. "My husband and the magepriests. They used magic on me like the storm, with lightning in my head, and that destroyed my memories. I hardly remember most of my life, except for small pieces at the palace. Then I started making myself remember in secret ways. But anything before the palace, that I don't remember."

She bit her lip and looked away as Mokin's eyes widened in new horror. He sucked more air through his teeth. Heat rose to her cheeks, as if she should be ashamed. She knew she shouldn't be. Tain had been the monster. Yet, even knowing Tain was the monster only slightly lessened shame's weight.

"I have no words," Mokin said softly. "Only my heart."

In her peripheral, she saw him press his hands to his chest again. She swallowed and nodded, having no words herself.

"The inked symbols you saw... My father tried to *force* magic into me. I didn't lose my memory, but it felt like a storm beneath my skin. For days sometimes. He said it was for protection, to help me find my way." His voice was becoming a growl again. "It was to make the magic *burn* if I didn't use it, and to make me feel ill if I should speak of what he did."

"What did you do?" Byria asked, though she still found herself studying her fingers rather than looking at her friend.

"There are herbs that pull infection and dirt from wounds. I cut the runes back open and covered them with a paste of those herbs, pulling out as much as I could."

He paused, and Byria could hear him rubbing his skin. She looked up to see him glaring at his arm. Though his skin *looked* unmarred now, Byria could still see in her mind the image of the black-scarred glyphs upon him. "The marks only healed so much, but the spells were undone."

Byria considered his words. "Why did he want you to do magic so much?"

Mokin snorted. "He leads because he's the strongest in magic. He keeps us hidden from you giants, from dragons... and it does other things. But he wants to be even stronger. I believe he figured if I worked alongside him, together we'd be more powerful."

Byria studied the lines on his face that illustrated a deeper struggle within him than any words could possibly say.

After a long sigh, he continued, "I think he still believes I'll someday change my mind. He's taken no apprentice, and I expect a day to come when he speaks of taking his last walk and there being no one to protect our village with magic. So I'd feel forced to study with him."

"Is there anyone else to help care for the women and babies as you do? I'd imagine that's just as important to the village."

Mokin gave her a half smile. "I would agree, but Koki's been assisting me for about a hundred years now—"

"What? How long?" Byria wondered if there was a problem with his communication magic.

"We've been soul-joined just over a hundred and eleven years."

"How old are you?" The oldest estimate of the high magepriest's age was only a hundred and fifty—and he looked far older than Mokin.

"Two hundred and nineteen. Almost two hundred twenty. We chose to join very young. From the way you've aged, I believe you giants age far faster than people do."

Byria pressed her lips together. Being called a "giant" sent a wave of indignation through her. "I'm a person, too. Not just some 'giant.' And I'm hardly a giant. I *do* remember a story of a giant, and he was almost *ten* times the size of a person—a my-sized person."

Mokin widened his eyes. "I didn't mean to offend, but while you're still small for your people, most are almost twice our size, and some even taller. When Ulhokeyen was with you, Koki balanced upon my shoulders, and she was still taller than both of us. We've never met any 'person' creatures bigger than your people."

"Nor I. I just remember hearing a story. And the giant was a monster, so I don't like being called that." She frowned, feeling a little childish, but firm in her statement. It was a silly thing to be bothered over, but she didn't like being labeled so. She hadn't thought of Mokin or Koki as anything but smaller, greener persons. Like how Patch was far taller and darker—and Patch didn't have the odd extra finger- and toe-joints, or the pointier nails, teeth, and ears, either.

"I apologize, then. I didn't mean to upset you." He inclined his head, and Byria sensed his earnestness.

"I accept your apology. So, since Koki's helped you for so long, your father thinks she could just take over?"

Mokin frowned deeply, anger darkening his eyes again, and nodded. "She's a hunter, not a healer. She cares very much, but she'd never be happy doing what I do. As much as I fear every time she goes out, I know hunting is as much part of her spirit as healing is part of mine. And one who enjoys hunting—though she doesn't enjoy *hurting* anything—is still not a good person to heal. She helps me, though, and she knows almost as much as I do."

"And you won't take an apprentice, because then your father would have an excuse to pull you away?"

Mokin pressed his lips together and picked up the clay bowl, studying it for a long minute. "One normally takes an apprentice when one's child has come of age and expressed interest in a different vocation, or if one has truly become too old to have children and has had none. Or if a child comes of choosing age, requests to apprentice with someone other than their parent or parents, and is accepted."

"Oh…"

"Koki and I are still very young. I should have apprenticed another half a century before taking over." The sharp-toothed sneer twisted his face again. "I didn't have that option, though."

Remembering his earlier words of joy that Byria had left her torturer, she understood what wasn't being said. However, Mokin had also said his father was the leader. He was Someone Important, like her father, and like Tain. "How—?"

"We have little time before the magic wears off," Mokin interrupted, pain etched as deeply as anger in his face. His voice caught as if someone had wrapped their hands around his neck. "There are other important things we should discuss."

"I'm sorry, but please. Let me ask first and then… if you don't want to answer, that's fine. I don't want to hurt you, but I think it's important."

His momentary glare made her wince, but it melted into a scowl as he said very softly, "Ask."

"You said your father was a leader. That he has power. My father is king, and my husband is prince, so no one can stop them from hurting people. That's why I had to run away. If your father still leads after what he's done, how does he not hurt you more? And how can you stop him from demanding I be given to him? Should I leave?"

She didn't want to leave. The realization dawned on her that she didn't want to leave *yet*. Tears stung her eyes, and she barely kept them from catching her words.

"No!" Mokin reached for her hand, but stopped and simply repeated. "No. You don't need to leave."

A warmth burst in Byria's heart's fire, one that made it impossible for her to keep tears from falling. She shivered with pleasant tingles that spread out from her chest, a feeling similar to when she'd heard Patch say her name the first time.

Biting her lip, she took Mokin's hand, and her heart's fire grew even more. Byria found herself without words again.

"You don't have to leave," Mokin said softly, though he squeezed her hand tightly as if he wanted to pass a sense of Truth to her beyond what words could give. "You can stay with us as long as you like, for the rest of your life. If you did choose to stay, and you wanted to learn, I would teach you what I know. I *am* the only Motherhealer of the village. More women have given birth, and more women have conceived children in my short time doing this work than even my mother's long years. The families I've helped, and Koki's family, would stand behind us if he challenged us, or if he tried to do anything to you. And he would never risk anyone finding out what he's done if he *were* to do something to you."

Byria scrunched her brows at him.

He paused, realizing the contradiction in his words; he *had* told Byria it wasn't a good idea for her to go out alone. He sighed. "It's complicated, but I *will* act against him if he harms you. I just don't want you to feel even a moment of his harm."

And if you did choose to stay…

Byria hadn't stopped to consider staying or leaving. When she'd arrived, she'd felt it was safe to rest. It *felt* like home. But in her mind, in her heart's fire, she knew this was only a place to stop, heal, and learn.

She needed to find the dragon.

The look on Mokin's face said he *wanted* her to stay. And he'd just offered to apprentice her, even though he still hoped he and Koki would have their own child to teach. Each of her heartbeats echoed in her ears and thrummed through her—not unpleasantly—and she found herself both sniffling and gripping Mokin's hand as if she needed to hold on to keep from falling.

After a few deep breaths, she loosened her fingers, then flexed them, letting go. She wiped away her tears and wiped her nose on her sleeve. After one more ragged breath, she trusted herself to look into Mokin's eyes. She swallowed hard at their intensity, but didn't look away.

"I must leave, though. Not *now*, but sometime," she finally said, speaking softly. "I need to find the dragon."

Mokin's face grew dark again, and he pressed his lips together tightly before asking, "What? Why?"

"Because I must. I know it. Here." She pressed her hand to her heart.

Her words and gesture only further darkened his face. "That's what Ulhokeyen said. She left and took you, and…" He made a gesture toward Byria's body. "Here you are."

"The dragon didn't do this to me! They kidnapped him, too. They came and captured both of us. I don't remember how, but I know that's what happened."

"He was unable to protect you," Mokin pointed out.

Byria shook her head. "I know I need to go. As soon as I'm well enough, and once I know better how to travel—for they stole all those memories, too."

More emotions flitted over his face than she could read, but his expression stayed dark. "Why did you even ask if you should leave if you were planning to?"

"I needed to know if I should leave *now*. If being here put you and Koki in danger, I would leave today."

Mokin raised his brows at her. "If you were to leave today, Koki would track you until you collapsed from pain, exhaustion, thirst, or whatever afflicted you first, and drag you back in her sledge, scolding you until well after you were awake. And while neither of us would force you to stay, she would repeat her tracking and bringing you back until you regained your senses."

Byria closed her eyes, blinking back even more tears. "She would be a very good mother."

"I believe that, too."

"And you, a very good father."

He looked away, cheeks growing greener. "I hope so."

"When I was with you and Koki before, with Patch, how long were we here before she took us to the dragon? How old was I?"

"I don't know your age, and I remember you grew faster than I expected. You were little more than an infant when you arrived, and it was nearly three years that you were here before Patch decided you were old enough to travel safely."

Byria smiled because she understood and heard Mokin trying to say Patch's name as Byria said it. "How did you meet her?"

Mokin snorted a chuckle. "Koki found you. She was out hunting and heard a baby fussing. She followed the sound and found you in a bush surrounded by a number of traps.

"She assumed a terrible giant was using its child as bait to catch a creature, so she undid the traps and decided to bring you home.

Patch, as I understand the story, tracked her, and attacked her for taking you."

Byria couldn't help but chuckle at imagining very small Koki and very tall Patch facing off.

"Somehow—you see how different our languages are—Patch managed to communicate to Koki that she wasn't using you for bait, but trying to hunt some food. You'd fallen asleep, so she wrapped you and surrounded you with traps so if anything tried to reach you, her magic would alert her and hurt or kill whatever was attacking you. Because Koki hadn't set off the traps, Patch didn't know you'd been taken, so she panicked."

The thought of Patch *panicking*—after seeing her intimidate Tain—intrigued Byria.

"Patch had never had a child of her own, so she was exhausted and willing to accept help. Koki, as you might imagine, was more than happy to bring a baby into our home."

"And you?"

Mokin smiled. "I felt the same. We don't have our own children yet, but we have much experience helping the parents in the village, so we taught Patch and helped her care for you."

He tilted his head and regarded her a moment. "Even if you had your full memories, I believe you might have been too young to remember much of your time here, despite how little time has passed for us. You'd still be a child, were you of our blood, not even old enough for a choosing ceremony. But you're an adult now, and have been married." He gritted his teeth at the last part.

Byria sighed as well. "I wish I hadn't been, but because he supposedly 'rescued' me from the dragon, my family gave me to him as his wife."

"What?" Mokin gave her a look of confusion.

"Once I had my first women's blood..." Byria had been taught women's blood was a thing never to discuss with men. Even the magepriests Tain had sent her to about their lack of children had hardly wanted to talk about her bleeding times. Mokin didn't cringe, so perhaps things were different among his people. "I was considered old enough to marry, and since he'd brought me and the dragon back, I was to marry him, so he'd be the next king."

Mokin blinked a few times, shaking his head slowly. "I don't understand."

Byria opened her mouth, then closed it. "I don't know how else to say it. Is the magic wearing off?"

He shook his head again. "It will soon, but I understand all your *words*. Your parents *gave* you to him? As soon as you had your first blood?"

Byria nodded.

"Did you *want* to marry him?"

Byria shrugged. "I don't remember, but I can't imagine so. I have no memory of caring for him, only being afraid, and the moments I wasn't afraid."

Mokin placed a hand to his stomach and paled as if he were about to be sick. "This is *normal* among giant—giant peoples?"

"Not everyone is supposedly 'rescued' from a dragon. Most women see matchmakers to find their husbands."

"I don't understand that, either." He looked between the empty bowls and Byria, shaking his head, and then looking crossly at the bowls. "If there isn't an *idea* for something among our people, perhaps no magic can make the words understandable? I don't understand how or why someone would need to *see* someone or something to find their beloved. Wouldn't they just know they're falling in love?"

Byria paused and sighed. "There are stories among my people of falling in love like that, but most people marry to elevate their status, acquire goods or land, because our God says such a union would be good for our people, or the families hire the matchmaker. A matchmaker, usually one of the priests, speaks to the God, and they're told whom the girl must marry. This usually happens on a girl's eleventh birthday, and the marriage happens on the birthday following her fifth cycle, because that's an auspicious time for a first child."

Mokin shook his head, eyes wide as if he was terrified. "That sounds like *you*—your women—are a trade of goods and services! And unless you grow even faster than I figured..." He scrunched his fingers through his hair, face twisted in disgust. "Are giant women really expected to bear children after only a few blood cycles?"

Byria shrugged again. "Many women conceive within a few years of marriage. Sometimes they die. It depends on their health and who's caring for them. We have many priest-healers, but they do need to be paid, and some people cannot afford—"

"Enough, enough." Mokin pressed his hands to his ears, looking even more ill than before. His eyes were watery with tears. "What about you? You have no children?"

"I had no children." Byria shook her head, heat prickling her face as she wondered how Mokin might react, might feel if she admitted she'd ended her one and only pregnancy. "How do *you* get married here, then, if it's so different?"

With an indignant chuff, Mokin said, "First of all, we don't marry when our women are barely more than children! There's no *giving* or trading someone away, and no one chooses for us! Pffft. Not even the *leaders* can choose against who we love."

Byria caught his brief flash of a dark smirk.

"Koki was very proud at first—I didn't care for her much—but she found me one day and helped me hide from my father. She never pressed me for more information and didn't ask when I didn't want to speak. She was just *there*. Then Koki and I would meet secretly— my father *hates* Koki and her family. Our dearest friend, Chimayo, would help. Her family, too. We're all close. We'd make our Trading Day plans so we'd cross each other's paths."

A smile spread across Byria's face to match the one spreading on Mokin's face as he spoke.

"That happened more than a few times, and that's how I grew to trust her more than anyone in the world. She says I made her a better person, questioning her assumptions, and making her think when she spoke arrogantly."

Their love story could be one we sing during Blossomtide, Byria thought.

Mokin shrugged, but he was beaming with a wide, sparkling grin. "But she has done even more for me. I don't have words, in any language. I believe she was always good at heart. You don't change someone if there isn't goodness *here*." He touched his chest.

Byria nodded in agreement.

"When I left my father's home, she helped me build this house. I didn't ask her to; she just did. I felt it was *our* home, but I didn't want to assume. She'd said she loved me, and I knew it was real. But…"

Byria recognized the dimming in his eyes, what he'd felt: that he wasn't good enough, he didn't deserve to be loved.

Mokin took a deep breath. "In any case, she wanted to stay with me. And we both wanted to spend our lives with each other, so we exchanged promise beads, and the following spring, we had a Souljoining Ceremony."

"That's beautiful," Byria said softly.

"That's how it *should* be," Mokin stated. "Anyone in the village, souljoined or not, will talk about their love for their partners, about their friendship, about the moment they knew they wanted to share their lives, and after, if we're souljoined." He fingered his necklace again.

Byria pressed her lips together. She agreed with what Mokin said, but a part of her bristled at his judgmental tone. Her ears began to ring. She touched them and looked at Mokin.

He did the same and nodded. "The spell will be wearing off soon. What else must we speak about?"

"I know you don't want me to leave and find the dragon, but will you still teach me what I need to know when I do leave? Please?"

Mokin frowned. "I will. We will. Koki knows better how to travel, how to avoid animals, how to hunt. I'll teach you what I know and think you should know for your health, but will you please consider staying? Will you promise me that?"

Byria paused. The ringing was growing, and his words seemed to unfold in her mind slower than he spoke them. But she understood. What if she did decide to stay?

She nodded. "I'll consider it." She raised her voice because the ringing had become so loud.

Mokin seemed to be feeling the same, gritting his teeth and rubbing around his pointed ears. Standing, he grabbed the bowls and backed away from her. As he moved away, the painful din subsided. He motioned for her to wait again as he left the room.

Byria massaged around her ears and down her jaw, which she'd been clenching. After she heard the back beads swing and the door close, the ringing faded to nothing. Turning her attention back to separating herbs, she ran through the conversation with Mokin in her head over and over. Each time, she stopped to consider staying with them.

Each time, her heart's fire said *no*.

* * * * *

Chapter Nine
A Mother's Touch

Koki burst through the front door before Mokin returned from the back patio. Her cheery greeting to Byria was muffled by the piles she carried. Then she called, "Come! Come!" as she just about skipped through the beads and doorways out to the patio.

Byria followed just in time to see that Koki had dropped the overflowing baskets and engaged Mokin in yet another indecent kissing session. Having heard Mokin talk about how they met and loved each other, and seeing the ridiculous and beautiful grin on his face as he spoke of Koki, made no difference in her discomfort at such unreserved affection.

And while she wasn't *meaning* to look out of the corner of her eye, she still managed to notice Koki's fingers moving just under the back of Mokin's loincloth. Had they not realized she'd followed right behind Koki?

While the moment was intense, it passed quickly (compared to other such moments). After one last kiss to Mokin's lips, Koki exclaimed in delight once more and filled her arms with the coarse yellow-green material—like the inner wood of a bush. She thrust the cloth at Byria, grabbed pots of cleaning scrub and brushes, and handed those to her, too.

She half-filled the pot they used for cleaning and bathing and brought that to the further corner of the patio, where Mokin would look at her injuries.

Even without Mokin's magic, she understood what Koki was asking. The woman's joy kept Byria from feeling offended at being asked to bathe and change. Grabbing Mokin's hand, Koki made it clear Byria should call when she was finished, and to ask for help if she needed it.

A long bath alone was luxurious, and it gave Byria a good chance to look at her scars and injuries. Her feet were healing well, and while the many other scars and burns she could see still looked ugly and reddish, the angry inflammation had faded quite a bit. Most hardly hurt, and all the purple-black bruises seemed gone.

As Byria bathed, she saw the three flat baskets Koki had brought lined up along one of the patio sides. Divine-smelling vegetables and fruits filled one. Another had wooden disks with glyphs carved or painted on them—none made Byria feel uncomfortable, fortunately. More strings of multi-colored beads were piled in the third.

Once she was satisfied with her cleanliness, Byria turned her attention to the garments Koki had given her. There were two pieces—and yet there seemed not to be enough material. Why did these small people wear so little? After several moments of frustration, she took the largest piece, pulled it around her, and squatted, trying to cover every inch of her body.

"Koki?" she called to the house, then amended, "Just Koki?"

Koki came out and looked at her, brow furrowed in confusion.

Byria raised her eyebrows and pleaded, "Help?"

Koki nodded and tried to direct her with gestures and simple commands. Mokin had been right; it was terribly frustrating to not have that level of communication they'd shared. Almost painful. Yet Koki didn't lose her patience, even as Byria wrapped the fabric even more tightly around her.

Koki fixed a firm but gentle gaze on Byria. Speaking slowly and using both their languages, she said, "Mokin said you saw his marks, scars from his father. I've seen them, too. All of them. I'm not bothered by them, and I *will not* hurt you. I will *never* hurt you. I only want to help."

"I know." Byria nodded. "Just..." She tried to get her mind to remember the words Mokin had used; she remembered both hearing them as he spoke as well as understanding them as if they were her tongue. "For giants." She scowled, still disliking that word in reference to herself, but she could think of nothing better. "Only marriage can see. Body. Some parts."

"What about mothers?" Koki asked softly. "Caretakers? You're born knowing how to dress?"

Byria shook her head and bit her lip. Swallowing hard, she loosened her grip on the fabric. It was rough, rougher than the servant's clothes she'd taken. Closing her eyes, she focused on the texture. As Byria relaxed her grip, Koki manipulated the material, pulling the hole in the center over her head.

With a stepstool and further patient communication whenever her fingers brushed Byria's skin, Koki secured the dress upon her charge.

The cloth only went down to Byria's elbow, and while the tied body did cover most of her side, if she were to lift her arms, she revealed her entire underarm and a little of her side. And the dress hardly brushed below her knees! It felt... indecent.

Tucking her arms into the material and folding them close to her, Byria asked, "Is more...?" She didn't know the word for "cloth" or "clothing." She crouched, trying to tuck her lower legs under the "skirt" to make her point more clearly.

Koki frowned and folded her arms, but Byria could tell it was a frown of thought, not disappointment.

After a few moments and a deep sigh, Koki retrieved the other garment she'd brought, a short tunic similar to her hunter's spotted skin. After another sad sigh, she took her knife and started cutting the fabric.

"Oh!" Byria said, shocked.

"It's all right," Koki murmured and shook her head. "Just wait..." Then she motioned for her to put on her slippers.

Byria nodded, and Koki approached with four strips of fabric. She gestured for Byria to sit and watch. Then, taking one of the longer pieces of fabric, she wrapped Byria's leg from ankle to just below her knee, where she tied it tightly, but not painfully. Handing Byria the next piece of fabric, she let her try.

With a nod, she did. It didn't feel as secure as the one Koki had done, but she could fix it later. With a smile, she thanked her friend, inspecting her new wrapped "stockings."

Smiling back, Koki took another strip of cloth and reached for Byria's right arm, ready to wrap that. Then she stopped.

When she saw the look on Koki's face, Byria tried to pull her arm back, but the woman held it tightly.

Byria squeaked at the strong grip.

"What? Is? This?" Koki spoke even slower, in both languages, pointing so close that one of her dagger-like fingernails almost touched the glyph just below Byria's elbow.

Gestures and words she knew wouldn't answer that question. Eyes wide, heart hammering, Byria stammered, "How I leave home. How I live. No magic now. Mokin saw. Ask?"

Koki released her with a nod and an apology, but she didn't call for Mokin. Byria bit her lip, pulling her arm to her. It didn't hurt, despite how firmly Koki had gripped it, and there wasn't a hint of redness.

The hunter apologized again, then said, slowly and deliberately, repeating some parts in both languages, "Mokin said you saw his father, and he told you what happened to him. I know how the marks can hurt, and that being near his father hurts you. I wanted to make sure…"

Byria frowned. "If he did this, how I know what it meant?"

Koki nodded. "If you didn't know, I would worry."

Surprising herself, Byria released her next breath in a wave of nervous chuckles and tears.

Koki stepped close to her, looking concerned. "What?"

"I no remember worry for me like you and Mokin. Except Patch—Urukyen."

Koki's eyes widened for a moment, then blinked back a glimmer of tears. She threw her arms around Byria, embracing her tightly, her face pressed to her stomach.

Byria stiffened, then relaxed. More of her own tears fell. She rested her hands on Koki's shoulders, returning the embrace awkwardly—deeply moved by the affection.

"I wish that weren't true," Koki murmured against her.

Whether it was the closeness or that Koki had magic similar to Mokin's, Byria understood her perfectly, despite her muffled voice.

She let go of Byria just as quickly, stepping away and wiping her eyes. "I didn't mean to make you uncomfortable. I'm sorry."

Byria shook her head and reached out her hands to Koki, squeezing her once she took them. Byria didn't even have words in her own language for what she wanted Koki to know, but she hoped the squeeze communicated it.

Koki smiled. A wide, beautiful smile—despite the sharp teeth—that said she did.

* * * * *

Chapter Ten
Women's Blood

When Byria went out to relieve and wash herself the next morning, she saw only Mokin stirring one of his clay pots. She wished him a good morning in his language, and he did the same, though he seemed distracted. Upon returning from the waste hole, she asked where Koki was.

He made a face of pain, touching his lower stomach, and said, "Her woman's blood is always difficult." As he spoke, he scooped out a bowl of broth for Byria, stirred in a small egg, and topped it with crisped deerpig fat.

Byria took the bowl and asked, "She'll be all right?"

"Yes. She needs rest. A day, two days, sometimes more."

"All the women here are like that?" Byria had had some difficult women's times, and especially bad upon making herself lose Tain's child, but she'd taken that suffering to be a fair punishment.

She thought upon how much Mokin and Koki wanted a child, but also upon how Mokin *still* suffered for having a parent who was like Tain. She thought of Mokin's face when she'd asked about his mother. *Na.* Just no. Her heart strongly suggested a similar fate would've been hers once Tain had an heir.

Mokin shook his head. "Some, yes, but not many."

"Is Koki in a lot of pain?" She finished drinking her soup and wiped her finger to get every tiny morsel. She studied the clay, anxious about the small woman hurting.

Mokin waggled his fingers over her bowl, making Byria jump. She handed the bowl to him, and he began to prepare another. "Koki…" His face wore both a smirk and the expression of trying to find the right words. "Doesn't talk about pain, even to her healer husband. I ask, and she'll say she doesn't hurt, or hurts only a little. She tells me now that she's tired. Sleepy." He gave Byria a knowing look and raised an eyebrow.

Byria nodded in understanding. She wasn't in the least surprised Koki would never admit to being in pain.

"So, I tell you she's sleepy. But this bowl is for Koki. Healing soup. This—" he held up a bowl of powder "—kuchu root." He waited for Byria to show her understanding. She nodded again, realizing he was teaching her healing things. She leaned in to pay close attention. "Most women, for women's pains, two of these." He showed her a very small wooden spoon with a small glyph carved on the handle. "For Koki, four. Never *more than* four. That can make it worse."

"So she is in a lot of pain."

"She won't say. I just know. Some healing is knowing what people won't say. A good healer discovers real truth and works on real truth. Do you understand?"

"I understand," Byria said. "And I think your magic is still working a little. I understand you better."

"I think you learn very fast, as well."

With a smile, Byria thanked him, pride blushing her cheeks.

"You like to bring this to Koki?" Mokin asked, stirring Koki's soup vigorously.

"I would. Please," she said.

He nodded, stirring it in the other direction just as quickly, then pointing. "You should see no grains, but she needs to drink quickly, or it'll settle back out."

He brought over another clay jar. Using a ridged stick, he dripped what looked like honey into the soup. "Terrible taste. This helps."

When Mokin had finished preparing it, Byria brought the bowl into the windowless room Koki and Mokin shared. The smell of blood pricked her nose. "Koki?"

A questioning grunt came from the middle of the room. Byria's eyes adjusted, and she saw Koki curled on her side amidst a circle of mats on top of skins. A thin cloth of the same material as her new dress blanketed her.

"I brought soup from Mokin," Byria said. "He said drink it all, quick as you can."

"I know, I know," she grumbled, propping herself up on one elbow. She gave Byria a weak smile. "Thank you."

Byria handed her the bowl.

She drank it quickly, making a few faces, then placed the empty bowl aside and laid back down with a soft groan.

Koki placed the empty bowl aside and laid back. Byria pursed her lips, wanting to do more for the woman who'd helped her so many times. The desire to help Koki loosed more memory stones. Stones about storysongs. When she'd been hurt, especially when she was younger, but even recently, she'd ask Syng, her primary handmaid, for a storysong.

Memories of storysongs flowed into her head.

"Beelheah?" Koki asked.

Byria wiped her nose as she realized the newly released memories were making her sniffle. She didn't have the words to explain herself to Koki, so she said, "I don't like seeing you in pain—"

"Not in pain. Just tired," the woman grumbled.

Byria continued, "When I was... tired, sometimes my caretaker would sing stories to me. And I rested better."

"You still sing?" Koki sounded interested. "I remember Ulhookee-en singing, and you repeating. You were still little, but you both had beautiful voices."

"Would you like me to sing something to you, then? My language, but..."

"I would like that, yes."

"All right, then." Byria hummed, looking for a tune she could remember the words for. It only took a moment of humming to recall the first story of the Demon-Wife Between. She smiled, remembering the servants singing during the last Between Moon festival. The day she'd gotten the gift of the glass shard—the tiny tool that had given her the bravery to find the dragon and release him.

She sang the song for Koki. While the small woman might not need more bravery, anyone could use a gift of strength while in pain.

Koki made a pleased sound when Byria stopped singing. "You have a beautiful voice."

"Thank you. Do you want me to try to explain the story?" Byria smiled, sensing Koki could see even in the darkened room.

"I think I understood it from the music." Koki propped herself up again. The light that filtered in through the woven walls reflected in her eyes, illuminating the coppery rings around her pupils.

Byria tilted her head, wondering if she was comprehending her friend.

Koki smiled a little more. "Our dear friend, Chimayo, is a storysinger for our people. And her mother sings…" Byria didn't understand what Koki said, but didn't want to interrupt. "They taught me to hear the story just in music."

When Byria made an incredulous face, Koki offered that Byria's story started out about family love, though one of the family could be a trickster. Not a hurtful one, but mischievous. And then a hurtful, *bad* trickster caused some problems, and the resolution, while not tragic, was not entirely happy.

"Oh!" Byria blinked several times, surprised at how close Koki's guess was to the story.

"You like the not-hurtful trickster in that storysong," she also said with a knowing smirk.

Byria nodded. Between storysongs *were* her favorites, since she used tricks and games to overcome obstacles. She was clever and unafraid, even when facing down monsters and evil people.

With a groan and a stretch, Koki sat up. Byria looked away as the sheet slipped off of her. A soft chuff from the woman had Byria peek at her from the corner of her eye.

Folding her arms, though not in modesty, Koki said, "Thank you for sharing your song. I do feel better, and I'll go outside. If you wish not to see my blood or me without clothes, go tell Mokin I'm doing better, and his broth helped."

Outside, Byria relayed the information to Mokin, and a relaxed smile spread across his face. He returned to his mentoring, explaining what different herbs and broths did, what herbs should be used to clean skin, and what should be used to clean pottery or wood.

Byria paid attention, repeating the information back to him to his satisfaction.

When Koki joined them, Mokin doted upon her until she shooed him away, grabbing some herbs and separating leaves from stems with ferocity until he returned to Byria's lessons.

After lunch, Byria asked Koki what she used to collect her blood, for she knew she'd need this information when she left on her own.

"I plan hunting when such isn't needed," said Koki with an approving nod, "but I still know to be prepared."

The rest of the day, the desire to stay with Koki and Mokin, as their apprentice, as their family, fought with her heart fire's need to leave soon and find the dragon.

* * * * *

Chapter Eleven
Emergency House Call

The next day, as Mokin was putting out the jasmine bush to show he'd see patients again, young Owi and Gyotan, whom Byria remembered from the jungle, ran up to him, looking worried and agitated.

Byria heard their frightened voices rising as she watched out the window. Matching their expression, Mokin nodded, said something softly, and brought the jasmine bush back beside his door. Calling for Koki, he rattled off something too quickly for Byria to understand, and headed to the back patio.

After another glance outside to see Owi clutching Gyotan's entire arm, Byria headed to the patio to see if she could help.

Mokin and Koki were throwing packets of herbs and bowls of salves into a basket. Koki, tight-mouthed and pale, caught Byria's eye first. With a pained grunt, she pointed to herbs on higher shelves.

Byria reached the items Koki requested as Mokin headed to the back door, paused, and gave Byria a firm look. He spoke slowly in his language and hers. "Stay here. *Back* here. Don't answer the door. If we need help, we'll send Owi, and *ti* will come right back here with instructions."

"But what is problem?" Byria's heart pounded in worry.

"Bebe has a cut that turned into a fever. I need to see her in her house, and I need Koki's help," he said slowly, though only in his tongue. Then, in both languages, he repeated emphatically, "Stay. Here. *Back* here. Don't answer the door. Owi will come in if I need something else from here."

"I understand," she said slowly in his language.

Nodding, he and Koki left. Resisting the urge to follow and watch out the front window, she did as Mokin had requested and stayed on the back patio.

To distract from her unexpected loneliness, Byria washed all their bowls, put them away, found herbs that still needed to be separated, weeded all the garden beds and pots in the back, put together a lunch from fruit and the always-cooking broth, and found herself with nothing else to do.

This was the first time she'd been entirely idle since she'd come to the village. It occurred to her she should take some time to think, possibly find more memories, and do something just for her.

Byria's gaze fell to the symbol on her arm. She'd carved it, copied it from Patch's writing. She'd written it on the mirror before the high magepriest had captured her again. She'd written to accomplish tasks; she hadn't had time to appreciate that she'd been *writing*.

She went and grabbed the pyut-gem. She hadn't looked at it much, since the triangle bothered Koki, but she needed that connection to Patch.

Sitting upon mats at the edge of the patio, she doodled in the dirt with a stick, pyut-gem clenched in her other hand. The doodling turned into shapes and symbols she recognized, ones that held memories, or ties to memory stones that wanted to wiggle free. Even if writing memories didn't come free, the act of writing felt deliciously empowering.

She must have known how to write before, though she remembered no lessons. Patch had offered to write on the map with a beautifully wicked and rebellious smile, so Patch likely had taught her. As she traced each symbol and glyph, she knew what it meant.

I can read!

When she left the village, she'd practice writing while thinking on her fire. Perhaps she could unearth more knowledge and more memories that way. Perhaps the dragon would teach her. Dragons were known for their wisdom.

Another thought occurred to her, and she rubbed out her writing. She started drawing a map. The map she remembered looking at in the dungeon.

Where is the dragon?

Even when she focused on her heart's fire, a clear answer didn't come. Had she remembered the map incorrectly? Pursing her lips, she scratched away and redrew the map again. And again.

With each new drawing, her heart's fire grew. Despite the happiness she felt with Koki and Mokin, she knew it would be *when* she left the village, not if.

* * * * *

Chapter Twelve
A Secret Promise

Mokin and Koki came back as the light through the leaves darkened to twilight. Koki, hands over her womb and face lined in pain, mumbled something too low for Byria to understand and shuffled to the outhouse. Mokin grabbed clean cloths and mosses and offered Byria a weak smile as he headed after his wife. He stopped as he saw the remnants of Byria's scribbling.

"Beelheah?"

"Yes?" She came over to him.

He closed his eyes and sighed. "Will you wait?" He took another deep breath, and his face wrinkled with his "trying to find words" expression.

Byria offered her hand to him, and he pulled away. "No magic. Must return to heal. I can't…" The lines on his face deepened, and he sounded exhausted.

Byria backed away, respecting what he was asking.

"Thank you." With another deep breath, he drew a toe lightly across the lines of her map. "This. Wait for Koki to feel better. Don't…" He clenched his teeth, frustration evident in his weariness. "She hurts too much…?" His voice lifted with a question at the end.

Byria didn't completely understand him this time, but she knew what he was asking. "I won't speak of leaving until Koki isn't hurting with blood."

Mokin's face relaxed, and he thanked her again. As he headed for the waste hole, Byria saw the glimmer of tears in his eyes.

After he helped Koki to bed, making her eat and drink another bowl of pain herbs, he told Byria he had to leave again and would be back in the morning.

* * * * *

Chapter Thirteen
Family Stories and Healing Songs

Bebe's fever broke in the night, and Mokin returned to spend half the day sleeping. Owi accompanied him back, carrying beads, food, and Mokin's basket of supplies.

Unsure of the proper hospitality, Byria offered Owi broth and water after taking Mokin's items as he stumbled to sleep.

Ti accepted, taking the time to tell Byria what had happened.

Bebe, ti's mother, had cut her foot badly on the way back home from their visit here. Owi's father had been out collecting seeds and other things to make beads. Bebe had tried to clean the cut herself, but being as pregnant as she was, she couldn't reach it well.

Owi added indignantly that ti's mother hadn't even thought to ask ti or ti's older sibling for help. The cut had become infected, and Bebe came to have a fever—which was very dangerous for one who's pregnant. Mokin had spent the prior day and night treating the cut and bringing down the fever before Bebe grew sicker and potentially miscarried.

Byria also found out Bebe and her husband had been friends with Mokin and Koki since long before they were even courting, and that Bebe had made their "soulbinding promise" necklaces and had refused to let them pay for them.

Owi thanked Byria and gave her another hug before leaving. She told ti to come back right away if Bebe had any other problems; it seemed like something Mokin would say. With more thanks, Owi promised to do so and left.

Byria spent the morning cleaning any dirty or used-looking supplies and returning everything to where it belonged.

Koki came out to the patio by the afternoon. Concern lined her face.

"What's wrong?" Byria asked.

Byria only understood Mokin's name from the woman's collection of grumbles and sighs. Following Koki as she dampened rags, Byria gave her a questioning look.

After another sigh, Koki offered in a very quiet voice, "Fever. He took the fever for himself."

"He—?" Byria began to ask, but Koki waved her hand at her and gave her a *look*.

Byria nodded, but chewed her lip. She'd heard of healers taking on the illness of the healed, but that required magic. And Mokin had explained magic shouldn't be used with pregnancy.

Reading Byria's face, Koki pressed her lips together. "Bebe was very sick. Waited too long." Shaking her head, she looked to the ground.

"Owi said Bebe was doing better," Byria offered.

"She will be." Koki disappeared back into the house.

Byria gathered the herbs Mokin had mentioned were good for fevers. Koki nodded in approval when she returned and showed Byria the amounts for steeping.

When the brew was done, Koki mixed it with broth and handed it to Byria. "Mokin likes music, too," she said.

Byria smiled, understanding. Carrying the fever-reducing soup, she knocked at the side of their bedroom doorway. "Mokin?"

Hearing a soft grunt, she entered. He was under a sheet, eyes half-closed, but looking at her curiously. She brought the bowl to him as he propped himself up on an elbow and thanked her.

"Koki said you like music, and she enjoyed when I sang to her when she was ill. Would you like that?"

He didn't answer as he sipped his broth. When he put the bowl down, he patted his face with the damp cloth and nodded. "I would."

Byria settled beside him and started humming. A different song came to her mind this time. It was still a Between story, though the Demon-Wife played only a small part. The tale was of a family she'd helped.

* * *

After many years of trying, a butcher and his wife finally had a child. They adored that child more than anything, doting on him and loving him, teaching him right and wrong—even though it broke their hearts if they ever had to discipline him. But he grew into a well-behaved and well-mannered child.

One day, the king sent out a notice to the butchers, bakers, fruit-cutters, fishermen, and more to choose among them who would provide food for his son's wedding. The child's parents were chosen for their excellent quality of cuts, and with the amount of food the king needed, both the father and the mother needed to go.

The father asked his younger brother to watch their child for them. He was worried, for his brother was a wanderer, and had changed vocations many times in his life. However, he figured his own blood would love and protect his son, as one should do.

The butcher and his wife didn't return home from the prince's wedding until the next morning, both exhausted. Before they retired, they wanted to see their little boy.

They went to the child's room, and to their dismay, they found the butcher's younger brother curled up on the child's mat. He awoke, confused and frightened, and then he remembered what had happened.

A demon! A demon had come and asked for hospitality. The brother knew one should always grant hospitality to strangers, but he didn't think to see if the stranger was a demon in disguise. The stranger was wonderful company, with many great stories, and he'd convinced the brother to play a game of chance—

"Say no more!" the butcher said, striking his brother, for he knew how games with demons always ended. "Leave! Leave this house! You are no longer my blood or my brother!"

Deeply shamed, the brother left the house in tears.

The butcher and his wife returned to the palace, hoping to get help, for they had done well to provide excellent food and service to the prince's wedding. However, no one at the palace would help. "Demons? You would ask the royal family to taint themselves with your demon problem?"

The butcher and his wife were thrown out and told they would be marked as traitors to the kingdom should they befoul the palace door with such requests again.

They visited a temple of magepriests and found no help there. Instead, they were ordered to leave an offering for bringing up such a topic in a sacred space. Then they sought out the ancient, hidden magic users: exiled sorcerers and witches. Some tried to help, and some didn't.

They used up all they'd made from the wedding, and their shop was left neglected. They traded all they owned, all their money, the butcher's best knives and second-best knives, everything, but all their attempts proved fruitless.

It was only after they had merely the clothes on their back to offer that a sorcerer offered them a map to the realm of demons so they might find their son and make a deal for themselves.

The map worked, and they found their way to the demon's realm. One attended to them upon their arrival and took them to their son. He'd aged a year, and had become emaciated and thin—for as good parents, they'd taught him to never eat nor drink what demons offered.

"We don't gamble or play chance," the butcher said, "and we've given up everything just to come here. What must we do to bring our son home?"

The demon offered a trade. One of them for the boy. The butcher and his wife argued; neither wanted to leave the other to the demons. Finally, the butcher begged his wife to go with their son, for her heart was stronger, and she was clever and would be the better parent.

She agreed, but only if he promised to not eat or drink for a year as well, to give her a chance to find a way to free him.

He agreed to that condition, but only if she promised she would neither sacrifice herself nor their son for him.

The wife agreed and left the demon realm with their son. Both could hardly walk home—the boy weakened from his stay in the demon realm, the wife weakened with grief.

They returned home to a house furnished with new things, with food in the cellar, and fresh clothing. The wife was suspicious. Was this a demon's trick?

No, the butcher's brother was there, trying to make things right.

Still angry, for this was a mess the man had made, she told him to take his things and leave. His brother now belonged to the demons because of his foolishness!

The brother took nothing from the house, but left and went to a nearby tributary of the Great River. As his tears hit the water, his reflection changed to that of a lovely woman who stepped from the water and sat beside him.

"What troubles you? You have the aura of one done wrong by demons," she said.

"I've made a grave mistake, and I would do anything to undo it."

"What have you done?"

He found himself crying into the woman's arms, telling her the whole tale. The woman, dressed in silks the color of water, comforted him for only a moment, then asked,. "Do you speak truly when you say you would do anything to undo your mistake?"

"I do!"

"Would you take your brother's place in the realm of demons, that he might return to his son and his wife?"

"I would."

"It would be for all eternity, and you would have to eat their food and drink their wine."

"I would do just that."

"Then I shall tell you how to get to the demon realm. Find your brother's clothing and wear it as your own, and come to me here when both moons are half dark."

It took time for the brother to find a full set of clothes that belonged to his brother—he purchased them piece by piece. The shirt still had the stain of pig's blood. He even found a pair of his brother's shoes that he'd traded. When the moon had waned to half-dark, he returned to the tributary where the woman waited for him.

He followed the woman into the water, refusing to be afraid, and took the flowing roads to the demon realm. As they walked, she instructed him further. She led him to where his brother lay on a luxurious padded mattress. There was a tray of food and wine untouched beside him.

He gently touched his brother's shoulder, waking him. Before he could curse or rebuke him, the younger brother asked in a whisper, "Do you still feel your tie to your wife and boy?"

"Of course I do! It pulls my heart every minute of every day."

"And you have not eaten, and you have not drunk anything from this realm?"

"I promised my wife I wouldn't."

With a nod, the brother ate a bite of rice and sipped from the warm cup of wine. His insides twisted, and he doubled over, but he croaked out the instructions: "Go! Now! Follow where your heart pulls, and you'll return to them."

The butcher did as his brother said and found himself in his wife's arms by morning. They cried together, and lit incense and candles for the brother—unsure what help it would be in the demon realm.

Their son kept up the practice every Remembrance Day. And sometimes, just sometimes, he saw the face of his uncle or a lovely woman in a shimmer upon running water.

* * *

As Byria sang, another memory loosed of Syng sitting at her bedside when she'd had a fever due to Tain not letting her dress the wounds he'd inflicted upon her days earlier. She'd asked about a set of meetings.

After punishing her for forgetting, or questioning him, or whatever she'd done, he'd forced her to stay by his side for the duration of the meetings. He'd wrapped the wounds, for he'd wanted no blood or seepage to mar her clothing, but he'd given her no balm for the pain. She'd fainted on the second day, feeling like her whole body was on fire.

She remembered looking in all the pools of water, every puddle and every pan, to see if the Between twin watched. She'd spent her healing time near the gardens' fountains, staring for hours at the water. Surely, the demon's realm couldn't be worse than the one she lived in.

"You *are* a healer." Mokin's voice splashed through her memories like a pebble into a pond.

Byria said nothing as she focused on the memories so they wouldn't be forgotten again. Then she processed what her friend had said, and that he was sitting up, eyes brighter, and the cloth from his head tossed aside.

"What do you mean?" she asked.

"How do you feel?" He held out his hand, and she let him take hers. He checked her pulse. Then, adjusting the sheet around his waist (thankfully), he reached for her face.

Byria was confused, but didn't pull away.

"I felt that. Your magic is healing, but you haven't taken my fever into you. Not even a little."

"I heal myself sometimes, but it takes a lot of rest and... thinking of doing so. I was only thinking of the song."

"But you said, when you came in, you wanted me to feel better."

"Um... yes. Koki said you like singing, and she liked when I sang. But..." She pressed her hand to her heart. A warmth tingled through her whole chest and hand. "I didn't—I mean..."

Mokin tilted his head. "Koki worked with me all day yesterday. Normally, during her bleeding time, she has no energy, or hurts too much to do anything. And she's awake now. She helped you make the broth?"

Byria nodded.

"You sang to her, and she felt better."

Byria shrugged, not sure what to make of Mokin's interpretation, unsure how she felt about someone knowing about her power—even someone she trusted.

"I thought your injuries healed faster than I expected. I didn't know if it was a giant—"

Byria failed at repressing her scowl.

He glanced at her with a shamed face. "I mean, a large-person trait. Or if it was the magic I sensed in you." With a pause, he looked at her again. "But you prefer to keep your magic hidden, too."

Swallowing a dry lump in her throat, Byria gave a little nod.

His voice hitched as he asked, "From Koki, too?"

Byria wasn't sure how to answer, so she shrugged.

"I... don't keep secrets from her." His voice was small.

With a frown, Byria chided, "You told me to wait about telling her about leaving."

"Only until she is better. Koki…" He paused. "… wears the skin of the small river dragons like her spotted cat skin. Only it's a glamour, like the skin you see."

"River dragon? Glamour? Skin I see?" Byria didn't understand.

Mokin held out his arm. Byria's eyes had adjusted enough to see the illusion of his skin shimmer away to reveal his scars and then shimmer back. "Glamour. She can hide with it, too. Better than anyone."

Byria nodded, now understanding that word. "River dragon?"

Mokin rolled back the edge of a mat to reveal the dirt floor and drew a quick sketch.

"Oh, crocodile." She said the word in her language before repeating what Mokin called it. "She wears an illusion of hard skin that doesn't stop her from getting hurt."

Mokin nodded. "She'll be hurt by your leaving. Deeply hurt. And hurt in her heart…" He tapped his chest. "She doesn't recover from that well."

"And you?" Byria looked away, ashamed she would ask such a thing. She knew she was leaving, and she didn't *want* to hurt Koki or Mokin.

He placed his hand on hers again, drawing her attention as his scars shimmered forth once more. "I have more experience in dealing with hurt than she does. From people I love. And scars make thick skin."

Byria's heart plummeted at his words, erupting in a fountain of tears. A buzz in her ears let her know he was using his magic to make sure she understood. She did; she also understood what he didn't say directly.

She pulled her hand away and stood as best she could in the small room. The feel of his power was fading, so she spoke fast. "I'm happy you're feeling better, and if I did help, I'm happy I could. But I think you're wrong. I'm not a healer. A healer shouldn't make people hurt, and as much as I don't want to hurt anyone, I will."

"Beelheah—" he began.

She shook her head. "Koki will be happy you're better. I should weed the gardens. I owe you for all you've taught me, and for healing me as much as you've done."

Wiping away tears, she walked out of the dark room. She paused in the central room until she had her emotions under control, focusing her heart's fire to ease the pain cracking through her chest. She decided to chance working on the herb beds in front of the house so Koki wouldn't see the tears burning her eyes.

*****

Chapter Fourteen
The Weight of Secrets

Byria's attempt to be alone in the front didn't last very long. A person approached. The person appeared to be a *she* beneath her necklaces.

Byria greeted her politely, though she bit her lip.

"Mokin isn't seeing people—?" the woman began, then stopped herself as she looked at Byria's face. "Is Mokin ill?"

Cursing to herself, as making more people worry was the last thing she wanted, Byria said, "A small fever, but it's getting better."

"What's wrong, then?"

Byria wiped her eyes, then saw the soil on her hands—now likely smeared over her face. Shaking her head, she gave a little chuckle. A small bit of truth would be the best way to answer. "Long time since people have been as kind to me as Koki and Mokin. I dislike seeing even a little sick."

"Aaah." The woman nodded and gave Byria a smile, patting her arm. "Koki and Mokin are very kind. Are giants not so kind? And will Mokin see people tomorrow?"

Byria considered her words a moment and said, "I believe Mokin will see people tomorrow."

"Not tomorrow." Koki came out the front door. "Day after tomorrow. He always waits to be healthy for a whole day before seeing people. And larger people can be as kind or not-kind as any people."

"People are people." The younger woman nodded, reached her hands out to Koki, and embraced her with kisses on the cheek. "I'll leave health prayers for Mokin with your mother."

"Thank you." Koki returned the woman's embrace and placed a hand on her belly. "We will see you in two days, then, Coin-Kaima? Are you well?"

"Well enough. Just… you know."

"Of course!" Koki kissed her again and bid her well. Once the woman was gone, she cast a chiding look at Byria. Crouching to weed alongside her, she said softly, "Mokin told me he told you to not be alone out here."

Looking away, Byria mumbled an apology.

"He's up and weeding the back gardens. I knew your singing would help him." Though she still whispered, her tone had the edge of a question and pointed statement.

"I'm happy it did."

"He said nothing about it?"

Byria pursed her lips. Next to the small woman, she felt she could be honest and candid—but she'd asked Mokin not to say anything about her abilities. To say something now would make him look bad.

"I found him quiet, like you, and your face speaks without words. You rushed out here, *alone*."

An explanation came to Byria. "He told you of our talking the other day? About his father?"

Koki nodded but said nothing.

"If neither of you know about me and things I do, you won't have so many problems with him. You can say 'We know nothing,' and not lie."

She hoped her words came out clearly. Since his spell, she'd found speaking and understanding easier, though she missed the absolute clarity they'd shared for that short time.

"I see," Koki said. "So he asked about singing, called it healing powers—I know he'd notice such things—and you said...?"

"I said nothing. He didn't argue."

"He wouldn't." Koki moved to the next row, facing the road, eyes darting. Still speaking lowly, she continued, "But I would think his patience wouldn't cause you tears or to avoid me."

Byria said nothing.

"Mokin would respect your wish for silence, but we don't hide things from each other. I understand his discomfort, but there was more."

Byria pressed her lips together. What should she say? "I don't want anyone hurt because of me. You're both kind, very kind, and don't deserve any pain in your lives."

"Seeing you again, knowing it was *you*, has brought far more joy than any pain you can imagine you would cause, for both Mokin and me."

Byria sighed, having no further or better words. She brushed her elbow against the woman's shoulder, hoping that was enough. Koki pressed her cheek to Byria's shoulder for a half second before snapping to taut attention.

Byria followed her gaze to see Mokin's father passing by. That same dark chill began to creep from her joints to her heart's fire, but she tried to match Koki's glare, willing her heart to burn hotter. The older man walked by, casting only a smug glance at them. As he left, he took his illness with him.

Koki said nothing more as they quickly finished weeding the front gardens. They brought the weeds to the back, where Mokin burned off the roots, and piled the rest in lumps of black soil along the borders of the gardens.

"My father tried to visit again?" he asked.

Either the small people were particularly good at reading faces, or Byria's face was easier to read than she wanted.

"He just walked by, nothing more. I was right there," Koki said.

Mokin nodded, giving Byria a reproachful look.

"I told Koki I didn't want to talk about my singing," Byria offered. "Because if I didn't say anything—if he asked—you could say 'I don't know' and not lie."

Mokin raised his eyebrows. "I could also tell him I have nothing to say to him and not lie."

Byria shrugged and cleaned her hands and face. She wanted to tell him, without making more trouble, that she hadn't meant to make him keep secrets.

As Mokin walked by to dump more roots into the fire bed, he tugged the end of Byria's washcloth. When she met his eye, he gave her a gentle smile and a nod.

A pressure she hadn't noticed earlier released in her chest.

Widening his smile, he rubbed his finger over his nose and left eye, then pointed to her. Byria scrubbed off the last stubborn bit of tear-stuck dirt, looking at him once more.

He nodded again and brought over a starchy root. Placing it on a smooth piece of wood beside a stone knife with an edge almost as smooth as metal, he asked, "Would you like to practice your cutting?"

* * * * *

Chapter Fifteen
Confessions in Lessons

The next day, Koki looked weary again. Byria noticed her still wearing a cloth between her legs; the tied rope that secured it showed through the hunting tunic. Byria had seen men in the same cut of animal skin, and Koki had said they were hunters, too.

This skin was what Byria remembered her wearing when they'd first met; its spots were two-colored, brown and black. The other she'd seen Koki wear had only black spots.

The prior night, Byria had decided she'd pay attention to every small detail. She didn't want to forget any time with Koki and Mokin, ever.

Koki invited her to gather some herbs and mushrooms that grew not far from the village. Since Koki's "invitation" sounded somewhere between a request and a command, Byria agreed to join her.

Koki pointed out particular trees and landmarks as they first circled around the village, "in case you should ever get lost." They continued in an outward spiral, the woman taking her time to explain the land, point out poisonous insects, and to reveal hiding spots for snakes.

They paused near two sets of mushrooms that looked identical to Byria. Koki pointed out subtle differences in the coloring and points of their caps—then proceeded to pick two and switch them between her hands, testing Byria on her knowledge before showing Byria how to properly harvest the ones that wouldn't kill them.

At an orange-green bush, Koki gave a particularly long lesson about using its leaves, fresh, to pack wounds, and its roots to help pain.

When Koki started walking away, Byria asked, "Are we not going to harvest that?"

"No. All its parts are best used fresh. They lose potency too quickly. But if you're injured and traveling, it'll save your life."

Byria froze. She'd kept her promise to Mokin and hadn't told Koki about her plans to leave; why would the woman take so much time with this lesson?

Koki took the basket off her shoulders and planted a hand on her hip. "Uhl-oh-kyen—Patch—told me my face spoke all my thoughts, even more than Mokin's, at least for her. I see what she means in yours."

Heat flushed through Byria's face.

"I noticed your bag has remained packed and secured, ready to leave at a moment's notice."

The embarrassment burned even more.

"And…" Koki paused for a very long moment; Byria couldn't help but squirm. "…Mokin has also thought the same." Further squirms. "And he's asked you to not speak your thoughts of leaving to me."

A whimper squeaked from Byria's throat to her lips that didn't make words, but ended in a questioning tone.

With a snort and a mirthless smile, Koki said, "I have many years practice in reading his face and body. He thinks I don't see the concerned glances he makes between you and me."

"Ehrmr... um... he didn't say *not* to tell you. Just to wait. Until you were less sick."

Koki gave an annoyed chuff and rolled her eyes, pausing to glance at the sky. It was growing dark, like another storm. "I teach you how to... in a storm. *Or* he might worry and become sicker if we don't return."

"Teach me what?" Byria hadn't understood all Koki's words, but part sounded like a jab at Mokin for worrying so much.

Koki said the words again, but Byria shook her head. With a sigh, Koki shrugged. "Another day. I shall return his *kindness* and not worry him further."

"I don't understand what you are saying about Mokin either."

"He's recovering from *illness*. I don't want him *worse* from *worry*. Is that what he said? That worrying for you would keep me from healing?"

Byria tried to remember his exact words, but could only shrug.

"Or he thinks it would *hurt* too much." Koki fumed as she led the way back to the village. The small woman half-gestured to more landmarks during short pauses in her rant.

Byria understood a little more than half of what she said. Many of the words were similar to what Mokin had said. "... thinks I'm delicate, easily hurt. I'm a hunter; I'm not delicate. I've had my bleeding like this my entire life. *He* should know!" There were several other words in there that Byria recognized as curses from when one or the other would stub a toe or drop a thing.

"Please, don't be angry at Mokin!" Byria found herself pleading. "He loves you more than I've seen any person love any other person. He doesn't ever want you to hurt for any reason."

Koki stopped and looked at Byria. "I know he loves me. He's my souljoined husband." She touched her marriage necklace the same way Mokin did. "And I'm his. I'm not *angry*. Just, he should know. He felt the same as I do now when I worried about him using magic on Bebe."

"When he uses magic, it makes him sick?"

Koki tilted her head from side to side, glanced up at the sky as thunder rumbled lowly, and gestured they should continue walking—almost jogging. Byria had to catch her breath, despite her strides being twice the size of Koki's.

The woman continued, "His magic can take another's illness to himself, *and* it makes him weak. *And* when he uses magic, he doesn't see a patient for a full day and a full night after. *And then* he worries for everyone in the village, 'What if they need me?'"

Byria would've nodded or shrugged, but she was too busy trying to keep up.

With a *hmmph*, Koki declared, "Truth: he worries *much* more than I do over *all* things."

Between her huffs, Byria smirked. In her short time with them, she'd observed similar.

"You all right?" Koki slowed her pace.

Byria's breath had begun to burn from her throat to her lungs. "Not walked so much, so fast... long time."

Koki frowned, though she thankfully slowed her pace. "You should walk more, or you'll have no strength... if you do leave."

Byria took a breath; she might as well be honest. "*When* I leave."

The woman flinched, though she tried to hide it with a shoulder roll, as if she were stretching. "You're so worried about Mokin's father?" Koki also tried to hide the hitch in her voice.

Mokin had been far more correct in his assessment than Koki would ever admit; Byria regretted her words, but decided truth was still the best option. "I need to find the dragon."

Koki shot Byria a glare that physically hurt. "A dragon? Why?"

"Mokin said that Patch—Urukyen—had told you the same."

"Yes. She did." Koki's tone was ice now.

"Please don't be angry at Mokin that I spoke with him. When he used the potion—"

"Why do you need to see a dragon?" Koki interrupted, voice unchanged.

"Because my heart says so."

Koki chuffed. "You're young, even for a giant. Why are you sure you know your heart so well?"

"Bigger-person. Not giant. Giant is an insult among people like me," Byria corrected, hoping the change of topic might soften her friend some.

It did. Koki's raised eyebrow held more curiosity than anger. "Is your youth an insult, too?"

"I'm a woman, not a child. I was married. I *do* know my heart. It's all I know anything certain about." She tried rearranging the words and using both their languages to emphasize her certainty.

Koki huffed again, but said nothing besides pointing out more landmarks as they approached the village.

Rain started to fall. Koki's shoulders sagged as it soaked into their clothing. Byria felt the same.

She also knew they shared relief that the rain disguised their tears.

* * * * *

Chapter Sixteen
A Different Side of Love

A sickness settled into Byria's stomach as Koki and Mokin spent the rest of the day not *arguing*, but not *not* arguing. They spoke in hushed anger whenever they thought she wasn't near enough to overhear. While she understood fewer words through the whispers and growls, she understood their emotions. Making it worse, both were being gentler and kinder to her.

For the first time since arriving at the village, she felt like she had to watch her words and actions. There wasn't the *fear* she'd felt at the palace, but *something* was there. Even after hearing them make up after they'd gone to bed, Byria couldn't sleep or stop the trembling in her limbs until she brought out the pyut-gem and clutched it to her chest.

Come morning, there was still tenseness between them. Byria would jump when either spoke with a hint of sharpness or loudness. When Mokin squatted in front of her, looking her in the eye, she nearly dropped her still-full bowl of broth.

"We're not upset at you, and we still love each other. No one is angry at you, and no one is going to get hurt." He spoke very slowly, repeating as much as he could in Byria's language.

Byria nodded, but couldn't keep from averting her gaze.

Mokin stayed until she looked him in the eye. "This is *not* you. We have this argument regularly. I promise you that."

Byria swallowed and nodded again. The broth still rippled in her bowl. In her head, she understood what Mokin was saying. But the word "argument"—and she recognized that word in both languages—kept her trembling.

Arguments were suspect. Every memory Byria had of arguments led to pain and scars.

Mokin reached for her bowl. With another nod, she let him take it. When he offered his hands to her, she placed hers in his, thinking he might say something that would make her shaking stop. She didn't *want* to feel this way.

Mokin said nothing. He turned her hands so they were palms up and began rubbing his thumb in a circle over her palm, putting pressure in a few places. His hands were warm. She hadn't realized how cold hers had been.

"Just breathe," he said; his voice had a song to its softness. "Do what you do when you heal yourself."

It took her a moment, but she found her heart's fire and grew it with each breath. When she felt its heat hitting the tips of her fingers, Mokin stopped the circles and squeezed.

"Better?"

Taking another deep breath and not feeling it waver, she smiled. "Yes."

"Good. Koki's going to take you back out while I see people today." He gave Byria a smirk. "She *will* ask you about everything she taught you yesterday." With a wink, he let her go. "A full belly will help." He gestured to the soup.

"I'll finish eating and think of remembering."

"Good." Mokin headed into the house.

* * * * *

Chapter Seventeen
True Friends and Powerful Glamour

Koki gave Byria the same assurances as Mokin, only in her own more direct way, and between constant questions (as Mokin had warned) on everything she'd gone over the prior day. They gathered more herbs, mushrooms, and some berries. Koki even allowed Byria to "rest" by instructing her to sit perfectly still and silent while she used her stones attached by thin leather strips to kill a few large, colorful birds.

By the time they returned to the village, Byria was mentally, emotionally, and physically exhausted. And Koki had four beautiful dead birds hanging over her shoulder that Byria couldn't stop staring at.

"We've covered almost double the paces today as we did yesterday," Koki said approvingly, guiding Byria to a different path than the ones they'd used to enter the town.

"No rain today," Byria countered, but found herself smiling.

Koki chuckled. "Yes. But know you are doing better."

Byria's smile grew. "Thank you."

While Byria didn't recognize the village path they followed, Koki walked it as she did the path to hers and Mokin's hut. She led them to a home almost completely surrounded by bamboo walls, adorned with several more dead birds hanging in varying states of unfeathered-ness.

As they approached, Byria wrinkled her nose at a perfumed smoke mingling with the scent of blood and the funk of meat in the humid air. She also noticed more birdcalls and chirps, and unexpectedly, the tinkling of small bells and a soft drumbeat coming from somewhere nearby.

This home was comprised of several huts, woven between branches of one very large tree with many thick branches and tiny leaves shaped like hearts. This set of houses, like Mokin's, was separated from the closer clusters that made up the rest of the village.

Koki trilled a long, musical whistle toward the higher boughs of the heart-leafed tree.

"Kokiiiiiiii!" came a singsongy squeal in response. The drumming stopped. From the highest of the three houses, a woman unhitched a handle attached to a rope, adjusted another rope, and then, holding onto the handle, whizzed down the tree in a few push-offs with her feet. She landed, running, and pulled Koki into a tight embrace, kissing her face several times.

Koki returned the affection with equal enthusiasm before pulling the dead birds from her shoulder and holding them up proudly.

The slenderer woman—who was also the first person Byria had noticed with longer hair, dark-green curls half down her back—made a disgusted face and excessively gagged, which only prompted Koki to hold them even closer to her.

"Daa-aaaaaaaaaaaa!" sang out the other woman loudly.

"Cheeeee-maaah-yooooo," came a deeper voice that sounded like it was mocking the woman's musical tones.

Koki's laughter and the other woman's dramatic eye roll affirmed the mockery.

"Daa-aaaa-aaaa!" Faux annoyance rang out in this call as the woman grandly turned to face a man who came out from behind the tree.

He had silvery-green hair, a bloodied smock over his strands of beads, and a smirk that glistened in mischievous eyes. Byria liked him immediately—despite the bloody smock. His gaze jumped from the other woman to Byria. Widening his eyes, he gave a small bow and welcomed Byria, adding quickly, "As I am sure my rude daughter didn't."

"Daa-aaa!" With a huff, the woman flung herself at Byria in an embrace that, despite the lack of muscles compared to Koki, still nearly knocked Byria off her feet. "Beelheah! Welcome to our house, and I'm happy to finally meet you grown up!"

Indeed, every word the long-haired woman spoke seemed sung, even more than the generally melodic tones of the villagers' language.

"Um. Thank you..." Byria stammered through what she'd learned as proper greetings and gratification for such a welcome, as she tried to find a way to free herself from the uncomfortable hug.

After handing the dead birds to the father, Koki gave the other woman a firm smack on the arm.

"Oh! That's right!" She quickly stepped away from Byria and bowed. "Koki said you don't like embraces much. Accept my apologies, please?"

The woman looked so immediately repentant, bowing with her hands folded, Byria was taken aback. "Y-yes. Of course."

Koki sighed. "Beelheah, Chimayo—" she began to introduce them, and Byria remembered both she and Mokin mentioning this friend.

"I'm the oldest and closest friend of Koki," the woman said proudly, then twisted her lips with a glinting wink, "that she didn't soul-join herself to."

After another sigh, Koki nodded. "Yes, my oldest and dearest friend who is not Mokin—"

"Truly, definitely oldest. We were friends when Mokin still thought Koki was..." Byria didn't know the words Chimayo spoke, but she would never want to be on the receiving end of the glare Koki gave her.

A purposeful throat-clearing drew their attention to the man with the dead birds over his shoulder and a hand on his hip.

"And this is my father." Chimayo didn't miss a beat and danced over to the man, planting a kiss upon his cheek. "Iwikon."

"It's nice to meet you, Iwikon, Chimayo," Byria said carefully and bowed. Not knowing what else to say, she smiled shyly and glanced at Koki.

"Chimayo is the friend I told you also sings stories," Koki explained. "Her father specializes in birds—meat, feathers, and eggs from live ones. Her mother uses the feathers for..." She paused, looking for the right word. "...special clothes."

"And she sings even better than me," Chimayo said, then sashayed closer to lean her head on Koki's shoulder, smiling sweetly. "And if... honeyberries, she... sing for us. *Just* singing."

"Just singing," Koki agreed and kissed her friend—almost on the lips!

With her particular accent, Byria didn't understand all Chimayo said. Even more distracting and uncomfortable was seeing Koki—*married* Koki—this affectionate with another person, another woman, even! To think of things other than their intimacy, Byria wondered about the distinction for "just singing," and became even more confused.

Honeyberries she understood. Koki had just taught her about honeyberries and had had her gather some. They were quite sweet, but Koki hadn't let her eat more than one. The berries had certain *effects* that Byria didn't understand until, a few moments after eating the single berry, she felt inexplicably happy, and her feet were no longer sore from walking. The effect only lasted a short time, but she knew of similar substances courtesans and palace supporters used.

Koki gave Byria a nod as she twined her arm around Chimayo and pinched her under her ribs. Chimayo squealed and jumped, fixing Koki with an exaggerated pout.

Byria pulled a small handful of the berries from one of the waist-pouches Koki had fitted her with, deciding she rather liked Chimayo and her family—despite their unusual affection. If nothing else, she'd never seen Koki so playful.

When Iwikon saw the berries, he mouthed his thanks to Byria and gave a quick glance between her and Koki to instruct her to pass on the message. Affirming she would with a nod and a smile, Byria watched him take another look at Koki and Chimayo, chuckle, roll his eyes, and walk behind another bamboo wall.

As for the two other women, they were hardly acting like women. They were fully absorbed in a giggling "fight" where each tried to tickle the other.

Or, rather, Chimayo was spectacularly failing in her zealous attempts to tickle Koki, while Koki danced around, taunting with successful little pinches under her friend's ribs, at the backs of her arms, in the crook of her neck—each time causing another tittering musical squeal and what Byria figured were profane insults.

After a few minutes of play, which had infected even Byria with quaking giggles, Chimayo darted behind Byria, grabbing either side of her dress as if she were a tree, and made a distinctive *pthththt* at Koki.

Byria jumped in surprise, yelped, and almost dropped the berries. Koki caught her hand and steadied her, giving Chimayo a particularly fierce look.

"Oh, you did bring them! Thank you very much!" Chimayo sang and twirled toward the house. "Come, come!"

Koki squeezed Byria's hand with a gentle and apologetic smile, but her eyes sparkled with joy.

With a little laugh, Byria nodded.

Koki smiled even more, planted a small kiss on Byria's knuckles, and led her after Chimayo into one of the small, connected huts.

It was far smaller than Koki and Mokin's—and with only one room. Byria had to hunch upon entering and, even inside, couldn't stand up fully. Chimayo and Koki fussed, helping her sit on a mat and taking the berries.

Byria found herself beside an old woman. Her face had more lines, and her hair, longer like Chimayo's, was entirely silver and white. A long cloth draped around her entire waist, covering her legs. The woman looked up from the berries in her lap and squinted with eyes that reflected almost white rather than greenish copper or silver.

Her gaze inspected Byria for several heavy minutes before the woman, with shaking fingers, picked up a berry and started eating it. As she chewed, she continued to stare at Byria. The woman was missing many teeth. Those that remained were stained orange, like the juice that burst from the yellow-skinned fruit.

She placed a second and third berry in her mouth, still staring.

Uncomfortable and done inspecting what she figured was the oldest person she'd ever seen, Byria cast her gaze to Koki and Chimayo, who were snuggling against each other, each eating a berry. Repressing a scowl, Byria took another berry from her pouch and decided to eat it. After all, she *was* sore and exhausted from all the walking, bending, and everything that day.

As she ate, the room grew clearer, and she noticed the old woman's pained breaths relaxing. With the fourth berry the old woman ate, her thick wrinkles moved to reveal a smile. Her voice, seeming too clear and too beautiful for the body that spoke it, declared great thanks for the berries and the visit.

Introductions were made again, and Byria tried not to be surprised to learn that this woman, Siheemo, was Chimayo's mother. She'd met Koki's mother, and the woman hadn't looked half this old! Byria managed to follow the small talk—Mokin was well; Iwikon was well; Koki's parents were well; Iji and Duan—perhaps brother and sister or sibling and spouse to Chimayo?—had been honored to sing at "New Rain" in a couple of moons; new birds had begun laying eggs.

During the talk, Koki put her hand on Byria's arm and shook her head as she was bringing several berries to her mouth. Feeling like she was floating on a cloud and not remembering how many she'd eaten, Byria giggled and shook her head back. She was enjoying the conversation.

Koki gripped her arm harder, stopping her from putting the berries in her mouth. "Enough," she hissed, eyes sharp.

Byria scowled but was distracted when Chimayo asked her mother to sing. The woman nodded and, without hesitation, began to create the most beautiful music Byria had ever heard. Enthralled with the sound coming from the haggard old woman, she hardly noticed Koki removing the berries from her hand.

Siheemo's voice rose beyond notes normally sung by children and deepened to those sung by the large men in theatre. All one voice. Tears came to Byria's eyes, and despite how few words she knew, she *understood* the song. Not as much as Koki had understood what Byria had sung, but Byria could feel love, triumph, fear, loss, and greater triumph by the end—and had quite soaked the fabric wrapped around her arms with tears and snot.

Koki was tearstained, herself. She wiped a cloth across her face with one hand while hugging Chimayo with the other. She met Byria's eye and looked away quickly, biting her lip with a shyness the hunter had never displayed before. "Did you understand?"

Byria paused. The effect of the berries was wearing off, leaving her feeling more exhausted and achier—and worse for the tears. "Not..." She patted her waist, not finding the pouch of berries. "Not like you did." She looked down and was surprised it wasn't there.

"I did understand a happy ending." Pressing her lips together and feeling an unexpected *need* to know where the berries had gone, she started looking around the room. The pouch leaned on Siheemo's lap. She considered snatching it back, but her mind suggested they'd collected the berries specifically for Siheemo. A part of Byria's mind schemed a way she might take the pouch back without being terribly rude.

Chimayo distracted her again—Byria felt odd being distracted so easily. "That was the story of how Koki saved my life after... stopped... friends." She pointed to Koki's spotted dress. "That was how she... saving me."

Koki, looking intently at the stains on her fingertips from the berries, mumbled something Byria couldn't make out, then made a dismissive gesture. Despite the lack of words she knew, Byria understood.

"Well, I suppose... *was* Mokin's fault." Chimayo smirked at the immediate glare from Koki. "In a way. He... said would never... you. Not if... last woman."

Byria was giggling uncontrollably again, despite the exhaustion and stiffness in her joints. She remembered Mokin saying he'd found Koki arrogant at one time. It wasn't a surprise observation to Byria, and she was enjoying how animated Chimayo spoke, even if she didn't understand her as well as she understood Koki or Mokin.

And she liked remembering things! It struck her as a great realization that she could think over this entire journey, over all her time in the village, and remember so much. She remembered when everything happened; she remembered sights, smells, facial expressions, and sounds. Perfectly! She laughed so hard her sides hurt.

The other women shared her mirth. In the little bit of conversation Byria picked up, she learned Chimayo had also been in love with Mokin. Seeing the other woman speak of him, Byria figured she likely still loved him.

Yet, she and Koki were incredibly close—enough that Byria had felt the same way as when she saw Mokin and Koki being passionate. The two had fought when Koki had pursued Mokin. Chimayo had sought to earn his affections by going into the deeper parts of the jungle, based on the songs of herbs she'd memorized, and finding him rare roots and leaves. Unfortunately, singing in the jungle attracted danger—and Chimayo had attracted a leopard.

Koki had felt horrible and knew Chimayo was no good in the jungles, so she'd gone after her to keep her safe. She'd seen the leopard stalking her friend and had attacked first.

Though she'd killed the cat, it had almost killed her. Chimayo had had to keep Koki alive and drag her back to the village. To illustrate the damage done by the leopard, Koki opened the side of her dress. A heat shimmer wavered over her skin, and Byria could see the twisting claw scars that curled all the way from her hip and buttock to just below her breast.

She wondered how many of the little people used glamour to hide scars or anything else ugly.

"And that's healed by both Mokin and his mother," Koki stated.

Mokin's mother. It was on the tip of her tongue to ask what had really happened to her when the room fell to an unsettling silence that sobered her giggles. A white pheasant-looking bird with a deep purple cap and matching splashes on its wings and tail strutted into the room.

Vicious sneers broke out on Koki and Chimayo's faces. A growl emanated from the old woman who, with all her wrinkles and stained teeth, looked monstrous.

"From the back," Chimayo said and walked to the flap of cloth that billowed in the wind.

Two voices wandered through it with the wind breaths, one of which chilled Byria's blood.

"The front." Chimayo moved to the door they entered. "Tatmi?"

The old woman gave an affirmative hum that turned into another song.

Koki pressed a finger to her lips and motioned for Byria to follow her.

Byria tried to stand, but found her legs had been replaced with rubber, or perhaps fabric. With a yelp, she fell into a tangle of limbs as the room spun, and another wave of giggles hit her.

Koki spat what Byria recognized as a definite and severe profanity. That made her giggle more, despite the rising chill in her chest indicating there was a good chance *he* would hear. Unable to control herself, she struggled almost violently to regain control over her body.

With another curse, Koki pounced upon her. One hand clamped over her mouth while two knuckles from the other jabbed into her neck. A sharp pain shivered down her body, and she couldn't move at all.

"I am sorry. Please trust me," she whispered in Byria's ear, pressing herself against her. "Don't move. Don't make a sound."

As Koki nestled against her, Byria calmed—despite being unable to move or speak. She thought upon her heart's fire, which felt like it was fizzling erratically. Another shimmer like a heat wave fell over Byria's eyes, but she didn't see any difference in the room.

Mokin's father strode into the small hut. Siheemo continued to hum, eyes closed, as if she didn't notice him. Chimayo bowed low and greeted him with a song of words Byria couldn't follow.

They spoke for a few moments, Chimayo all but flirting with the monster of a man... keeping her eyes lowered demurely, fluttering her lashes every so often. She gestured to her mother and apologized, mentioning the berries. "The pain is getting worse."

Mokin's father—it struck Byria that she didn't even know the man's name—placed his hand on Chimayo's arm. If Byria didn't know him to be a monster, it would almost look comforting. His eyes glanced to the floor before Siheemo.

He's going to see us! Why doesn't he see us? Byria's heart hammered, its fire growing choked and cold.

"Ssssss," she felt more than heard from Koki, who was rubbing her cheek against Byria's hair as if trying to soothe her. It worked. She took a few deep breaths and fed her heart's fire.

As he stepped closer, Byria willed more heat to her heart's fire. If he *did* try to hurt them, she would *not* make it easy.

He didn't see them. Somehow. Byria still felt a chill from his presence, but it wasn't the oppressing, stifling cold she remembered.

This close, she could get a good look at his face. She decided Mokin was fortunate to get his features from his mother; even as the sorcerer was being cordial to Chimayo, he looked beastly. His too-wide smile showed off his pointed teeth, and his cheeks looked... ragged. No, more than that. Like the heat shimmer of Koki and Mokin's illusions, his face wavered, and she thought she saw jagged black scars.

Chimayo changed her stance, drawing Byria's attention back to the conversation.

"Three mats? Guests?" Mokin's father asked.

Chimayo gave him a big smile. "*Had* guests. Koki and her daughter."

Daughter? The word struck Byria in the heart with a welcome, but shocking, warmth. *Does she really call me that when she speaks to others? Her closest friend?*

"... berries. But visiting Koki's mother... had to hurry." Chimayo's voice was filled with sweet innocence and a desire to be helpful.

A dark look flickered across the sorcerer's face. It deepened after the purple-crested, pheasant-looking bird pecked especially close to his feet.

Chimayo seemed to crumple. "Is something wrong? Have you heard ill news about Bles-Ama?"

He blinked and refocused on her, eyes narrowing as if he were searching for some deceit. After a moment of scrutiny, he relaxed and shook his head with a chuckle. "No, no. She and I... recent argument. I remembered it."

"Oh, I'm sorry to hear! I do hope you... heal from it."

His chuckle this time had no warmth, and his following words spoke of his birds being ready. With a proper dismissal greeting, he left out the billowing back cloth. With another sneer at the curtain once he'd left, Chimayo rubbed where he'd touched her as if she were scrubbing off filth and leaned just inside the doorway, watching.

Her mother, who was still singing, sent a very-aware and sharp look at Byria, as if reminding her to stay put and stay silent.

It felt like an hour, but finally, Chimayo gave a nod. Byria saw that heat shimmer wave again as Koki released her and hopped off. The woman made an uncomfortable face and wiggled her arms and legs down to her fingers and toes. After a few moments, Byria felt her limbs awaken with pins and needles, and she managed to sit back up.

"You still have the best glamour in the village." Chimayo smiled.

Koki embraced her with thanks, and then went to the old woman, embracing and kissing her, too. "Your mother made it work. That was too close." She glanced at the bird eating some seeds in front of Siheemo. "Good that your father remembered."

"Remembered?" Byria asked, deciding she could try to stand—well, hunch—once more.

Chimayo spat a word Byria didn't know out the back door, then explained. "Sometimes Mokin would stay with us when he needed... especially if Koki was around." She gave a little eye roll, but her face wasn't unkind. "If Da saw *him* coming, he'd send in a Pupu hen from the door he approached. Koki and Mokin would hurry out the other door."

Byria nodded. Koki gave Siheemo another two kisses on each of her cheeks and followed Chimayo out the front door. They embraced and kissed quickly, Koki hurrying Byria back into the jungle, taking her the long way around to her and Mokin's home.

When they were halfway back, at least according to Byria's landmark guesses, she touched Koki's shoulder. "You see? It's better I leave. I *am* causing problems."

"No. Nanana," Koki insisted. "You heard Chimayo. We did this long before you were even born."

"But Mokin has left. He's on his own. Safe with you. His father wants me and will hurt again to get me."

Koki took both of Byria's hands. "No. He. Will. Not. We will not let him." After squeezing her hands, the small woman turned away. "Now, come. Mokin *will* worry if we're too late."

Despite tears that wanted a reason to fall, or perhaps because of them, she blurted, "You call me your daughter to other people?"

The woman stopped, but didn't turn around. "Yes. Does that bother you?"

Byria felt a smile stretching at her mouth as she sniffled. "No. It fits."

She heard Koki sniffle, too. As she quickly wiped her eyes, the woman hardened her voice with command. "You and I both hate seeing Mokin worry. Come."

The slightest hitch in Koki's voice warmed Byria's heart more.

* * * * *

Chapter Eighteen
Another House Call, Another Emergency

"**K**oki! Mokin! Mokin! Koki!"

Byria sat up with a start. The high-pitched, musical voice sounded terrified. Then she heard a *bang* on the back door, rattling the beads. Chimayo. It was Chimayo's voice, and something was wrong.

Koki ran from the bedroom to the back door and returned, just about carrying Chimayo.

Tears ran down the other woman's face as she choked out, "Mother... my mother. Please."

"We'll come. Sit with Byria."

Not entirely awake, Byria caught the small, sobbing woman Koki handed to her. She let Chimayo cry against her, gingerly putting an arm around her heaving shoulders as Koki disappeared back into her and Mokin's room. She understood a few of the words the woman was gasping out. "Not wake up. Not breathing. Cold."

Dressed—fortunately—Mokin came out and squatted beside Chimayo, taking her hands and asking soothing questions. Byria was relieved he'd taken over, but watched Mokin work with Chimayo keenly.

He asked several questions over and over, nodding and massaging her hands as her breathing slowed, and her answers became longer, more coherent and detailed. He pulled her close and kissed her face several times, saying something Byria didn't understand but that sounded assuring. Chimayo nodded, though she still shook.

Mokin gave Byria a look she did understand, and she put her arm back around Chimayo's shoulders, letting her lean on her. With a grateful smile, Mokin squeezed Chimayo's hands once more and got up. "I need to get some things."

Chimayo didn't say anything at first, but snuggled against Byria. After a moment, she murmured, "Thank you." Then she tensed, pulling away. "Sorry? Thank you?"

"It's all right," Byria assured her, her heart going out to the woman. She squeezed Chimayo's shoulders, wanting to make the woman feel better. "It'll be all right."

"Thank you," she murmured again with a sniffle.

After a few moments, Koki and Mokin came back into the front room. Mokin carried a basket of supplies, while Koki collected Chimayo from Byria, mouthing thanks to Byria. She ushered Chimayo out the front door, still mostly carrying her.

Mokin lingered a moment, then nodded toward the patio. "Stay here. Stay safe."

Byria nodded and quickly folded her sleeping mats, heading outside as Mokin had requested. She helped herself to some broth, cracking in an egg as Mokin did for breakfast. Surveying the patio, she found very little to keep herself busy. Mokin had been cleaning and rearranging last night. The gardens were all recently weeded, and Byria couldn't tell if any of the hanging herbs were ready to be separated or processed.

Her mind wandered. What did she still need to learn before she left? Could she survive on her own? When would she even know if she could?

Pressing her lips together, she sat down at the far end of the patio, where a slender beam of sun had made its way through the tree canopy, and decided to sort through her memories further. How happy she'd felt yesterday, realizing she could remember almost every moment since she'd left the palace, and perhaps even since she'd freed the dragon.

If she took the time to remember all the recent things, perhaps it would remind her *how* to remember.

Byria started going backward, day by day, replaying each in her mind, and assembling every detail.

The sounds of voices, birds, and heavy rain.

The tastes of Mokin's broth—also an earlier memory!

The fruits she'd never seen before, and fresh roasted deerpig fat.

The smell of moisture, ripeness, and earth.

The many shades of green, how sun filtered through a leaf canopy, and the bright jewel tones of birds, flowers, and beads.

The touch that didn't cause pain but healed injuries, a kiss that expected nothing in return, and the feel of tears that were happy.

Her tears fell on the dirt just outside the patio area, where she'd been drawing again. She'd made another version of the map Patch had marked for Tain. As she looked at the lines, she felt it was a True rendering. Something she remembered.

She didn't have much time to consider her map. Through the house she heard a different voice calling, "Hunt-Koki? Heal-Mokin? Heal-Mokin? Hunt-Koki?"

Mokin had told her to stay in the patio—but surely he wouldn't want her to ignore a child calling. It sounded like Owi. Could Bebe have taken sick again? What could they do if Mokin was already with a patient who desperately needed him? She certainly hadn't learned enough to be much help!

Still, she unlatched the front door and crouched to look Owi in the face. "What's wrong?" she asked.

"Eh… nothing wrong." Ti looked nervous, glancing around the gardens. "Is Hunt-Koki or Heal-Mokin here?"

Nervous pricks itched all over Byria's skin as she also looked around, only mildly noting that Owi added their jobs to their names. None of the other villagers were near. That wasn't unusual, though. Mokin's home was out of the way.

"Something is wrong," Byria stated, feeling that was a True Thing as soon as it left her lips. Was someone following Owi? Had someone threatened ti? Something *felt* very wrong. "You can trust me. Come in, come in."

The child hesitated. "But, are they here?"

"No, but I can try to help as best I can."

Chewing on ti's bottom lip, Owi pulled a string of beads from a pouch. "Mom wanted Koki and Mokin to have this. For coming and healing her."

Byria almost didn't understand Owi's words. They were simple sentences that she understood, but the message didn't fit with how Owi was acting.

"Koki has a basket she keeps those in. Come in." She didn't know why, but she felt she had to protect Owi, and the only protection Byria could think of was to bring ti to the patio. "Come, come."

She found herself mimicking Koki's "you will listen to me" sounding "Koa, koa."

Owi seemed to flinch, but obeyed. Byria closed the door behind ti and latched the rope back around the frame. Resting a hand on Owi's shoulder, as seemed common for the jungle folk, Byria headed to the patio.

As the back door shut behind her, a chill all but froze her in place. Owi whimpered beside her.

"Owi-ki, you were supposed to give her the beads and leave."

Whimpering again, Owi edged closer to Byria, who stepped away. Owi had betrayed her? She looked between the child and the man standing just outside the stones of the patio.

Mokin's father.

He smiled at Byria. Even his smile was like Tain's—but with pointed teeth like a monster.

Owi glanced between them, eyes looking too large to be real. A stab of guilt pained Byria's heart, and she stepped back to comfort the child. Ti had had no choice. She glared at Mokin's father.

He smiled even more in return. "We can finally speak, Beelheah."

Byria cringed as he spoke her name. She edged closer to the door. Would he follow them into the house? Surely, Owi must know where Koki's parents lived—or where Chimayo lived, whichever was closer. They could run.

"Owi-ki, come here." There was a crack in the air when the sorcerer spoke.

With another frightened chirp, Owi moved toward him. Ti's little hand still clenched the beads the child had tried to give Byria.

"Na!" Byria said just as sharply, grabbing Owi's shoulder to keep ti near her. That was about all the bravery she could muster. Her knees were growing rubbery. She tried to pull Owi to the door.

Owi pulled from Byria's grip and began walking stiffly toward Mokin's father, each move jerked, like a theatre puppet. The child's wide eyes darted back and forth with wild fear.

"What are you doing to Owi?" This time, Byria's voice was more of a squeak. She pressed her hand to her chest, trying to warm her heart's fire. She wanted to go after Owi, but her legs weren't listening.

"I want to speak with you, but that would be hard if you should leave." He gave a knowing look at the door behind her.

Byria bit her lip until it hurt. She clenched her hands into fists and dug her nails into her palms. She had, in fact, kept the points she'd filed on the wall in the dungeon. They weren't as fearsome as Koki's, but they were *her* claws. It occurred to her that she understood Mokin's father quite well.

She clenched her fists harder, fighting to keep her breaths steady, to feed her heart's fire.

It was no help. She shivered as if covered in ice.

The sorcerer's eyes narrowed, and she felt a buffet of air or pressure. His lips curled into a sneer, and he grabbed Owi and drew the child close.

"Now, you step away from the door and come to me."

His voice sounded… off… and her ears hurt, like when Mokin's spell had worn off.

She lifted her head high. "Na," she said with the same tones as the jungle people. Her heart hammered. Without thinking, she took one more step toward the door. Surely she could find someone somewhere who'd help.

Baring his teeth more, the sorcerer dug his nails into Owi's shoulders. The child cried out in pain, clutching the beads ti still carried. Tears ran down Owi's cheeks. Ti shook even more than Byria.

"Come. Here," the sorcerer repeated.

This time Byria saw it—a heat shimmer like when Mokin or Koki removed the glamour that hid their scars. She felt the tiniest threads pulling her toward Mokin's father. With another step toward the door—she could touch it with her heel—she felt those little threads break.

"Na." Her voice still cracked, she was barely standing on rubber knees, and her breath came in shallow gasps, but she didn't move toward the man.

She could see him better now—or rather, his monstrous face. Cut into each of his cheeks were ragged, blackened scars. Between the shimmers of illusion, they stood out like the dark symbols he'd carved into his son.

The fierceness in his eyes grew, and he clenched his fingers into the child's shoulders. Thin lines of green trickled down ti's arms. "I'm sure Mokin and Koki have told you much about me." He didn't need more of a threat than that and Owi's sobbing and bleeding.

Byria whimpered.

"Come. To. Me."

She couldn't. She couldn't make herself go to him. Shaking her head, she sent an apology to Owi.

Her hand was on the edge of the door, but she wasn't going any further.

"Why?" she squeaked out the question.

He was too far away to beat her, as Tain would have for such an impertinent question. And his magic didn't seem to be affecting her outside the icy fear spreading through her body.

His answer was exactly what Tain would have said. "Because I said so."

Her knees finally buckled, and she slid down the side of the hut, ignoring—no, appreciating—the pain of grass and wood splinters digging into her back.

They gave her clarity. The sorcerer hadn't come onto the patio stones. He likely couldn't. Mokin must have some protection spell—magepriests did that to the palace. That's why he needed her to come to him.

And if she wouldn't come to him, and his magic couldn't make her come to him…

He began to drag his nail across Owi's chest and shoulder, drawing more streams of green blood.

"Beelheah!" the child whimpered.

Could she run and pull Owi from the sorcerer? No, her legs wouldn't even move. She'd let him hurt the child—what kind of horrible person was she to let someone be punished for her?

I'm sorry, Owi. I'm so sorry! Byria wrapped her arms around her knees, and wherever she found flesh, she gouged herself until she felt the stickiness of blood. She had to pay attention. She deserved this. She must remember this.

As if he were pulling the thoughts from her mind, the sorcerer spoke, "You would let a child suffer for you? You're hurting ti quite a bit. Do you *want* me to hurt Owi?"

Byria managed to shake her head just a little. She couldn't stop this.

"You can make it stop if you just come out here and speak with me."

Byria squeezed her eyes shut, then forced them back open to look at Owi.

"This is your fault—"

No sound introduced the spear that landed but a breath from the sorcerer's body.

Koki? Byria gasped in hope.

"I would think—" it was another man's voice, deep and slow as if he wanted to ensure Byria understood "—it's the fault of the person whose hands are *on* the child."

"Pakin." At least, that was what the bestial growl from the sorcerer sounded like to Byria. "You...?" He threw Owi to the ground and reached for the spear, then recoiled.

"*You?*" The other man strolled over—as if he had no care in the world—and looked down at the sorcerer. He was the tallest, most muscular villager Byria had seen. He nodded his head in the direction of the covered patio and hut. Owi scrambled like a crab toward the fire. Smears of green colored the rocks as ti moved.

The sorcerer didn't back down. He spoke lowly, still growling. Byria couldn't make out his words.

The other man continued to appear unflapped. He casually reached for his spear, plucked it from the ground, and laid it over his shoulder. When he spoke, it was loud and slow enough for Byria to follow. "As I understand, you're not welcome at this home. In these gardens, even."

The sorcerer sniffed in his direction. "The cuts on the child are nothing for my son to fix, and the child is *not* going to say anything to ti's parents." He fixed Owi with a glare. The child flinched and nodded. Byria felt another knife in her heart.

The spear man must have felt the same. His face revealed a fury every bit as fearsome as the sorcerer's. "The child is free to speak to whomever! That's not your choice."

Turning his back to the spearman, the sorcerer moved with the swagger of a victor in battle. "Na. It *is* my choice."

Clenching his fist and gripping his spear so hard it trembled on his shoulder, the other man stood tall and watched Mokin's father leave.

As with the other encounters, the growing distance of the sorcerer came as a physical relief to Byria, as if her lungs opened up and her heart was freed from a clenched grip.

The spearman softened his stance and came over. Putting down his weapon, he knelt beside Owi, though he kept casting glances at Byria. She gave the slightest gesture with her chin that he ought to see to the child first. Giving her a nod, he spoke softly to Owi.

Byria watched as the child stopped shaking and allowed the man to clean ti's wounds. He brushed tears away from Owi's eyes with his fingers and thumb, kissing the top of ti's head a few times. He made faces until a tiny smile and giggle escaped Owi's pale lips.

His movements and mannerisms were familiar to Byria. Not like Mokin, but just as comforting. The man had confidence and revealed a smile both mischievous and kind as he dressed Owi's cuts.

Bringing over a mat, he bade the child to lie down. Owi grew nervous, mentioning ti's mother and "worry." They spoke a little more, Owi growing more agitated before settling down.

Kissing Owi's brow once more, the man approached Byria.

She couldn't stop herself from cringing. He dropped to a knee several feet from her.

"Beelheah?" he asked softly.

She nodded slowly, wishing she could relax her arms, but unable to stop clutching her knees to her chest—or digging her nails into her own flesh.

"Pakin." He touched his chest and bowed his head. "Koki's father."

"Oh," she managed. That explained the familiarity. She didn't know what else to say.

"Ama's gone to get Koki and Mokin. Koki asked us to watch you, protect while they… with Siheemo." With a frown, he swallowed. "I'm sorry. I should have visited sooner."

Byria shook her head, trying to remember and mumble some word of forgiveness.

"Cht," he said. "And you. He spoke only lies. It was *his* choice to disrespect his son's wishes, *his* choice to hurt Owi so he might hurt you. Not you. Not you."

Byria made a noncommittal noise. What if she'd listened to Mokin earlier and hadn't answered the door? What if she'd held onto Owi tighter, keeping the child near her? What if she'd gone to—she didn't even know the sorcerer's name—to him when he'd asked?

"Look at me, Beelheah." Pakin edged closer, making Byria start again, but getting her to look at him. "Not. Your. Fault."

She looked away again, blinking at tears. *But what if—?*

"Beelheah." Pakin's voice was firmer now.

"But…" Byria didn't have words in any language to fit how she felt, other than that it *was* her fault. It was her fault for being in the village, for staying with Mokin, for somehow getting the sorcerer's attention, and perhaps a million more reasons.

"Na. Look at me. Look at me again." He inched closer once more. While Byria still cringed, it brought her gaze to him. "He told Mokin that, too, you know. Did Mokin tell you?"

With a sniffle, Byria shook her head.

Pakin sighed. "Mokin shares little, but I believe he'd want you to know, so you wouldn't feel as he did—still does. When Lakan would hurt Choli—Mokin's mother—he told Mokin it was his fault. If he would only study magic, do as he was told, his mother wouldn't be hurt so. Do you think it was Mokin's fault his mother was hurt?"

Byria shook her head. *No. No, it wasn't.* Lakan—now she had a name for the monster—was the cruel beast. She *knew* this. She comprehended what Pakin was saying, but guilt still weighed upon her heart. She nodded to ease Pakin's concern.

"You're hurt," he stated. "What did he do to you? How—?"

Byria shook her head harder. "Will you please bring me things for washing and healing balm?"

Pakin raised his eyebrows, as if expecting her to change her answer. When she didn't, he got the washing cloths and balm.

When he didn't turn away, Byria tensed more. "Would you check on Owi?" How could she explain that she didn't like anyone looking upon her skin, not even a healer or the one who called her daughter? "Please?"

"You're hurt," he repeated.

She nodded. "Mokin has taught me to heal. Please?" She gestured toward Owi, who appeared to have fallen asleep.

Raising his brows once again, Pakin turned away and attended to Owi. Byria quickly cleaned and balmed the cuts she'd made upon herself, then adjusted her dress and arm and leg wrappings to hide the marks. In doing so, she managed to unclench herself and stand. Her back still burned from slivers, but she could ask Koki to help with those.

When she came over to the fire to deposit the cloths in the cleaning pot, Pakin looked up at her and, with the end of his spear, picked up the beads Owi had been carrying. He lay them on the stones of the patio, scooped coals from the fire with the broad end of the spear, and poured them on top. The strings of beads hissed and sparked as they burned. Byria cringed back toward the hut, and Owi winced in ti's sleep.

Lakan meant for me to take those beads from Owi, Byria thought. As they burned, they sent a similar chill over her as Lakan's presence created.

Pakin frowned. "Perhaps we should send Owi home. I don't know how Koki or Mokin will react when they see ti's cuts."

Byria paused, thinking, then shook her head. "They'll be more upset by not knowing or seeing. They'll think worse."

Pakin nodded. "True. They would."

Byria got two more mats and offered one to Pakin to sit upon, and then spooned broth into two clay bowls. He'd saved her and Owi; the least she could do was be hospitable. Still, she set up her mat away from him.

He thanked her for the broth, and if he noticed how far away she sat, he said nothing of it.

After a strained silence, Byria thought she might broach a question. "Pakin?"

"What?"

"What happened Mokin's mother?"

Pakin's face grew dark. After a long, even more uncomfortable silence, he said, "It's not for me to speak of."

Byria pressed her lips together. Before she could say more, Pakin looked toward the hut. Byria followed his gaze and picked up familiar voices. Tears welled up her throat and into her eyes, surprising her with how relieved she felt upon Koki and Mokin's approach. Likely Ama's, too.

Taking a deep breath, she reached out and brushed Pakin's arm. He looked at her in surprise. "Lakan is a monster. Why is he a leader? What can he do?"

Pakin blinked and nodded slowly, then he sighed.

Byria heard the voices coming through the front gardens. "Pakin?" she hissed.

"It's complicated, Beelheah."

She couldn't ask the most important question before Mokin, Koki, and Ama burst through to the patio. Koki threw her arms around Byria, who winced before letting herself relax into the embrace.

She had no good answers to their question of "Are you all right?"

As Pakin moved away, pulling his own wife into a deep kiss and hug, Byria realized she didn't have the right words to ask him what she needed to know. Besides, she had her answer.

She needed to leave the village. Now.

* * * * *

Chapter Nineteen
Unforgiveable Acts

When Owi had awoken to Mokin's care, ti had grown anxious again. Koki had turned her attention to ti, and Byria gently pushed her in their direction. With a nod of thanks, the hunter woman joined her husband comforting the child.

Pakin and Ama spoke heatedly off to the side.

Byria hesitated, her heart still hammering from the incident with Lakan, what he'd done to Owi, what he would've done to her. Koki and Mokin would try to make her stay, and she couldn't. She needed to leave now. It was better to go without say goodbye. That would just make things more difficult.

Mokin would be upset his father had been there, that he'd come after her. If she were gone, they could move past that. Perhaps they'd realize the trouble she'd brought to them, and Koki wouldn't come tracking her—she wasn't entirely sure how to hide her tracks. Certainly not from an accomplished hunter.

But she was fairly certain she'd learned enough to survive on her own. Mokin had said she learned well, and Koki had been pleased with her responses to all her testing questions. She needed to follow where her heart pulled her, and she'd find where she needed to go.

If only it didn't feel like all it wanted was to beat out of her chest.

As she considered all this, as the two couples seemed preoccupied, Byria moved on legs with their own mind into the main room of the hut. Her arms twined around her bag, wrapping it to her body to secure it. Then her feet, on tiptoes, though she doubted sound made any difference at this point, took her out of the hut and onto the patio.

Her eyes, seeing things sharper than she expected, scanned the area before her mind realized that was the proper thing to do.

Owi had left, and Mokin and Koki argued even louder. Mokin had something in his hand that made Byria's stomach twist in fear, though she couldn't quite make out what it was. His face was a deep green and furious, and his whole body looked ready to attack.

Koki was in front of him, looking like she was trying to stop him from doing something. Though she heard their words, her mind wasn't ready to decipher their language through the thick emotion.

Koki's parents were farther away, on the other side of the gardens, looking less angry, but no less intense. They were all focused on each other and not her.

Moving at an even pace, one that wouldn't draw attention to herself, Byria headed toward the jungle beyond Mokin's garden. Her head said she was doing something dangerous—what if Mokin's father waited? What if she didn't know enough to survive? What if a leopard attacked her like it had Chimayo, and Koki wasn't there to save her?

Battling even more strongly than her mind's doubts, something else drove her to run. A feeling like a trapped animal in her chest, the pounding in her ears, the familiar terror that screamed in her blood that she had a way to put as much distance between herself and Lakan as possible, so she *must* do just that.

Once she passed the gardens and entered the thicker trees, she found she couldn't hear the others. Byria told herself it didn't matter; she ought to get used to being alone until she found the dragon. Even as her mind weighed such thoughts, she stopped and yelped before her eyes and mind connected why.

Pakin stood in front of her, leaning casually on his spear, an amused smile on his face.

Byria let out a defeated whimper once she recognized him, and surprisingly, felt relieved.

"Where are you going?" he asked, voice as easygoing as his posture. The tiniest glitter in his copper-green eyes, though, reminded Byria he was an expert hunter. She wouldn't get by him if he didn't want her to.

"Away," she mumbled, needing to look away from his piercing gaze and unsure if she should mention the dragon.

She heard him sigh. "We won't let that happen again, Beelheah. I promise. You will be safe."

Her eyes snapped to him with a wave of unexpected anger. "You don't know that!"

His blink was the only thing that showed the small man's surprise.

Before he could respond, she continued, "He'll come for Mokin and Koki to get to me. He will hurt them. He'll hurt whoever he needs to. You cannot stop that."

The fire in her heart burned with a fury that lapped over the fear and made the village language fall more easily from her tongue.

After a short pause, Pakin responded, "And how do *you* know that?"

"Because he's still a leader in the village. Because no one did anything to him for what he did to Mokin and his mother. And no one will do anything for what he did to Owi."

"Your words are mostly true. He is still leader. Owi will say nothing, so no one will act against him, because no accusation will be made. But he didn't go entirely unpunished for his other crimes."

Byria frowned, taking a deep breath as her anger and fear evened out. She was about to learn an Important Thing, so she paid close attention.

"Right now, my daughter argues with the strongest healer in the village—regardless of magic—our only Motherhealer, so that he doesn't kill his own father."

He took a deep breath and Byria recognized the "trying to find the right words" look on his face that, despite his similarity to Koki, reminded her more of Mokin.

"To betray—you know that word in our tongue? Betray?"

Byria nodded. She didn't remember from which conversation she'd learned it, but she understood what he was saying.

"To betray one's family is to choose to leave the village forever. To say you'll never return. To kill another person is to ask the village to kill you. To kill you and destroy your body, that you may never return to our ancestors and loved ones who have left us."

Byria weighed his words carefully, and then scowled. "Then why was his father not killed by the village, and his body destroyed?" While no one had yet told her what had truly happened to Mokin's mother, she had a strong suspicion that Pakin's answer would confirm or deny.

He narrowed his eyes, understanding what she asked—and what more she asked—with her question. "Lakan leads the council. He's one of the last of our people to remember dragon attacks, attacks from giants, and his magic hides us so we need not train more people to fight beyond hunting. Mokin is his son and doesn't follow the path of magic. There's no one to replace Lakan. Choli said nothing and stood beside Lakan until she was gone. There are none besides Mokin who'd say Lakan betrayed family. Mokin has never said Lakan has killed family, but if he did, it would be his words against Lakan's. And once a good person has cooled from fury, it's not easy to condemn another to death."

Byria frowned. Perhaps she wasn't a good person, but she would easily condemn both Lakan and Tain to death if she could. It would keep them from hurting anyone else.

Pakin continued, "I have no doubt in this moment, if Koki wasn't with Mokin, our village would be without both magic protector and Motherhealer by sundown."

The thought of Mokin killed by the people of the village, of his body defiled in some way to prevent a trip to the afterlife... That thought made her stomach churn, and she pressed her hands to it. But Pakin hadn't told her enough.

"You said Lakan was punished. *How* was he punished?" Byria pressed, though she doubted whatever Pakin said would satisfy her. Lakan still breathed and was *still* hurting people.

The thin smile on Pakin's face held no mirth. "You saw his face." He gave her a weighty look and a nod.

But when he didn't elaborate further, Byria pressed, "What does that mean?"

Pakin appeared confused a moment, but then he seemed to remember that Byria knew only so much about the village culture. He spoke slowly and chose his words carefully. "You must know what it is to be souljoined?"

Byria nodded.

"You spend all your life together. Then you walk together to the Ancestor Grove. All together."

Byria nodded once more.

With a sigh—clearly less used to explaining things to giants or others—he continued, "If something happens to one of a souljoined, the other or others mark themselves for mourning. The cuts become scars, always there, until they walk to the ancestor trees to join again, all scars healed."

Byria pursed her lips, taking in the information—particularly the oddness of there potentially being more than two in a souljoin union—but she found herself able to piece together what Pakin said with words and without words. "His face had that ink like Mokin's scars…"

Pakin nodded again. The two were silent for a moment. Then the man moved toward her—not quickly or aggressively—and reached for her arm.

Byria jumped away, shaking her head. "More reason for me to go. Everything you said."

Pakin frowned. "How so?"

"Everything I said before. Lakan *is* still in power. He *will* hurt Mokin or Koki—or do something that'll make them get hurt. Or hurt people they care about."

Like Siheemo, Byria thought. The idea had been on her mind. Lakan had clearly planned his arrival. Had he purposely done something to Chimayo's mother to get both Koki and Mokin to leave?

"I *must* go."

Pakin folded his arms and gave her a firm look that, at one time, might have made a child-Koki listen to him. She did find herself backing away and strongly considering turning around, but she also found a surprise streak of indignance.

After a sigh, he leaned his spear in the crook of his arm and counted on his fingers. "If you leave here, now, I must follow you, or Koki will never forgive me. And I'd leave a trail for her to follow. And your concern: Koki and Mokin *will* be hurt. It will hurt them if you sneak away. If you leave now. You don't want them hurt, so don't be what hurts them."

Unable to keep herself from scowling, Byria found no other argument. Her heart was hammering less after speaking to Pakin; she was thinking more clearly. He'd seen her reasoning, so Koki and Mokin should, too.

She'd say her goodbyes properly, then.

* * * * *

Chapter Twenty
Knife and Broth

As she followed Pakin back to the patio, she noticed Koki's mother staring with her arms folded at Mokin, who had a defiant look on his face and his hand over what looked like a sheathed knife on his hip. It wasn't one of the knives with which he prepared herbs.

Koki looked between them with concern, as if she were ready to break up a fight.

The fire in Mokin's eyes hadn't cooled. There was an excellent chance he might kill his father. Her own fire burned with him, but such an action wasn't worth the cost.

If I had the chance, could I kill Tain? Or Lakan? Myself?

Studying her hands, she decided such a chance should likely never happen. She'd been a coward today, and Owi had suffered for her cowardice. Even if she wasn't a coward, she hadn't any training. There was no way she could stand up to—well, not even a child Owi's size.

A soft whistle from Pakin startled her. The three looked at them.

"Beelheah!" Koki ran to her, taking her hands. A glimmer of tears moistened her lashes.

The other two forgot their fight for the moment.

Mokin approached just behind Koki. "I'm so sorry! I'm sorry." The anger in his face melted into a wash of guilty tears.

She crouched, pulling one hand from Koki and reaching out to Mokin. Her own tears stole her voice, but she squeezed his hand tightly, hoping he understood the emotions she could only partly put together in her own head. Her heart beat hard and fast.

After a moment, she stood, pulled her hands from both, and hugged herself. She found her voice long enough to choke out, "I leave tonight."

Despite what felt like horrible pronunciation of their language, Koki and Mokin both froze and stared. They shook their heads hard.

"You're not ready to travel," he said.

"There's still much for you to learn," added Koki.

"We won't let him hurt you," declared Pakin.

There were more arguments Byria only partly understood as their voices grew louder. She hugged herself tighter and took a step away, shaking her head hard.

They stopped.

After a tense moment of silence, Koki snapped her gaze to the side of Byria and gave a little headshake, lips pressed tightly together.

Following the look, Byria saw Koki's mother edging closer to Mokin with narrow eyes. The woman was reaching toward Mokin, returning a *look* to both Koki and Mokin.

Byria didn't quite comprehend the following conversation of more *looks* as well as a few hissed words that didn't exactly sound like the regular language of the villagers.

It ended with Mokin stepping away from Koki's mother, but closer to Koki, and Pakin clearing his throat and stating that he and Ama had "things to do."

Koki and Mokin seemed to agree. Both Koki's parents took her hand and wished her well, Ama giving her another blessing. Tension thickened the air enough for Byria to taste it with each heavy breath.

Once Ama and Pakin left the yard, Byria turned her attention back to her hosts—no, they were more than that. She turned her attention to her adoptive parents.

Byria's eyes were drawn to the knife Mokin still kept his hand over.

Pointing, she blurted out, "What? That knife?"

Koki frowned deeply, but Mokin put a hand on her arm. Closing his eyes in thought, he took a deep breath and spoke slowly. "I took it from my father when he used it on my mother."

His expression said what he probably didn't have words for, and Ama's earlier reaction spoke even more. What he said was enough of an answer.

Byria nodded, feeling strangely more relaxed after his confession.

With a nod to the fire, she took three bowls and filled them with Mokin's herbed broth. There was much to discuss, and she'd learned well that whatever Mokin kept simmering over his fire healed more than just the body.

* * * * *

Chapter Twenty-One
The Truest Things

Byria had stayed firm in her decision that it was time to leave, but had compromised from "now" to "with dawn."

While it was clear her decision pained both Koki and Mokin, they accepted and, while tending to the splinters on her back, worked on making the best plan for her.

They put together traveling rations, and were as stubborn about her taking *all* of them as she was about leaving. She let them win that battle.

Koki packed her more cloth and women's supplies—who knew what she might or might not find once she left the jungle? Mokin put together herbs in cloth wraps and sealed clay jars, going over what each did no less than three times.

Freeing a variety of colored beads from various strands, he coded each parcel with a beaded string, insisting Byria repeat his codes back to him.

Before the sun started to set, Byria remembered the map she'd drawn and took them over to it. Mokin paused and frowned upon seeing the scuffed over lines.

"My father see this?" he asked in a tight voice. The drawing was just outside the patio, where Lakan had stood.

Byria froze a moment, rubbing her arms and the scars she'd created as she replayed the interaction in her head. "Didn't act like he did."

He gave a quick nod and said nothing more on the topic. Koki was already retracing lines and changing things on the map. Mokin then added to it. The two argued back and forth about little details.

Byria noticed they still leaned very close to one another, brushing each other frequently. Sitting on her heels, she found herself blinking back tears at their little affections, even as she was entranced as the map seemed to grow more and more... *True.*

Mountains bordered the jungle moving northward from the west until they came to the ocean. Further west, the mountains were a border between the jungle and some sort of wasteland Koki and Mokin agreed Byria shouldn't go to and had gouged with angry X marks and zigzags. The other thing they seemed to agree on was that dragons lived in mountains, which was why the people always stayed under the trees.

Even as they made the map, one or the other would turn and ask her to reconsider.

"You do know every dragon in every story eats people—giant people, too."

"He will not eat me."

"How do you know he did not go to...?"

Byria made out that they were referencing another world, which she figured was like going to the demon realm. "I know he's where I can find him."

"You know you don't have to leave. We *can* keep you safe."

"It's not just that. I *must* leave. I must find the dragon." With a sigh, Byria pressed both hands to her heart to show she knew this thing as a Truth.

With sad sighs, Koki and Mokin began a new argument, each pointing to a different place in the mountains, one area closer to the wasteland, another closer to the ocean. Both cited songs and stories, debating which was more true and more recent, as proof for their suggested location for where a dragon might be.

An idea came to Byria, and she went over to her satchel, which she'd left to the side. "We can try my magic."

Koki scowled, but Mokin had an expression of both apprehension and curiosity.

Pulling out her pyut-gem, though keeping the eyeball hidden, she placed the small stone with the glimmering triangle center upon where the drawn map depicted the village.

For a few moments, the stone did nothing, but as the sun set, it glowed brighter. Then it began to spin, slowly at first.

It then darted to the area in the mountains Mokin had indicated—the one closer to the wasteland. It spun, shooting up a tiny cyclone of hot dust, then stopped. The tiny triangle within continued to glow.

Koki's face was frozen in neither a smile nor a frown. Mokin took a deep breath and blew it out through pursed lips.

"I *need* to go there." Byria picked up the stone, but pressed her index finger to the spot.

Mokin nodded before Koki, giving one more deep sigh as he sat back.

Biting her lip, Byria stared at Koki, who remained staring at the indentation in the dirt. Her lips trembled just a little.

Then with a start, she looked away, blinking her eyes. With a soft sigh, she pointed to an area where the jungle met the mountains. "I can bring you here. That's all I can travel."

"That's enough. Thank you. For everything." Byria reached for Koki's hand, but for the first time, it was the small woman who pulled away.

"We sleep. It won't be easy travel." She spoke shortly and headed into the hut.

Tasting blood as she bit her lip again, Byria watched her leave. A brush against her hand made her jump.

Mokin apologized softly, holding out his hands to her with a serious look in his eyes.

She knelt facing him and took his hands. Warmth passed between them, and the dusky light around them shimmered. Familiar clarity rang in her ears with his words.

"Don't be hurt. She wouldn't have you see her pain. She loves you. We both love you."

Byria hiccoughed over a sniffle.

"She'll wake you before I wake. Especially after using this magic, adding protection to our home. I want you to know, you can always return, and I won't let my father hurt you."

Byria opened her mouth, but didn't get to speak.

His eyes hardened. "I've needed to… deal… with this for a long time. If you find trouble, anything…"

Byria let him move both of her hands into one of his. Then he lifted the wooden disk that hung from his belt, his mark as a Motherhealer. But, she realized, it was also unique to him.

"Think on my spirit symbol. Call on me. I know you know how."

Furrowing her brows, Byria shook her head.

He reached toward her arm wrappings. When she nodded permission for him to unwrap them a little, he revealed the glyph she'd carved to remember how to travel through the black glass as Patch had instructed. "Always. You can always return."

She bit her lip. His words felt True, but how? *I'll learn.* That also rang True.

Catching her eye again, he went to take both her hands. When she allowed it, he squeezed them, closed his eyes, and swallowed hard. Tears dripped from his eyes. "We will always love you."

Uncontrolled and unexpectedly beautiful emotion overcame her. She tugged Mokin's hands, and they embraced. He didn't feel that much smaller than she when he hugged her back or cradled her head on his shoulder to cry upon.

"I love you and Koki." It was the first time she could remember saying such words out loud.

* * * * *

Chapter Twenty-Two
Departure in Darkness

Barely any light from dawn lit up the inside of the hut when a gentle touch on her shoulder woke Byria. She gasped, hands in fists. She hadn't been dreaming—not that she remembered—though she'd replayed the memory of freeing the dragon before she'd fallen asleep.

"It's me," Koki said, pulling back. Her copper-green eyes were wide.

Byria nodded and wiped her nose on the cleaned servant's clothes she'd changed into. She'd save the clothes Koki had made her as extras. The servant's clothes covered her more, made her remember more, and were more comfortable—more like *Byria*.

"Are you sure you still wish to leave?" Koki's lips trembled a little, but she had a look on her face that said she refused to cry. The swelling around her eyes and the deepened lines said she'd already been crying.

Byria nodded and started folding all the skins and putting them to the side. Koki helped, though she kept her eyes averted. Once she'd tidied the room, Byria tied on a belt Mokin had given her, upon which hung more pouches of food and skins of water. She slung her full courier's satchel over her shoulder.

Koki pursed her lips in thought, then motioned for Byria to follow her outside. On the patio, Koki put on her own gear: two different belts with pouches and knives, the rolled piece of bark sledge that Byria knew she used to carry heavier game, and her spear.

She gestured for Byria to turn around and squat, then adjusted her bag strap around her shoulders and neck, muttering something about balance and how some idiot—further described with more colorful words—must have designed the bag. They certainly hadn't made it for long travel or not-sore backs.

When Koki stepped away with a nod, Byria stood, and the bag, now hanging at her back, seemed to weigh less. She smiled and thanked her friend.

With another nod and half smile, Koki gestured for Byria to follow again. She started to do so, then paused, looking over her shoulder to the dark hut beyond a smoldering fire bed. "Is Mokin all right? Will his father...?"

"My parents will visit him today. I woke early... and asked them so. He'll be unbothered."

Byria smiled and let out a sigh.

"Here." Koki threw a small bag of berries and nuts at her, which she caught with little flailing. "Eat this slowly as we walk. Drink after." Lifting her chin and one eyebrow, Koki further explained, "Lessons in traveling for many days start now."

"Thank you," Byria said, also silently thanking her friend for returning to the hunter-teacher role. She wasn't sure her heart's fire, which burned even hotter as they moved, could handle it if Koki was holding back tears the whole time they headed to the mountains.

* * * * *

Chapter Twenty-Three
Finding Patterns

Teacher Koki stayed with Byria for most of the travel, quizzing her on her previously taught lessons on herbs, plants, fruits, nuts, and roots. She even showed her how to set traps.

She flatly refused to let Byria touch the dried food they'd packed in her bag. "You may need that in the mountains."

Koki was equally tough about water, showing her how to find and gather fresh water. Byria lost count of how many times Koki reminded her how dry she'd found Byria not even half a moon's phase ago. Being too dry kept wounds from healing, and made muscles hurt more and tire faster.

However, whether it was the effectiveness of Koki's teaching, or the fact that Mokin had said more than once that he found Byria learned things very well, Byria began to notice they were taking a circuitous route from what they'd mapped out.

"Koki?" She stopped walking. "We've been this way before."

"Why do you say that?"

With that question, Byria knew this was purposeful and frowned angrily. Why would the woman deceive her? She pointed out the trees, the hard-to-find bush that grew berries just after the rainy season, and even some marks she was certain were from their camp three days ago.

Koki turned and gave Byria a half smile, blinking her eyes a few times. "You noticed." She took a deep breath and lifted her chin—as if she felt the need to be defiant or pull herself together. "I wanted to know you were prepared when I left you. It took you some time…"

Byria pressed her lips together and stared hard at Koki for a moment before saying, "You also hope more time may change my mind?"

Koki shrugged with nonchalance. "If you changed your mind, I wouldn't argue."

Frowning again, Byria asked, "We'll go to mountains now? I passed your test."

"Yes. Come." Koki turned away, adjusted her route through the trees, and walked at a much faster pace than before.

It tired Byria to keep up, but she didn't complain.

* * * * *

Chapter Twenty-Four
Byria's Blood

Byria awoke earlier than usual, rubbing just below her stomach as grinding pains pulled her knees to her chest, and she felt a stickiness between her legs. She hissed out a few curses and remembered seeing the moons close to their half-full points. It was, in fact, time for her woman's blood.

After taking a few deep breaths, sending her heart's fire to tame the ragged cramps, she looked around. It was still pre-dawn dark, and she didn't see Koki anywhere.

With a grumble, she pulled off the servant's trousers, annoyed that she would have to clean them and wear her other clothes, annoyed she was moving so slowly, and annoyed to have to search for the moss Koki had shown her. This would slow them down even more!

As she shuffled toward the shallow stream that twisted through many crooked roots, she chided herself for being so impatient. She had no deadline to find the dragon, and she truly wasn't eager to say goodbye to Koki.

That someone cared for her so—no, *loved* her so—wasn't something anyone *should* want to run away from.

But here she was. Running away. No, running *to*. Running to the dragon. The clawing ache within her screwed her mouth to a scowl.

When she arrived near the water, she stopped, seeing Koki kneeling, head lowered. She was placing a broad, heart-shaped leaf upon the fast-moving current. Upon the leaf were several feathers and a sticky ball of something black, burning and smoking. Incense.

Farther down the stream, another leaf-boat with a glowing ember and scented smoke twirled away upon its own journey.

Koki made several gestures with her hands, kissing them and offering them to the air, to the water. She murmured in words too soft for Byria to understand.

After a final bow when her face touched the earth upon the water's edge, she spoke so Byria could hear. "That last was good wishes for you. That one—" she pointed to the other, further downstream "—for Mokin, as I cannot be with him now, and I know things aren't easy for him."

Byria pressed her lips together, a hollow ache in her heart.

Koki sniffed and turned quickly, eyes widening with compassion when she saw the stains on Byria's clothes. "Do you need help?"

"No. I can wash. I can change clothes," she muttered, shaking the fresh clothes in her hands.

Koki simply nodded. "I'll make the appropriate drink."

As the woman left, Byria chided herself for her lack of manners and called, "Thank you," after Koki.

After cleaning and changing, Byria returned to the camp, eager for anything to ease the pain throbbing waves all over her body, especially behind her eyes and in her ears. She gulped down the bowl Koki offered, though it scalded her lips and throat.

"Drink quickly, but not *that* quickly!" Koki said.

Byria managed to hold her tongue and only scowl in the woman's direction, smacking her lips at the bitter herbs and honey without Mokin's ever-simmering broth to flavor it.

Once the clenching pain receded, Byria stood and began packing up the camp.

"You still want to travel?"

"Yes. I'll be fine."

Koki raised her brows, but didn't argue. They travelled for less than half a day, covering less than a quarter-day's distance, when Byria finally groaned for a rest. Koki adjusted Byria's dress as she sat on stone and then put an arm around her.

"This not normal. My blood not normal this bad." Even trying to make her mouth form simple sentences in Koki's language proved to be more difficult. "Not like yo—" Byria tried to turn her last word into a cough as she cursed herself for such insensitive words.

You're not in a palace with many women taking care of everything you want, princess, teased a cruel voice in her head. *You have only primitive herbs—no wine, no soft silks and linens…*

I. Am. Free! shouted another voice in her head, one who very much didn't want to be called princess again.

This is the cost of being "free."

Then I shall bear it! Now be silent!

"Byria?" Koki's voice was soft, gentle, and concerned.

Hoping she hadn't actually been speaking her argument aloud, Byria asked, "Yes?"

"It's all right to rest. I promise I'm taking you the most direct route to where your stone said to go."

With a deep sigh, Byria nodded.

"It's only two or three more days until the… edge."

"Edge?"

"Trees and mountains?"

Byria gasped, not realizing they'd gotten so close. "Only two or three days?"

Koki nodded, studying Byria's face so intently, the former princess needed to look away. How long had they been traveling? While she sensed the question in the air, she appreciated Koki not asking, again, if she wanted to return to the village.

"Sit here," the woman said.

Byria didn't have the desire to argue. She watched Koki circle around them, then nod in approval. She began to set up a fire.

"We are camping?"

Koki nodded. "You should rest, and your blood will attract predators. I can fight them better if we're not moving."

Everything the small woman said made sense, but Byria found herself scowling again, and for no good reason, as the thought of only having two or three more days of Koki's company chilled her stomach.

"Should I climb a tree?" Byria asked, grimacing at the thought of predators. "Avoid predators?"

Koki looked up and gave Byria a look of incredulity. "Leopards, big spotted cats—" she pulled on her spotted tunic to ensure her clarity "—climb trees. *Like* trees. Safer here, near me."

With that, she drew her spear, spun it, then put it back in its holder on her back—all in less than a second's time.

Byria couldn't argue with that logic, so she glanced around nervously and slouched on the rock. After some time, Koki brought her another bowl of broth and bade her to change her absorbents. She took Byria's bag and laid out her sleeping mat with several leaves and cloths over it. She led Byria to rest upon it.

When Byria protested, repeating that she normally wasn't affected so by her woman's blood, Koki gave reasons it would be unusually bad: Byria was upset and anxious; Byria had never traveled like this—or at least not for many years; Byria was still healing from other injuries; Byria was eating differently; the village magics might still not agree with Byria.

The small woman counted these things off as she finished setting up the camp and took the damp clothes Byria had washed earlier in the day. Using water that had begun to steam over the fire, she gave them another scrub with herbs that lessened the bloodstain and, she explained, the scent they might still carry. When she was done, she sat beside the finally-reclining Byria, handing her a fresh bowl of the pain herbs and honey.

After a moment, she gently ran her fingers through Byria's hair and down her arm. "I'm not a gifted storysinger, but I'll sing a story for you if you think it'll help."

The touch did feel good, and Byria had resigned herself to a day of rest. It would do her no good if she was attacked by a leopard or managed to injure herself before she got to the dragon. With a nod, she said, "I would like that."

Like with Siheemo's song, Byria didn't quite understand the words, but she *felt* the song. Koki's voice wasn't exceptional, but Byria enjoyed hearing it. The former princess let herself relax and press into Koki's caresses.

* * * * *

Chapter Twenty-Five
The Edge and The End

It had taken three days. Three days *after* that day of rest. Byria had still bled for a day and a half after, but she could move, and she had.

Now Koki and she stood at a place where the trees finally gave way to mountains. Unlike the sudden appearance of a wall of jungle from the fields of grass, this change had come more gradually. The ground had become harder, with more stones, and the air had become cooler and less humid. As space between the trees had grown and grown, Koki spoke less and less.

It was their last night together; they would part ways in the morning. Byria would ascend into the mountains, and Koki would return to the village, likely bringing back an animal or several upon her bark sledge.

They sat across from each other, eating the roasted meat of what Byria thought looked like another oversized rat.

The former princess found the strength to break the silence. "I know you still don't want me to go, but I must. It's the proper thing for me to do." She pressed her hands to her heart. As she did so, the familiar warmth of her heart's fire grew.

"I don't have to be happy about it," was all Koki said in reply.

"I understand," Byria said, "and I thank you, because that means much to me."

Koki tilted her head, then stood and held out both hands. Byria took them as Koki said, "I don't have Mokin's magic, but you did speak with him?"

Byria nodded, squeezing Koki's hands tightly, and then pulling them to her lips to kiss, nodding harder and sniffling.

Tears ran down Koki's face. She looked like she wanted to say more, but her lips and jaw shook from holding back sobs.

Finding some composure, Byria managed, "He said you both..." What was the word? Closing her eyes, Byria tried to remember; her emotions were getting in the way of her thoughts and memories.

"We love you," Koki said, choking on a sob for a moment, "since you were a baby with Uhlokee-en. Always love. Even when gone."

Byria wrapped her arms around Koki, kissing both her cheeks as the villagers kissed each other.

Having heard the word again, she could say it back. "I love you..." Catching her breath with another sob, she added one more word she'd learned in the village. "Mother."

* * * * *

Chapter Twenty-Six
Into the Mountains

Byria and Koki shared few words the morning they parted. Everything that had needed to be said had been spoken.

They hugged and kissed once more before Koki headed into the jungle. She looked over her shoulder once, pausing and giving Byria one more chance to return with her.

She shook her head. Koki disappeared into the trees, like magic, the way she'd appeared when they'd first met.

Facing the mountains, feeling cooler air swirling around her through the sparse, remaining trees, Byria adjusted her bag and swallowed her remaining tears.

* * * * *

Chapter Twenty-Seven
Muscle Memory, Magic Memory

Traveling the mountain paths was far different from traveling in jungles or grasslands. This fact didn't surprise Byria as much as it annoyed her.

Byria preferred annoyance to the occasional threat of tears if she thought too hard of Koki and Mokin.

Sometimes, as she climbed, Byria would feel her body moving instinctually, as if she'd traversed this type of terrain before. And then, it was as if her body forgot all that and stumbled over boulders, lost its footing, or—the worst one—misstepped so badly she tumbled into a crevice with a small rockslide.

That worst one required her to take a day off from traveling, because her foot hurt so badly, she dared not put weight on it. All the tests Mokin had given her seemed to prove it wasn't broken, but his advice for such injuries had required at least a day of rest if possible.

Very. Annoying.

She tried not to let tears fall as she carefully wrapped the injury and made a paste of herbs for the scrapes as Mokin had shown her.

Also annoying was there was far less moisture in the air now, so she had to watch her water consumption, even with all that Koki and Mokin had packed for her. Worse, the wind often picked up the fine, ashy sand that covered everything. It sucked moisture from the air and her skin, which made the scrapes and abrasions from this fall and the prior ones itch maddeningly.

Where Byria camped to rest her ankle, she was in a valley that still had dry grass and some small, twisted trees. Two great walls of stone, carved by time or gods, met in a corner that protected her camp on two sides. It cut down the wind, and Byria noticed less ash. Clean looking water trickled down one side, so Byria gathered all she could.

She hadn't gone far upward yet in her days of traveling alone. According to the dirt map, her destination was almost to the wasteland area. From where she sat, she could somewhat see the tops of four different mountains. Closer ones loomed too high or had ledges that obscured their peaks.

The valley wasn't very big; Byria could see almost all of it. Sheer faces of mountains bordered the two sides across from her, as if some giant god or such had cleaved them from something even bigger. When the sun rose, shiny, sparkling veins of stone first reflected the beautiful pinks and oranges. She'd had to turn away and shade herself, as the reflection blinded her.

Further away, one mountain seemed to have an entire side of rubble and loose boulders, as if caused by massive landslides upon landslides over the years, or one giant catastrophe. Just looking at the piles made her stomach turn for no particular reason—besides an especially horrible smell when the wind came from that direction. She decided she'd stay far away from that area as she passed through the mountain range.

As the darkness of night fell early due to the high mountains, she took out her pyut-gem and held it to her chest, eyes closed. Her intent had been to will some of her heart's fire into her ankle and foot so it would heal faster, and she could continue traveling tomorrow. But something more happened.

Close.

Her eyes shot open. Feeling became a word. Not a voice in her head like she'd heard from the dragon or from Patch, or when Mokin used magic to help them communicate, but she understood it.

She closed her eyes again, pressing the small gem harder to her chest.

Close.

Acknowledging the message, she moved on to healing herself. When she'd finished, something still nagged at her heart, and the gem grew warm in her hand. Holding it in her palm, she looked at it.

It started spinning immediately, then bounced over to her satchel.

After her initial surprise, Byria collected the stone and looked through her things. A soft glow came from the jar holding the eye. She hadn't looked at it a single time since she'd arrived at the jungle village, as it had unsettled Koki so much.

When she pulled it out, she noticed the eye wasn't looking at her as it usually did. It aimed its pupil up and away. Shifting it around, repositioning herself, and then carefully moving to a more open area of the valley, Byria tried to follow its gaze.

The eye stared at a blurry, dark fuzz that dimmed the stars around the top of one of the nearby mountains—right above the rockslide mess she'd decided to avoid.

Byria licked her lips to moisten them, tasting ash despite her protected campsite. Her nose prickled with a new scent of hot rock.

Ash came from fire, and she'd smelled hot rock before.

Looking back up to that dark-haloed mountain, she planned her course for the next day.

She was, indeed, close.

*****

Chapter Twenty-Eight
Dragon's Grip

A damp cloth around her mouth and nose made it easier to breathe with the ash in the air. She tried to remember having worn such a thing, or having seen Patch wear something. Surely if they'd spent time near a dragon or a volcano, they'd have needed to.

While the sensation of wearing it was familiar, she could pull up no visual memories.

In fact, since leaving Koki and Mokin, Byria still hadn't been able to pull up any new memories prior to her palace time. The clearest pre-palace memories she *did* have had just been food.

Memories of the palace, of Tain, and even some more pleasant ones with her serving girls singing or just sitting in the gardens had started to become clearer, but those—even the pleasant ones—only made her long more for the missing memories.

She'd even tried writing in the ash on her resting day after the big fall. She'd pulled many things from her head as she'd drawn them. She understood all their meanings, but she had no memories of having learned them, having been taught them, or having used them—save the one she'd stabbed on the dragon's cage that had freed him.

When she'd written *that* one, the image of stabbing that rune had flashed in her head, and the sensation of crawling bugs upon her very bones—just as she'd experienced strapped to that damned memory-stealing bed—had hit her instantly.

She'd kicked at the dust to destroy the glyph. As the ash had puffed into the air, the awful prickling had eased, and the memory had returned to the recesses of her mind, no longer obscuring her vision with its presence, but still there.

Byria didn't want to *lose* any memories—even the frightening and painful ones.

It had taken one whole day of travel just to get to the foot of this mountain. Not only had she been moving slower with the pain in her ankle, she'd given wide berth to the stinking rockslide. Even individual boulders that had rolled from the mess caused prickles up and down Byria's spine.

Her pyut-gem didn't seem to "like" them either, growing painfully hot in her hand whenever she checked it for direction. Once she'd passed them, she, and the gem, had felt much better.

After breaking camp as soon as the sky had begun to lighten with coming dawn, it had still taken almost a half day of hiking to entirely break away from all trees and vegetation. Her world became nothing but stones, sky, and herself.

As she continued upward, she slipped a few more times, but managed to catch herself. She decided to risk cutting her feet again—they now had scars and calluses from their prior injuries—and put her shoes in her bag. She imagined her hands and feet like dragon's claws, or the strong claw-nails of the villagers, gripping when the path became nothing more than a sense that carried her over boulders and had her clinging along thin ledges.

About midway through the following day, it was becoming harder to breathe the higher she went—and not only for the ash. A memory of knowledge told her air in the mountains was thinner, and she should move more slowly, because it could make her mind do odd things, like feel as if it were spinning. Listening to that knowledge, she slowed herself, pausing more often to drink water and just breathe, and to strengthen her heart's fire.

Then she came to where there wasn't even a *sense* of a path. There was only a rock wall and the thought she needed to go *up*.

Her heart hammered. If she fell from here, she'd surely die. If her death wasn't immediate, it would be long and painful.

Byria didn't know how long she stared at the wall, but the sweat beading on her brow cooled and chilled her. She pulled out her pyut-gem and the eye. The gem warmed her heart's fire, and the eye looked straight up. This was the correct path.

If she was going to do this, she should do it while there was still light to see.

And she *was* going to do this.

Stowing the pyut-gem and the eye securely, she tied her satchel to her body as Koki had taught her for better balance. After a few stretches and a test that her ankle would hold, Byria took a deep breath and started to climb.

She willed her heart's fire to help her grip, and she felt stronger. Looking down was a bad idea, she knew, so she only looked at the wall and up.

Cold gusts of wind cut. With no barrier but clothing, the sun pricked hot needles against Byria's skin. Despite the damp cloth, the smells of hot stone and frost burned her nostrils. The joints of her fingers ached, along with the muscles of her stomach, and the growing throb of her injured ankle.

Byria kept climbing. In the back of her mind, she kept stoking her heart's fire. She'd make it. She would.

One pause taught her it was harder to hold on while stopped, so she kept moving. *How much farther?*

Close.

One glance up while she still climbed suggested a ledge near, perhaps the length of one or two people away—or so it looked. Memories of knowledge dropped cold stones in her stomach that whispered distances looked shorter than they were.

It doesn't matter. I'm climbing.

Sweat dripped and prickled uncomfortably down her face, neck, and back. Wind continued to send chills across her skin and deep into her stomach. The familiar burn of pain crept outward from all her joints and the skin of her hands and feet.

Her injured ankle sent one warning shot of pain all the way up her leg and back before she felt nothing. It gave.

And she slipped.

She fell for half a second before another sharp pain jolted from her shoulder to her spine as she stopped. Her feet dangled against the stone, toes scraping. Sticky blood pasted small stones to her fingers where sparkling rock crumbled in her grip.

Massive fingers of stone wrapped around her other arm. No, not stone. They were soft and warm, and shifted to a grayish, greenish shimmer of scales. She followed those fingers up and saw the stone beside and above her shiver and fade to scales.

Two red eyes of flame blinked at her.

"You're here," came the familiar rumbling voice that also echoed in her head.

Taking a gasp of air—she'd momentarily forgotten to breathe—Byria found she could only nod.

She'd found her dragon, and he'd saved her life.

* * * * *

Chapter Twenty-Nine
All in a Name

"Why did you not call for me?" the dragon asked as he gently placed her upon the ledge. Byria's heart was pounding from the short flight. After grabbing her, he'd launched off the side and into the air. It had been but a few seconds of flight, but she still felt as if she were spinning and falling. The roar of his fire wings, though he'd already dismissed them—or whatever a dragon did with his fire wings—still rang in her ears.

Call for him?

In a rare moment, a bloom of pride outweighed Byria's confusion at his immediate question and the swell of other emotions upon seeing him again. Lifting her chin defiantly, she stated, "I needed to make this journey."

As she spoke the words, they rang like True Things. There was no need to reveal that she'd had no recollection of being *able* to call for him.

He lowered his head and closed his eyes. She picked up the same sadness and shame she'd sensed upon first discovering he was real and imprisoned. Like when he'd asked her to forgive him, those emotions were tangible, physical.

"I suppose you did," he said.

In her heart, she knew these weren't normal feelings for a dragon, and these were *his* feelings. If her heart's fire didn't tell her so, his very posture and demeanor gave it away.

In silence, the two studied each other. He crouched on all four of his feet—hands and feet? Byria was unsure of dragon anatomy—like a hunting dog being chastised. His tail, while not between his legs, curled close, rigid between his torso and Byria.

A neck almost as long as his torso hovered just above the ground, well below his tightly coiled shoulders and hips that appeared ready to leap away at any moment. His coloring shifted between green-gold scales and dull stone colors, and his pupils were wide slits that almost entirely covered the flame-red irises. His head was larger than Byria's body. He had bat-like ears and long feelers—similar to those on catfish—that quivered and shifted color even more than the rest of his body. His crocodile-like lips pulled back some, but not in aggression.

Byria's observation of his proportions didn't seem much different than what she remembered upon seeing him fly away, but with only the mountain and sky as contrast, he now appeared much smaller.

And what must he think of me?

Byria looked at herself. She sat with one knee folded under her and her bad ankle outstretched, beginning to swell again. As she frowned at the injury, he came nearer, as if also just noticing.

"You are hurt."

Byria flinched at his approach—so much faster than she expected from a creature so big.

He stopped immediately and met her eyes. "Do you wish me to heal you?"

The swell of pride lost its blossom, and Byria was without words again, so she took a deep breath and simply nodded.

He didn't move, and Byria could feel his stare boring into her. She closed her eyes. It felt like he was reading her soul, and she wasn't ready for that yet.

"Are you sure, my princess?" he asked, voice like wind moving gravel.

Byria's eyes flew open. "Don't call me that!"

Now the dragon flinched.

The *dragon*. Flinched.

She shook her head in disbelief. In but one snap of his jaws, the beast could eat half her body. One claw swipe, and he could disembowel her. One breath, and he could cook her to the bone.

"I would never hurt you," he said.

"Are you reading my mind?" She averted her gaze again.

"No. You never liked when I did that. But I can smell your fear and surprise, and I see how you sit."

Byria snorted, refraining from saying she'd seen that same fear in him. After a few more moments of tense silence, she hazarded another glance in his direction.

His eyes, unblinking, were fixed on her. This close, she could see his mustache and beard of feelers. His ears quivered as they leaned toward her. Byria was surprised to find that she was more curious than anything as she studied his face and features.

Finally, she asked, "You know my name?"

"I know the name I and my lady called you."

My lady? Byria didn't ponder on how he referenced Patch. Not yet. There was the present issue of how he addressed her. "That would be my name, yes."

"It wasn't the one you were born with. I know that, too."

Byria hesitated. "But it's who I am. Will you speak my name?"

"Byria."

A smile touched her lips. His voice saying her name was familiar. Tears pricked her eyes. The sound loosed memories. Real memories, old ones. The feel of sleeping against scales and on top of animal skins. How utterly dark the depths of a cave became. A feeling of safety.

"Again... please?" she whispered.

"Byria?" There was concern in his voice, and that, too, felt familiar. She remembered that sound, that tone.

With a sniffle, she wiped her hand across her eyes, then made a face at the sticky sensation and scent of copper she was smearing over herself. Blood oozed from broken fingernails and cuts on her palm. Moving her gaze back to the dragon, she slid nearer and held out the injured hand.

"Would you... please?" Tears cracked her voice, but she didn't care. She could feel the smile on her face.

The dragon nodded and reached his snout to her. His long, snake-like tongue darted at first, then slowly brushed against her skin. Hot-stone-scented breath warmed her stiff, chilled fingers. She edged closer, though her shoulder still ached, and her ankle bumped painfully on the rocks with her movement.

When the dragon stopped licking and breathing on her hand, she pulled it back to inspect it. There were no scars or scabs, even. Her fingernails, ragged and broken long before she'd started climbing, appeared fresh and new, as if she'd never left the palace.

She bit her lip, feeling even more tears.

"And the rest of your injuries, Byria?"

Smiling again, and using her tears and her sleeve to wipe most of the blood from her face, she shifted so her ankle was closer to the dragon. The swelling went down with his warm breath, and the pain ebbed away from the brush of his tongue.

Byria came closer until she sat in the shadow of his long neck. He turned to look at her, his pupils less wide now, his head a little higher, his muscles a little less tense. He flicked his tongue in her direction and sighed over her whole body.

His breath pulled away the pain in her shoulder, as well as smaller aches and discomforts, carrying it up and away just as the wind pulled away the white petals from cherry blossoms. More tears came, and Byria buried her face in her hands.

Even with his nearness releasing more memories, memories she wasn't yet ready to confront, one eluded her. An important one.

He has a name. What is his name?

A few ragged sobs escaped her throat. She rocked back and forth as she scrubbed at her face and eyes, trying to force her mind to release that one thing. Only one thing...

"Byria?" His voice made her choke, but she peeked between her fingers to see him lie down. His body almost made a circle around her. Protecting her. Cradling her.

Another sob gave her painful hiccoughs, and she covered her face again. He knew *her* name.

"What is it?"

She had to admit her failing. She'd done so with Patch, but it felt worse to tell *him*. He'd be hurt, knowing the extent of how damaged she was.

But she remembered—a different memory, but an important one—he valued honesty. He'd promised he would never lie to her, and he'd warned her he wouldn't tolerate any lie from her. Dragons could smell a lie.

"I'm sorry," she apologized first. "I can't remember... I don't remember..." she barely breathed the words between her lips and fingers as she covered her face, "...your name."

His body warmed her more as he scraped closer. Then she felt the slightest tickle against the shins of her folded legs. Lowering her hands, she saw his head—the edge of his nose wider than the edges of her bent knees—only inches from her. The feelers on his face brushed against her filthy trousers. She certainly hadn't washed them since she'd started hiking in the dryer mountains.

Why where such thoughts occurring to her now? Before she could further argue with herself, he lifted his head until his eyes—each bigger than the largest mango fruits—were the same level as hers.

"You truly do not remember?"

Byria shook her head, ready to bury her face once more, but he flicked his tongue, brushing her fingers gently to stop her.

"You have nothing to apologize for, and no apology I can give you will ever be sufficient."

"Don't say that. Please... just... will you tell me your name?" Another thought occurred to her about names. Something she Knew before. Something her time in the village—Mokin's promise of how she could find him if she ever needed—solidified. "Or at least what you would have me call you? You needn't say your True Name."

"But I will, to you. And if you use it, well..." He sighed, and more waves of shame and pain rolled from his body. He moved even closer, his neck circling almost around her shoulders. His words came on a hot breath in a voice as soft as a whisper. "If you use it, if

I am at all able, I will come to you. Which is not the promise I want to give, but what I can."

"It's enough." Byria reached out as if to caress his face, then stopped. Not only was he a dragon—a beast no mortal should touch—but how long had it taken her to share affection with Koki and Mokin?

He gave a small nod, granting permission for her to touch him. Biting her lip, Byria brushed the underside of his jaw. Besides the thicker feelers, almost as thick as her wrist, smaller ones like coarse hairs also grew from his scales. She'd only meant to touch him briefly, but found herself rubbing his jaw. That, also, felt familiar. Right.

Pressing against her hand and arm, he whispered his True Name into her ear.

She gasped. She *did* know that name. Hearing it set loose a landslide of memories. Byria fell to the ground, overcome with them.

"Byria?"

Blindly, she reached for *him* and found his face beside her. She gripped the base of a larger feeler, perhaps the edge of his lip. She couldn't quite tell, because the memories made her dizzy. Byria needed to clutch something, anything, while her mind reeled and sobs shook her body.

The waterfall was short, and the images blurred together, but Byria knew she could sort them later, for they were free in her mind. Some memories had ragged edges, some were incomplete, but they were something.

And they were hers.

As she found her breath, she loosened her grip on him. One of his taloned hands cupped her back. As she released his face and clutched his thumb, he pulled his head away with a shake. His lips parted and flexed as his feelers curled and flipped.

"Sorry," she whispered against the scales of his hand; the ones closest to where the talons grew were the size of her thumbnail. As she focused on breathing, on controlling her wild mind and hammering heart, she traced the edges of the scales. They felt familiar. Comforting. This was a thing she'd done when frightened. He'd held her when she'd been frightened or hurt. She remembered that.

"I told you that you never need to apologize to me." He lowered his head close to her face once more.

She nodded, wiping her face against his thumb—loving that she remembered doing this before. At one time, she'd loved being held, loved giving and receiving affection. Feeling in control again, she asked, "And what shall I simply call you?"

He tilted his head again. "Do you not remember that, either? You gave me the name you always called me."

Byria blinked, trying to sift through the freshly loosed memories. The sound of his wings, of fire bursting in flight. That memory was strongest. She felt the heat and wind, saw the undulating flames, smelled the burning—tasted it, even. *Heard* it.

"Hawusshhh," she said softly, mimicking that sound, drawing it out. That felt True on her lips. "Hawush. I called you Hawush, because that's the sound you make with your wings."

She saw the smile in Hawush's eyes as his feelers caressed her cheeks.

"Yes. You named me Hawush. And that is who I am."

* * * * *

Book III
Child of Earth and Fire

* * * * *

Chapter One
Dragonhome

Byria snuggled against Hawush's chest and into the crook of his elbow... or front knee. She still wasn't quite sure of dragon anatomy. When he walked, it was on all four of his limbs. Yet he'd carried her, touched her, and seemed to manipulate things with his front claws, which were shaped more like hands than feet.

Hawush had curved his neck and tail so she was within a circle of his body, his face right beside where she'd curled up in his arms—she'd call them arms. His breathing was slow and even, but his eyes, their burning irises the only part she could actually see, were only half-closed and looking at her.

She didn't mind. It matched the memories she was putting together in her head. When she was young, a child, he'd never fall asleep until she did. And he always woke easily—be it from her having a nightmare, or Patch moving in restlessness, or someone or something coming near the cave.

After running from Tain and Lakan—at least one of whom might still be searching for her—knowing he woke easily, knowing he was holding her, knowing he wanted to protect her felt even more welcome than Mokin and Koki's cozy hut with healing broth and animal skins to sleep on. Curling in Hawush's embrace felt more at "home" than she could remember.

This was where she was supposed to be. *This* was the feeling she'd known was missing with Koki and Mokin, though she knew they loved her. Home was with Hawush.

Though *this* was a different cave from the one she was finding in her memory pieces. At one time, she'd have been able to tell why it was so different, but at the moment it was enough that she recognized it was so.

There was quite a bit of ash in the air inside, and the very stones smelled of heat. Hawush had darted his tongue around her face, and that seemed to help her breathe. She'd removed her face cloth when she'd curled herself against him to sleep. Byria had wanted to feel his scales against her cheek, as the newly-found memories suggested she'd regularly slept against him as he held her.

Dragon scales had a scent. She remembered the scent now—sour sulfur mixed with a warm metal and leather. It wasn't the most pleasant scent to Byria's nose, but she welcomed it. It was familiar, and the smell made it easier to piece together and organize the fragments of memories that had come back when he'd spoken his True Name.

Her stomach rumbled, and she ignored it. Hawush had offered to get food earlier, but she hadn't wanted him to leave. Opening one of her eyes, she saw his eyes open in question again. She shook her head, rubbing her face against his scales.

Reaching into her satchel with as little movement as possible, she pulled out what was left of the rations Koki and Mokin had given her. She let the memories of their caring and teaching play in her head as she offered to share their gifts of food with the dragon. Hawush wrinkled his snout and shook his head, also moving very little.

Byria refrained from asking all the questions that tumbled around her mind; she wanted to order the memories first. That would help her find what holes remained and ask better questions—she could tell a lot of memories were still missing.

Hawush had asked nothing of her, aside from if she'd wanted him to bring her food or heal the other injuries he could sense on her.

She'd turned down his offer of more healing, just as she'd done with Mokin. So many scars on her body—she wasn't ready to lose them yet. Every time she looked at the hand and foot that Hawush had healed, she was amazed. They looked brand new, untouched by either Tain or herself.

Some of the scars that had healed were ones Byria had made, ones she'd meant to keep. The marks she'd made to help her remember Patch's instructions—seeing those gone had made her stomach twitch uncomfortably. Only half her forearm had been healed, just past where his tongue had touched. The rest of her list and the symbol she'd needed to draw upon the black mirror, though, those were still there.

Hawush released a soft, rumbling sigh. The vibrations of that felt familiar, too—comforting, secure, happy.

Comforted, secure, and happy in the place she'd been taught to fear for so many years, a new sensation moved in Byria. Not a memory, but a shift. She was no longer afraid of not having fear.

* * * * *

Chapter Two
A Dragon's Laugh

Byria awoke, rested and comfortable, and still in Hawush's hold. The impatient thump of his tail against the cave's floor and the dim light of day had been the first things she'd noticed.

He carefully released her as she stood up. While he stretched his limbs, neck, and tail in several directions and curves with great almost-roaring yawns, Byria crossed her legs, hoping to think of some delicate way to ask where she might relieve herself—for she certainly didn't want to leave her filth in his—in *their*—home.

When he saw her posture, he smirked. That expression would be Byria's second favorite memory of the morning—for a smirk was quite a thing to see upon a dragon's face, especially when his burning eyes sparkled in amusement.

Understanding her dilemma, he took her through a short passage in the cave to a small exit with its own ledge.

He waited, back turned to her, while she took care of her body's needs off the ledge. When she returned, Byria blurted, "Where do you go?" He certainly couldn't fit where she'd just been.

That had made him laugh, and the sound of his laughter was Byria's favorite memory of the morning. He tossed his head back toward the larger entrance and chuckled all the way to the ledge, launching into the air with the sound of his name as flaming wings had flared from his side.

"Anywhere I want."

His voice came into her head, a momentary surprise, until Byria realized she would've had a hard time hearing him while he flew and his wings whooshed and crackled.

With a dive toward the mountainside covered in the rubble that had made Byria's skin prickle, he added, *"But usually, somewhere specifically there."*

Byria realized there was an importance to his actions, but didn't quite know what it was. It didn't feel as if there were a memory attached to that piece of Truth. She wondered if her distaste for the area came from it likely being comprised of large amounts of dragon piss and shit. Certainly, that explained the smell.

But something else in her mind suggested the reason the area felt so off was the reason Hawush preferred to excrete upon it.

He returned briefly to tell her he was going hunting and she should make herself at home in the cave. There was a pool of clean water—though it was hot—deeper inside, should she need it.

The thought of a pool of hot, clean water had been welcome in Byria's mind, so once she could no longer see even a speck of Hawush in the distance, she'd decided to explore.

In what Byria calculated as four full Hawush-lengths into the cave, it was pitch dark. She took the pyut-gem from her satchel along with a few clean cloths. As in the jungle, it didn't cast much light, just enough that it might be found if dropped. It was something, though.

Slipping bare feet over stone, feeling the wall, smelling and feeling the air, she went deeper into the cave. The trickle of water grew closer. Moisture thickened the air. A tiny dot of light on the floor before her surprised her. As her eyes adjusted, the darkness pulled away to reveal reflective glimmers on moist walls. Byria was seeing the reflection of her token in water—and that reflected off all the moist, shiny surfaces.

Crouching and wiping moisture from her face, she found the edge of the pool. Leaning so close was like leaning over a pot of boiling water. Hawush hadn't been exaggerating when he'd said it was hot!

The smell of sulfur and heated stones was stronger, but breathing the moisture felt good. Above her head, the walls and ceiling dripped like slow rain. When she moved the stone close to the walls, she found clinging, delicate, pale leaves on bone-white vines that looked and felt like flaps of moist skin, which fluttered as if breathing. Every so often, she heard a skittering, like a small animal, or a splash in the water that sounded much bigger than a drop of condensation.

The steam suggested the water was too hot to bathe in. Knowing she was filthy, and unsure if this was also the drinking water, Byria didn't want to contaminate anything. That occasional loud splash also unsettled her. Still crouching, she followed the edge of the water. It wasn't still; it lapped back and forth. Every so often, a breeze cooled the perspiration dripping from her face and neck.

Byria headed into the breeze, then paused to pluck a leaf from a vine. Reaching as far over the water as she could, she dropped the leaf and held her glowing pyut-gem tightly.

Something that looked to be the size of a koi, but pure white and with far more feelers, splashed out of the water, ate the leaf, and promptly spat it out. Its tail slapped the surface in annoyance. The leaf drifted in the direction from whence came the cool breezes.

Following the shore further, Byria noticed a little more light filtering in from a big pile of rocks where the hot pond ended. The sound of water trickling was louder here.

From between the edges of what looked like a very old rockslide, light entered in beams that reflected the steam and moisture. Plants and lichen, greener, tinted the rays. Drizzles of water, like sun-shimmering ribbons, tinkled and dripped into the pool from between the stones.

Near the end that was all boulders, Byria could see the pool was very shallow. Shafts of light danced through a fine fur of plant tendrils. A few small fish, some pure black, but a few pure white or metallic, skimmed through the shallows. There weren't many, less than a dozen, even if Byria weren't counting a few twice, but she was entranced, watching them dart around.

Where the pool grew deeper, more in the darkness, the plants became fewer, and Byria couldn't see very many fish. She considered the pond more, then walked back along the pond's edge.

Just into where she couldn't see without the help of her pyutgem, Byria dipped the cloth into the water. She hissed as the scalding water soaked into the cloth and right up to her recently healed fingers.

With a grimace, she gripped the cloth partly between her nails and fingertips and shook it out. When it had cooled some, she draped it over her shoulder and pulled out another dry cloth. Walking halfway to the rock-pile wall, she dipped in the fresh cloth. Here, the pool was more like freshly drawn bathwater. Hot to the touch, but not painful.

Moving to the shallowest point near the stones, she dipped another cloth and found the temperature to be just below tepid, almost cool. Reaching up to the fine stream of water that dripped from outside, Byria flinched at the unexpectedly icy temperature.

A smile played on her lips as she stepped back from the boulders. Even if whatever had caused this particular collapse or landslide had happened some time ago, she wanted to take no chance of stepping somewhere weak or rotten.

She circled around and looked at the cavern that surrounded her, her smile growing. Her eyes had adjusted to the dimness, and she could see more of the plants, the sparkling walls of glossy black, the deceptive stillness of the water. It was beautiful.

Absolutely beautiful.

Choosing a spot near the freshly-poured-bathwater temperature, Byria undressed and slipped her foot into the pool. The incline was steep, but not as slippery as she'd expected. The rock beneath was firm and almost ridged—textured by years of gentle laps—and the hot water on the bottoms of her feet felt amazing.

Sitting on the ground, she edged into the water and began to wash herself. Since it was flowing toward the boulders and out of the pool, she had little fear of contaminating the water.

She cupped some of the water in her hand and drank. It tasted of sulfur and minerals, not really pleasant, but certainly not dank or spoiled. Perhaps the cold water dripping in would taste better; she could try that when she was done bathing.

Though her eyes had adjusted, she found that once she'd slipped into the water, she could hardly see her scars. She ran her fingers over the remaining cuts up her left arm and over the rune she'd cut into her flesh, as well as over the rippling pattern of waves from the flame she'd created to escape that awful bed.

Still below that, she felt the raised welts of the older scars. She traced each one she could reach with her fingers, cataloging what memories she could associate with each, which scars were caused by others, and which ones she'd made herself.

Some of the fresher cuts from her climb were already mostly healed, but still stung in the water. Byria figured the proximity to Hawush made things heal faster.

There was a fine silt further in that clouded the water as Byria bathed. It pulled and smoothed away the dead skin, loose scabs, and the deepest dirt stains upon her.

After she'd washed herself, she washed her clothes as well. It was too moist for them to dry, so she wrung them out as best she could and put them back on. A taste of the trickling ice-cold water invited several more, prompting her stomach to twist painfully from the difference in temperature. Byria decided to bring her waterskins back and fill them so they could warm up.

Collecting the cloths and her pyut-gem, she headed back toward the cave mouth's ledge, where she could let the sun and wind dry her clothes and hair, which had grown faster than she'd expected in her travels and time in the village.

As she settled and stared at the painfully clear sky, Byria found herself smiling once more. In that moment, she didn't need to think of any memories; she just needed to rest in the sun.

She was entirely happy.

* * * * *

Chapter Three
Magnificence

Hawush returned with a giant tuna. It looked like one of the fishes the palace chefs would cut up for special occasions. Byria's eyes widened, and hunger panged in her stomach, reminding her she'd only eaten some dried fruit before her bath. She licked her lips.

The dragon put the fish down and stepped on it, just in time to keep it from flipping itself with its thick tail. Its gills strained, opening wide to reveal blood red gashes.

"That's one of my favorites!" Byria said, and a lightness touched her voice as she spoke.

A smile stretched at Hawush's crocodile-like lips, and he nodded. "I thought so."

"How close are we to the ocean? I thought it was much farther away."

"If you were walking, perhaps." His smile quirked, and he stretched from his neck to the end of his tail. Sharp fins spiked up from his spine in a wave as he flexed. Byria hadn't noticed them before, but found herself smiling even more as they caught the sun in an iridescent glimmer.

He tilted his head and stretched again, his posture resembling one of the peacocks in the garden as it preened and spread its tail.

"You are magnificent," she told him.

He bowed his head gracefully in response, though his chest puffed out more, and the fire in his eyes seemed to glow brighter. Arching his neck like a parade horse, he flexed his taloned fingers and cut into the fish with the precision of a high-ranking chef. He split its stomach and pulled out its innards, setting them aside as he licked his own lips. Then he carved off several small squares of flesh and placed them before Byria, skin side down.

Kneeling primly, as if she were at a fancy dinner—she'd rather be here than any palace dinner—Byria delicately picked up one of the squares of fish. As soon as she did, Hawush swallowed the fish's innards and then bit off its head, crunching its bones between his teeth.

Not needing to say any more to each other, they enjoyed their late lunch.

* * * * *

Chapter Four
A Learning of Dragons and Forgiveness

Dragons cleaned themselves, Byria learned, by rolling and wiping themselves in stone and dirt, then scattering the dirt away from their home. Or, as in Hawush's case, blown off the ledge and into the wind.

Despite the apparent dexterity of their clawed hands, dragons were very messy eaters, and they ate almost every part of their prey. Fluid, blood, and flesh bits clung to Hawush's lips and teeth, and he licked as much of it off as possible, but the thin, darting muscle wasn't as efficient as the tongues of dogs or cats, Byria observed.

Watching him eat fascinated Byria more than she expected.

When he was finally finished cleaning, he rolled onto his side and stretched once more. The ledge, which faced southeast, was now bathed in full sun, and getting warm.

"I can hardly even feel the winds now," Byria said.

"That is because I do not want them. I can keep them away the way I keep away the ash that would harm your lungs."

Byria looked at him curiously, then lay beside him to also enjoy the sun. "Did you teach me about dragons before, and I've forgotten? Or did you not teach me of dragons?"

Hawush didn't answer right away, and Byria worried she'd offended him or made him feel sad and ashamed again for not having protected her.

"I had not intended to teach you, but you always had many questions. At first, I feared to tell a human so much but I had promised you I would be honest. If I expected you to be honest with me, I would have to be the same. I answered all the questions you asked me."

"Hmm," was all she said. She closed her eyes and let the heat of the sun warm her face.

"How long have you been out in the sun?" Hawush asked after a moment.

Not opening her eyes, Byria thought. "Perhaps less than half the time you were gone. I took a long bath."

"Do you not feel how red your face is?"

Byria wrinkled her face, and there came a burning tightness.

There was a reason women kept parasols outside. She'd had her head covered when she'd first run, the jungle had shadowed her while she was there, and the mountains, themselves, had kept her fairly shadowed until she'd begun her climb yesterday.

Today she'd spent a particularly long time just sleeping in the sun. The memories of the sensation made her happy—but now she remembered the dry pain after.

She pursed her lips in annoyance. "I assume the sun doesn't affect you so?"

"I have scales, not skin, and I am a creature of fire and earth." His voice was gentle and teasing as he rolled over and flicked his snout in the direction of the cave.

"I want to be near you," she protested, though she stood and slumped in the direction of the cave's shady opening. "And can you not just heal me anyway?"

He chuckled, still herding her. "Would you wish to be a continual drain on my power for foolish, avoidable reasons?"

"No." Byria felt childish as she spoke, but she liked feeling so.

As she leaned on the cave's cool wall, he breathed over her again, his tongue flicking over her face. The heat burned initially, and his licks stung, but the dry, painful heat pulled from her skin.

"Thank you," she told him when he was done.

With a diving roll, he flopped back on the ground, stretching in the sun and across the opening of the cave. "We are still near."

"Good," Byria said.

"Have you other questions you wish to ask of me?"

"I have many, but I don't want to ask right now."

He twisted his neck to look at her better.

"It hurts to ask. You're upset, too, and I don't want to do that to you. I want... I want to just feel like this, because I remember feeling like this, and it was good."

Hawush repositioned himself so his head was nearer to her. Byria stroked her fingers over the feelers that grew from his chin and nose like the long beard and moustache of an old man. They twitched on the stone beside her. As she touched them, they slowed, and a sense of calmness and pleasure flowed from him.

"That feels good to you?" she asked.

"Yes." He moved even closer so her fingers brushed his chin as well. "When you were a child, we discovered that." He sighed, creating a warm breeze that gently caressed her.

"What do you wish to ask me?" Byria glanced to his eyes shyly.

"Nothing that would hurt you any further, either."

She chewed her lip a moment, then said, "One thing I've learned in the palace is that sometimes you have to make something hurt to have power over it."

"I do not wish to hurt *you*. I can sense you have been hurt more than I could measure at this point. Possibly more than I could even heal if you would let me try."

"And I don't wish to hurt you, so that leaves us at an impasse. Except, if I say you can ask me questions that might hurt, that makes it my choice to suffer the pain, so while it *hurts*, it's not you hurting me."

Hawush lifted his head, looking down his snout, and flicked his tongue at her. "You have grown wise, Byria."

"Hardly. There are some small things I've learned that I wish I'd learned earlier or, perhaps, not forgotten if I *had* learned them before."

Hawush chuffed slightly in her direction, then put his head back down, giving a little shake so his feelers rested across Byria's legs.

She went back to stroking the tendrils, but when he didn't ask anything after a while, she suggested, "Perhaps we can make a plan, and that gives us even more control. You should ask me all you want today, and tomorrow, after we eat and if you would permit me, I can ask you the questions I have."

He sighed once again. A silence passed, long enough for Byria to notice his shadow lengthen and blend into the darkness of the cave. His feelers, warm and heavier than she expected, were unmoving across her lap when he finally spoke.

"That is a fair plan. And I appreciate your perception of power and pain. I would have permitted you ask me anything, regardless, but I do feel less uncomfortable about it. Of course, asking you questions will also be painful, and I acknowledge and accept that, too."

Byria pressed her hand against his feelers. An older memory of her handmaid Syng came to mind. She'd secretly squeeze Byria's hand in comfort when Tain was in a foul mood. More recently, and less painfully, she remembered Koki and Mokin giving her comfort with a pat or squeeze—and giving them comfort similarly.

Hawush sighed again, then moved his head so the side of his snout rubbed against Byria's legs. His scales were almost hot to the touch, but she ran her hands along his face. He rolled onto his belly, all his claws tucked beneath him the way Byria had seen the menagerie wildcats do. His neck curved so his head was at almost the same level as hers.

He studied her, and she sensed he was considering his first question carefully.

When he finally asked, his voice was a whisper—the deep, thundering whisper of a faraway storm. "Did you truly forget me?"

The words rumbled into Byria's stomach. Tears immediately stung her eyes. Sighing herself, she leaned her head on the cave's hard stone wall. "For a time, I think I did. I let myself forget, because it was easier. Any time I thought of 'dragon' anything, I was either punished or told that you did awful things to me. That *he* rescued me from you, that all the scars were from you. I couldn't remember where the scars had come from, and it hurt to try to remember, so it was easier to believe the story."

She stopped herself before apologizing to him again. While he'd said she had nothing to apologize for, Byria sensed that each time she apologized, he felt more guilt. She wanted to ask him why he blamed himself for her capture, but tonight wasn't her night to ask. Only to answer—and she wasn't done answering.

"But..."

He tilted his head and blinked his eyes. A shimmer of tears reflected in them. In the sunset, the tiny detail that he had two sets of eyelids stuck out to Byria, as if her mind were reaching for something, anything, to distract her.

She shook her head. "But I didn't forget all the way. I couldn't have. I looked upon you every parade, and it would make my mind work. Then you talked to me. And then I found you. Every time I tried to find you again, every moment I got closer, when I found you now, and every moment I've been with you, I remember more."

He nodded slowly and blinked again. Byria took a deep breath and waited. Could another question be as difficult?

For a moment, he gave his head a shake, then turned away and sneezed before twisting his neck and rubbing his face in his elbow. He blinked a few more times, particularly with the inner, more opaque eyelids. He cocked his hips to the side and stretched both back feet out from underneath him.

After all that adjusting—was he hesitating because the next question was difficult for him, too?—he looked at her again and twisted his lips. "It is foolish to ask what you have forgotten. That is not exactly what I mean, either, but I suppose... What is the extent they harmed—changed—your memories? And how?"

Byria sighed. At least this question dealt with specific things she could recount, as painful as they were. "The 'how' is easier to answer. They tried to do it again after you escaped, to find out where you might hide. Except I remembered before they did it, and I remembered—well, I discovered how I could fight back. They used the bed in the room they kept you in. That wooden plank on an angle with the wires and metal crown. It..."

Hawush's face stilled as if frozen, save for the trembling of his feelers.

Byria found herself shivering again and rubbed her hands over her arms. "It was like putting a storm in my head, except they controlled the lightning, and used it to pull memories and destroy them."

Hawush's claws flexed, then relaxed as he regained control.

"But I don't think they were all destroyed, not with some coming back still," she continued. "I think it just changed how my mind worked. It was like a landslide, or after a storm, when things are knocked over, and stones and trees have tumbled, and things are trapped under them. Sometimes I don't know what rocks or trees the memories are hiding under. Other times, the rock or tree is really heavy, and the memory can't get out, and I can't move the thing out of the way to get to it. I don't know if that makes sense, but that's how I've come to think of it."

Hawush closed his eyes. "I smelled you upon that thing. Your blood and your fear. I didn't know..."

"They wanted to keep us apart. That's why they only allowed me to see you during the parades and told me I should never look upon the dragon statue. Perhaps they knew or had a feeling that we could still reach each other. I know every year except the last two, I was told I had a 'break' during the parade and couldn't finish. I think that was you trying to reach me, which would go against the stories they put in my head to try to replace my memories, and it was working, but I couldn't figure it out, and it frightened me."

Lowering his head more, Hawush shook it in the negative. "I tried to reach you during the first two parades. I saw him hurt you the second time, and I stopped. Then you reached out to me."

Byria shook her head. "I don't remember before… the last two parades." She took a deep breath. "As for the extent, I remember… I *remember* bits and pieces of the days since my wedding. I remember little bits of preparing for my wedding. Easy things, like clothing and dressing, and even the specific words I had to say. I remember moments in the gardens, moments eating, moments during celebrations. I remember being told stories, and the stories… but I can't always put what I remember in order or remember why certain memories come. Except simple things: a moment I wasn't afraid, a moment Tain said something kind, a moment I was told I had to remember. From when I was brought to the palace until the parade last year, that's all I have."

He sighed, but nodded for her to continue.

"When I heard you during the parade last year, something changed. Something made me *want* to remember, so I started finding ways to remember, even when it hurt. Especially when it hurt. I tried hurting myself, realizing I could remember better when I made myself hurt, and I wasn't afraid if it was me doing the hurting. I remember deciding I would never have a child with Tain, and punching myself when I found myself pregnant, and how much blood there was. And I remember how, as painful and sick as that made me feel, I was entirely *un*afraid for the first time I could remember."

Scales up and down Hawush's face and body twitched, and the feelers twisted upon themselves.

She offered a small smile she hoped would calm him some. "Then this year's parade happened, and I decided I needed to see you. I remember all of that, and I remember the memories I hadn't known I'd forgotten coming back—being in a volcano, being at the beach, and just feelings. I remember everything after you escaped, at least when I was conscious. I made myself remember. And I remember how I escaped, how I ran, how I met the people in the village, and Koki and Mokin, and everything that happened since the moment I set you free."

The anxious tics in his body slowed some, but his expression—or what emotions she felt from him and tried to attach to his expression—still spoke of his discomfort and guilt.

She paused, then frowned. *You must be completely honest*, she reminded herself. "Though sometimes... still not perfectly. Still not in the right order, or only after I think very hard about remembering." She spoke in a whisper, lowering her eyes.

Hawush flicked his tongue, and she sensed he wanted to comfort her. She reached to stroke his feelers, but he pulled away and laid his head down, eyes closed, for a few moments.

When he lifted it again and looked at Byria, he asked, "And that is all you remember? What about from before...?"

"Only the pieces that have come to me since I traveled to find you. They're like fragments of a beautiful mosaic that have scattered far and wide. I didn't even remember Patch when I met her again."

Byria bit her lip over a tearful hiccough. She hadn't remembered Koki or Mokin, either, but even they had said she might have been too young to remember. That she'd forgotten Patch... hurt most. "And now Patch is likely dead."

Hawush turned his head to her. "My lady may be dead?"

"Your lady?" It wasn't her turn to ask questions, but hearing Hawush call Patch "my lady" for a second time...

"I know what *you* called her, but she saved my life. More than my life... I would never regard her with any less honor. I helped her care for you in return for such a debt as I owed. Is she truly dead?" Tears dripped from the dragon's eyes as he blinked furiously, nostrils flaring.

"... They said she was killed when they collapsed the dungeons."

"Your voice and eyes say you are not sure."

Byria bit her bottom lip, then held up a finger. She went to her bag, pulled out the jar with the eye in it, and presented it to Hawush.

He hissed with a heat and force that made Byria stagger back. Not speaking, but sending a sentiment of apology, he turned away and roared toward the southwest, the direction of the palace. A blaze of fire almost twice the length of his body flashed in the dusk.

Byria cringed from the prickling heat, though she was several paces into the cave and almost his body length's distance away from him.

"That *is what happened to her eye?* They *did that to her?*"

His tail darted back and forth in anger.

Byria had to step back to keep from being whipped with its end.

She hugged the jar to her chest, making herself breathe. As much as he'd promised he would never hurt her, how could one *not* be terrified when a dragon displayed his fury?

Swallowing, she pressed against the inside of the cave and watched his ribs flex with several deep breaths that crackled with spouts of flame. When nothing more than puffs of smoke escaped his mouth and nostrils, and his breathing slowed, he turned back to Byria, giving a shake from head to tail, flittering the spikes on his back again and sending another mental message of apology for frightening her.

With a shrug—her own breathing had normalized in time with his—she returned to the edge of the cave and slid down the stone to sit, waiting for him to join her.

He didn't. He paced along the ledge, which wasn't an optimal size for such a large beast to pace, so he'd take a few steps, turn, take a few steps, and turn several times over.

"She is not dead, at least," he finally said.

Byria sat up. "What?"

Hawush gestured to the jar she held. "If she were dead, that would have withered and died, as well."

"And you know it's hers?"

"I have looked her in it when it was still within her face."

Byria hugged the jar again, tears streaming down her face. "Then perhaps she'll find us. She said she'd try to find me if she could escape. She didn't think she could. She made me promise to find you even if she didn't make it. I begged and begged her to promise she'd come with me, but she only promised she'd *try*."

"She has likely worked whatever magic she has left to lead them away from you. In the time I knew her, there was nothing she desired more than to keep you safe. She never told me why, and I do not know if she even knew why herself, but she'd taken you from certain death and sworn to protect you as her own."

With a sniffle, Byria pressed her cheek to the top of the jar and let herself cry more. *Why?* she wondered. *Why protect me?*

Hawush stopped pacing and turning and settled back down so his nose was just in front of her folded legs again. When she lifted her head, she saw him blink slowly, then wipe his cheeks on the stone, leaving wet marks.

She stroked his nose and feelers. "What else would you like to know?"

Hawush took another deep breath and released it with a rumbling, "Hmmm…"

Byria found it easier than expected to be patient. Now that she was reunited with Hawush, there was no needing to rush, no needing to actually *do* anything.

Tightening his lips and then swallowing, Hawush spoke his next question in a tentative rumble. "If you remember nothing from before but fragments…"

Byria barely kept from flinching from the sight of his pained grimace.

"How could you say you forgive me for something you do not remember?"

After a short pause to consider the question, Byria found this the easiest to answer. "Because I *knew* I did. There are things I've done because, while I don't have the memories, I *know*. Things just come to me as True Things. Such as when I broke your prison. I have no memory of reading or writing, but I knew where I should stab the writing, how to stab it, how to break it. I *knew* certain things to do that helped me survive while I came here. When you asked me to forgive you, I *knew* I did. And I still know it."

He chuffed at her as he jerked his head back up. Byria winced from the edge of hot air that hit her, even though he'd quickly turned to avoid her. "But you *don't know!*"

"I *know*. I just don't *remember*."

"How can you know if you do not remember?" Another puff of ember-filled smoke flew into the breeze as he spoke.

"The same way I knew I needed to recognize you in the parade, the same way I knew where I had to go after I finally heard you, and the same way I knew how to set you free after I told you I forgave you."

Hawush shook his head hard and stood, returning to his circular pacing on the ledge. "You should *know* what you think you have forgiven me for."

Byria paused. "I know it's not my turn to ask questions, and we can wait until tomorrow if you want… but do you want to tell me?"

"Of *course* I do not want to tell you." He hissed over his shoulder, tail wagging angrily. After another turn, he said, voice slightly more subdued, though still a bitter growl, "But I will. And it is foolish to wait a day, as we are speaking of it now."

Byria nodded, resettling herself to sit and listen.

Hawush turned a few more times, his growl still reverberating as stars appeared in the sky behind him. Finally, he sat on his rear legs, tail still swishing, and he looked toward the sky as he spoke.

"I remember you begging me to help you more than anything. Begging me not to let them take you. You had fought and lost, and they had bound you. You were scared, and I was scared for you, but not as much as I was of—" A shudder chopped through his growl and shivered from the top of his head all the way to the end of his tail. Byria put the jar with Patch's eye down and hugged her knees to her chest. *What can scare a dragon so…?*

"I had not felt my power—my *being*—pulled from me like that since my first prison." He glanced over his shoulder at Byria; the red in his eyes sparkled like a bed of embers in a fireplace. "The one my lady saved me from. I had not felt like that for so long. I have never felt terror like that."

Her memories were her being. A part of it, anyway. Byria at least knew some of his terror.

He took a deep breath, blowing out another flume of smoke. "But it should *not* have been more terrifying than letting them take you."

He lay down, head just over the edge of the cave's ledge. "I told myself I was no help to you if they weakened me like that, that if I left and came back for you, I could still save you. So while you screamed and cried for me, I flew away and hid."

Still holding her knees, Byria leaned forward and stared at Hawush. She said nothing for a long time. When the silence became too chilled and painful, she finally asked, "If you flew away and hid, how did they capture you? You must have come back for me."

"I did, but I was too late. When I hid, I fell into a deep sleep, healing what they stole from me. I knew I had done that when my lady rescued me, but I had not expected they had taken so much that I would do so again. I do not know how long I slept, only that when I finally found you, you were at the palace. I stalked, hid, and waited until you were with only your women in the garden, figuring they would run, and I would take you. Only I was too late. They had attacked your mind already, and you did not recognize me."

Byria swallowed hard, searching all her recently loosed memories for that one.

He looked out over the mountainside. "You fled with your serving women. When I followed, you were utterly terrified of me. I did not know what to do; I could not leave you, but you would come nowhere near me. Seeing that fear in your eyes—seeing you in so much pain…" His voice wavered with the sound of more tears.

"Your every movement looked like it hurt when you tried to escape me... That was when they captured me. I did not even fight them."

After another moment of silence, Byria whispered, "I don't remember any of that."

"But it happened. I let them take you, which allowed them to torture you. Had I not run, I could have saved you and kept my word to my lady that I would protect you with my life. Just as she had done for me." His breath came out through his nose in loud, angry, smoking snorts. Byria could see his ribs spasm with each pant.

Pressing her lips together, Byria picked up the eye jar once more. She traced her finger around it. Within the jar, the eye looked at her, then slowly turned to look at the dragon. As she held the jar, she felt no anger and no bitterness.

Slowly the eye turned back to her. She nodded and put the jar back down so she could stand. "Hawush—"

The spiny fins on his back flexed up, and he stretched his back as flames erupted to each side of him.

"Wait!" She took a step toward him, surprised that she felt little heat from his massive wingspan.

Turning, he lifted his wings and looked under them at her with his burning, sad eyes. "I will not leave you like that again, but I need to fly." He spoke barely loud enough to be heard over the crackle of his fiery wings.

"Wait. First, I still forgive you. Now that I know, I still forgive you. And so does Patch." She lifted the jar so he could see what she saw, perhaps feel what she'd just felt. The eye turned to look at him.

He stared at her—at her and the eye—for a few moments before bowing his head. "I will return shortly, and I *swear* I will never abandon you again."

With that, he leaped off the ledge and soared into the distance. Byria wiped the tears flowing from her eyes with her sleeve. Watching until she couldn't even see a spark of his wings, she carefully stowed the eye again.

It would be some time before he no longer carried the guilt; this was a True Thing. Her own healing, she sensed, as well as her memories, were tied to his healing.

She would continue to remind him that she forgave him.

Moreso, that she still loved him.

* * * * *

Chapter Five
Keeping Fruit

Hawush returned with a heavy bough laden with ripe mangoes. He said only, "I recall you need more than animal or fish flesh to be healthy, and I remembered you liked this."

"I do," Byria said.

"Do you remember how to prepare it so it lasts? You and my lady would do that, not I."

Byria nodded, giving him space to talk about something simple, like food and good memories. She liked food and the memories she recalled about food. "When I was in the village in the jungle, the two who helped Patch when I was a baby, Koki and Mokin, took me in and helped me get to the mountains. They taught me a lot while I was there, but I felt I'd known some things before, so I learned it very quickly."

He paused, as if confused by her words, but nodded. "I also recall you need to eat several times in a day."

Rubbing her stomach, Byria affirmed that, too. She *had* been getting hungry again. "Would you like some?"

Hawush made a face of disgust. "Dragons eat only flesh and bones and such. Things we kill." His eyes narrowed, as if seeing what Byria thought of such a fact.

She nodded and shrugged. In her satchel was a stone knife Mokin had given her that was better suited for cutting and preparing food. She retrieved that and peeled a fruit, cutting chunks to eat until she got to the massive seed in the center. Hawush lay outside the front of the cave and watched.

After tossing the uneaten skins and seeds off the side of the ledge, Byria stated, "I'll take care of the rest in the morning." After a moment's hesitation, she asked, "Did you want to talk or ask more? Or, I don't know... perhaps just rest?"

The dragon didn't answer right away. He stood and stretched, then pulled the fruit branch mostly into the cave. "If the wind takes it, it will fall, and the fruit will be lost."

After repositioning it a few times, he stretched once more, and then curled up in the worn dent in the stone where he slept. "You may forgive me, but do you still wish to stay with me?"

"I do," Byria answered without hesitation and went over to him.

He lowered his head as she ran her hands over his face and feelers then planted a small kiss just above his nose, similar to the ones she'd planted on Koki's cheeks or upon the jar with Patch's eye. He ducked his head, almost shyly. Then he curled up as he did for sleep and held his arms out to her.

Smiling, she crawled into his embrace.

* * * * *

Chapter Six
Fire and Other True Things That Hurt

The next day, Hawush went to hunt more meat.

Byria settled in to cut up more mangoes and do her best to remember how to properly dry them. She didn't have the many-leveled fire with clay grates and stones from Mokin's outdoor hearth, but she had an idea.

The wind was enough, and the air was dry, which she knew was better than the still, humid air of the jungle for preserving food, but she needed fire. A smile touched her lips, and the spark in her chest called to her.

Moreso, she *wanted* to show Hawush what she'd discovered about herself and ask him about it. After all, he was a dragon who created fire for wings and breathed it at will; surely, he could teach her more of this ability.

She wanted to practice first.

By the time Hawush returned with another fish, Byria had created a small fire protected from the wind with stones she'd found near the hot pond. She'd even woven layers of the tiny, fresh green sticks and flatter stones to hold the drying mango slices.

He put down the fish, holding it with his rear foot as he inspected her little chimney. "I could have done that for you." He sniffed.

"I know, but I wanted to show you what I could do."

"I am aware that humans can create fire."

"Well, yes, but not like I do."

He tilted his head curiously.

With a smile, Byria held out the palm of her left hand, the one he'd healed completely. It took her a little longer than she wanted, but she managed to summon a small flame—no larger than a candle's flame—from the palm of her hand.

Hawush blinked and snorted in surprise.

"There's more. I *just* learned what I'll show you." She made the flame engulf her index finger, and then stuck her finger into one of the holes in the side of her little chimney where orange flame flickered. She held it in until she felt the heat, and then pulled it out. The flame around her finger disappeared, revealing a layer of black soot. She wiped it off to reveal the same pristine skin as before her experiment.

After another blink, the dragon leaned closer and took a deep sniff of her. His feelers and tendrils reached past his snout to touch her face and under the hat she'd remembered to wear to keep the sun from her face.

Byria let him, but also let her expression convey her confusion at his response.

"I knew you had magic, but I would think I would have recognized fire within you as I did my lady."

"You knew I had magic before?"

"I knew you healed faster than humans, and my lady confirmed that as well. And you managed to get into all sorts of trouble I did not expect." He gave a little chuckle. "But you should eat now. You have the rest of the day to ask me whatever questions you wish."

"May I ask you things while you cut up the fish again?"

"I suppose you already are." There was more amusement than chiding in his eyes and voice.

"How far away is the ocean? I appreciate you wanting to bring me my favorite food, but I wasn't a picky eater at the palace. Was I a picky eater when I stayed with you?"

"No. You were easy to keep fed, and you were beginning to learn to hunt on your own. However, the beasts around here are tainted with magic. Hunting those in the jungles, I could potentially run into the fey who helped you, and the history between their people and mine is far from friendly."

He gutted the fish as he'd done the day before. "I want to make sure the food is safe for you, so I would rather take the time to go out to the ocean. I have already eaten, so perhaps you can make the extra meat from the fish last for some days, too."

He cut the fish's flesh into smaller chunks.

Byria tilted her head and looked at her little chimney, lips pursed. "Would it be safe to assume you can touch hot rocks without injury or pain?"

"It would."

"Then yes. I'll need your help to make this bigger, though."

"I can do that."

"How are the animals around here tainted? Are you sure it would hurt me?"

"I do not know if it would hurt you. I just *know*—in the sense you say you *know* things—magical flesh is not meant for mortals to consume, human or fey. The folk of the jungle do not hunt outside of their trees."

"They don't even like coming here," Byria added.

"They are tied to their lands, as are most fey. It is uncomfortable for them to leave. Shall I cut the rest of this flesh as I remember we would in planning for your eating needs? Your fire looks different than what I recall."

Byria shrugged and picked up the chunks of fish. "If you look inside, you can see how I cut the mangoes. Did Patch teach me how to properly build a drying fire?"

"My lady left you in my care after a few years; she needed to lead away assassins coming for you."

"Assassins? For me?"

"Eat first, and then I will answer your questions." Hawush waited for her to begin eating, then slurped up the innards of the fish before checking on the chimney. After studying it awhile, he appeared satisfied and cut up the rest of the fish, eating everything that wasn't flesh.

Once they'd finished eating, Hawush rebuilt the chimney to dry the fish as well as the mangoes. Then the dragon lay on his stomach and waited, crossing his hands in front of him much like a cat.

With a shy smile, Byria sat beside him. He gave her a nod as she silently asked if she could lean on his side. Upon settling against him, warm as he was and her face properly shaded from the sun, she sighed deeply, not sure where to begin with her questions.

After a long silence, Hawush stretched and rolled on his side. Byria readjusted herself so she rested on his stomach, which had the largest and most pliable scales. His belly was hotter than his side, but it felt good against Byria's back. She'd been hunched and moving stones all day.

Finally, a question she liked hit her. "What do you think is the most important thing I should be asking about?"

Lifting his head, he regarded her with half-closed eyes and a snort.

She pouted at him, conceding without words that it was almost a cheat of a question. But where else would she begin?

"You asked earlier about assassins," he said. "So, I suppose why there would be assassins coming for you is as good a start as any. I would imagine people would be coming for you again in time—"

"What?" Byria sat up and stared at him, fear widening her eyes. "Would they find me here? *Why?* Is that how they found you and captured you? They were coming for *me*? Have I put you in danger?"

"Ssssshhhh," he soothed, flicking his tongue at her gently. "I invited you to stay here, and I promised I would never abandon you again, did I not? Besides, they have many obstacles to cross to find me here, and they have never known me to be here before. Also, you said you stayed with the fey. I would imagine they would not want humans anywhere near them, so they will mislead them any way possible."

"You weren't here before? But Koki and the other—fey, you called them?—remembered me and Patch. We passed through when I was little and stayed with them for some years. The couple, Koki and Mokin, they tried to talk Patch out of coming to find you. Me, too."

"I was in the mountains, but not *here*, specifically. I was much closer to the ocean."

"Oh." Byria remembered Koki marking the map near the ocean. "But they *did* mark here, or near here."

Hawush snorted. "Well, it *is* a fair guess on their part, but that begins a much longer answer. I will tell you what my lady told me about you when she asked me to help her care for you."

"Please." Byria nodded and settled back against him.

"You were very young, needing to be carried more than you were able to walk, when my lady arrived here with you. You slept a lot, and asked ridiculous questions, and cried when you did not like my answers. I was *not* accustomed to human children, so the fact that I was indebted to my lady was definitely in favor of your survival."

He gave a teasing chuff in her direction, and she chuckled.

"She told me she had been captured by your family and made to be your nursemaid. I did not get details on *why* or *how* that happened, just that it did. She also had *not* specifically said your family had been the ones who removed her marked eye."

Byria winced.

Another snort produced smoke. "In any case, another family came in one night and killed your family. My lady had heard them and stole away with you as the palace guards fought the assassins. She took you, for while she had not wanted to be enslaved by your family, she had grown fond of you. She stayed in the jungle for some time, years, as you say, but she felt you would be safer protected by a dragon than a village of small fey."

His voice grew bitter as he spoke the last part. "And I did owe my life to her, so I could not refuse."

"So you were stuck with me?" Byria asked softly.

Hawush regarded her. "I was annoyed at your crying and whining, but I never resented that my lady brought you to me. I enjoyed her company very much, as I soon grew to enjoy yours." Curling his neck, he gave her shoulder a gentle nuzzle.

With a smile, Byria rubbed under his chin, gently scratching around the feelers.

He half closed his eyes, smiling and rumbling with pleasure. After a moment, he pulled away and continued. "Some years later, word came from the jungle fey that humans were tearing apart the jungles to find you. My lady assumed it was the same assassins, so she left us to lead them away... and never returned."

Byria bit her lip and swallowed hard.

Sadness colored his voice, and he blinked the glimmer of tears from his eyes. "I still had you to protect, and I would not abandon you to go look for her. No word came about her from the jungle fey, and no others came, so I had hoped she had done well in leading them away. When they did finally return, several years later, they were disguised—even to me. And that they were able to drain me as they did..." His sentence trailed off in a low growl.

"They must've had a very powerful magepriest with them."

"Their intent was to kill neither of us. That much was certain. Had they been assassins—"

"They'd have simply killed me on sight. No." Byria shook her head. "If they knew a dragon was involved, they wouldn't try to kill you, either. The story I was told was that a dragon had kidnapped me as a child, and Tain—" she said his name as if slime were on her tongue "—came to rescue me and reclaim the power of the dragon for my family, in exchange for the right to marry me."

Hawush growled again.

"Patch said she hadn't told them anything about me or you when she was captured. I believe her."

Hawush nodded. "I do as well."

"So, how did they know I was with a dragon?"

He sighed. "A number of reasons. Or, perhaps, they figured you *were* the dragon."

"What?"

"You said they told you *he* was reclaiming the power of the dragon for your family. How long were you told your 'family' ruled the lands?"

"Over two hundred years. Paintings are all over the palace of the different emperors and their families. But if they really aren't my family, if they're imposter assassins…" Byria frowned.

"That makes no sense unless they were disguised by some magic. Would the humans you ruled over not notice that, all of a sudden, their rulers for so many generations now had different faces?"

"No. They wouldn't," Byria said softly. "My family is considered sacred, so no one but our most trusted servants, the highest court officials, and the highest ranking magepriests are allowed to look upon our faces. Even during great holidays, we go out painted and shaded and, as you saw, on high floats. If they came in quietly, and the magepriests supported these imposter assassins, then…"

"No one would know the difference." Hawush sighed and nuzzled her again. "If *your* family did have magic in their blood, and the imposters did not, they would want to reclaim you to bring the magic back to the bloodline. That is why they wanted to change your memories, keep you alive, and marry you off to one of their choosing."

"The fact that I had a dragon protecting me didn't hurt, either, or their story that you'd kidnapped me for yourself." Byria also glared in the direction of the palace, blinking back stinging tears.

Hawush growled again, sending curls of smoke and sparks out through his nostrils.

"If I was that young, would I even remember my parents' true faces? Likely not. I wouldn't know, though they always told me I looked ugly."

She held out her arms that, even though she still wore the long-sleeved shirt, had grown darker from the sun's exposure. Her skin had been a slightly different color from that of her "parents," and her face never had looked right compared to theirs. It was more angular, with a longer nose and flatter cheekbones.

"I am no judge of human physique, but I have never found you ugly."

Byria chuckled and rolled over, tucking her knees up so she leaned the side of her face and arm against him now. "So, that explains much about... well, almost everything. Not what actually happened, but at least why. And why is important."

"Yes."

Byria hesitated, then said, "You know I have magic, and maybe it's from my family that was assassinated. I see it as my heart's fire. You're a creature of fire and earth. I'm only just learning what I can do with this magic. Would you...?"

"I can try to teach you. I cannot imagine it would be easy."

She laughed. "It's *never* been easy."

"Then yes, I will help." Hawush laid his head and neck back down on the sandy stone, rubbing it as if it itched. He said nothing more, awaiting her next question.

Byria felt she'd discovered quite enough about herself. Any other things she needed to know would be memories of her time with him and Patch, things she'd learned, experiences they'd shared. Some of those memories would be painful or difficult, but she could handle them. Tonight was her night to ask difficult *questions*, and one had been pinging in her head since Hawush had brought up his relationship with Patch.

"How did you come to owe Patch such a debt that you took on an annoying human child and vowed to protect her with your life?"

Hawush's groaning sigh was so great, the movement in his belly nearly knocked Byria over. She gently rubbed her hand against his scales, but didn't rescind her question.

After a very, very long wait—Byria was *quite* proud of her patience—he gave a short answer. "She set me free from another prison that was also draining my power and my spirit."

Byria waited for elaboration that didn't come. Finally, she prodded. "Who imprisoned you, and how?"

Further groaning, only stronger, had Byria grasping his elbow to keep from rolling to the ground. At least the time it took for him to respond wasn't as long.

"I was born there. My mother was imprisoned before she even laid her clutch of eggs. I was the only one who hatched." He sighed again. "Sometimes she would care for me, make sure I ate, but as time drew on, I stopped growing, and remained ever a dragonling. She grew to resent me, and I had to even fight her for my food. And that was the least of our issues."

"The least of your issues?" She thought of Mokin and his father.

He stretched his side more gently, so as not to send Byria tumbling. "They are not easily apparent to your human eyes, but I still have scars. The uneven lines of my scales show it somewhat."

Byria stood and ran her fingers down the length of his side. He snorted, but stayed still for her to touch him. She said nothing, letting him continue.

"Most of the scars are from her, particularly the long ones, from our fights over what rats or goats may have found their way into the prison. Besides that, not nearly as often but more memorable, strangers would come in and attack us. Always humans. Sometimes my mother killed them. Those were the hardest fights with her, because she would not share those prizes."

A shiver ran down his body from his head to his tail, nearly knocking Byria over again.

"Other times, they won, and I thought my mother was dead. She never let me fight them, either." He took a deep breath. "After some time, she would begin breathing again, not dead, but angrier and... less the mother I remembered from my youngest days."

Byria sat back down as Hawush closed his eyes and was silent a moment.

"My lady ended up being one of those humans we would meet. She was escaping humans, herself. She had run to the mountains, hid in the creation that imprisoned me, and found herself attacked by magic. As she had her own magic, she fought it off and ended up facing my mother and me.

"My mother, starving, for it had been a very, very long time since anything had stumbled upon us, attacked me first—perhaps intending to keep me from eating what she wanted. My lady did *not* do what I still believe would have been the logical choice: run."

Byria nodded. "She wouldn't."

He nodded. "Instead, she turned upon my mother, protecting me. She slew her—pulling her very magic from her in an arc of fire that she sent to me, taking none for herself. In that moment, I *knew* my mother was truly dead. But I also knew, by that time, there was likely nothing left of who she had been."

Leaning against him, she stroked his scales, hoping it brought some comfort.

He let out a ragged sigh and swallowed. "I do not know whether it was the energy it took, or the sheer amount of fire, but the prison began to fall around us. That was when my rescuer, my lady, finally ran, looking back at me to ensure I was unhurt. I followed her out. She threw fire and energy at boulders and cracks and safely led us away from that prison. When we were clear, she collapsed."

"Collapsed?"

"Yes. She had given all for me. I was exhausted, too, but I still had the energy of my mother inside of me; I could feel it. I sent some to her, then finally collapsed myself. When I woke, she was already tending to my injuries, and her eye was marked."

Byria blinked a few times, wondering how having a mark put on one's eye like that felt.

He paused, taking another deep breath. "My prison, the only place I had known since birth, was nothing but a pile of stones and boulders."

Byria lay herself across his stomach and looked over the valley as he rested his neck and head flat upon the stone. "One you make sure to piss and shit on every day now?"

Hawush chuckled beneath her, but said nothing.

"And that's why you don't think they'd look for you here? Because you wouldn't choose to be so close to it?"

"Mmm-hmm."

"And is that why the animals are tainted with magic you're worried about me eating?"

"Mmm-hmm." He lifted his head to speak more clearly. "But for the jungle animals. I am fairly sure my prison's freed magic did not affect the fey territory. They would not permit such abomination."

Byria sighed against him, rubbing her cheek with the grain of his scales—for their edges were sharp and hard. "I'm sorry that happened to you."

His chuckle this time was dry. "I would say the same for you."

"Mmm-hmm."

More of a laugh than a chuckle this time, his mirth vibrated beneath Byria enough to make her stand up and move closer to his face, where she sat, cross-legged, in front of him.

"One more important question, and I believe I'm done for now," she said solemnly, fighting her lips that wanted to quirk up on either corner of her mouth.

Hawush lifted his head and regarded her, his feelers dangling in her lap. The hint of a smile and twinkle in his eye let her know she wasn't fooling him. "Since I have plenty of food, and you say you've eaten well, what shall we do with our time tomorrow? In our time together, did you ever take me for a fly?"

"In our time together, that was one of your favorite ways to pass a day."

* * * * *

Chapter Seven
A History of The World, One Story

The next few days passed with Byria remembering the thrill of flying.

Hawush started by carrying her in his hands. Before she'd been taken, he'd explained, Byria had only begun trying to balance at his shoulders (without being in the way of the fin scales that helped him steer in the air).

He took her over "the tainted lands" to see some of the animals. Besides the palace menagerie, Byria remembered animals more from pictures in paintings and on tapestries, which made animals look different. For some of the deer and wild water buffalo, and the birds, she didn't notice the changes immediately—unless they were a more unnatural color, or she caught them breathing fire. Or water. Or, in one case, even ice!

She recognized the sacred and magical beasts from tapestries, statues, carved art—and even the knives she recalled in the high magepriest's hidden room. A peacock of flame was clearly a phoenix. A beast chasing after a normal-looking deer was definitely a manticore—which Byria remembered came from the deserts east across the vast ocean, or from the very far west. Other creatures she didn't recognize at all. Often, these looked like two or three beasts sewn together, or simply shades of two- and four-legged things with teeth and claws. Even Hawush stayed away from those creatures.

"They're all here because Patch destroyed your prison?" Byria asked as they found a high ledge to rest on. Below them stretched a puzzlework of terrains to the north and west horizons. Swaths of black desert sand ran into copses of trees Byria didn't recognize; tufts of fine plains grasses patterned against the thick, reedy grasses and thorny vine bushes. Here and there, ponds reflected patches of perfect blue sky, some steaming hot and simmering like the water in the mountain, others perfectly still even when the wind bent the vegetation around them.

"The world is full of pockets of magic, places the oldest of magic still exists under the layers created by the old gods, and then their children. Creatures like us, some created by the First Ones, the Elements, are drawn here naturally. We have some effect on the land around us."

He paused and took a breath, curling his body more closely around Byria, who rested against his side. "If a thing happens that disturbs those layers, a wild magic is born, and that *does* affect, well, just about everything."

"Even you?"

"I am affected some, but not as much as others. Dragons were the first... *special* creations by the Elements. There were plants, fish, birds, but the Elements wanted beings who might recognize them, who had a measure of power over the land and its energies and its inhabitants. So they created dragons. They created two kinds, those whose parents were Earth, Fire, and Magic, and those whose parents were Water, Air, and Magic. When they saw they liked what they created, they began creating other things: the various types of unicorns, the phoenix and the storm birds, the great whales and golden fish…"

"And the sea serpents?" Byria asked. Byria had heard stories of the giant water snakes destroying trade ships over the great ocean. In that meeting Tain had forced her to sit through with fever, she remembered a discussion of serpent attacks having become so frequent, there'd grown a whole new industry of insuring trade goods that came from overseas.

Hawush chuffed at the mention of the sea serpents. "They are *not* among the original magical beasts created by the Elements. They were made by the ancient gods in a weak attempt to recreate dragons. A poor mimicry, at best."

Byria smiled at the pride in his tone. She imagined, if a dragon hadn't been as abused as Hawush had been for so much of his life, it would speak as he was now—only all the time. Especially if they claimed to be older than ancient gods.

Of course, Hawush's history of all things sounded different than the one she'd heard over and over from the high magepriests at the regular services to the God.

"Is this how the world is, the Elements and ancient gods and ancient gods' children? Is this something you've told me before?" She pressed her cheek against his flank. Nearness to him often loosened more memories, but there was nothing for this.

He tilted his head, considering. "Not much. You never specifically asked. And like our Creators now, dragons pay little mind to those who came after us."

"Will you tell me what you know?"

"Mmm," he rumbled, stretching in thought, but mindful not to jostle her. "When things began, in darkness and light and energy becoming physical, the first things to become aware were the Elements of Earth, Fire, Water, Air, and Magic. The first four created materials for themselves, and those materials were in many forms. Magic never wanted to have a form, but would bind with each regularly."

Byria giggled; if nothing else, spending time among her serving girls and Syng had taught her there was a name for such loose people. Of course, such people would have never been considered as one of the Beings that likely created the universe.

Hawush raised an eyebrow at her and smirked. She wondered how much he knew of human culture, but didn't want to interrupt the lesson to ask. She gestured for him to continue.

"As I said, they turned their many parts—combining them and separating them and more—into the world we see, only younger, and with fewer plants and creatures. But the Creator Elements set in place all the groundwork—stone, volcanoes, oceans, winds, lands. After creating all of that, after watching for so long, after seeing many creations live and die to extinction, they wished to create something different. Those that they made bore offspring and had relationships with, rather than simply watched, those offspring…"

His voice trailed off; Byria figured he was thinking of his "relationship" with his mother. She stroked her hand over his side, and he gave a little shake to dismiss it.

"And the Elements wanted that, so they birthed the beings most now call the Ancient Gods. The Elements do not have personalities or spirits as you and I know. They just… are. The personalities and spirits of the dragons and the beasts whose lines survived until now, those developed over time, influenced by the world around us.

"That process began with the Ancient Gods, who, unlike their Elemental parents, *very much* developed individual personalities. Some were selfless creatures of pure love; others were cruel, selfish, and hateful; most fell between those extremes.

"Most importantly, the Ancient Gods wanted to create bigger and better things than the Elements had. They wanted the world to be theirs, and they developed a desire to be worshipped—something the Elements did not crave. So, the Elements left the world in the hands of their children.

"It was the Ancient Gods who created the fey beings, as well as other types of magical beasts—sea serpents among them—and the world changed greatly in their care."

"For better, or for worse?" Byria asked, wondering how her kingdom had been before the imposter assassins had come. How much had changed? Had it been better before?

"Does it need to be better or worse?" Hawush asked.

That made her pause. "I suppose not."

"Of course, like their parents before them, some of the Ancient Gods eventually wanted to create 'children' rather than just beings who worshipped them. And then those children wanted to be as their parents and have this world and its worship for themselves.

"As the Ancient Gods were not like the Elements and did *not* want to relinquish control, this became a war that would leave the world more changed than anything, leaving both scars and beauty. The Deivim, as is the most common term for the Ancient Gods' children, created their own persons—humans, like you—and promised them control over the world's resources if they could wrest it from the creations of the Ancient Gods and the creatures before them. Battle broke out between the different races and creations of the gods and the elements.

"As you might imagine, such things never end well. Many of the fey races were decimated or went into hiding. Most of the magical beasts were hunted to extinction or near extinction. Even dragons."

"We were taught dragons hunted humans."

He shook his head. "To *survive*. There are so few of us now. And being hunted to death was not even the worst." A shudder ran down the length of Hawush's body.

"The prisons?" Byria asked.

Hawush nodded. "They are more than that; I cannot begin to explain, and I was born within one, so my experience was limited."

"How old are you, then? I mean, if that's not a rude question to ask."

Hawush managed to get one of his clawed hands around Byria for protection as a massive laugh had him rolling back and forth. She chuckled nervously, not sensing any offense, but not sure why he found her question so hilarious.

"You have asked me more questions that delve up painful memories in less than a moon's quarter phase than I have ever answered in all my life prior. My age is hardly a thing I would find rude to ask about."

"Oh." Byria's cheeks flushed.

"Not that I am upset. I gave you permission to ask such questions." He gently placed her back on the ledge. "As for my age, I honestly could not tell you. I was freed from my prison but four or five years before I met you, you were with me for seven, perhaps eight years, and I was imprisoned by your imposter family for an additional six. Before that, I could not tell you how long I was imprisoned, or even if I matured at the proper rate, for I lacked space to grow and sufficient food to eat. It could have been centuries. I have not even a glimpse of this world to compare for any passage of time. My guess is, for one of my kind, I am still especially young."

"How do you know all of what happened, then? I mean…"

"Did my mother tell me?" He chuffed. "In a sense. All dragons are born with a collective memory separate from our own that goes back to the very first dragons created."

"Oh." Byria blinked several times. While she knew it was the fault of Tain and the high magepriest that she could hardly keep track of the memories she had and was still discovering, she wondered how a dragon's mind managed hundreds and hundreds, perhaps thousands of years of one's own memory, plus the memories of all dragons that had ever lived.

As if he understood her unspoken bewilderment, he continued. "I know my own thoughts and memories, and there are things I just *know*. I may not have thought about them prior to being asked, but I *know*."

"Do you think I'll get the rest of my memories back? And that the ones I make now won't slip away?" They hadn't yet, though they sometimes felt fuzzy and out of order.

Hawush said nothing for a moment, then spoke very softly. "I do not know. But I do know that you are still hurt, and you do not seem to want those things to heal. I believe that affects things, too."

Byria pressed her lips together. She didn't entirely understand her own behavior, either. She trusted Hawush with her life. In her heart, she also felt if he were attacked, she might not fail him as she'd failed Owi. She would offer her life in trade for his, yet…

She hugged herself.

What she'd done to her body, what she did to it now—let it be healed or not healed, touch scars she'd given herself—she was in control of that. It was her power. She wasn't ready to give that up.

Giving a little shake, Hawush let her know she should stand. Stretching, he said, "We should probably return to the cave." He pointed with his chin toward a nearby clump of trees. Shadows within them moved out of turn with the wind and branches. "I do not *know* all the creatures I see out here, and I would rather not chance their abilities this close."

* * * * *

Chapter Eight
Questions from a Nightmare

That night, Byria had her first nightmare since finding Hawush.

As she stood upon the stone floor, gasping for breath and shaking, she remembered punching and kicking his taloned hands that held her. Her ears still rang with her scream. Her muscles ached, and her hands and feet felt bruised.

Hawush still stood near, both protectively—eyes flicking between the mouth of the cave and Byria—and apprehensively, leaning a little away from her. He held one of his front hand-feet off the ground, flexing it. A tiny piece of the shirt Byria wore clung to one of the claws.

She checked herself, finding the tear on her shoulder, but feeling no blood nor the pain of a cut.

"Byria?" the dragon asked after a few moments.

Byria stopped rubbing her shoulders. Hawush took a step nearer, and she instinctively backed away, her mind struggling to pull apart the dream pieces from *Real* and *Now*. When she flinched, he did, too, nostrils twitching and tongue flicking from his mouth.

Scrunching her feet against the cool rock, Byria felt her toenails drag. It wasn't a comfortable sensation, but she did it again and again, grounding herself, helping her sort her mind. She'd tucked her hands under her arms, digging her long nails into her underarms; pain helped her focus.

She'd been bound in the dream, held down by Tain and bound. Glancing at the material on Hawush's claw, she figured she must've gotten caught on him, and that had added to her trapped feeling. The nightmare lashes and punches ghost-ached over where she knew real scars recorded Tain's abuse. Of course, he'd said he was punishing her, helping her, but there was more.

Was it a memory? One of the awful ones her mind worked so hard to hide?

Or just a fear?

"Does your knowing include anything about the God my people worship?"

"What is his name? What do you call him?"

"We are never to use his name. We call him Great God, True God, Giver of High Magic, Enemy of Demons."

Hawush lowered his head. "That is all I remember, too, and no, I do not *know* more. They invoked him when they harvested my energy."

She paused. "They harvested your energy?"

His lips twitched, then he snarled. "Yes. That is why they wanted me and kept me as they did."

Byria blinked. "How?"

"Painfully," he said flatly.

Byria unfolded her arms and looked at her hands, one in perfect condition from Hawush's healing, the other with the ends of scars extending past her wrist and up her forearm. Outside of the irregularities in Hawush's scales, which she hadn't noticed until he'd pointed them out, she hadn't seen other scars upon him. Perhaps scaled creatures hid their injuries differently. It wasn't as if his softest skin was all that was between him and the awful world.

She paced a few times, rubbing herself as a cool wind came in through the cave mouth; the stone she walked on chilled her bare feet. What time of year had she left? Had she even thought of that? Would the cooler, rainy season be coming soon?

Pressing her lips together, she tried counting all her days of travel and imprisonment. She'd had her woman's blood while traveling with Koki to the mountains, and there had barely been half of either moon's phase since. As she counted these recent memories, the nightmare flashed in her mind, and they flowed together.

No!

She pinched her underarms hard, knowing her skin would bruise; Hawush might smell if she drew her own blood. Why did the memories still flow together?

Tears blurred her vision, so she lowered her head to watch her feet. Her hair, which had grown faster than expected, curtained her face, but it didn't hide her loud sniffles.

She heard nothing from Hawush, but she felt his eyes on her every so often. When she didn't sense him looking at her, she gave her head a tiny flick and looked at him through her hair. He was licking his hand and flexing it.

"Did I hurt you?" she asked, just connecting that fact at the moment.

"Some bruises, I think. They will be gone by morning."

"I'm sorry, and you can't tell me I don't get to apologize for that."

"Then I accept your apology, Byria."

She smiled, appreciating him saying so, even though his voice suggested she needn't apologize. Taking a deep breath, she walked back to him and leaned her face on his shoulder. He nuzzled her softly, his feelers brushing her back. She uncrossed her arms and rubbed her hands over his scales, feeling irregularities up his neck where they didn't quite align smoothly.

"We should probably go back to sleep," she murmured against him.

He chuffed against her, his breath hot. He was too agitated, worried for her to sleep.

"We should try. You were going to take me to the beach in the morning, and I want to be well rested."

"I suppose we should make a trip to the jungle soon so I might kill you something with a pelt to sleep on." He shook the piece of material from his claw.

"I'm comfortable sleeping as you hold me. Unless you'd rather not?"

"I do not mind holding you, but it is getting colder. We made you a bed when you were with me before…" His voice trailed off.

Byria nodded, arranging herself beside him as he opened his arms to cradle her again.

"I remember sleeping on skins. I remembered that the first night I was here. You still held me."

"I did. And I will, unless you ever ask me not to."

* * * * *

Chapter Nine
The Beach Memory

The beach sand by the ocean was a silvery pink. A returning memory told Byria the color came from certain sea creature shells and local stones. Hawush confirmed so when she asked.

During the morning, they practiced flying with her on his back; he was concerned about her falling, even when he focused his magic to keep her on. Byria didn't argue; as brave as she was becoming, she didn't want to fall from even the low heights and slow speeds at which he moved when she was atop him.

Come afternoon, Hawush left Byria on the beach so he could hunt himself something to eat. She rolled up her trousers and walked along the shore as the waves lapped at her feet. The water was clear. Even walking up to her knees, she could see the bottom.

Further out, the water deepened into a most beautiful turquoise that met in a clear line of the cloudless sky's sharp, pale blue.

Smelling, feeling, hearing, even tasting the salty ocean air helped Byria with her memories. There'd been many memories at the beach, but they were scattered, with ragged edges. Splashing in the water. Digging in the sand. Watching the birds dart and dive. Mimicking the bird's cries back at them as if they were conversing. Shoving hair out of her face. Wind sticking salty hair to her cheeks. Collecting shells and organizing them into patterns of colors and shapes.

As she played with that last memory, wondering where it went in the whole pattern of broken memories, a shell of rich purple rolled over her foot. Feeling a childhood smile tug at her lips, she reached for it, but it slipped between her fingers.

Pouting, she took a few steps farther in, pulling her trousers up more. It was a small shell, but she wanted a closer look at it. A large wave soaked her to the waist, so she gave up trying to stay dry.

Finally, her hand wrapped around the shell. Between waves, the water was just above her waist. As the larger swells came in—she was beyond the breakers—she let herself bob just a little off the sand. Able to stand through a series of smaller swells, Byria studied the shell. It wasn't quite as brilliant as it had looked beneath the water, but it was still a lovely swirl of blues and purples, with fine white lines like marble veins. Tiny in the palm of her hand, it was a perfect nautilus without a crack or hole.

Clasping it, she turned toward the shore and froze.

How had she gotten so far in? The length from herself to where the waves broke on the shore was at least twice the length of Hawush.

Whether it was a memory not quite loosed or just the thought of being so far into the water, a shock of fear shot through her. She quickly headed toward the shore.

Water yanked at her legs, and her feet sank deeper as she tried to leave. One of the larger swells lifted her again, and an undertow pulled her deeper. She gasped, dropped the shell, and fought, trying to swim.

No memories of swimming came to her, so she did her best to flail her feet and pull with her arms. Her feet touched sand again, and the beach looked even farther away! She tried to run and swim at the same time, scrambling to get closer to the shore.

She didn't get far before another swell snagged her. And then there was *no* sand below her feet! She kicked bottomless water.

Byria spun in the water, trying to find the shoreline so she could attempt to swim in that direction. A movement further away in the water caught her attention and gave her another shock of fear. Something she should remember... something she should get away from rippled through the water. Came toward her. She tried swimming to the shore again.

Why couldn't she remember swimming? Had she known? The shore wasn't getting closer.

From above came a roar, and then the water and world flew away from her. She screamed in surprise, curling up as a gaping mouth full of teeth closed just below her. The jaw's *snap* popped the air around her, and she screamed again.

Byria sensed a fury from Hawush as he repositioned her in his front claws. The world spun again, and fire poured from his mouth at the sea serpent in the water. The ocean steamed hot clouds as the dragon arched upward.

Byria saw sky and water and beach; her stomach flipped even more times than they did. The water below—now behind them—churned in a whirlpool.

Hawush deposited her in the sand less gently than he normally did when putting her down. "*What* were you *thinking?*"

As she stumbled in the sand, as she felt his emotion, as she heard his chastisement, another memory came. A complete memory, a strong one.

Though tears flowed down her face, a smile broke through, and she ran to Hawush and embraced his leg. "I'm sorry! But I remember! I remember!"

He cocked his head curiously, though anger still narrowed his eyes.

"I don't know how to swim, and I walked too far, and I was trying to pick up a pretty shell—just like today—and I shouldn't go in the water so far. You were so angry, because there was a serpent then, too. And you grabbed me just in time, just like today. Your claw cut my shoulder because I was still struggling, and I was so scared. You wouldn't heal it all the way so that I wouldn't forget, but I did. I did. I won't again, I promise."

Hawush's eyes widened, anger fading to comfort and relief as he sat on his haunches.

Byria rubbed her runny nose on her wet sleeve. "I remember all of it, all of it! None of my other memories are all together like this."

Hawush tenderly ran a finger down her back as Byria cried happy tears against him, replaying the recent memory and the complete earlier memory, over and over.

* * * * *

Chapter Ten
Fireglass and Hot Water

They were flying back after another day at the beach when Hawush caught sight of something small and greenish moving through the valley. He circled, pointing the movement out to Byria, and swooped closer.

It was one of the jungle fey.

"Let's go see. They might need help," Byria said. In addition to sensing his thoughts and emotions, she'd grown stronger at speaking with him in her mind. There was no better way to communicate whilst wind and fire rushed around one's ears.

Hawush growled lowly—Byria could feel it against her back where he held her to his chest—and sent a mild disagreement, but circled lower.

The jungle fey had stopped moving. It looked like it had fallen. Hawush took in a deep breath through his mouth and nose and groaned slightly as he widened his wings for a landing.

He placed Byria down carefully as he stretched his rear legs to the ground. She caught her balance, close enough to finally see, and—

"Koki! Oh, Koki!" Heart hammering and anxious tears wetting her cheeks, Byria ran to the small woman, falling beside her. "Koki! Talk to me!" Forcing herself to take a deep breath, trying to pretend she could be calm like Mokin in an emergency—could he be calm for an unresponsive Koki?—Byria inspected the woman for injuries.

There was a hole in her shoulder, bleeding and soaking her leopardskin tunic. But it didn't look right; the appearance made Byria nauseous. Instead of the deep green she'd seen of their blood, a sticky mess of black flowed. And blackness colored the veins around her injury, not unlike the blackness of Mokin's scars.

The small woman shook, breath catching like she was choking.

"Hawush! Help! She's hurt!"

Hawush took another sniff of her. "Her blood is tainted. Upon my back. Hold with all your strength and all your heart's magic!"

Byria did so, barely containing her own choking sobs—she had to focus her heart's magic. For Koki. Hawush scooped up the small woman and leapt upward.

It was all Byria could do to cling to him at this speed of ascent. Her ears popped painfully, and his fin scales pricked her stomach and chest as he tried to steer. As he climbed so fast, she pressed flat against him, binding the fins. Even if she hadn't been so sick with worry, this flight was the least pleasant she'd ever experienced, with all the darting, writhing, and extra-hard wing beats.

When they got to their home ledge, Hawush gently laid Koki down. Byria was already trying to slide off before he crouched to help her, hardly keeping her feet. Her arms and legs were iron coils of pain; she did her best to shake them out.

"Get your token and my lady's eye," he commanded.

Byria hesitated, looking at the now-very-still Koki. Was she even breathing?

"Now! I will heal her."

Swallowing hard, Byria did as he bade and returned to Koki's side.

"Hold them close and call upon your heart's fire."

She nodded again, using the techniques Hawush had been teaching her so it flared to almost bonfire levels quickly.

Once Byria's chest burned as hot and wild as his wings, Hawush breathed upon her. His feelers tickled her face and eyes. "Keep watch and report to me anything you see."

Byria blinked as her vision grew clearer. The valley came into focus as if she were moving within it. She could see every blade of grass. All the colors became both brighter and sharper, and *different*, though she couldn't describe how.

"Tell me of any movement you see while I help your friend. Anything."

"Yes," she said, coughing over another emotional wave that choked up her throat. Koki would be all right. She was a fighter, a hunter. And Byria trusted Hawush.

After one more breath to release the tightness squeezing her chest, Byria saw to her task. Her eyes darted across the valley, looking for any movement whatsoever. All was still. Even the perpetual wind seemed calmer. The exact opposite of what she felt.

As her vision adjusted to almost grays in the growing length of the mountains' shadows, Hawush announced, "Your friend will live."

Byria turned around and fell to her knees at Koki's side. The woman was breathing, though her brow was still pale and tense. Her eyes fluttered.

Looking up to thank Hawush, she saw the dragon's colors looking drab, and crust around his eyes and nose. She reached to touch him, but he shook his head and took her place on the ledge.

"Hawush!"

"You should get her some water," Hawush said over his shoulder; his voice sounded tired.

"You're hurt! What—?"

"That... that blood poison, magic taint is... difficult. But I will be fine."

"Hawush—"

"You should have her drink. Is that not what they insisted you do when you were injured?"

Byria scowled slightly, understanding how Koki had felt about Mokin taking Bebe's fever. Then her own guilt attacked.

Had her need to save Koki hurt Hawush?

Swallowing anxious dryness, Byria put Patch's eye and her token back and grabbed one of the water skins. Cradling Koki's head, she dribbled water into her mouth and stroked her throat, as Mokin had also taught her. It had to be slow, and only a little water at a time so that one wouldn't accidentally breathe it and cause other problems.

The small woman lifted a hand and weakly gripped the skin, taking a gulp, sloshing it around her mouth, and spitting it out. Her eyes were crusted shut, so Byria helped clean as Koki tried to blink them open.

When she saw Byria, she threw her arms around her. "Beelheah!"

Byria hugged her back, kissing her forehead.

Just as quickly, Koki pushed her away. She reached behind her, grabbing air where her spear would be. Frustration joined the concern and anxiety spreading over her face.

"They coming from village. I follow. Leave now. Must leave now!" She tried to stand, but seemed unable to find her feet for the moment.

"Wait, you're hurt. What—?" Byria began, not quite able to make out all of what Koki said between her haste and slurring.

Hawush, on the other hand, clearly understood and asked, "How long ago?"

Byria blinked. His words sounded like both her tongue *and* the jungle fey tongue—similar to the way Mokin had used magic to help them communicate.

Koki jerked her head in his direction, then squawked in fear, jumping right into Byria, and nearly falling again.

"I give you my word upon my name and your Ancestor Trees, I will not harm you. I would protect the human." His tail swished in irritation, and he glanced over his shoulder at the two of them. "But I must know how much time we have."

Koki looked up at the sky and frowned. "No time."

Byria understood that.

Hawush lowered his head and bared his teeth.

Koki gathered her breath. "Leave now. They hide in illusion and see through illusion. We sent them the wrong direction, and they knew we lied."

As Koki spoke, Byria felt that sense of magical speaking and understanding again. Was Hawush doing something with his dragon magic?

"Pack everything in your bag and tie it to you as when you tried climbing the mountain," Hawush ordered Byria before a ball of lightning erupted on the edge of the ledge he stood on.

His wings appeared immediately as he scrambled to the mouth of the cave, and he blew a blaze of fire down the side of the mountain.

Byria had never packed or tied her bag faster. She was ready as soon as Hawush shoved them both inside with his tail. "Keep moving in! You know where to go."

An image of the cave pond flashed in Byria's head. She grabbed for Koki's hand and ran. The cave vibrated around them as Hawush roared deeper and louder than any sound she'd ever heard.

Everything fell dark, and a series of loud crashes thundered behind them. The quaking knocked Byria and Koki to the ground.

Hot smoke hissed over them as Hawush growled. His claws scraped and screeched on the rocks. Small sparks barely hinted at his silhouette.

"Keep moving!" he ordered.

"I can't see!" Byria cried as she scrambled to her feet.

There was another hot chuff behind her, and he said in the jungle fey tongue, "Continue. You can see, no?"

"Yes," Koki affirmed, taking Byria's hand and pulling her along.

It was all Byria could do to keep from tripping again. She wished she'd grabbed her pyut-gem from the bag.

When they got to the water, Byria and Koki slipped again. Koki cried out in pain with a splash and backed right into Byria. Drops of scalding water hit Byria's legs, and she yelped, too, backing until she found the cooler wall, pulling Koki with her.

Her eyes adjusted to the filtered light from the rockslide's end. She edged that way, mindful of the floor that seemed far slipperier than any of the other times she'd visited.

"We need to cross it," Hawush said, still speaking so they all could understand, in a somewhat whisper. She sensed his anxiety and anger.

Even if she hadn't been able to see in the dim light, Byria could feel Koki shake her head in a violent *No!*

"We must. The shaking you still feel is no longer me. They are moving through what I collapsed. This magic user is stronger than any I have seen among the humans."

"You go. I will hold them—" Koki began.

"Absolutely not. You will not even slow them down, so such a sacrifice is useless. Hold on to Byria as she holds on to me—"

"Na! I do not cross water! Bad choice!"

"If that's Tain or anyone working for him, they're far worse than the water or crossing it!" Byria said, trusting Hawush's dragon magic to make Koki understand.

Koki shook her head again.

Hawush growled and looked between the two women and the hall behind them. He snorted again. In the sulfury humidity, his smoke only added to the unpleasant smell. With a gesture of his head, he told Byria to bring Koki to the furthest end.

As she did so, he inhaled deeply. The roar of his fire shook the floor so they could barely stand. He blasted the wall. The room heated as flames flew in many directions. Sweat pricked painfully on Byria's skin, which felt dry and hard like another sunburn.

Koki yowled and edged toward the much colder water. It was shallower on this end, but…

The rocks behind them shifted. "Hawush!" she called, stepping nearer to him, feet in the water. A school of the smaller fish gathered at this end, and Byria saw more ripples and splashes in the deeper, darker, hotter water.

Perhaps Koki was correct in being afraid to cross.

Behind them, the rocks transitioned from shifting to falling. Chunks of sunlight appeared and disappeared. Byria and Koki moved toward Hawush as cracks formed in the floor.

"Hawush!" Byria called again. The water flowed harder as the rocks and floor began breaking away and falling down the mountain.

Hawush finally stopped firing the wall and turned to them, to Koki in particular.

"Your mate, can you write his name or a symbol for his name?"

Koki nodded hesitantly, looking between the growing cracks on the floor and the dragon, her eyes wider than the totin coins of Huotaro.

"Come closer and give me your hand. Quickly now!"

Byria had never seen Koki so frightened. The woman froze beside her, staring at the dragon and trembling.

Streams of stone dust and water slicked down the walls and from the ceiling as everything shook around them. Byria felt she should be blinking her eyes as Koki was, wiping away the gritty dust, but it all seemed to avoid her face—though it pasted to her clothes, stiffening them.

The sound of gurgling, flowing water mixed with the sound of falling rocks. Byria looked behind. The room had been halved in a rockslide that threw stones back into the cave. She just barely avoided one hitting her head.

One of Hawush's wings appeared to bat another away, then disappeared just as quickly.

He scratched his claw on Koki's palm. The small woman screamed, pressing harder against Byria. She held out her hand limply; green blood dripped from her fingers.

"Write it! Write your mate's name on this now!" Hawush's voice rose with his worry.

Byria finally noticed that the wall he'd fired was a smooth, black glass.

More rumbling came from the hall. The sound of rocks crumbling and moving echoed unnaturally, as if a god moved and destroyed them.

Koki, shaking like a leaf in a windy rainstorm, drew the symbol Mokin wore on his belt on the black glass.

As she did so, Hawush bit his own front claw and drew another symbol over it. The one Byria had carved on her forearm.

Koki gasped. A shimmer rippled out from the symbols. Hawush shoved the small woman through.

Just in time. A spiderweb of cracks spread from the two cave-ins—the one by where they'd lived, and the one still happening in the pond. The mirror lost its magical sheen.

"On me now," came Hawush's voice in her head. *"And... imagine your entire being covered with your heart's flame. Just as we practiced."*

Byria widened her eyes. In their practice, she'd managed to cover one arm and shoulder, and that had exhausted her. Her *entire being* was far bigger!

There was no time to argue. More of the room was collapsing around them. She gripped Hawush's neck as he launched into the hot water. She screamed in pain for just a moment before she had to close her mouth to conserve air. Her skin felt like it was peeling off, *and she couldn't breathe!* How could she nurse her heart's fire if she couldn't breathe, when it burned so much?

"Out of the water! Out of the water! Out of the water!" she mentally screamed at him. She tried to grip, but the edges of his scales cut her

fingertips. All she could do was squeeze until she could barely link her feet and fingers together around his neck, fighting painful, burning shakes. Her head burst from the water, and she took a breath almost as cold as ice.

She couldn't see, but *felt* the brush of stone just above her head.

"Breathe!" At this point, she couldn't differentiate between her own mental voice and Hawush's.

She listened anyway. *"Breathe in. Out. Breathe in. Out."* She found her heart's fire and willed it out in waves over her skin, as when everything had hurt after Tain had punished her for freeing Hawush. She breathed in cold air and pushed fire over her skin as she exhaled.

Her skin's searing lessened slowly. She kept focusing on the breathing, on her own fire, on holding onto Hawush.

"Going under," he warned.

Byria took a deep breath in. Her face burned a moment before she willed her heart's fire over herself again. Underwater, clinging to the dragon, she could hear her heart in her head. With every beat, she sent out a little more fire.

Her lungs started to hurt. She let out a bubble. That helped some. She let out another. Byria started timing the release of her heart's fire with bubbles.

She was running out of air.

The water felt like it was moving past her quickly. How much longer?

She only let out tiny bubbles now, and her heart's fire was dimming. Pain tore up from her lungs, as if a beast would pry her mouth open from the inside. She could hardly feel her hands to keep holding onto Hawush.

And then she wasn't.

She wasn't in the water, either. Not entirely. She rolled off him sideways, only able to think of breathing.

Water scalded her lower legs before Hawush pulled her onto cooler stone. He was panting. He kept one hand-foot upon her, and that seemed to lessen the pain.

He was shaking.

After taking a few moments to rekindle and regrow her heart's fire, Byria willed it to heal herself—and calm Hawush if possible. Once his breathing slowed some, she asked, "Where are we?"

He was silent a moment and lay down, close beside her. "A place I never wished to return to in all my life."

* * * * *

Chapter Eleven
Mouth of the Monster

Byria couldn't see, but she could smell, and it stank. She remembered Hawush's statement regarding where he regularly relieved himself and wrinkled her nose from the musky ammonia stench.

"Now what?" Byria asked, sitting up and feeling his shaking claw slide from her as she moved.

Hawush had no answer. She pressed her own hand to his arm and felt his trembling. Despite the humidity and the hot water, he felt colder. It felt like a True Thing that coolness wasn't good for dragons. At least not fire and earth dragons like Hawush.

With a sigh, she fought with the bag she'd tied to herself, keeping one foot touching the side of the dragon so she wouldn't lose him in the perfect darkness. The knots were waterlogged and tight, cutting into her chest and shoulders. It took a fair amount of wriggling and two torn nails, but she loosened it enough to remove it.

Hawush hardly noticed.

Everything inside was soaked. She fished the pyut-gem out first. Taking a few breaths, she closed her eyes and focused on her barely-burning heart's fire, willing it hotter and brighter. She imagined the fire moving through her arms, hands, and fingers into the gem. *Just a little more light.*

When she opened her eyes, she smiled. The small stone glowed almost as brightly as a candle flame. She held it up for Hawush to see, but the dragon didn't move. The light didn't reach far enough to see his face. Byria always seemed to know when he was watching her—and she didn't feel that now. If she hadn't felt him breathing, she'd be even more worried.

He was definitely unwell.

She kissed his side and decided at least one of them needed to be practical. Sitting with her back against him, she balanced her glowing gem on her knee and assessed what was left of her possessions.

The belt Mokin had given her hadn't been ruined by water. One pouch and one filled waterskin still seemed serviceable. Wringing out the cloths, she wrapped one around Patch's eye jar to keep it safe, and placed it in the one good pouch with the stone knife from Mokin. With another cloth, she did her best to wrap the blade of the dragon knife and attach it to her belt.

Not knowing when her next meal would be, she ate as much of the fish and mango as she could—though the sulfurous hot water had made them hardly palatable. She threw what she didn't eat into the water. If it wasn't already bad, it would be soon.

All the remaining herbs from Mokin were entirely soaked, if not completely disintegrated. Useless. Nothing more was worth packing in her belt. She abandoned the messenger bag in a sodden heap.

Hawush had still not moved.

Picking up her pyut-gem, Byria stood and moved along his neck. He started as if surprised by her presence. Her time going through things had let her heart's fire grow. Gently, she rubbed him, willing her warmth to affect him, heal him, give him the courage it always gave her.

After a moment, she felt the heat of his breath and the touch of his feelers on her back. He said nothing, but she sensed his unspoken gratitude. Turning around, she kissed the side of his nose and rubbed his face and feelers.

She asked, "Can you direct my heart's fire to let me see as you do?"

He lightly brushed her hand and the gem with his snout. "You have done well."

"But it doesn't let me see far. I can't see more than the glowing red of your eyes."

He nuzzled her again, then breathed over her as his feelers brushed against her. A shot of warmth rose from her heart to her eyes.

As Byria blinked, the room came into view like it was lit with grayish-purple lights, only clearer, sharper. After the initial burst of energy, her heart's fire burned steadily, untaxed. She put the pyutgem into the pouch with Patch's eye, pulling her energy back out of it to conserve her fire.

Directly in front of them was what had once been a grand portico, now almost entirely collapsed, but for a small, sharply angled opening of carved stones. Around it were piled pieces of carved columns and supports, chunks of sculpted magical creatures and plants and shining stones beneath a fine layer of dust.

As Byria looked at the ruins, it felt as if squirming bugs and spiders crawled over her bones—much like when she'd been strapped to the lightning-storm bed. She kept herself from reacting. Pain and terror still flowed from Hawush. It was her time to be strong.

"Come on," she said, heading toward the only other direction for them to go. The entrance.

One of the framing pillars that had held up the top cross-stone had completely collapsed. The carved top frame, a cracked relief sculpture of two dragons facing each other, angled down onto the pile of rubble. The other column, decorated with a spiral of flowering vines, still stood, though cracks lined it.

Hawush balked, edging just a little closer to the water that had brought them there.

"Staying here is as much a prison, and we'll both surely die of starvation," Byria said, imagining she was Hawush speaking to a young Byria.

The dragon tilted his head at her tone and stance, blinked a few times, then took a deep breath and headed toward the entrance.

* * * * *

Chapter Twelve
Earth and Fire, Heed My Call

The humidity lessened after leaving the water behind, but the smell lingered. Byria was unsure how far they'd walked, but it was enough for her clothes to start chafing.

The awful sensation of *things* crawling over her bones, particularly at her back, didn't abate.

Hawush had said nothing thus far, so when he nudged Byria's shoulder and telepathically sent her a message of *"Hold,"* she just about jumped out of her skin.

"What?" she asked. As she stopped, she felt it. *"Oh."*

There was the slightest crosswind where they stood. Byria and Hawush each took one side to investigate. Byria gasped at the same time she heard the dragon snort in surprise. He must've found what she had.

The wall became another corridor.

She stopped herself from asking Hawush which way they should go: continue onward, or take one of the two directions at this crossroad. She could sense his confusion and doubt already. Instead, she pulled out her pyut-gem.

And promptly dropped it.

It glowed and burned as if flame covered it.

With a frown, Byria willed her heart's fire to her hand. Tendrils of fire sprouted from her skin. She picked up the stone, and it spun in her hand. After watching it for a few moments, she got the sense it wouldn't give a direction. Gripping it tightly, she squeezed it back into her belt pouch, and pulled out the jar with Patch's eye.

It looked at her, spun, then looked down the hall on Hawush's side. The dragon nodded, and they headed in that direction. Byria kept the eye out in case they needed Patch's help further.

A different feeling crept through Byria, similar to when she'd known she was being watched in the jungle, but colder. The sensation made her stomach churn with sickness. A low growl from Hawush let her know he felt it, too. They both moved slower and walked closer, Byria resting a hand on his side.

"We should go back. We are getting deeper below." Hawush was trembling again.

He was right about them getting deeper. Byria had noticed the decline as they'd walked.

But hadn't they felt a cool breeze from this direction? Had Patch's eye not sent them this way?

The stones below her feet were warm, almost hot. The air was dryer now, but more sulfur-smelling.

These are volcanoes, too, Byria thought to herself. *I've been in a volcano before*. Fire and earth. It made sense a dragon like Hawush would make his home near these elements.

Hawush nudged Byria again and began to turn—no small feat for a creature his size in the narrow passage.

As he turned, the whistle of arrows pierced the air.

Hawush snarled and cried out in pain as one buried itself in the ridge of his fin scales. The other two glanced off his hide, sparking lightning.

Byria crouched, drawing her knife—not that it would do much against arrows, but she wanted to hold something. It felt warm and *right* in her hand. That angry buzz worsened, and she looked at the arrow in the dragon's back.

It sparked lightning still. Its feathers faced to their left. Another hidden hall? *"Fire that way!"* she ordered, then stood. With a quick jump against his side, she grasped the arrow and yanked. Just touching it sent shocks up her arm, but not enough to disable her. Hawush yowled as she pulled it out and sent a stream of fire as she'd directed.

It *was* another hidden hallway. Cries of men echoed back. She tucked Patch's eye away and saw blood running down Hawush's side. The injury still jumped with sparks.

Out of breath, Hawush finished the tight turn in the hall, putting himself between Byria and their attackers.

The whistle of more arrows followed immediately. Hawush put up his fin scales.

The sound of three *clinks* let Byria know the arrows had grazed off again. They broke into a run toward the intersection they'd come from, with Hawush lifting his head to breathe a few fireballs behind them.

As she looked behind them, the men emerged from the passage.

She stumbled as her heart jumped.

Tain.

Hawush paused to make sure she was all right.

From the diamond medallion on Tain's chest—the blinding, sparkling medallion she'd seen at so many parades and Important Events—shot a web of lightning that wrapped around Hawush's tail.

The dragon's scream of pain deafened Byria and shook the hall around them. As he tried to breathe another fireball, only smoke and sparks left his mouth. A glowing sheen of gold—the only color she could see, despite the grays and lavenders of her "dragon vision"—started to cover him.

"Run!" Hawush ordered.

"No!" Byria turned around, ducked between Hawush and the wall, and ran full speed at Tain, brandishing her knife.

There were no scars upon his face. She hated that fact as she saw it. There was no evidence of her injury upon him. She slashed her knife at Tain, hoping to make a scar that would stay.

Without dropping his gemstone, he drew his own sword and easily parried her aside. His withering look froze her just long enough for a soldier to grab her from behind.

The touch relit her heart's fire, and she fought, stomping and stabbing blindly. Why hadn't she thought to have Koki teach her to fight? The soldier avoided all but one cut, a small one that slipped into the elbow joint of his armor.

That was enough.

With a yowl, he released her and fell to the ground, clutching his arm. A fiery glow burst from beneath his armor as he howled in agony.

Seeing what she'd done, hearing his shrieks as tortured as Hawush's, stunned her. The two other soldiers hesitated, but another person wrapped his arms around her from behind, this time pinning her arms better.

This one wore fancy, silk robes colored with the most expensive dyes...

Byria didn't fight. She willed her heart's fire all over her body once more. The high magepriest cried out, and she pulled from his grip. This time, he didn't go up in flames. With a growl and a glare, he shrugged, and the flames on his robe extinguished.

Without thinking, Byria threw herself to the ground to escape his next grab. In the direction of Tain. She stabbed her knife into Tain's calf, where his armor didn't cover.

He cried out in pain, but his response was less than that of the soldier's. She rolled away from both his strikes and the high magepriest's. Finding her feet faster than she expected, she crouched, almost on instinct, knife ready.

Tain leaned heavily upon the high magepriest. "Get her!" he choked out at the remaining two soldiers.

Both men looked at each other, at the struggling Tain, at the pile of smoldering ash and bone that was the first soldier she'd cut, and hesitated.

Byria swung the dragon knife at them a few times. She watched them back up in her peripheral vision, focusing instead on Tain and the high magepriest.

Lightning no longer shot from Tain's necklace, though the necklace glowed like a lamp. Smaller sparks and twinkles now covered Tain's body, all the way down to his leg. Where she'd stabbed, an ash-gray hole of embers was already closing.

Byria muttered a particularly potent curse of mixed languages and looked at Hawush.

The gold was fading from his body. His rear feet clumsily scrambling as if just getting feeling back, the dragon tried to turn in the small corridor again. In her "dragon vision," Byria saw him as deathly pale.

The two soldiers, likely seeing—wait, how could *they* see?—her attention on Hawush, lunged at her. She swung her knife, but they came at her from two sides. Her bare feet, elbows, and punches did little through leather boots and traveling armor. And both now knew to avoid even the slightest cut from her blade.

Another pained cry from Hawush cut into Byria's heart. She feigned a limp fall. The nearest solder caught her. With a twist, she bit at his throat. She gagged on the taste of blood. The soldier cried out and released her. The other rushed her and pinned her, facedown, to the floor.

She turned her head some to see Hawush's face and neck frozen, turned to gold. "No!" she cried out, but the soldier planted his weight where he pressed one knee into her back. She tried to flail, but he pinned both her hands to the ground above her head.

No more noise came from Hawush now, but she could *feel* him.

There were no words. It was worse than what she remembered from Tain's torture. Hawush's very essence was being pulled from him, dragged out through burning pinpricks.

Byria went limp once more. The soldier tightened his grip. "I won't fall for that again."

"Good!" she growled and thrashed her head back.

He avoided being hit by her skull, but that pulled some pressure from her wrists.

With a jerk, she freed the hand with the dagger, slashing at his hands. He caught her wrist, keeping the blade from touching him, and dug his thumb beneath hers, sending jolts of pain through her fingers. She could barely keep her grip on the knife.

The feel of Hawush's pain in her mind was fading.

She was losing him. She had to do something. She needed help.

I'm in a volcano.

Byria pushed into the soldier's grip, giving her a moment's reprieve, and then slammed the blade into the back of her own hand, willing the blade to cut all the way into the stone.

Burning, searing pain choked out a cry from her throat. She sent all her heart's fire into the wound and deep into the stone beneath her. Everything went pitch black, but she could still hear, still feel.

"Earth and Fire, Earth and Fire, Earth and Fire!" she screamed out in her mind. She *summoned* in her mind.

The blackness erupted into an equally blinding blaze that surrounded her.

Byria was vaguely aware of the soldier jumping off her, crying out in pain.

"Earth and Fire, Earth and Fire, Earth and Fire!" She spoke aloud now, not in her native language, Patch's language, or the language of the jungle fey, yet she understood them anyway. "Earth and Fire, Earth and Fire, Earth and Fire—*heed my call!*"

Byria called, summoned, begged. She spoke the words without thought, letting them pour from her mouth as her blood poured into the stone beneath her.

"Earth and Fire, attend to your son! Stop your children's children's children from harming your first! Lend your power. Lend your strength that imbues all things since before the world had memories. Grant sanctuary and protection. Heal his wounds. My heart's fire is my sacrifice for this!"

The earth shifted and moved beneath her. Screams and protests from Tain, the high magepriest, and the soldiers sounded so far away. Liquid rock bubbled up. It burned worse than the hot water, tore her nostrils worse than the acidic fumes Tain had held her over, blistered her skin so it felt like it was tearing off in strips.

She stopped screaming and breathed.

The pain was her choice.

Letting go of the dragon knife, she embraced the hot molten stone as if she'd embrace Hawush one last time.

"*Save him!*"

* * * * *

Chapter Thirteen
In the Darkness

Byria awoke to no pain, but she couldn't move.

Am I dead? Is this what death feels like?

The high magepriests promised an afterlife of golden warmth and no pain for those true to the Great God. Those who were unfaithful would have nothing and cease to exist, forgotten to all.

It was warm, and she was in no pain, but there was no golden light.

After a few blinks, Byria saw similarly to her prior "dragon vision," but that sent a dull ache through her head like looking at the sun after coming out from the cave. She squeezed her eyes closed.

There *was* pain. She was very likely *not* dead.

Hawush? Was *he* dead? Her very heartbeat hurt at the thought!

A low rumble and a wave of emotion soothed that pounding pain.

"Hawush?" she whispered.

He didn't speak, but she felt his presence. Keeping her eyes closed, she tried to move again. It felt like he was holding her, as he did when she slept, only... more.

More was neither good nor bad. It just was.

She could wriggle some, so she did until she felt her back nestle against a familiar warmth. It didn't feel like flesh and scales, but soft stone. Still, she knew it was him.

Hawush...

* * * * *

Chapter Fourteen
Ways of Flight

Byria woke to the soft *whoosh* of already-burning dragon wings and the sound of scraping and crumbling stones. She blinked her eyes open.

Everything was so bright!

She blinked more, and the painful brightness faded to a firelight flickering on stone. Stonefalls of pebbles, rocks, and dust slid from Hawush's blazing wing to pile along the perimeter of the tiny cavern or wherever they were. She followed the glow of his firewing to see its glimmer on dragonscales.

"Hawush," she croaked, smiling. His wing was over her, obscuring her view of anything besides his stomach, rear legs, and the tight, stone quarters around them. The scraping and rock crumbling stopped.

"Byria?"

The sound of him saying her name sent a pleasant shiver through her body. She embraced his leg, the only part of him she could easily reach. Hot tears ran from her eyes, and small sobs escaped her lips. She couldn't bring herself to talk, so she thought to him, *"You're alive!"*

"As are you." He wriggled his shoulders and front legs until he curled his neck and fit his head into the small area beneath his wing, which pressed Byria tightly against his flank. When she saw his face, she embraced it, crying even more—happy to be crying. Happy to be touching her warm, alive dragon.

The glow of his wings glistened in his tears. His wings didn't burn. Byria felt only a gentle warmth from them. Hardly able to sit up, she edged over to kiss below his eye.

He rubbed his face against her slightly, then shook and shimmied away. This time his wing shimmered as if it were going out, but only long enough for his head to disappear through the flames. "I need to get us out of here. Stay close; I do not want any stones falling upon you."

Nothing fell upon Byria. She rested against his side, watching more rocks and dust rain over his wing as he scraped and pushed. She napped at least once, if not twice, and her stomach had begun to rumble fiercely.

She reached for her belt. She still had it! Taking off the one waterskin, she sipped. It was warm and stale, but it felt good. Remembering what Koki and Mokin had taught her, she sloshed it around in her mouth and spit most of it out. The little that trickled down her throat burned like tiny knife blades.

She forced herself to take two more mouth-washes and tiny sips. How long had they been here?

Hawush had moved more. She could now see part of his tail. The rest was entrapped in obsidian stone that shimmered like tiny black mirrors. His muscles weren't so tight now. He stretched as he clawed his way through.

Shafts of silvery light made lines in the falling dust and stones. Hawush gave a proud snort and nudged Byria away from him with his belly. She moved to the center of the ceiling of fire created by his wing. He coiled his muscles once more, and with a growl and a great heave, he broke through the remaining shell of stone. He pulled back, holding Byria to his chest, then pushed free into the night where two three-quarter-full moons shone through a hazy but cloudless sky.

The valley between the mountains looked eerie and foreign, bathed in their light. Byria still felt the uncomfortable energy of the destroyed prison—as she figured Hawush did—so she moved slowly and carefully.

A soft layer of ash cushioned each of her steps with a small puff. An inch or two covered the ground. Byria ran her hand around the solid black rock that had housed them. Cooled lava. It had encased them during the volcano's eruption that had spewed this much ash. Lines of cooled black stone now overlaid the boulders and rubble Byria remembered avoiding when she'd crossed the valley, the remnants of Hawush's prison. The appearance made Byria think of a giant serving balls of sticky rice drizzled with a squid-ink sauce down the side of the mountain.

Hawush stayed close to Byria, circling her as they moved. His tail drew lines through the ash, hiding their footprints, and creating the appearance of waves or drifts. He said nothing, but Byria sensed he was ready to leave, to go somewhere far away.

She moved farther out into the valley to see the mountain she'd called home for a short time. While there were no lines of black stone, steaming water now dribbled over a beard of rubble that covered the entire facing side. The very top was sheered almost flat; there was no sign of their cave or the ledge, and from the valley floor halfway up, more boulders and stones piled.

More sadness than she'd expected weighed on her heart upon seeing its destruction. She turned to Hawush. Its loss was worth the fact that they were both alive and together. As she walked toward him, she kicked something hard in the ash.

Furrowing her brow, she looked down. A glimmer in the moonlight made her stomach twist. She snatched the diamond necklace and glared at it. Inside flickered tiny darts of lightning.

With a dragon-like snarl of her own, she ran to the closest pile of stones and whipped the gem against them. A blast of energy and a *crash* like thunder almost threw her back, but fury grounded her.

She pictured her heart's fire all over her body, anchoring her to the earth—had she not called the Earth and Fire? Had they not found her worthy to live after she'd called upon them?

Byria smashed the necklace over and over. She imagined the rune she'd stabbed that had imprisoned Hawush, imagined it fracturing with each strike.

"Byria!" Hawush called.

"Stay back!" she roared as winds whipped around her, and the earth rumbled at her feet. Ash spiraled up around her, lightning flashing in its dusty clouds.

She pictured the bed Tain and the high magepriest had strapped her to. She imagined that rune upon it. She imagined it cracking and splintering and burning.

Byria willed her heart's fire into the stone with one last flog.

It shattered with a deafening *boom*, and she flew without wings.

No, she saw fiery wings in the tiny seconds she could bear to keep her burning eyes open. She didn't hear the familiar *hawoosh*, but she felt the familiar clawed hands. Her ears rang, and her bones buzzed, yet she still clenched the chain.

Everything felt like it was moving slower than life.

The gold chain was light in her hand, below it the bent, charred, *empty* setting. She smelled blood, tasted it, and felt lines of zinging, burning everywhere. Hundreds of tiny lines of blood, as if painted by an artist's fine brush, flicked over her shirt, trousers, and arms.

"Byria?" At the sound of Hawush's voice in her head, she smiled. Even that hurt.

Well, at least she wasn't dead.

"Take me home?" she asked.

"And where would home be?"

"Wherever you feel it is." With her free hand, she adjusted herself in his grip. Home was wherever Hawush was.

That, she knew, was a Real Thing.

* * * * *

About the Author

Trisha J. Wooldridge writes stuff that occasionally wins awards—child-friendly ones as T.J. Wooldridge. Find her in the Shirley Jackson Award-winning *The Twisted Book of Shadows*; *HWA Poetry Showcase 5, 6* and *8*; all of the New England Horror Writer anthologies (that she didn't edit); *Don't Turn Out the Lights: A Tribute to Alvin Schwartz's Scary Stories to Tell in the Dark*; *More Lore from the Mythos Volume 2*; *Paranormal Contact: A Quiet Horror Confessional*; and *34 Orchard* literary journal.

Owner of A Novel Friend Writing and Editing and part of the editing team of The Writer's Ally (www.thewritersally), Trish lovingly tortures consenting authors with her editing talents, sometimes resulting in wickedly fantastic anthologies, and is a fan and advocate for properly used semicolons and Oxford commas.

Prior word-loving, fandom-friendly employment has included editing the MMORPG *Dungeons & Dragons: Stormreach*; interviewing Goth and Metal bands for various magazines; teaching creepy things to college students and creating a study guide for *Frankenstein*; getting paid to write researched opinions about food, alcohol, and the business thereof; acquiring middle grade and YA titles for a mid-size press; and coordinating events and PR for Annie's Book Stop of Worcester.

Former president of Broad Universe, an organization promoting and supporting women and other underrepresented voices in writing,

Trisha now serves on the board for the New England Horror Writers and is an active member of HWA, SCBWI, and SFPA.

She spends rare moments of mystical "free time" with a very patient Husband-of-Awesome; a tiny witch kitty; a rescued bay gelding; and a matronly calico mare. If you see her at one of the many conventions she haunts, ask if she has her Tarot—and if she'll give you a reading.

Find her at: anovelfriend.com.

* * * * *

Author's Note

I was very fortunate to have had a childhood and life full of genuine affection.

But not everyone does.

I've had several vocations and positions that have included helping people who've suffered the trauma of abuse and domestic violence. While there are several fantasy novels that include these issues, I've been disappointed in those that don't always treat these topics with respectful authenticity. I cannot represent the diverse experiences of trauma victims, and what is a True Thing for one person isn't always so for another, but being as True as possible, honoring and respecting the experience so many suffer is intrinsic to my writing, particularly in this series.

With that in mind, I wanted to include some resources for readers who may be suffering from trauma, abuse, or domestic violence collected from the professionals who helped me in writing and in helping those I worked with.

If you're in danger, please consider calling:

- 911 – for police or medical assistance
- 988 – for mental health assistance

If you're a survivor in need of help, please contact:

National Domestic Violence Hotline

24 hours a day, seven days a week, 365 days a year, the National Domestic Violence Hotline provides essential tools and support to help survivors of domestic violence so they can live their lives free of abuse. Contacts to The Hotline can expect highly-trained, expert advocates to offer free, confidential, and compassionate support, crisis intervention information, education, and referral services in over 200 languages.
- thehotline.org
- 1-800-799-7233 (SAFE)
- TTY 1-800-787-3224
- SMS: Text START to 88788

* * *

Love is Respect – the National Dating Abuse Helpline

A project of the National Domestic Violence Hotline, love is respect offers 24/7 information, support, and advocacy to young people between the ages of 13 and 26 who have questions or concerns about their romantic relationships. We also provide support to concerned friends and family members, teachers, counselors, and other service providers through the same free and confidential services via phone, text, and live chat.

We aim to be a safe and inclusive space for young people to access help and information in a setting specifically for them. We provide comprehensive education through resources including quizzes, interactive pages, and testimonials, as well as training, toolkits, and curriculum for educators, peers, and parents to promote healthy relationships and prevent future abuse.

- loveisrespect.org
- 1-866-331-9474
- TTY 1-866-331-8453
- Text "loveis" to 22522
- Live chat at loveisrespect.org

* * *

StrongHearts Native Helpline

American Indian and Alaska Native women suffer some of the highest rates of violence and murder in the United States, a crisis that has diminished the honored status of women and safety in tribal communities. In spite of the high rates of violence experienced by AI/AN persons, only a small percentage reached out for assistance to The Hotline at the National Domestic Violence Hotline. By dialing 1-844-7NATIVE (1-844-762-8483), nationwide 24/7, callers can connect at no cost, one-on-one with knowledgeable StrongHearts advocates who can provide lifesaving tools and immediate support to enable survivors to find safety and live lives free of abuse.

- strongheartshelpline.org
- 1-844-762-8483 (call or text)

* * *

RAINN—the Rape Abuse Incest National Network

Every 68 seconds, an American is sexually assaulted. And every 9 minutes, that victim is a child. RAINN (Rape, Abuse & Incest National Network) is the nation's largest anti-sexual violence organization. RAINN created and operates the National Sexual Assault Hotline (800.656.HOPE, online at rainn.org y rainn.org/es) in partnership with more than 1,000 local sexual assault service providers across the country and operates the DoD Safe Helpline for the Department of Defense. RAINN also carries out programs to prevent sexual violence, help survivors, and ensure that perpetrators are brought to justice.

- rainn.org
- 1-800-656-4673 (HOPE)
- Secure, online private chat: hotline.rainn.org/online

* * *

Resources for those Looking to Support Current Efforts

National Resource Center on Domestic Violence

The National Resource Center on Domestic Violence (NRCDV) is online at: nrcdv.org. It provides a wide range of free, comprehensive, and individualized technical assistance, training, and specialized resource materials and key initiatives designed to enhance current domestic violence intervention and prevention strategies.

Please note that NRCDV works to support those working on behalf of survivors.

To request technical assistance, please contact an NRCDV Technical Assistance Specialist at 1-800-537-2238 or email at nrcdvTA@nrcdv.org. Please allow 3-5 business days for response.

* * *

National Center on Domestic Violence, Trauma, and Mental Health

The National Center on Domestic Violence, Trauma, and Mental Health promotes survivor-defined healing, liberation, and equity by transforming the systems that impact survivors of domestic and sexual violence and their families. We envision a society where all people are free of systemic, collective, and individual trauma. They maintain a long list of resources available around the United States of America.

Online at: nationalcenterdvtraumamh.org/resources/national-domestic-violence-organizations/

* * * * *

Excerpt from
Khyven the Unkillable

Book One of Legacy of Shadows
An Eldros Legacy Novel

Todd Fahnestock

Available from New Mythology Press
eBook, Hardcover, and Paperback

Excerpt from *Khyven the Unkillable*:

Two knights threw open the door of the tavern, and the scent of last night's rain blew in with them. Khyven heard their boots thump on the rough planks, heard the creak of leather and clink of chainmail as they shifted. He sat with his back to them, but he didn't need to see them to know where they were.

The room went silent. This dockside drinking hole didn't see knights very often, and their appearance had rendered the entire place speechless. That was respect. That was what being a knight meant in the kingdom of Usara.

They paused just inside the threshold, perhaps hoping to spook the fearful, but Khyven wasn't a jumper. He had more in common with the newcomers than those who fled from them.

Ayla, the pretty barmaid sitting across from him, looked past Khyven, her eyes wide. She had been a lively conversationalist a moment ago and he'd been daydreaming about what it would be like to kiss those lips.

Now she looked like an alley cat who'd spotted an alley dog. Reflexively, she stood up, the wooden stool scraping loudly on the floor. She froze, perhaps realizing belatedly that when the powerful—the predators—were in the room, it was best not to draw attention to yourself.

Khyven heard the metallic rustle of the fighters' chain mail and Ayla's face drained of color. He envisioned the alley dogs turning at the sound, focusing on her.

She needn't have worried. They weren't here for her or any other patron of the Mariner's Rest. They were here for Khyven.

He had killed a man in the Night Ring two days ago, and not just any man—a duke's son. The entitled whelp had actually been a talented swordsman, but his ambition had outstripped his skill. And the Night Ring was an unforgiving place to discover such a weakness.

After Khyven had run the boy through, Duke Bericourt had sworn revenge. No doubt he had been waiting for an opportunity to find Khyven alone, vulnerable, to send in his butcher knights.

Men like these, sent to enforce a lord's will or show his displeasure, were called butcher knights. Usually of the lowest caste—Knights of the Steel—butcher knights didn't chase glory on the battlefield or renown in the Night Ring. They were sent to do bloody, back-alley work at their lord's bidding.

Khyven took a deep breath of the smoky air, sipped from the glass of Triadan whiskey, and enjoyed the fading burn down his throat.

The booted feet thumped to a stop next to his table.

"Khyven the Unkillable?" One of the men spoke, using Khyven's ringer name—the flamboyant moniker the crowd had laid upon him.

Khyven glanced over his shoulder. Indeed. He had guessed right. The pair were Knights of the Steel.

There were three castes of knights in Usara: Knights of the Sun, Knights of the Dark, and Knights of the Steel, which was the lowest caste and the only one available to most lords. The pair wore chainmail shirts instead of full plate, conical steel caps with nose guards instead of full helms, and leather greaves and bracers.

As predicted, they wore Duke Bericourt's crest on their left shoulders.

There was a code of honor among knights—even butcher knights. Except in cases of war, civility was required before gutting a man, especially when there were onlookers. Often a knight would give a flowery speech—including the offense he'd been sent to address—before drawing weapons. This was enough to justify murder.

Sometimes there was no flowery speech, but a knight would always at least say their victim's name. If the victim acknowledged their name, that was all it took to bring out the blades.

Khyven didn't give them the satisfaction. He took another sip of his whiskey and said nothing.

"Did you hear me?" the knight demanded, his hand touching his sword hilt.

If Khyven had been a normal ringer—a caged slave thrown into the Night Ring to slay or be slain for the sport of the crowd—these men would probably have forgone their code of honor and drawn their swords already.

But Khyven wasn't just any ringer. He was the Champion of the Night Ring, and the king had afforded him special privileges because of that fact, like a room at the palace. Khyven had survived forty-eight bouts, the longest string of victories since…

Well, since Vex the Victorious had claimed fifty, won a knighthood and become the king's personal bodyguard.

Steel scraped on steel, bringing Khyven back to the present. The second knight drew his dagger and placed it against Khyven's throat.

Ayla gasped and backed away.

"You think you're protected," the second knight growled in Khyven's ear. "You're not."

Of course, if Khyven didn't acknowledge his name, there were other ways for the butcher knights to start the fight. If Khyven attacked them, for example, they could retaliate. The powerful could always push a victim into a corner when they needed to. That's what the powerful did. Khyven had learned that long ago.

That was why, when Khyven had won his fortieth bout and his freedom from the Night Ring, he'd continued fighting, risking his life in every bloody bout. For the prize at the end of ten more bouts. For the power that would come with it.

When Khyven won his fiftieth bout, he would be elevated to the knighthood, just like Vex the Victorious. And no one would look at him as a victim again.

The blade broke the skin, just barely, and a bead of blood trickled down Khyven's neck. His pulse quickened. The familiar euphoria filled him, the rush of pleasure that came with the threat of death.

The euphoria brought vision, and Khyven saw with new eyes, his battle eyes. He saw his foe's strengths and weaknesses as a swirling, blue-colored wind.

"You are Khyven the Unkillable," the man breathed in his ear.

Khyven chuckled.

The second knight's face turned red. He slashed—

But Khyven was already moving.

* * *

Get Khyven the Unkillable on Amazon at: amazon.com/gp/product/B09Z9W3ZSH

Find out more about Todd Fahnestock and the Eldros Legacy at: chriskennedypublishing.com.

* * * * *

Excerpt from
A Reluctant Druid

Book One of The Milesian Accords

Jon R. Osborne

Now Available from New Mythology Press
eBook, Paperback, and Audio

Excerpt from A Reluctant Druid:

"**D**on't crank on it; you'll strip it."

Liam paused from trying to loosen the stubborn bolt holding the oil filter housing on his Yamaha motorcycle, looking for the source of the unsolicited advice. The voice was gruff, with an accent and cadence that made Liam think of the Swedish Chef from the Muppets. The garage door was open for air circulation, and two figures were standing in the driveway, illuminated by the setting sun. As they approached and stepped into the shadows of the house, Liam could see they were Pixel and a short, stout man with a graying beard that would do ZZ Top proud. The breeze blowing into the garage carried a hint of flowers.

Liam experienced a moment of double vision as he looked at the pair. Pixel's eyes took on the violet glow he thought he'd seen before, while her companion lost six inches in height, until he was only as tall as Pixel. What the short man lacked in height, he made up for in physique; he was built like a fireplug. He was packed into blue jeans and a biker's leather jacket, and goggles were perched over the bandana covering his salt and pepper hair. Leather biker boots crunched the gravel as he walked toward the garage. Pixel followed him, having traded her workout clothes for black jeans and a pink t-shirt that left her midriff exposed. A pair of sunglasses dangled from the neckline of her t-shirt.

"He's seeing through the glamour," the short, bearded man grumbled to Pixel, his bushy eyebrows furrowing.

"Well duh. We're on his home turf, and this is his place of power" Pixel replied nonchalantly. "He was pushing back against my glamour yesterday, and I'm not adding two hands to my height."

Liam set down the socket wrench and ran through the mental inventory of items in the garage that were weapons or could be used as them. The back half of the garage was a workshop, which included the results of his dabbling with blacksmithing and sword-crafting, so the list was considerable. But the most suitable were also the farthest away.

"Can I help you?" Liam stood and brushed off his jeans; a crowbar was three steps away. Where had they come from? Liam hadn't heard a car or motorcycle outside, and the house was a mile and a half outside of town.

"Ja, you can." The stout man stopped at the threshold of the garage. His steel-gray eyes flicked from Liam to the workbench and back. He held his hands out, palms down. The hands were larger than his and weren't strangers to hard work and possibly violence. "And there's no need to be unhospitable; we come as friends. My name is Einar, and you've already met Pixel."

"Hi, Liam." Pixel was as bubbly as yesterday. While she didn't seem to be making the same connection as Einar regarding the workbench, her eyes darted about the cluttered garage and the dim workshop behind it. "Wow, you have a lot of junk."

"What's this about?" Liam sidled a half step toward the workbench, regretting he hadn't kept up on his martial arts. He had three brown belts, a year of kendo, and some miscellaneous weapons training scattered over two decades but not much experience in the way of real fighting. He could probably hold his own in a brawl as long as his opponent didn't have serious skills. He suspected Einar was more than a Friday night brawler in the local watering hole. "Is she your daughter?"

Einar turned to the purple-haired girl, his caterpillar-like eyebrows gathering. "What did you do?"

"What? I only asked him a few questions and checked him out," Pixel protested, her hands going to her hips as she squared off with Einar. "It's not as if I tried to jump his bones right there in the store or something."

"Look mister, if you think something untoward happened between me and your daughter –" Liam began.

"She's not my pocking daughter, and I don't give a troll's ass if you diddled her," Einar interrupted, his accent thickening with his agitation. He took a deep breath, his barrel chest heaving. "Now, will you hear me out without you trying to brain me with that tire iron you've been eyeing?"

"You said diddle." Pixel giggled.

"Can you be serious for five minutes, you pocking faerie?" Einar glowered, his leather jacket creaking as he crossed his arms.

"Remember 'dwarf,' you're here as an 'advisor.'" Pixel included air quotes with the last word, her eyes turning magenta. "The Nine Realms are only involved out of politeness."

"Politeness! If you pocking Tuatha and Tylwyth Teg hadn't folded up when the Milesians came at you, maybe we wouldn't be here to begin with!" Spittle accompanied Einar's protest. "Tylwyth? More like Toothless!"

"Like your jarls didn't roll over and show their bellies when the Avramites showed up with their One God and their gold!" Pixel rose up on her toes. "Your people took their god and took their gold and then attacked our ancestral lands!"

"Guys!" Liam had stepped over to the workbench but hadn't picked up the crowbar. "Are you playing one of those live-action role playing games or something? Because if you are, I'm calling my garage out of bounds. Take your LARP somewhere else."

"We've come a long way to speak to you," Einar replied, looking away from Pixel. "I'm from Asgard."

"Asgard? You mean like Thor and Odin? What kind of game are you playing?" Liam hadn't moved from the workbench, but he'd mapped in his mind the steps he'd need to take to reach a stout pole which would serve as a staff while he back-pedaled to his workshop, where a half-dozen half-finished sword prototypes rested. From where he stood, though, he didn't feel as threatened. He knew a bit about gamers because there were a fair number of them among the pagan community, and he'd absorbed bits and pieces of it. Maybe someone had pointed Liam out to Pixel as research about druids for one of these games—an over-enthusiastic player who wanted to more convincingly roleplay one.

"Gods I hate those pocking things," Einar grumbled, rubbing his forehead while Pixel stifled another giggle. "Look, can we sit down and talk to you? This is much more serious than some pocking games you folk play with your costumes and your toy weapons."

"This isn't a game, and we aren't hippies with New Age books and a need for self-validation." Pixel added. Her eyes had faded to a lavender color. "Liam, we need your help."

* * *

Get *"A Reluctant Druid"* at:
amazon.com/dp/B07716V2RN

Find out more about Jon R. Osborne and "A Reluctant Druid" at:
chriskennedypublishing.com/imprints-authors/jon-r-osborne/

* * * * *

Made in the USA
Middletown, DE
05 October 2022

12017785R00268